Kim Stanley Robinson was born in 1952. Af...
traveling and working in different p...
now returned to his beloved Cali...

One of the finest science fiction...
Robinson has won many awards...
Asimov, John W. Campbell, Locu... ...wards.

His previous books include *The W... ...*, *The Gold Coast*, *Pacific Edge* and *Escape from Kathm...du*.

KIM STANLEY ROBINSON

Down and Out in the Year 2000

Grafton
An Imprint of HarperCollinsPublishers

Grafton
An Imprint of HarperCollins*Publishers*
77–85 Fulham Palace Road,
Hammersmith, London W6 8JB

A Grafton Original 1992
9 8 7 6 5 4 3 2 1

A catalogue record for this book
is available from the British Library

ISBN 0 586 21497 6

Set in Times

Printed in Great Britain by
HarperCollinsManufacturing Glasgow

Contents

A Short Sharp Shock

CHAPTER 1

The Night Beach

When he came to he was drowning. The water was black and he bobbed up in it swiftly, obscurely aware that it was dangerous to do so, but he was helpless to stop; he tumbled over and swam downward, arms loose and thrusting like tentacles, but it was useless. Air popped out of him in a stream of white bubbles that flattened and shimmied as they squashed upward, all clustered around bearing him to the surface. He glanced up, suddenly aware of the idea of surface; and there it was, an undulating sheet of obsidian silk on which chips of raw silver skittered wildly back and forth. A flock of startled birds turning all at once – no – it was, he thought as the world began to roar, the shattered image of a crescent moon. At the thought a whole cosmology bloomed in him –

And broke apart like the moon's image, as he crashed up into the air and gasped. He flailed at the water whooping and kicking hard to stay afloat; he felt a wave lift him, and flopped around to face it. A cold smack in the face and he tumbled again, thrashed through a somersault and came up breathing, barking like a seal to suck in more air.

The next time under he rammed a sandbar and then he was rolling on a steep shorebreak, sluiced by sandy water and struck repeatedly by small silver fish. He crawled up through rushing foam, mouth full of salty grit, hands sinking wrist-deep in the wet sand. The little fish leaped in the phosphorescent foam, banged into his arms and legs. The beach was bouncing with silver fish, it was like an infestation of insects. On hands and knees he couldn't avoid squashing some into the sand.

At the high water mark he collapsed. He looked across a gleaming black strand, filigreed with sea foam receding on a wave. Coarse-grained sand sparked with reflected moonlight, and the fish arched to the shape of the crescent moon, which hung over the horizon at the end of a mirrorflake path of water. Such a dense, intricate, shifting texture of black and white –

A large wave caught him, rolled him back down among the suffocating fish. He clawed the sand without effect, then slammed into another body, warm and as naked as he was. The receding wave rushed down to the triple ripple of the low water mark, leaving them behind: he and a woman, a woman with close-cropped hair. She appeared senseless and he tried to pull her up, but the next wave knocked them down and rolled them like driftwood. He untangled himself from her and got to his knees, took her arms and pulled her up the wet sand, shifting one knee at a time, the little silver fish bouncing all around them. When he had gotten her a few body lengths into dry sand he fell beside her. He couldn't move.

From down the beach came shrill birdy cries. Children ran up to them shouting, buckets swinging at the ends of their arms like great deformed hands. When they ran on he could not move his head to track them. They returned to his field of vision, with taller people whose heads scraped the moon. The children dashed up and down the strand on the lace edge of the waves. They dumped full buckets of wriggling silver leaves in a pile beyond his head. Fire bloomed and driftwood was thrown on it, until transparent gold ribbons leaped up into the night.

Then another wave caught them and rolled them back down to the sea; the tide was rising and they would have perished, but the cords of a thrown net stopped them short, and they were hauled back and dumped closer to the fire, which hissed and sizzled. The children were laughing.

Later, fighting unconsciousness, he lifted the great stone at the end of his neck. The fire had died, the moon sat on the beach. He looked at the woman beside him. She lay on her stomach, one knee to the side. Dry sand stuck to her skin and the moonlight reflecting from her was gritty; it sparkled as she breathed. Powerful thighs met in a rounded muscly bottom, which curved the light into the dip of her lower back. Her upper back was broad, her spine in a deep trough of muscle, her shoulders rangy, her biceps thick. Short-cropped hair, dark under the moon's glaze, curled tight to her head; and the profile glimpsed over one shoulder was straight-nosed and somehow classical: a swimmer, he thought as his head fell back, with the big chest and smooth hard muscling of a sponge diver, or a sea goddess, something from the myths of a world he couldn't remember.

Then her arm shifted out, and her hand came to rest against his flank, and the feel of her coursed all through him: a short, sharp, shock. He caught his breath and found he was sitting up facing her, her palm both cool and warm against his side. He watched her catch the moon on her skin and fling it away.

CHAPTER 2
Sea Wrack

When he woke in the morning, the woman was gone. The sun burned just over the water. He lay on a crumbling sand cliff, the high mark of the previous tide's assault on the beach. With his head resting on one ear, he saw a wet slick foam-flecked strand of silvery brown, and the sea; resting on the other, he saw a lumpy expanse of blond beach, dotted with driftwood. Behind the beach was a forest, which rose steeply to a very tall cliff of white stone; its top edge made a brilliant border with the deep blue sky above.

He lifted his head and noticed that the sand cliff under him was a tiny model of the granite cliff standing over the forest – a transient replica, already falling into the sea. But then again the immense rock cliff was also falling into the sea, the forest its beach, the beach its strand. It repeated the little sand cliff's dissolution on a scale of time so much vaster that the idea of it made him dizzy. The tide ebbs and the stars die.

On the wet strand a troop of birds ran back and forth. They seemed a kind of sandpiper, except their feathers were a dark metallic red. They stabbed away at dead grunion rolling in the wrack, and then dashed madly up the strand chased by waves, their stick legs pumping over blurred reflections of themselves. They made one of these frantic cavalry charges right under a thick white fishing line; surprised at the sight, he raised himself up on his elbows and looked behind him.

A surf fisher sat on a big driftwood log. In fact there were several of them, scattered down the beach at more or less regular intervals. The one closest to him was all in brown, an old brown woman in a baggy coat and floppy hat, who waved briefly at him and did not stir from her log.

He stood and walked to her. Beside her a bucket stood on the sand, filled with the little silver fish from the previous night. She gestured at the bucket, offering him some of the fish, and he saw that her hand was a thick mass of shiny dark brown, her fingers long tubes of lighter hollow brown, with bulbs at their ends. Like tubes of seaweed. And her coat was a brown frond of kelp, and her face a wrinkled brown bulb, popped by the slit of her mouth; and her eyes were polyps, smooth and wet.

An animated bundle of seaweed. He knew this was wrong, but there she sat, and the sun was bright and it was hard to think. Many things inside his head had broken or gone away. He felt no particular emotion. He sat on the sand beside her fishing pole, trying to think. There was a thick tendril that fell from her lower back to her driftwood log, attaching her to it.

He found he was puzzled. 'Were you here last night?' he croaked.

The old woman cackled. 'A wild one. The stars fell and the fish tried to become birds again. Spring.' She had a wet hissing voice, a strange accent. But it was his language, or a language he knew. He couldn't decide if he knew any others or not.

She gestured again at her bucket, repeating her offer. Noticing suddenly the pangs of his hunger, he took a few grunion from the bucket and swallowed them.

When he had finished he said, 'Where is the woman who washed up with me?'

She jerked a thumb at the forest behind them. 'Sold to the spine kings.'

'Sold?'

'They took her, but they gave us some hooks.'

He looked up at the stone cliff above the trees, and she nodded.

'Up there, yes. But they'll take her on to Kataptron Cove.'

'Why not me?'

'They didn't want you.'

A child ran down the beach toward them, stepping on the edge of the sand cliff and collapsing it with her passage. She too wore a baggy frond coat and a floppy hat. He noticed that each of the seated surf fishers had a child running about in its area. Buckets

13

sat on the sand like discarded party hats. For a long time he sat and watched the child approach. It was hard to think. The sunlight hurt his eyes.

'Who am I?' he said.

'You can't expect me to tell you that,' the fisherwoman said.

'No.' He shook his head. 'But I . . . I don't know who I am.'

'We say, the fish knows it's a fish when we yank it into the air.'

He got to his feet, laughed oddly, waited for the blood to return to his head. 'Perhaps I'm a fish, then. But . . . I don't know what's happened to me. I don't know what happened.'

'Whatever happened, you're here.' She shrugged and began to reel in her line. 'It's now that matters, we say.'

He considered it.

'Which way is the cove you mentioned?' he said at last.

She pointed down the beach, away from the sun. 'But the beach ends, and the cliff falls straight into the sea. It's best to climb it here.'

He looked at the cliff. It would be a hard climb. He took a few more grunion from the bucket. Fellow fish, dead of self-discovery. The seaweed woman grubbed in a dark mass of stuff in the lee of her log, then offered him a skirt of woven seaweed. He tied it around his waist, thanked her and took off across the beach.

'You'd better hurry,' she called after him. 'Kataptron Cove is a long way west, and the spine kings are fast.'

CHAPTER 3

The Spine

The forest was thick and damp, with leaves scattered at every level, from the rotting logs embedded in the carpet of ferns to the sunbroken ceiling of leaves overhead. Streams gurgled down the slope, but apparently it had not rained for some time, as smaller creekbeds held only trickles; one served him as a pebble-bottomed trail, broken by networks of exposed roots. In the cool gloom he hiked uphill, moving from glade to glade as if from one green room to the next, each sculpted according to a different theory of space and color. Leaves everywhere gave proof of his eye's infinite depth of field, and all was still except for the water falling to the sea – and an occasional flash in his peripheral vision, birds, perhaps, which he could never quite see.

The forest ended at the bottom of the cliff, which rose overhead like the side of an enormous continent. Boulders taller than the trees were scattered about at the foot of the cliff. Ferns and mosses covered the tumble of rotten granite between boulders. The cliff itself was riven by deep gullies, which were almost as steep as the buttresses separating them. He clambered between boulders looking for a likely way up, in a constant fine mist: far above waterfalls had broken apart, and to the left against the white rock was a broad faint rainbow.

Just as he was concluding that he would have to scramble up one of the gulleys he came on a trail going up the side of one, beginning abruptly in the ferny talus. The trail was wide enough for two people to walk side by side, and had been hacked out of the granite side wall of the gully, where it switch-backed frequently. When the side wall became completely vertical, the trail wound out over the buttress to the left and zigzagged up that steep finger of stone, in stubborn defiance of the breathtaking exposure. It was impossible to imagine how the trail had been built, and it was also true that a break anywhere in the supporting walls would have cut the trail as neatly as miles of empty air; but there were no breaks, and the weedless gravel and polished bedrock he walked over indicated frequent use. He climbed as if on a staircase in a dream, endlessly ascending in hairpin turns, until the forest and beach below became no more than green and blond stripes running as far as he could see in both directions, between the sunbeaten blue of the ocean and the sunbeaten white of the granite.

Then the cliff laid back, and the trail led straight ahead on an incline that got less and less steep, until he saw ahead a skyline of shattered granite, running right to left as far as he could see. The rock stood stark against the sky. He hurried forward and suddenly he was on the crest of a ridge extending to his left and right, and before him he saw ocean again – ocean far below, spread out in front of him exactly as it was behind. Surprised, he walked automatically to a point where he could see all the way down: a steep cliff, a strip of forest, a strip of sand, the white-on-blue tapestry of breaking waves, the intense cobalt of the sea. He stepped back and staggered a little, trying to look in every direction at once.

He was standing on the crest of a tall peninsula, which snaked through an empty ocean for as far as he could see. It was a narrow ridge of white granite, running roughly east to west, bisecting the blue plate of the sea and twice marring the circular of the horizon. The ridge rose to peaks again and again, higher perhaps in the talcum of afternoon light to the west; it also undulated back and forth, big S shapes making a frozen sine wave. The horizon was an enormous distance away, so far away that it seemed wrong to him, as wrong as the seaweed woman. In fact the whole prospect was fantastically strange; but there he stood, feeling the wind rake hard over the lichen-stained ridge, watching it shove at low shrubs and tufts of sedge.

It occurred to him that the peninsula extended all the way around the world. A big ocean world, and this lofty ring of rock its only land: he was sure of it. It was as if it were something he remembered.

16

CHAPTER 4

Beauty Is the Promise of Happiness

And the only happiness is action. So he roused himself and headed west, thinking that a bend in the peninsula out that way might hide Kataptron Cove. The sun fell just to the right of the rock, slowing as it fell, flattening as if reluctant to touch the horizon, breaking into bands of glowing orange light that stretched until they were sucked down by the sea. The twilight was long, a mauve and purple half day, and he hiked rapidly over the crest's shattered granite, which was studded with crystals of translucent quartz. As he walked over the rough edges of stones, feeling liberty in the twisting ligaments of his ankles, he kept an eye out for some sort of shelter for the night. The trail he had followed onto the spine had disappeared, no doubt because the crest itself served as a broad high trail; but at one point a deep transverse cleft had been filled at a single spot by boulders, confirming his notion that the trail still ran, and would reappear when needed.

So he was not surprised when he came upon a low circular stone hut, next to a small pool of water. In this area stone broke away from the bedrock in irregular plates, and a great number of these had been gathered and stacked in rings that grew successively smaller as they got higher off the ground, until a final large capstone topped things off. The stones had been sized and placed so precisely that it would have been difficult to get more than a fingernail between any two of them. A short chimney made of smaller stones protruded from one side of the roof.

Opening a wooden door in the wall opposite the chimney, he entered and found a wooden shelf circling the interior of the wall. Next to the fireplace was a stack of kindling and logs; other

17

than that the hut was empty. He was without the means to start a fire, and it was fairly warm in any case, so he went back outside and drank from the pool, then sat against the west wall to eat the last of the fisherwoman's grunion, in the final hour of twilight. As the light leaked out of the sky it turned a deep rich blue, dark but not quite black: and across this strangely palpable firmament the stars popped into existence, thousands upon thousands of them, from bright disks that might have been nearby planets to dots so faint that he could only see them by looking slightly to the side. Eventually the sky was packed with stars, so densely that they defined perfectly the dome of sky; and frightened him. 'Where I come from there are not so many stars,' he said shakily to the hut, and then felt acutely his solitude, and the emptinesses inside his mind, the black membranes he could not penetrate. He retreated into the hut. After a long time lying on the hard wooden shelf, he fell asleep.

Sometime before dawn he was awakened by a crowd of folk banging in the doorway. They held him down and searched under his skirt. They had broad hard hands. Cloaks made of small leaves sewn together clicked in the dark, and it smelled like oranges.

'Are you the spine kings?' he asked, drunk with sleep.

They laughed, an airy sound. One said, 'If we were you'd be strangled with your own guts by now.'

'Or tossed down the cliff.'

The first voice said, 'Or both. The spine kings' hello.'

They all had lumps on their left shoulders, irregular dark masses that looked like shrubs. They took him out of the hut, and under the sea-colored sky he saw that the lumps were in fact shrubs – miniature fruit trees, it appeared, growing out of their left shoulders. The fruits were fragrant and still reminded him of oranges, although the smell had been altered by the salt tang, made more bitter. Round fruit, in any case, of a washed-out color that in better light might have been pale green.

The members of this group arranged themselves in a circle facing inward, took off their leaf cloaks and sat down. He sat in the circle between two of them, glancing at the shoulder tree to his right. It definitely grew directly out of the creature's skin –

the gnarled little roots dove into the flesh just as a wart would, leaving an overgrown fissure between bark and skin.

With a jerk he looked away. It was almost dawn, and the treefolk began singing a low monophonic chant, in a language he didn't recognize. The sky lightened to its day blue, slightly thickened by the sun's absence, and the wind suddenly picked up, as if a door had banged open somewhere – a cool fresh breeze, peeling over the spine in the same moment that the sun pricked the distant gray line of the horizon, a green point stretching to a line of hot yellow and then a band of white fire, throwing the sea's surface into shadow and revealing a scree of low diaphanous cloud. Before the sun had detached itself from the sea each member of the circle had plucked a fruit from the shoulder of the person on their right, and when the sun was clear and the horizon sinking rapidly away from it, they ate. Their bites caused a faint crystalline ringing, and the odor of bitter oranges was strong. He felt his stomach muscles contract, and saliva ran down his throat. The celebrant nearest the sun glanced at him and said, 'Treeless here will be hungry.'

He almost nodded, but held himself still.

'What's your name?' the celebrant asked. He had been the first speaker in the hut.

'I don't know.'

'No?' The creature considered it. 'Treeless will be good enough, then. In our naming language, that is *Thel*.'

In his mind he called himself Thel. But his real name . . . black space, behind his nose, in the sky under his skull . . . 'It will do here,' he said, and waved a hand. 'It is accurate enough.'

The man laughed. 'So it is. I am Julo.' He looked across the circle. 'Garth, come here.'

A young man stood. He had been sitting opposite Julo, facing out from the circle, and now Thel noticed his tree grew from the right shoulder rather than the left.

'This is Garth, which means Rightbush. Garth, give Thel here an apple.' Garth hesitated, and Julo strode across the circle of watchers and cuffed him on the arm. 'Do it!'

Garth approached Thel and stood before him, looked down. Thel said to him, 'Which should I choose?'

19

With a grateful glance up the youth indicated the largest fruit, on a lower branch. Thel took the round green sphere in his fingers and pulled sharply, noting Garth's involuntary wince. Then he sniffed the stem, and bit through the skin. The bitter taste of orange, he sat in a small dark room, watching the wick of a lamp lit by a match held in long fingers, the flame turned up and burning poorly, in a library with bookcases for walls and a huge old leather globe in one corner ... He shook his head, back on the windy dawn spine, Julo's laughter in his ear, behind that a crystalline ringing. A bird hovered in the updraft, a windhover searching the lee cliff for prey. 'Thank you,' Thel said to Garth.

The treefolk gathered around him, touched his bare shoulders, asked him questions. He had nothing but questions in reply. Who were the spine kings? he asked, and their faces darkened. 'Why do you ask?' Julo said. 'Why don't you know?'

Thel explained. 'The fisherfolk pulled me from the sea. Before that – I don't know. I can't ...' He shook his head. 'They pulled out a woman with me, a swimmer, and sold her to the spine kings.' He gestured helplessly, the thought of her painful. Already the memory of her was fading, he knew. But that touch in the moonlight – 'I want to find her.'

'They have some of our people as well,' Julo said. 'We're going after them.' He reached into his bag and threw Thel a leaf cloak and a pair of leather moccasins with thick soles. 'You can come along. They're at Kataptron Cove, for the sacrifices.'

The boy's fruit was suddenly heavy on his stomach, and he shuddered as if every cell in him had tasted something bitter.

CHAPTER 5

The Snake and the Tree

The treefolk hiked long and hard, following a line on the broad crest that minimized the ups and downs, nearly running along a rock road that Thel judged to be some three thousand feet above the sea. After a few days, the south side of the sinuous peninsula became a fairly gentle slope, cut by ravines and covered with tall redwood trees; in places on this side the beach was a wide expanse, dotted with ponds and green with rippling dune grass. The north side, on the other hand, remained a nearly vertical cliff, falling directly into waves, which slapped against the rock unbroken and sent bowed counterwaves back out to the north, stippling the blue surface of the water with intersecting arcs.

Once their ridge road narrowed, and big blocky towers of pink granite stood in their way. The trail reappeared then, on the sunny southern slope, and they followed it along a contoured traverse below the boulders, passing small pools that looked hacked into the rock. Half a day of this and they had passed the sharp peaks and were back on the ridge, looking ahead down its back as it snaked through the blue ocean. 'How long is this peninsula?' Thel asked, but they only stared at him.

Every morning at sunrise Julo ordered young Garth to provide a shoulder apple for Thel's consumption, and in the absence of any other food Thel accepted it and ate hungrily. He saw no more hallucinations, but each time experienced a sudden flush of pinkness in his vision, and felt the bitter tang of the taste to his bones. His right shoulder began to ache as he lay down to sleep. He ignored it and hiked on. He noticed that on cloudy days his companions hiked more slowly, and that when they stopped by pools to rest on those days, they took off their boots

21

and stuck their feet between cracks in the rock, looking weary and relaxed.

Some days later the peninsula took a broad curve to the north, and for the first time the sun set on the south side of it. They stopped at a hut set on a particularly high knob on the ridge, and Thel looked around at the peninsula, splitting the ocean all the way to the distant horizon. It was a big world, no doubt of it; and the days and nights were much longer than what he had been used to, he was sure. He grew tired at midday, and often woke for a time in the middle of the long nights. 'It doesn't make sense,' he said to Garth, waving perplexed at the mountainous mound zigzagging across the sea. 'There isn't any geological process that could create a feature like this.'

This was said almost in jest, given the other more important mysteries of his existence. But Garth stared at him, eyes feverish. He was lying exhausted, his feet deep in a crack; seeing this in the evenings Thel always resolved not to eat, and every morning he awoke too ravenous to refuse. Now, as if to pay Garth back with conversation, he added, 'Land floats like wood, thick cakes of it drifting on slow currents of melted rock below, and a peninsula like this, as tall as this ... I suppose it could be a mid-oceanic ridge, but in that case it would be volcanic, and this is all granite. I don't understand.'

Garth said, 'It's here, so it must be possible.'

Thel laughed. 'The basis of your world's philosophy. You didn't tell me you were a philosopher.'

Garth smiled bitterly. 'Live like me and you too will become one. Maybe it's happening already, eh? Maybe before you swam ashore you didn't concern yourself with questions like that.'

'No,' Thel said, considering it. 'I was always curious. I think.' And to Garth's laugh: 'So it feels, you see. Perhaps not everything is gone.' It seemed possible that the questions came from the shattered side of his mind, from some past self he couldn't recall but which shaped his thinking anyway. 'Perhaps I studied rock.'

At sunset the wind tended to die, just as the sunrise quickened it; now it slackened. Perhaps I have died like the wind, he thought; perhaps the only thing that survives after death are the questions, or the habit of questioning.

The two of them watched the sun sink, just to the left of the bump of the spine on the horizon. 'It's as if it's a river in reverse,' Thel said. 'If a deep river ran across a desert land, and then you reversed the landscape, water and earth, you would get something that looked like this.'

'The earth river,' Garth said. 'The priests of the birdfolk call it that.'

'Are there any tributaries? Any lakes-turned-into-islands?'

'I've never seen any.'

The air darkened and the salt air grew chill. Garth was breathing deeply, about to fall asleep, when he said in a voice not his, a voice pleasant but at the same time chilling: 'Through mirrors we see things right way round at last.'

In the days that followed, this image of a landscape in reverse haunted Thel, though in the end it explained nothing. The stony spine continued to split the water, and it got taller, the south side becoming as steep as the north again. In places they walked on a strip of level granite no wider than a person, and on each side the cliffs plunged some five thousand feet into white foam tapestries that shifted back and forth over deep water, as if something below the blue were lightly breathing: it disturbed one's balance to look down at it, and though the strip was wide enough to walk on comfortably, the sheer airiness of it gave Thel vertigo. Garth walked over it with a pinched expression, and Julo laughed at him, cuffed him hard so that he had to go to his knees to avoid falling over the side; then Julo forced him to walk backwards, which served the others as amusement.

Eventually the north side grew less steep, splaying out until the peninsula was wider than ever. In this section a hot white cliff faced south, a cool forested slope faced north. On the north slope were scattered stands of enormous evergreens, the tallest trees three or four hundred feet high. One of these giants stood on a ledge just below the crest, and had grown up above the ridge, where the winds had flattened it so that its branches grew horizontally in all directions, some laying over the ridge, others fanning out into the air over the beach and the sea far below.

The treefolk greeted this flat-topped giant as an ancestor, and clambered out over the horizontal branches to the tree's mighty trunk, over it, and out the other side. They ended up on three or four lightning-blasted gnarly branches, ten feet wide and so solid that jumping up and down would not move them, though the whole tree swayed gently in a fitful west wind. Big shallow circular depressions had been cut into the tops of these branches, and the exposed wood had been polished till it gleamed.

They spent the night in these open-roofed rooms, under the star-flooded sky. By starlight Thel looked at the wood by his head and saw the grain of centuries of growth exposed. The peninsula had been here for thousands of years, millions of years – both the plant life and the erosion of the granite showed that. But how had it begun? 'When you talk among yourselves about the spine,' he said to the treefolk, 'do you ever talk about where it came from? Do you have a story that explains it?'

Julo was looking down into the grain of the floor beneath him, still and rapt as if he had not heard Thel; but after a while he said, in a low voice, 'We tell a story about it. Traveling in silent majesty along their ordered ways, the gods tree and snake were lovers in the time without time. But they fell into time, and snake saw a vision of a lover as mobile as he, and he chased round the sky until he saw the vision was his own tail. He bit the tail in anger and began to bleed, and his blood flowed out into a single great drop, bound by the circle his long body made. He died of the loss, and tree climbed on his back and drove her roots deep into his body, trying to feed his blood into him, trying to bring him back to life, and all her acorns dropped and grew to join in the attempt. And here we are, accidents of her effort, trying to help her as we can, and some day the snake will live again, and we will all sail off among the stars, traveling in silent majesty.'

'Ah,' Thel said. And then: 'I see.'

But he didn't see, and he arranged himself for sleep and looked up into the thickets of stars, disappointed. Garth lay next to him, and much later, when the others were asleep, he whispered to him, 'You don't know where you came from. You have no idea how you came here or what you are. Worry about that, and when you know those things, then worry about the great spine.'

CHAPTER 6

Kataptron Cove

The next dawn it was bitterly cold out on the swaying branches, and they sat back against the curved wall of the biggest room shivering as Julo watched the sky to determine the exact moment of sunrise, hidden behind the ridge. When he turned to pluck the fruit from the man next to him he took three, and the others did the same. Thel restricted himself to his usual one of Garth's, and asked him why the others had eaten more.

'We'll reach Kataptron Cove this evening.'

And so they did. It was on the south side, in an arc the peninsula made. Here the granite side of the peninsula was marred by the shattered walls of a small crater – a horseshoe ring of jagged black rock, extending into the sea and broken open to it at its outermost point, so that the inside of the crater was a small lagoon. Clearly it was an old volcanic vent, and as it was the first sign of vulcanism that Thel had seen, he approached it with interest.

But he was soon distracted by the grim faces of the treefolk, who marched around him as if going into battle. Foreboding charged the air, and the treefolk abandoned the trail that descended the southern slope in a long traverse to the crater bay, and struggled through dense woods above the trail.

They descended into thick salt air filled with the sound of waves, gliding from tree to tree like spirits, moving very slowly onto the high crumbly rim of the crater, overlooking the inner lagoon. The curving inner wall of the crater was a reddish cliff, overgrown with green. Where the crater met the spine a stream fell down the inner wall and across the sand into the lagoon; on the banks of the stream there was a permanent camp, built in a grove of trees that had been cleared of undergrowth. In the shadows of these trees people moved, and smoke spiraled up through the sunbeams lancing among the branches.

In the depths of the grove there was a hubbub, and a crowd emerged onto the open beach, a gang wearing leather skirts and belted short swords, and tight golden helmets. They chivvied along a short row of prisoners, naked and in chains, and Thel heard Garth whimper softly. He looked around and saw that the treefolk had their eyes fixed on the beach in horror, and unwilling fascination. 'What is it?' he said.

Garth pointed at where the grove met the beach. Two tall tree trunks standing beside each other had been stripped bare; behind the trunks stood a platform about half their height. 'It's the flex X,' Garth whispered, and would not elaborate. He sat with his back to the scene, head in hands.

Thel and the rest of the treefolk watched as a prisoner was hauled up the steps of the platform. Two crews on the ground set about winding ropes tied to the top of each tree trunk, until the trunks were crossing each other at about the level of the platform. Intuitively Thel understood the function of the large bowed X the trees made, and his stomach contracted to a hard knot of tension and vicarious terror; still he watched as the first prisoner was tied to the two trees, and the thick ropes holding the trees in position were knocked off notched stumps, and the two tall trunks returned to an upright position, with a stately swaying motion that had not the slightest hitch in it when the prisoner was ripped apart. Blood fountained from the head and the body, now separated. Thel saw that the beach around the two trees was littered with lumps here and there, all a dark brown, now splattered with red: the wreckage of lives.

At that distance people were the size of dolls, and they heard nothing of them over the sounds of waves. The executioners tied each prisoner to the two trees in a different manner, so that the second came apart at the limbs, and the third in the middle, leaving a long loop of intestine hanging between the two poles.

Thel found he was sitting. His skin was covered with a sour sweat. He felt cold. He moved in front of Garth, took his face in his hands. 'The spine kings?'

Garth nodded miserably.

'Who are they?'

No response. Feeling the futility of the question, Thel stood and went to Julo, who laughed maliciously as he saw Thel's face.

'What will you do?' Thel asked.

'Go have a look. They'll be drinking tonight, they'll all get drunk and there'll be little watch kept. They fear no one in any case. We can be quiet, and some of us will go have a look for our kind. If we can find them, we can see what kind of lock they're under. It may be possible to slip them out on a night like this. We're lucky to have seen that,' he said, ironic to the point of snarling. 'We know they'll be off guard.'

Thel nodded, impressed despite himself by Julo's courage. 'I want to come with you,' he said. 'I can look for the swimmer.'

'She'll be under stronger guard,' Julo warned him. 'But you're welcome to try. It's why you're here, right?'

CHAPTER 7

Two Xs

So in the long indigo twilight they made their way around the rim of the crater bay like ghosts, stepping so silently that the loudest sound coming from them was their heartbeats, tocking at the backs of their open mouths. Shadows with heartbeats, as silent as the fear of death, slipping from trunk to trunk and searching the forest ahead with the acute gaze of hunted beasts . . . the spine king sentinels carried crossbows, Julo had said. They descended the crater wall well away from the village, and then worked their way back to it through a thin forest of pines, stepping across a carpet of brown needles.

Ahead came the sound of voices, and the beach stream. The leaves of the treefolk's shoulder bushes rustled when they moved too quickly. It was getting dark, the color draining out of everything except the pinpricks of fire dancing in the black needles ahead.

Drumming began, parodying their heavy heartbeats. They hugged the crater wall, circled to the edge of a firelit clearing. In the clearing were huts, cages, and platforms, all made of straight branches with the bark still on them. Some of the cages held huddled figures.

Thel froze. Reflection of torchlight from a pair of eyes, the shaggy head of a wild beast captured and caged, brilliant whites defiant and exhausted: it was her. Thel stared and stared at the black lump of the body, heavy in the dark, clothed only in dirt – the tangled hair backlit by fire – eyes reflecting torchlight. He had no idea why he was so certain. But he knew it was the swimmer.

The treefolk were clustered around him. When guards with torches arrived in the clearing, the prisoners sat up, and around him Thel heard a faint rustling of leaves. He peered more closely and saw that the cage beside the swimmer's held seated figures, slumped over. One of them begged for water and the guards approached. In the sharply flickering torchlight Thel could see slack faces, eyes shut against the light, odd hunched shoulders – ah. Trunks, stalks, stumps: their shoulder bushes had been chopped off. One of the captured treefolk, lying flat on the ground, was hauled up; he still had his little tree, its fruit gone, its leaves drooping. 'The fire's low,' one guard said drunkenly, and drew his short broad sword and hacked away. It took several blows, *thunk, thunk*, the victim weeping, his companions listless, looking away, the other guards holding the victim upright and steady and finally bending the trunk of the miniature tree until it broke with a dull crack. The victim flopped to the ground and the guards left the cage and tossed the little tree onto the embers of a big fire: it flared up white and burned well for several minutes, as if the wood were resinous.

Thel's companions had watched this scene without moving; only the rustle of leaves betrayed their distress. The guards left and they slipped back into the black forest, and Thel followed them. When they showed no signs of stopping he crashed forward recklessly, and pulled at Julo's arm; when Julo shrugged him off and continued on, Thel reached out and grabbed the trunk of Julo's shoulder tree and yanked him around, and then had to defend himself immediately from a vicious rain of blows, which stopped only when the other treefolk threw themselves between the two, protesting in anxious mutters, whispering *shh, shh, shhh*.

'What are you doing?' Thel cried softly.

'Leaving,' Julo said between his teeth.

'Aren't you going to free them?'

'They're dead.' Julo turned away, clearly too disgusted and furious to discuss it further. With a fierce chopping gesture he led the others away.

'What about the swimmer?'

They didn't stop. Suddenly the black forest seemed filled with distant voices, with drunken bodies crashing into underbrush, with yellow winking torches bouncing through the trees. Thel backed into a tree, leaned against the shaggy bark. He took deep deliberate breaths. The cage had been made of lashed branches, but out in the center of the clearing like that . . .

'I'll help you,' Garth said out of the darkness, giving Thel a start. 'It's me, Garth.'

They held each other's forearms in the dark. 'You'll lose the others if you stay,' Thel said.

'I know,' Garth said, voice low and bitter. 'You've seen how he treats me. I want to be free of them all, forever. I'll make my own life from now on.'

'That's not an easy thing,' Thel said.

Without replying Garth turned back the way they had come, and they crept back to the clearing. Once there they lay behind a fallen log and looked into the firelit cages. Garth's fellow folk sat there listlessly.

'Their trees won't grow back?'

'Would your arm?'

'And so they'll die?'

'Yes.'

Garth slipped away, and after a time Thel saw an orange light like a sort of firefly bobbing through the trees: Garth, holding a branch tipped by a glowing ember. Thel joined him, and they crept to the back of the treefolk's cage, and Garth held the tip of the branch to the lashings at the bottom of one pole. As they blew on the coal the treefolk inside watched, without a sound or any sign of interest.

Garth begged those inside to emerge, and got no reply. Thel stared at the orange ember which brightened as they blew on it, embarrassed for Garth, and worried about what he could do alone. When the cage lashing caught fire with a miniature explosion of white flame, Garth looked at his comrades through the smoke and said fiercely, 'You know what the spine kings have done to you! You know what they'll do to you next! Come out and exact some revenge, meet your end like trees should. While you do we can rescue a friend who yet lives, and you'll either make a quick end to it, or escape to be free on the great spine when your time comes.' He jerked hard on the pole and it came loose. 'Come on, get out there among them and remember the part of you they threw on their fires.'

One of them started forward and crawled under the lifted pole, and the rest looked at each other, at the raw stumps protruding from their shoulders; they too slipped from the cage. In a moment they had all disappeared into the dark.

'It would be better if we had something else for the other cage,' Garth said to Thel. 'The ember is dying.'

'There are a lot more in the fire.'

'My kin's lives.'

'They can free these others.'

Garth nodded. 'We burn hot. But one of those swords they carry would be helpful.' And he disappeared again.

Thel waited, as near the swimmer's cage as he could get without emerging into the light. From the hut beside the bonfire and the central cage came the sounds of laughter, then those of an argument turning ugly. Around him in the forest were odd noises, sudden silences, and he imagined the treeless treefolk wandering murderously in the dark, jumping drunken guards as they stumbled off to piss in the trees, bludgeoning them and then stealing their swords to slip between the ribs of others. The spine kings feared no one and now they would pay, ambushed in their own village in the midst of their death bacchanal. Sick with images of brutal murder, keyed to the highest pitch of tension, Thel leaped to his feet involuntarily as a crash and cries came from the direction of the beach, and the guards in the clearing's hut rushed out and down a path. 'The platform!' someone was shouting in the distance as Thel ran to the bonfire and snatched up a brand. Sparks streamed in a wide arc from the burning end as he ran to the cage and crushed the red ember tip against the lashings at the bottom of a pole. This cage was better constructed and it was going to take longer. A twig cracked behind him and the swimmer croaked a warning; he swung the brand around and caught an onrushing guard in the face. The guard's raised broadsword flew into the cage, cutting one prisoner who cried out; the guard himself couldn't do more than grunt, as Thel beat him furiously across the neck and head. When Thel turned back to the cage the prisoners had cut the lashing with the sword and were squeezing out of the cage and cursing one another under their breath. Thel took the swimmer woman by the arm and pulled her out; she was thicker than the others and barely fit through the gap. She appeared dazed, but when Thel held her face in his hands and caught her eye, she recognized him. Garth had reappeared, and Thel was about to lead the swimmer out of the clearing when one of the other prisoners said urgently, 'Wonderful saviors, thank you eternally, please, follow me, I know where the trailhead is that leads up to the spine!' So they followed him, but it seemed to Thel he went straight for the center of the camp. Shrieks cut the night and torches had been tossed high into the trees, some of which had caught fire and become great torches themselves, so that there was far too much light for their purpose. 'Wait one moment please,' the prisoner who claimed to know the way said, and he ran into the largest house in the camp.

Apparently some of the treefolk amputees had found the flex X and set it alight. The crater wall enclosing the lagoon appeared out of the darkness, faintly illuminated by the burning village. Sparks wafted among the stars, it seemed the cosmos was winking out fire by fire. The prisoner ran out of the house carrying a sack. 'Follow me now,' he cried jubilantly, 'and run for your lives!'

They ran after him. Thel took the swimmer by the arm, determined not to lose her in the mayhem. But now the prisoner was true to his word, and he led them through firebroken shadows to a wide cobbled trail, ignoring the shouts and cries around them. The trail ran up to the crater's rim and then along it, to the point where the crater wall diverged from the great slope of the spine ridge. The trail began to switchback up the slope. Looking across an arc of the lagoon they saw the village dotted with burning trees and smaller patches of fire, the flex X burning high on a beach glossy as a seal's back, and there were two images of everything: one burning whitely over the beach, another, inverted, burning a clear yellow in the calm black water of the bay.

CHAPTER 8

The Mirror

Afraid of the spine king's pursuit, they ran the trail west for many days, scarcely pausing to loot caches located by the prisoner who led them. The caches contained clothing and shoes, and also buried jugs of dried meat and fruit, lumps so hard and dry they couldn't tell what anything was until chewing it; good food, but because there were seven of them they were still hungry. 'We'll come to my village soon,' the prisoner said one evening after doling out a meager dinner, and outfitting Thel and the swimmer in pants and tunics, and boots that were a lucky fit. The prisoner's name was Tinou, and he had a wonderful big smile; he seemed astonished and delighted to have escaped the spine kings, and often he thanked Thel and Garth for their rescue. 'When we get there we'll eat like the lords of the ocean deep.'

The sun had set an hour before, and a line of clouds over the western horizon was the pink of azaleas, set in a sky the color of lapis. The seven sat around a small fire: Thel, the swimmer, Garth, Tinou, and three women. These women all had faces cast in the same mold, and a strange mold it was; where their right eye should have been the skin bulged out into another, smaller face, lively and animated, with features that did not look like the larger one around it – except for the fact that its own little right eye was again replaced by a face, a very little face – which had an even tinier face where its right eye should have been, and so on and so on, down in a short curve to the limit of visibility, and no doubt beyond.

This oddity made the three women's faces impressive and even frightening, and because the three full-sized faces seldom spoke, Thel always felt that when talking to them he was really

33

conversing with one of the smaller faces – perhaps the very
smallest, beyond the limit of visibility – who might reply in a tiny
high squeak at any time.

But now the three women stood before Tinou, and one said,
'We want to know what you took from Kataptron Cove.'

'I took this bag,' Tinou said, 'and it's mine.'

'It is all of ours,' the middle woman said, her voice heavy and
slow. Her companions moved to Tinou's sides. 'Show us what it
is.'

In the dusk it was hard to tell if expressions or firelight were
flickering across Tinou's long and mobile face. Thel and the
swimmer leaned forward together to see better this small
confrontation, and Tinou flashed them his friendly smile. 'I
suppose there is justice in that,' he said, and picked up his
shoulder bag. Untying the drawstring he said, 'Here,' and slipped
something out of the bag, a small shiny plate of some sort.

'Gold,' the middle facewoman said.

Tinou nodded, 'Yes, in a manner of speaking. But it is more
than that, in fact. It is a mirror, see?'

He held it up – a round smooth mirror with no rim, the glass
of it golden rather than silver. Held up against the dark eastern
sky it gleamed like a lamp, revealing a rich blue line in a field
of pink.

'It is no ordinary mirror,' Tinou said. 'My people will reward
us generously when we arrive with it, I assure you.'

He put it back in the bag, and for a moment it seemed to Thel
he was stuffing light into the bag as well, until with a hard jerk
he closed the drawstring. Wind riffled over them, below lay the
calm surface of the sea, and in the east the moon rose, its blasted
face round and brilliant; looking from it to the quick yellow
banners of their fire, Thel suddenly felt he walked in a world of
riches. Night beach and big-handed children, running the mirrorflake road on the sea . . .

The next dawn they were off again. At first Thel had been shy
of the swimmer, even a bit frightened of her; she couldn't know
how important her image had been to him before the rescue, and
he didn't know what to say to her. But now he walked behind
her or beside her, depending on the width of the trail, and as

they walked he asked her questions. Who was she? What did she remember from before the night they had washed into the beach? What had gotten them to that point under the water? What was her name?

She only shook her head. She remembered the night on the beach; beyond that she was unable to say. She concentrated her gaze on her long feet, which seemed to have trouble negotiating the rock, and rarely looked at him. He didn't mind. It was a comfort to be walking with her and to know that someone shared the mystery of his arrival on the peninsula. She was a fellow exile, moving like a dancer caught in heavier gravity than she was used to, and it was a pleasure just to watch her as the sun roasted her brown hair white at the tips, and burned her pale skin red-brown. Often aspects of her reminded Thel of that first night: the set of her rangy shoulders, the profile of her long nose. With speech or without, she reassured him.

And Garth – Garth too was an exile, a new one, and he hiked with them but in himself, skittish, distracted, sad. Thel hiked with him as well, and told him more stories of the rock under their feet, and Garth nodded to show he was listening; but he wasn't entirely there. The leaves on his little tree drooped, as if they needed watering.

So they moved westward, and the peninsula got steep and narrow again, the granite as hard as iron and a gray near black, flecked with rose quartz nodules. The dropoffs on both sides became so extreme that they could see nothing but a short curved slope of rock, and then ocean, a few thousand feet below. Tinou told them that here the walls of the sea cliffs were concave, so that they walked on a tube of rock that rested on a thin vertical sheet of stone, layered like an onion. 'Exfoliating granite,' Thel said. Tinou nodded, interested, and went on to say that in places the two cliffsides had fallen away to nothing, so that they were walking on arches over open holes, called the Serpent's Gates. 'If you were on the tide trail, you could climb up into them and sit under a giant rainbow of stone, the wind howling through the hole.'

Instead they tramped a trail set right down the edge of a fishback ridge. In places the trail had been hacked waist-deep into the dense dark rock, to give some protection from falls. Every day Tinou said they were getting close to his village, and to support the claim (for somehow his cheerful assurances made Thel doubt him), the trail changed under their feet, shifting imperceptibly from barely touched broken rock to a loose riprap, and then to cobblestones set in rings of concentric overlapping arcs, and finally, early one morning shortly after they started off, to a smoothly laid mosaic, made of small polished segments of the rose quartz. Longer swirls of dark hornblende were set into this pink road, forming letters in a cursive alphabet, and Tinou sang out the words they spelled in a jubilant tenor, the 'Song of Mystic Arrival in Oia' as he explained, fluid syllables like the sound of a beach stream's highest gurgling. At one point for their benefit he sang in the language they all shared:

> We walk the edge of pain and death
> And carve in waves our only hearth
> And nothing ever brings us home
>
> But something makes us want to climb:
> The sight of water cut like stone
> A village hanging in the sky.
>
> A village hanging in the sky
> And nothing ever brings us home
> But something makes us climb.

And climb they did, all that long day, until they came over a rise in the ridge, and there facing the southern sea, tucked in a steep scoop in the top of the cliff, was a cluster of whitewashed blocky buildings, lined in tight rows so that the narrow lanes were protected from the wind. Terrace after terrace cut the incurved slope, until it reached an escarpment hanging over the sea; from there a white staircase zigzagged down a gully to a tiny harbor below, three white buildings and a dock, gleaming like a pendant hanging from Oia.

CHAPTER 9
The Sorcerers of Oia

A crowd greeted them as they entered the village, men and women convening almost as though by coincidence, as though if Tinou and his retinue had not appeared they would have gathered anyway; but when they saw Tinou they smiled, for the most part, and congratulated him on his return. 'Not many escape the spine kings,' one woman said, and laughing the others crushed in on them to touch Tinou and his companions, while Tinou sang the trail's mosaic song, ending with an exuberant leap in the air.

'I thought I would never return here again,' he cried, 'and I never would have if not for Thel here, who slipped into the spine king's village the night we were to be torn apart on the crossing trees. He set us free, he saved our lives!' Jubilantly he embraced Thel, then added, 'He made it possible for all of us to return to Oia – ' and he took the mirror out of his shoulder bag.

Silence fell, and the crowd seemed both to step back and to press in at once. Thel thought he could hear the sound of the sea, murmuring far below. A woman dressed in a saffron dress said, 'Well, Tinou, your return was one thing, but *this* – '

General laughter, and then they were being led into the narrow streets of the village. These either contoured across town, making simple arcs, or ascended it in steep marble staircases, each step bowed in the middle from centuries of wear. Every lane and alley was lined by blocky whitewashed buildings, often painted with the graceful cursive lettering. By the time they came to a tiny plaza on the far side of the village, the sun was low on the horizon, it broke under clouds and suddenly every west wall was as gold as Tinou's mirror, and many of the west-facing windows were blinding white.

Restaurants ringed the plaza, each sporting a cluster of outdoor tables, and as dusk seeped into things lanterns were hung in small gnarled trees or put on windowsills, and the people ate and drank long into the night. Thel and the swimmer and the three facewomen ate voraciously, and became drunk on the fiery spirits poured for them, and the villagers danced, their long pantaloons and dresses swirling like the colors in a kaleidoscope, yards of cloth spinning under strong wiry naked torsos, both men and women dancing like gods, so that the watchers were shocked when a bottle shattered and the color of blood spurted into their field of vision, off to the side; a fight, quickly broken up, overridden by the gaiety of the sorcerers of Oia. The mirror was back.

In the days that followed, the celebration continued. Eventually it became clear that this was the permanent state of things in Oia, that this was the way the sorcerers lived. They poured sea water into stone vats, and later drew their spirits from taps at the vats' bottoms. Sea lions brought them their daily fish in exchange for drinks of this liquor; the creatures swam right up to the dock at the cliff bottom, barking hoarsely as they deposited long three-eyed fish on the dock. Later the sorcerers turned some of the fish meat into tough dark red steak, which tasted nothing like the flaking fish. Their gardens and goats were tended by their children – and in short, they lived lives of leisure, playing complex games, undergoing abstruse studies, and performing rituals and ceremonies. Tinou took his fellow travelers with him wherever he went, and introduced them as his saviors, and they were fêted to exhaustion.

One day to escape it Thel and the swimmer walked down the staircase trail that switch-backed precipitously to the sea. On the way they passed grown-over foundations, and roofless walls filled with weeds: vestiges of earlier Oias, shaken by earthquakes into the sea. On the dock below some of the sorcerers stood talking to the sea lions, taking their bloody catch and pouring tankards of the liquor down their throats. Even their vilest imprecations couldn't keep a flock of gulls away, and the gulls wheeled overhead crying madly until the barking sea lions breached far into the air, thick sleek sluglike bodies twisting adroitly as they snagged birds and crushed them in their small powerful mouths. Eventually the gulls departed and the lions swam off, a wrack of feathered corpses left on the groundswell.

After they were gone, Thel and the swimmer shed their garments and dove in. Underwater Thel became instantly afraid, but the sight of the swimmer stroking downward was somehow familiar, and strangely reassuring. He stayed under for as long as he could hold his breath, and then joined her in body-surfing the groundswells that rose up to strike the cliffs. As the two rode the waves they remained completely inside the water, surfing as the sea lions did, and they were drawn swiftly forward in the wave until they ducked down and out to avoid crashing into the cliff or the dock. During these rides, slung through the water by two curves of spacetime rushing across each other, Thel would look over at the swimmer's long naked body and feel his own flowing in the water, until it was hard to hold his breath, not because he was winded but because he needed to shout for joy.

When they pulled themselves back onto the worn stones of the dock, Tinou was there, except now he was a woman, laughing in a contralto at their expressions as she stripped and dove in; her face was clearly Tinou's, unmistakable despite the fact that it was slimmer, more feminine – yet clearly not a sister or twin, no, nothing but Tinou himself, shape-changed into a svelte female form. Thel and the swimmer looked at each other, baffled by this transformation; and halfway through the long climb up the stairs Tinou caught up with them, a man again, coquettishly embracing first the swimmer and then Thel (slim wet arms quick around his shoulders), and then laughing uproariously at their expressions.

That sunset he led them and the facewomen down into the ruins of the previous village. Here broken buildings had dropped their barrel roofs onto their floors, and worn splintered sticks of old furniture still stuck out between the bowed bricks. Other sorcerers set lanterns in a circle around what appeared to be an abandoned plaza, smaller even than the one above, and in the long lavender dusk more of the sorcerers gathered, somber for once and drinking hard. In the sky above a windhover caught the last rays of the sun, a white kestrel turned pink by the sunset, fluttering its wings in the rapid complex pattern that allows it to stay fixed in the air.

Tinou took the stolen mirror from his bag and set it on a short wooden stand, on the eastern edge of the circle the sorcerers made. Against the starry east it was a circle of pure pink sheen. When Tinou sat down the circle of seated sorcerers was complete, and they began to sing, their faces upturned to the windhover riding the last rays of the sun. The light leaked out of the sky and the wind riffled the enormous space of dusk and the sea, and Thel, surprising himself, feeling the old compulsion, said, 'As you can change your shape, and bend the world to serve you, perhaps you can tell me how this world came to be the way it is.'

They all stared at him. 'We have only a story,' Tinou said finally in a kind tone, 'just like anyone else.'

Another voice took over, that of an old woman; but it was impossible to pick out the speaker from the circle of faces. 'The universe burst from a bubble the size of an eye, some fifteen billion years ago, and it has been flying apart ever since. It will achieve its maximum reach outward in our lifetimes, and fall back into that eye of density which is God's eye, and then all will begin again, just as it was the time before, and the time before that, eternally. So that every breath that you take has occurred in just that way an infinity of times, and none of us are but statues in time to the eye of God.'

'As for this world,' said the voice of an old man, a cold, hard voice, 'this road of mountain across an empty sea, an equatorial peninsula circumnavigating the great globe: it came about like this.

'Gods fly through space in bubbles of glass, and their powers exceed ours as ours exceed those of the stones we stand on, who know only to endure. And once long ago gods voyaged through this forgotten bay of the night sea, and to pass the time they argued a point of philosophy.' And here the speaker's voice grew harsh, the edge of every word sharper, until they were as edged as the taste of Garth's shoulder fruit, sending the same kind of bitter shock through Thel. 'They argued aesthetics, the most metaphysical of philosophical problems. One of them said that beauty was a quality of the universe independent of any other, that it was inlaid in the fabric of being like gravity, in a pattern that no one could pull out. Another disagreed: beauty is the ache of mortality, this god said, an attribute of consciousness, and nothing is beautiful except perceived through the love of lost time, so that wherever there is beauty, love was there also, and first.'

Here another voice spoke, on the breaking edge of bitterness. 'And so they agreed to put it to a test, and being gods and therefore just like us, less ignorant but no less cruel, they decided to transform and populate one of the planets they sailed by, sinking all its land but this spine under an endless sea, and then making what remained as beautiful as they could imagine; but leeching every living thing of love, to see if the beauty would yet remain. And here we are.'

Silence. For a moment Thel felt he was falling.

A tray was passed around, and Thel did as the rest and took from it a thin white wafer, feeling a powerful compulsion. He ate it and his skin tingled as if crystallizing. Looking up he thought he could still see the kestrel hovering overhead, a black star among the sparkling white ones. The mirror's surface was a dark lustrous violet now, nothing like the western sky which had grown as dark as the east; as his gaze began to fall into the drop of rich glossy color there was a disturbance across the circle, and one of the sorcerer children burst among them. 'The spine kings,' she gasped, 'at the Thera Gate.'

All the sorcerers rose to their feet.

'So,' Tinou said, 'we must hurry a little.'

Quickly several of them seized Thel by the arms and legs; when he struggled he might as well have been thrashing on an iron rack. His skin was shattering. The swimmer and the three facewomen were being held back. Thel was lifted up, carried to the mirror.

Tinou appeared beside him, touched his temple. His smile was solicitous. 'My thanks for the rescue,' he said jovially, then in more formal tone: 'Through mirrors we see things right way round at last.'

41

They shoved his left foot into the surface, which was as smooth as a glass of water full over the rim, completely violet and completely gold at one and the same time; and the foot went in to the ankle. Now he had a left foot made of fire, it seemed, and he twisted in the implacable grip, cried out. Tinou nodded sympathetically, cocked his head. 'It's pain most proves we live. Nothing serves better to focus our attention on our bodies and the flesh metronomes ticking inside them, timing the bombs that will go off some day and end the universe. Remember!'

He stepped forward and leaned over Thel's face, looked at him curiously. 'There are so many kinds of pain, really.' They shoved his leg in to the hip. 'Is it pulsing, throbbing, shooting, lancing, cutting, stabbing, scalding? Is it pressing, gnawing, cramping, wrenching, burning, searing, ripping? Is it smarting, stinging, pricking, pounding, itching, freezing, drilling? Is it superficial or profound? Can you think of anything else? Can you tell me what eight times six equals? Can you take a full breath and hold it?'

And with each question Thel was thrust further in. A brief flare of genitals, the sickening twist of the gut, all his skin an organ of pain, every atom of him spinning in vain efforts to fly off – and Tinou, smiling, leaning over his face and questioning still, each word slower, louder, more drawn out: 'Is it dull, sore, taut, tender? Is it rasping, splitting, exhausting, sickening? Is it suffocating, frightful, punishing? Vicious, wretched? Blinding? Horrible? Killing? Excruciating? Unbearable?'

Then they got his face to the glossy surface, and the reflected visage within was that of a complete stranger, puffy and thick-necked, eyes bulging out – 'I have never looked like that,' Thel tried to say, certain he was dying. Compared to this the flex X would have been bliss, he thought, and with one last glimpse of Tinou's laughing face he was through the glass and gone.

CHAPTER 10
Through the Mirror

Blue stars ahead, red behind. Flare of an oil lamp in the library. We know more than our senses ever tell us, but how? How? Old brown globe, bookcases, beyond it a glassine sphere, the image of a wall. Milky black of the galactic core, tumbling down, down, down, down. Emergency landing. Emergence. The sensuous rise to consciousness.

Splayed on riprap, the taste of ocean wrack in his throat. Once with his parents he tripped and smashed his nose, vivid image of sunny pain and a chocolate ice cream, down by the canals filled with trash, a glassy sheen like the taste of blood suffusing every sundrenched manifestation of the world. Filled with sudden grief at the lost past, Thel sat up shakily and wiped his nose, spat red. Bloody spit on uneven paving stones, crowded with dead weeds. The whole village of Oia was in ruins, the walls just a block or two high. Dark wind was keening through him and the weeds rustled, it had been centuries and clearly he would never see the swimmer on the night beach again, it was past and irrecoverable. All his past was gone for good even if he could remember it; given the sense of loss for what little he could remember, it was perhaps for the best that so much was forgotten. But he knew he had had a life, childhood, adolescence, he felt its intensity and knew it would never return no matter what he did, even if he remembered every instant of it perfectly, as he felt he did, all of it right there behind some impermeable membrane in his mind, pressing against his thoughts until the ache of it filled everything.

And yet really it didn't matter if he remembered or not. Live a life and seize it to you with an infant's fierce clench of the fist, it still would slip away as lovely as the mountain sky at dusk and *never come back again*: not the moment in the dim library, the noon by the poolside, that moonlit beach and the warm sandy touch, none of it, none of it, none of it. How he loved his past in that moment, how he wanted it back! Eternal recurrence, as the sorcerers had said; ah, it would almost be worth it to be a clockwork mechanism, a bronze creature of destiny, if you could then have it over and over and over. As long as it felt new at every recurrence, who cared? He was a creature of destiny in any case, impelled by forces utterly beyond his control. To move his forefinger left rather than right was an enormous exertion against fate, anything more was too much to ask, it would be only water splashing uphill for a moment; he would bend to the curve of spacetime at last, which leads to the sea in the end. Fate is the path of least action. And if you never know it is all recurrence then it only means you feel the loss, over and over and over. But he had loved his life, he knew he had, the bad and the good and he wanted to keep it forever, all of it, to observe it from some eternal beach and perhaps step back into it, a moment here, a moment there, looking out a bay window at streetlight, bare branch, falling snow, listening to a snatch of piano by the coals of a fire, those moments of being when all the past seemed in him and alive, suffusing the moment and the only moment with a feeling – with every feeling, all at once.

Wind soughed in the weeds. Inside him the flesh metronome went tick, tick. Life slipped away hadon by hadon, limning every joy with a rime of grief; and he walked backward into the future, waving and crying out 'Good-bye! Good-bye! Good-bye!'

It was dark. There were only pinprick stars, a dozen at most though the sky was black as an eye's pupil. Shivering with fear, he stood and staggered up one of the marble staircases, now littered with blocks of stone which glowed whitely underfoot, apparently from some internal luminance, so faint it was at the edge of the visible. He was seeing the skeleton of the world.

On the spine the view of both seas was disorienting, literally in that he became aware that the sun would dawn in the west, and that he would have to trek east to new ground to escape the spine kings. Still it was reassuring to see both the oceans, to straddle the high edge of the peninsula, riding the back of the present as it snaked through past and future. He stood there for a minute, savoring the view and the bitter bite of the wind.

Looking back down at the dark luminous ruins of Oia, he saw a figure moving up terrace after terrace, flitting between walls and seeming at times to jump from place to place instantaneously. The figure looked up, and its eyes gleamed like two stars in its dark face. Thel shivered and waited, knowing the figure was coming to join him; and so it did, taking much of the night though it moved rapidly.

Finally it approached him: a man, though it was a man so slight and fluid in his movement that he seemed androgynous, or feminine. His skin was blacker than the sky, so that his smile and the whites of his eyes seemed disembodied above clothing that glowed like the stones of Oia, outlining his slim form. 'The spine kings are upon us,' he said in a bright, friendly voice. 'Side-stepping them only works for so long. If you want to escape you'll have to move fast. I can show you the way.'

'Lead on,' Thel said. He knew he could trust this figure, at the same time that another part of his mind was aware that it was a manifestation of Tinou. The intonation of the voice was the same, but it didn't matter. This one could be trusted. 'What is your name?' Thel asked, to be sure.

'I am Naousa,' the figure said, and reached forward in a confidential way to touch Thel lightly on the upper arm, a touch suasive and erotic. 'This way.'

He led Thel to a steep drop-off in the ridge, unlike anything Thel had seen before. Here the spine of the peninsula planed down and away in a smooth flat incline, as if an enormous blade had shaved off the mountain range, cutting at a hard angle down toward the beaches. Cliffs on the sides to north and south remained, while the cut itself descended at nearly a forty-five degree angle. The exposed stone of the cut was as smooth as glass, and a black that somehow indicated it would be dark gray in daylight. Descending this slippery slope would be extremely difficult on foot, but Naousa reached deep into a cleft in the granite and pulled out two lightweight bobsleds, both a whitish color. The sleds' bottoms were smoother than the glassy rock slope, and had no runners or steering mechanism. 'You lean in the direction you want to go,' Naousa said. 'The drop isn't entirely level left to right, so you have to steer a little to keep from going over the cliffs. Just follow me, and look out for bumps.' And before Thel could nod he had jumped on his bobsled and was off.

Thel threw his sled down and sat on it, and quickly was sliding down the slope. Naousa was an obvious dot below, cutting big slalom curves down an invisible course. The cut slope was only a couple hundred feet wide, though it broadened as they dropped lower. Bumps and curves invisible to the eye threw Thel left and right as he picked up speed, accelerating at what seemed an accelerating rate; he realized the only hope for survival was to follow Naousa's every move, even if it meant going as fast as Naousa and staying right on his tail. Naousa was flying down the slope, carving wide curves and crying out for joy – Thel could hear the shouts wafting back at him as another impossible turn by Naousa skirted the cliffs. It was thrilling to watch and Thel shouted himself, leaning hard left or right to follow Naousa's bold track, and despite the fact that it was like bob-sledding on an open ice slope with cliffs on both sides, Thel began to enjoy himself – to enjoy the contemplation of Naousa's expertise, and his own reproduction of it, and the sheer noise of the sleds and the wind smashing his face and the tears streaming back over his ears and off the cliff edges into space, falling down like dewdrop stars into the original salt.

It was a long ride but did not take much time. At the bottom they sledded out onto the grass of a meadow and tumbled head over heels. Naousa picked up the sleds and tucked them behind a round boulder perched on the ridge. Down here the peninsula was different in character: the stone old and weathered and graying, the spine only fifty to a hundred feet above the noisy sea, and the beaches to both sides wide, with sand white as could be, even in the starless night. 'The south side is the easiest walking,' Naousa said, and headed down to the north side.

Thel shouted thanks, and dropped to the south side, and walked west toward the sunrise. The sun would be up soon, the sky to the west was blueing. The white sand underfoot was tightly packed; scuffing it made a squeaking sound, *squick, squick*, and the scuffed sand sprayed ahead of Thel's feet in brief blazes of phosphorus. The dunes behind the tidal stretch were neatly scalloped, and covered with dense short grass all blown flat, pointing west to the dawn. The dome of the sky was higher down here and fuzzier, the blues of dawn glowing pastels. Then as he walked stars began popping into sight overhead and he stepped knee deep into the beach, as if the sand were gel; he was sinking in it, the sky was the pink of cherry blossoms and he was in sand to his cheekbones, drowning in it.

CHAPTER 11

Inside the Wave

The sun was hot on his cheek. There was too much light. He rolled on sand, shaded his eyes with a hand and cracked a lid: his brain pulsed painfully and the eyelash-blurred gold-on-white pattern meant nothing to him, then coalesced with a jolt that jerked his body up. The swimmer lay on the wide morning beach. Beyond her lay Garth and the three facewomen, leaves in their hair and long scratches on their arms and legs. Then he saw the shape of the mirror, in a bag tucked under the swimmer's outstretched arm. He was sitting and he almost rolled to her side, every muscle creaking as if carved of wood. He shook her arm, afraid to touch the bag holding the mirror.

She woke, and he asked her what had happened. She stared at him.

'I don't remember,' he explained. 'I mean, Tinou and the others pushed me through that,' pointing at the mirror bag. 'After that . . .'

She spoke slowly. 'The spine kings attacked and everything caught fire. The sorcerers left you on the plaza, and the mirror as well. We picked you up and carried you away, and took the mirror too. Then you woke and told us to follow you, and we did. We climbed out on the cliff face beside Oia to escape the sorcerers and the spine kings, and the next night we climbed to the spine and started west. You talked most of the time but we couldn't see who you talked to. Garth carried the mirror. The spine dropped into a forest and you ran all the way, and we chased you. Then it seemed you were never going to see us, and so Garth said we should push you back through the mirror. We did that and you fell through, unconscious – '

'You could just push me through?'

48

'No, it wouldn't work at first, it was hard as glass when I tried it, but Garth said it had to be at sunset, on the spine, with a kessel hawk hunting in the western sky. We waited three days until we saw one, and then it worked. But after we got you through you were asleep again. So we waited and then we fell asleep too. I'm hungry.'

The others were stirring at the sound of their voices. They woke and the beach air was filled with the chatter of voices over the hiss of broken waves. As they shared their stories they walked to the sea without volition, drawn by their hunger. The peninsula had changed to something like what Thel had traversed in his time beyond the mirror: a low forested mound snaking through the sea, sandy moon bays alternating with chalky headlands. They walked to the next bay, which faced north. Here the beach was a steep pebbly shingle that roared and grumbled at every wave's swift attack and retreat, and among the millions of shifting oval pebbles, which when wet looked like semiprecious stones, they found crabs, beach eels, scraps of seaweed that the facewomen declared edible, and one surprised-looking fish, tossed up by a wave and snatched by Garth. As they made their catch they wandered west, marking the sine curve of the hours with their passage until the sun was low. Knobs of old worn sandstone stood here and there like vertebrae out of the scrubby forest, and they climbed to one of these bony boulder knots collecting dead wood as they went, and in the sunset made a fire using Garth's firestone and knocker. Every scrap of the sea's provender tasted better than the last, the least scrap finer than a master chef's creation. Clouds came in from the south as if a roll of carpet had been kicked over them, and the sinking sun tinted the frilly undersurface a delicate yellow. Their fire blazed through the long dusk, and in the wind the whitecaps tossed, so that it felt like they were on the deck of a ship.

Each day they foraged west, and spent the night on knolls. 'We'll reach your folk soon?' Thel asked the facewomen.

'No. Many days. But when we do, you can continue on your way speeded by our horses.'

They hurried on, their hunger not quite held in check by the wrack of the waves. The peninsula straightened, and looking back they could see the big curve of land rising to the great ridge of Oia. Ahead of them the spit seemed, judging from the high points, to continue its gentle rise and fall indefinitely. They hiked on the beaches, over wet round stones that clacked together all the day long. Thel and the swimmer dove into the waist-high shore break more than once, ostensibly to try to catch briefly glimpsed fish, but really just for the feel of the dive and the wave's dizzying lift. In the evenings around the fire they pulled the mirror from its bag and contemplated it cautiously. Each of them saw different things in it, and they couldn't agree on its color. Salmon, gold, copper, lapis; such divergence of perception was frightening, and they snapped at each other and put it away, and slept uneasily.

One dawn Thel woke. The night before the mirror had been left face up on a rock, and he circled his hand over it, looking down at eyes, hair, red stones, years. The swimmer inched over the sandstone and lay prone beside him, their heads together as they peered down into it, as if looking down a well. 'What is it?' Thel said.

'It shows the truth,' the swimmer said, then smiled. 'Or maybe it just makes things pretty.'

They tilted it so it reflected their two faces.

'Hey!' Thel exclaimed. 'That's me.'

It was the face he knew from a million beard burns: narrow jaw, round forehead, long nose, wide mouth. He would have looked a long time but the reflection of the swimmer stole his gaze; it was her face, but subtly transformed, the harsh strong lines emphasized and given a pattern, a human face before anything else but so purely human that it was, he thought happily, that of a god.

They broke their gazes at the same time and looked at each other; grinning like children who have gotten away with something forbidden, they let the mirror drop and rolled together. Blood surged through Thel as they kissed and made love, he sank into her as if into a wave, riding inside the wave on an endless rise, pulled along as when body-surfing. Touch was everything then, her skin, the stone under his knees and elbows;

but once he looked up and saw the mirror beyond her head and filled with joy he waved a hand over it: gold light flashed up into the chill salt predawn air.

CHAPTER 12

The Facewomen

After that Thel carried the mirror bag himself. And the next night they saw bonfires ahead of them, to the west. As they progressed along the low line of the old sandstone ridge, the air thick with salt and the roar of waves, the peninsula took a pronounced swing to the north, making an immense arc thrown in the sea. And to the west where the horizon washed over the black mark of the spit, a short line of bonfires sparked against the late twilight sky. Apparently where these fires burnt the peninsula was quite a bit taller, for the dots of yellow light were a good distance above the obsidian sea; nevertheless they flickered to the point of disappearing briefly from sight. The three facewomen stood and watched intently. 'They are our signal beacons,' one said and after a while added, 'They say we are being pursued.'

So they began to hike all through the long days, and in the dawns and dusks, and each night the three facewomen talked among themselves, and then one night their eyefaces talked among themselves, in high-pitched voices; and yet they said to the other three travelers only, 'We are being pursued.' Until the distance between the bonfires began to decrease, and the line of four was almost one wide fire, growing brighter from right to left. Then they said, 'We are being pursued; but we have almost reached our home.'

Wearily they hiked on, spurred by this pronouncement, and slept one more night out, and then the next day in the late morning they came to a deep stone-ringed firepit. The leader of the facewomen crouched and touched one of the stones. 'We are home,' her eyeface said. She and her two companions led the way thereafter, skipping from knob to knob and touching each fire ring, then running downhill into the next swale between knobs. The peninsula became broader and more verdant: between the bonfire tors the crest ridge split in two broad lines of hilltops, holding between them sunken meadows spotted with vernal ponds that were in this season patches of bright grass strewn with wildflowers, dots of pure color. These meadows, strung like green stones on a necklace, grew larger and larger until they came on one that was broad and flat, and ringed by a split log fence and a number of low twisty pines. At the far side of the fenced-in enclosure clustered a herd of small quick dark horses, flowing along the fence like a single organism. In the trees behind the fence stood hexagonal buildings with wood walls and hide roofs. These were arranged in circles, like their firepits or their corral.

The three facewomen ran to one of the huts and burst into it, and emerged with a small gang of other facewomen clinging to them and shouting. When they had calmed down, Thel, the swimmer and Garth were welcomed with a fluid formality, recursive smiles of welcome shrinking away into the infinity of the facewomen's right eyes. It seemed to Thel that all the inhabitants of the meadow were women, but he noticed children among them, and saw that they tended to clump in groups of three; Garth confirmed that these were reproductive units.

Their threesome took them to what appeared to be the oldest threesome, village elders who greeted them and thanked them for rescuing their granddaughters. Thel took the opportunity to ask how the bonfire messengers had known they were being pursued.

'We saw the pursuers,' one of the threesome said.

Thel frowned. 'How?'

They led him to the knob above the village. There in the rocks stood a short pyramid of black fitted stone, holding up a long hollow tube carved from the same stone, set with a thick clear lens at each end.

'A telescope!' Thel said.

The old women nodded. 'You know the principle?'

'Yes.' Thel waited while one of them aimed the glass, then stooped to look through it. 'It's powerful!'

'Yes. More powerful than that, in fact. But that is sufficient to see the spine kings.'

So it was; in the pale colors of the image, swimming on the air, Thel saw ant-like soldiers, tramping in a line along the ridge. He looked over the top of the glass and saw it was pointed some halfway along the visible peninsula. 'They're far behind.'

'They stopped for other business. They will be here in a few days, at their pace. They will certainly come. We saw through the glass what you are carrying, you see. When the spine kings arrive you must not be here. But we will provide you with horses to speed you on your way west, in thanks for helping our daughters. And you may spend two nights here resting.'

They slept in a storage hut on piles of woven blankets, feeling so luxurious that they could scarcely get comfortable. The next day they were taken to the big meadow pasture's corral, and introduced to three of the small horses. 'These are young ones,' the facewoman in charge of the corral told them. 'They're wild but they have no habits – they should accept you. Here, you hold their mane and jump on.' The horses' hair was the chestnut red of certain fir trees Thel had seen back on the high spine, and their manes, long and rough, felt exactly like handfuls of the trees' hairy fibrous bark: indeed, looking closely at it, he couldn't see any difference. He laughed. Then the small herd in the enclosure bolted and ran around the inside of the fence, all in a mass, their manes and long russet hair flowing behind them as if they were underwater, and he laughed again. 'A horse is a fish made of trees,' he told the startled swimmer, and leaped on his animal and rode head pressed into the stiff rough red mane, feeling the sea wind course over him as it had during his wild ride on the other side of the mirror. Jerking the animal's head to one side or another influenced its direction, and pulling back on the mane slowed it, as kicking it spurred it on. The corral mistress said as he leaped off, 'Ride these until you come to the brough – they can take you no further. Set them free and they will return to us. They know to hide from the spine kings.'

'Thanks for your help,' Thel said.

One of the smallest visible eyefaces grinned. 'With what you are carrying,' it said in a small voice, 'we want you as far away as possible when the spine kings arrive.'

'Ah.'

That night they built a massive bonfire, and when the flames were leaping as high as the treetops and higher, the eldest three facewomen brought the telescope into the clearing and put it on a portable stand, and stood Thel next to the fire, and pointed the glass at him and looked at him through it. Feeling scorched at the back of his neck, he looked into the lens at the leader's face. She had the telescope placed against her eyeface, and in the little curved circle of glass he saw two eyes, blinking as they observed him: her smallest face, no doubt, too small for the naked eye to see. So there was an end to the recession after all, he thought. The ultimate leader of the facewomen, perhaps; and she said in a squeak, 'Stand still. Don't blink so much. Look straight into the glass.' He did as he was told, almost laughing because it felt like a kind of eye examination. 'How far back can you see?' he asked. The bonfire pushed roasted air past him.

'To your birth,' the high voice shrilled. 'You have been through the mirror and back. You are not from this world. You fell into this world, one night, into the ocean with seahorses.'

'Before that?' Thel asked, finding it suddenly hard to breathe. The clothes on his back were hot.

'A man in a bubble, flying through the stars. Others like you and not like you. When you were a child, you lived by a lake. The lake was circular and had high cliffs surrounding it. One day you tried to climb the steepest cliff, and fell. You hit the water feet first and survived the impact, plunging deep. The water of the lake was said to be bottomless and so when your feet hit a submerged outcropping of the cliff you were astonished, and in that state of panic these moments of your future came to you, intense as any memory, for every vision is a memory, and every memory a vision of a world that never existed until called up in the mind. You saw then your immersion in our ocean, your step through the mirror, your stand before our glass, the fire behind you, all of it seen in that instant. Remember?'

Falling water in his eyes, the sudden heat at his back. 'Yes,' Thel said, wondering, looking within frantically to see all he

55

could of that lost lake, his boyhood, his parents, the cat leaping from the table onto the dog, the old man who loved the clouds –

'Everything which we really are and never quite live,' the little voice said, and the whole thing snatched itself away from him and he was only aware of the heat on his back and his hair curling. He walked away, out of the telescope's view and into the purple night, feeling his back radiate against the wet salty air. The face of his mother – he snatched at it, lost it. Dune grass flowing like seaweed, rustling against the chewing sound of waves: clouds drifting through the stars. Never to be in anything but the present, trapped in the moment which is always receding, never ours to have and hold – the swimmer came out after him and found him, and he collapsed onto the sand, sat there with an arm around her strong thigh. 'I want to be a stone,' he said, 'a stone man lying on the beach forever, never to think, never to feel the future sifting through me. I want to be a stone.'

'It's the same for them,' she said.

CHAPTER 13

Garth's Apples

The following morning they woke with the dawn and the facewomen led them to their horses and waved farewell as they rode off. The horses were exuberant with running and galloped over the dunes waving their heads from side to side like blind things, eating the air and snapping at their riders if they were interfered with. So they hung on and rode: Garth's horse led, the swimmer's brought up the rear. Thick white thunderheads grew over the water to the south, and the colors of everything in the long morning light were richer than they remembered them being, the water a dark glassy blue outside jade green shallows, the foam on the breakers as white as the clouds, the dune grass subtle dusty greens, the red barky hair of their horses an irresistible magnet for the eye. The horses ran along the beach until midday, then cantered up onto the dunes and browsed on the sparse grass. The three riders dismounted stiffly and hobbled them, then walked down to the beach to forage for beach food to supplement the little the facewomen had been able to give them. They ate on the beach, returned to the horses and slept, then in the mid-afternoon rode again. They traveled so much faster than they could have on foot that it was hard to grasp: they were already far from the facewomen's meadow, and the horses ran on tirelessly through the long glarey stretches of late afternoon, until at sunset they trotted to a halt and stood in a wind-protected dip between two dunes, browsing easily through the mauve dusk.

They rode like that for days. Each day the peninsula became lower, narrower, more stripped of life. The thick mats of dune grass reduced to occasional patches, the tufts of grass as sparse as the hair on a balding man. Each tuft had been blown in every direction by the winds, creating a perfect circle of smoothed hard sand around it, deepest at the outer edge; the dunes became geometrical worksheets, sine waves covered with circles. One sunset walking in this deeply patterned sand Thel looked down at a tuft of grass and the perfect circle around it, and thought, That is your life: a stalk of living stuff blown in every direction, leaving a brief pattern in sand.

They had emptied the facewomen's bags of food, and went hungry as the beach provided less and less. One morning Garth plucked two of the fruit from his shoulder tree and offered them to Thel and the swimmer. 'I can eat grass,' he told them. 'More grass, more fruit. Really. Please. We can't afford to spend all day on the beach foraging.'

Thel said, 'If we stopped in the later afternoon instead of at dusk, we could forage more, and you could eat more too.' He scuffed dubiously at the tough dune grass, so sharp-edged you could easily cut skin with it. Garth also spent every evening with his feet buried in the sand; presumably more of that would help too, but it was something Garth didn't talk about.

He did agree to the early stops, however, and so every morning after that Thel and the swimmer ate one of his bitter electric shoulder apples, and felt the chemical tang of it course through them. It was wonderful how well the apples satisfied their appetites, how long they could subsist on them. And Garth ate dune grass in the evenings, and spent time with his feet buried in the sand, and got thinner; but the apples continued to bloom on his shoulder tree, tiny fragrant white blossoms giving way to hard green nubs, which grew quickly into edible fruit.

Then as they rode down the endless spit of the peninsula, even the grasses disappeared. They were on a desert shore, beach on both sides of a low mound of dunes; even the horses had to be fed from Garth's tree, and he had to spend the whole of every afternoon with his body stretched out to the sun, and his feet stuck deep in the sand – haggard, exhausted, a small smile playing over his mouth. 'I was told tales of this, how one of us could grow enough to sustain his fellows in a time of need. Like having children, they always said, and now I know what they mean.' And he looked at them with a gaze they could scarcely return, so filled was it with a kind of amused maternal affection.

Every morning thunderheads billowed up and sidled across the southern sky, but never hit their stretch of the coast, piling up instead against the mountainous spine far behind them. They found pools of water in holes in the sandstone, proof of storms past, but these had grown brackish with beach dew, and the travelers became thirsty as well.

After many days of this deprivation, they saw in the distance ahead a small knob in the peninsula. Dune grasses returned to the central mound, and they came across more pools of water. Days passed and it seemed they would reach the knob the following afternoon for several days running, but it was bigger than they had first thought, and kept receding.

Finally it loomed up, several hundred feet tall, like a sandstone lighthouse. They skirted it on the wide southern beach, and on the other side discovered a most extraordinary thing: the beach stretched out into the blue sea, and got thinner and lower, until it sank under the water. 'It's the end!' Thel cried.

'No no,' Garth said. 'It's the water gate. I've heard stories about it. Look out there, see that smudge? It's the other cape, where the peninsula proper begins again. In between is a tidal bar. This is the lowest part of the spine, nothing more. At low tide a strip of sand will emerge as fine as any road, and stay above the waves for half the day.'

It proved to be true. As the afternoon progressed the beach extended farther into the water, which was racing from north to south in a strong current, breaking whitely in a straight line that divided the sea. This stretch of white foam boiled furiously in a line to the horizon and the distant smudge of the farther cape. Then in a matter of moments, it seemed, the whitewater divided and fell away into two sets of waves rolling in from right and left, leaving a strip of wet gray sand and wet brown rock standing between them. The breakers tumbled in over rocky shallows on both sides, but the bar stood clear of them. And the spine trail extended even here; squarish blocks of water-holed rock had been laid in a path over the bar, making a causeway a foot or two higher than the bar itself. 'The horses can't cross that,' Garth said. 'The rock would tear up their hooves.'

'But surely it's more than one tide's walk across?' the swimmer said.

Garth nodded. 'Still we must send the horses back, as we said we would.' And he kicked and shouted at the horses, threw rocks at them until they cantered off, and circled nervously; then regarded each other and broke for home, flowing down the beach like a school of red fish darting through the sea.

Something moved on the side of the knob and they jumped, turned to look. It was a man the same color as the sandstone, his skin the same grainy dark brown. As he approached they saw he was naked, and that his eyes, his hair, everything was the brown of the rock. In his eyes the color seemed darker, the way the rock did when it was wet.

He stopped before them and said, 'I am Birsay the guide. It is more than one tide's walk to cross the brough, as you noted. This is how we do it; there is a rise near the halfway point, and we run to that in one low tide, on a path that I have built. It is just possible, though you get your legs wet. There on the rise I have left several large holed rocks. We tie ropes I have made to those anchors, and as the water rises we rise on it, floated by slings I have made of kelp bladders and wood. The current pushes us out, usually to the south, but we are tied by the ropes to the anchor rocks, and when the tide ebbs, we float down to a landing, and complete the crossing of the brough to the other cape.'

'Why have you made these things?' Thel asked. 'Why do you do this?'

The sandstone-colored man shrugged. 'The peninsula extends around the world, and there is no land but it. And this is the only place in its circumference where the sea has chewed the peninsula down almost to its level. And naturally the peninsula must be passable. Traders come through, and circumnavigators on pilgrimages – believers of more religious persuasions than I'd care to recall. It is simply the natural order of things. The land itself calls forth a guide to sustain that order, and I am the forty-ninth reincarnation of that guide, Birsay.'

He led them to a tall cave entrance in the side of the knob, down stone steps to a dry sand floor. Against one wall were circles of coiled rope, made of some sort of animal hair or plantlike fiber – impossible in this world to be sure which, it occurred to Thel as he examined it. It was thick in the hand, and would certainly hold against any current. The floats Birsay had mentioned were there too, made of the big bulbs one saw at the base of kelp tubes, tied by flat cords to a wooden framework that held them under the arms, and around the chest and back. 'You spend almost half a day suspended in the tide,' Birsay said. 'The water is warm, though by the end it doesn't feel so. The bath is good for the skin. Then the distance from the rise to the western cape is not as great as the distance from here to the rise.'

The three travelers conferred by eye. Garth said, 'When would you have us leave?'

'We've wasted too much of this ebb. And they are getting longer every day now, for twenty more days. The next one will begin in the dark before dawn.'

'The next, then,' Thel said, and the other two nodded their agreement.

They spent the night in the cave, around a small warm driftwood fire, the twisted shapes of the wood burning in bright flames tinged with blue, green, salmon. What little smoke there was rose through a blowhole in the roof of the cave. The guide fed them broiled conch, seasoned with wild onions and a gingery seaweed, wonderful after their week of subsistence on Garth's bitter apples.

Birsay had a place for everything, and he moved neatly and quickly around the fire, catching its light just as the cave walls did, so that sometimes it was hard to see him. He brought out a tray of black loam for Garth to stick his feet into after the regular meal was done, and with a blush and a grateful look, Garth silently buried his feet in the dirt.

'Do you guide all travelers that appear here?' Thel asked.

'I do.'

'You make no distinctions?'

'What do you mean?'

'Those that follow us are murderers, intent on our lives.'

'Is that so?' The wet pebble eyes regarded them with interest. 'Well, I wish you all speed. I make no distinctions of that kind,

61

no. Good, evil, right, wrong – they are personal matters, shifting from one to the next. These murderers may regard themselves as righteous folk, and you as great criminals perhaps, thieves of something they cherish, perhaps, who knows?' Though he glanced at Thel's mirror bag as if he did know. 'How am I to judge? By your stories? By the looks on your faces?' He dismissed the idea with a flip of the hand. 'My task is to lead travelers across the low point in the world road. Their purposes, their identity – none of my concern. One winter I led death himself across the brough, you can still see his footprints in the rock where a wave splashed him and he got angry ...' And as the firelight played over his face he told them stories of travelers who had passed, men and women and creatures it sometimes took him the burning of a branch to describe. One such had had the legs and waist of a man, his chest then rising up into the rounded and feathered body of a giant eagle. This creature had spoken to him in grim croaks, and after a while Birsay had guessed the truth; it walked across the brough because it had had its wing muscles clipped, so that it could no longer fly. The guide laughed at Thel: 'How judge that, eh? How judge that?'

CHAPTER 14

Crossing the Bar

In the middle of the night Birsay crouched by their warm sand beds and roused them. 'The brough comes clear soon.' They rose and ate more conch, and at Birsay's instruction drank from a jug of fresh water until their stomachs were heavy and cold.

The star flood still lit the beach as they walked onto the wet sand. Birsay watched each wave closely, and as one ran up the sand he pointed. 'Last high wave,' he said. 'From now on they ebb.'

Then more and more of the beach was revealed as each wave sluiced back and hopped over the nonexistent rail where the water regrouped and turned again. A point emerged, wet tan sand with a crosshatched stippling of black. Then the waves fell back to left and right as they had the afternoon before, and the line of boiling white water appeared. The bar emerged, at first just as an extension of their point of sand, receding away from them at a walking pace: then, in the blue of dawn, the water simply ran away from them to right and left, and they walked on a sandbar that extended all the way to the horizon.

Struck silent at the uncanny sight, the three travelers strode quickly after Birsay, their ropes coiled and hung over their shoulders, their floats hanging on straps tied over their own backpacks and bags. The sun rose and cast long faint shadows ahead of them. The seas rolled up flat wet sand to right and left, the northern and southern seas separated only by their spit of wet sand.

They crunched through patches dense with seashells, or squishy with living anemones. It was a blue day, the air clear as glass and the sea and sky darker and lighter shades of the same full blue. The sand and Birsay were a color composed of tan and

63

black sand, mixed thoroughly. A handful of it washed thin by water revealed clear grains, smaller white and brown grains, and tiny floating black flecks.

Then the sand began to grow thin over bedrock of the same color, which broke through as if it were a little model of the spine, here worn to ankle-high knobs and nubs, split by the sea down its grain of stratification, running across the bar from sea to sea. Eventually they walked on bare rock, sharp ribs of brown that ran out under the white waves, which grumbled toward them to nothing in hundreds of parallel grooves. Eventually the shallow faults turned the brough into a stretch of pitted knife edges, set across their way. Walking over these edges would have devastated first sandals and then feet, but Birsay or his predecessors had filled a rough narrow path through the faults with blocks of loose stone – an old path, it seemed, for the blocks were worn in their settings, and in places had been washed away.

They hurried over this low causeway, until when they looked behind they could see no sign of Birsay's knob, or the low peninsula beyond it; ahead they saw no sign of the knob at the halfway point, nor the farther cape. The brough extended all the way to the horizon in both directions, a horizon nearly at eye level, so that it seemed they crossed the bottom of a flattish bowl of ocean, which would sooner or later rush in on them. It was a strange sight.

In late mid-afternoon they came to Birsay's knob, first seen as a bulge in the bar, a widening of the white water to the sides. 'We've made good time,' Birsay said, 'but it's always a close thing. By sunset we'll be floating.'

Once on the knob it seemed not much different from the rest of the brough: slightly wider, minutely taller, pocked and runnelled like all the rest of the rock they had traversed. In the largest potholes were big blocks of rock that had had holes chiseled through them, and following Birsay's instructions they tied the ends of their ropes through these holes. Birsay chose the anchor rocks very carefully, after observing the surging mush and the wind, and his charges' bodies; he spread them out at intervals along the bar, Thel, Birsay, Garth, the swimmer. Their few possessions they placed in other potholes, with stones placed over them.

They sat on the damp rock, and waited. The tide began to come in.

It was impossible not to be frightened at the sight. Each broken wave rushed at them, at first as thick as the wave had been high, and boiling over the reef below; it thinned as it made its furious rush, until it was bubbling water trickling up the furrows in the rock, and then receding. But each final gurgle was closer than the last.

'Usually the south reaches us first,' Birsay said, 'because that's where the prevailing winds come from. But today – ' he frowned, sniffing – 'the wind is from the east. And the north side is closing faster.' He turned and turned again on the nob's highest point, sniffing. 'It may be windy tonight.'

Then, in the surge of just a few waves, the four of them were sitting on a tiny rock island in a sea of boiling whitewater, waves from the two seas running together and slapping up into the air, in lines of wind-tossed spray. Then a big wave from the north ran up the rock and right over their feet and backs. Quicker than Thel would have believed possible, every wave rolled over the rock and their lower legs. They stood around Birsay on the peak, and then waves from the south sea piled in as well, and up and down the brough to east and west they could see long sheets of whitewater squirting up into the air, underneath them a chaos of wave and backwash, the sea white with foam, millions of bubbles hissing out their lives, sending a fine rain into the air and creating a tremendous loud roar, a roar made of glugs and hisses that individually would scarcely be heard across a room.

When the water got waist high they were shoved hard this way and that, and Birsay told them in a loud voice to hang on – that this was the only tricky part – and that they should soon cast off and get away from the knob, trusting to their floats and anchors. When the waves were chest high they were forced to take his advice, and they swam off after him to the south, floating easily on their miniature rafts and spreading out as they were pushed straight out from their anchors.

As the tide rose the water grew calmer, until the only signs of the brough were long snaking lines of crusty foam floating away to the south, and an occasional brief mushy break at the top of the largest waves as they crossed the bar. The waves, and the current that pushed them, were from the northwest. So they floated to the southeast of the knob, connected to it like kites flying in the wind of the tidal current. If they rested they were some thirty feet from each other, and they were about two hundred feet from the submerged knob, so that Thel and the swimmer, on the outsides, could easily paddle over to talk to the middle two. Garth's shoulder tree looked odd indeed sticking up out of the water, like the last remnant of a deluged land. Garth's face was sputtering and apprehensive beside it; he couldn't swim and had to trust his float, clearly a difficult act of faith.

It was a strange sunset. Now the horizon was closer and higher than ever, the dome of the sky taller: all as blue as they had been at dawn. The sun dropped through the air yellow as a daisy and sank without fanfare, turning green at the end as if the last rays had shone through water. During the long dusk a line of puffy white clouds appeared to the northwest, so tall they redefined the height of the sky. These clouds eventually took on copper and iron hues, and cast their color over everything else, so that the sea took on a coppery sheen, and the air was dark and metallic.

Birsay watched this development nervously, and when the wind shifted and picked up suddenly, he swam to Thel's side and said, 'It may be a cold night. The northerlies are hard.'

Thel swallowed salt and nodded. Already the water felt warmer than the air, so that his head was cold, and it was warming to duck it into the brine. Birsay said the southern current was warmer still; Thel was content with the northern one, which felt just a touch below body temperature.

But the northwest wind was cold, and the swells rolling by began to steam a little. In the last light of the dusk they saw the line of tall clouds approaching, blocking out the stars that were just popping into salt-blurred existence. The travelers rose and fell on dark swells that steamed whitely. They rose and fell, rose and fell.

The wind strengthened and waves began to break on the bar, emerging from the dark several hundred feet away from them, on the northern shallows. There low dark surges in the sea's surface reared up and toppled over in a white roar, water shattered and tumbled chaotically, in a line as far as they could see. The broken waves rolled over the bar in a low continuous thunder, but as the water deepened again each wave would reconstitute itself out of its own mush, the whitewater shrinking back up the side of the swell until it was only a whitecap; and then it was only a groundswell again, on which they rose and fell, rose and fell, crest to trough and back again.

But the wind got stronger, and the waves bigger. A ground-swell breaks when the depth of water below it is equal to the height of the swell, trough to crest; now the swells were as high as the water beneath their feet, and they were at the ends of their ropes, they couldn't get any farther out onto the south sea. The wind picked up again, and now each time they rose on a swell there was broken water at the crest, so that they had to plunge under it and hold their breath until their floats pulled through the wave and out into the air again.

It was raining, Thel noticed once when he came up, a cold rain that roiled the ocean surface and threw up more steam. Now the wind howled, and the waves became big rolling walls of broken white mush, wild and powerful. It was all Thel could do to hold his breath as he was thrashed up and down under these broken waves; he held his float to him, waited grimly each time for it to pull him back up into the roaring black night. When it did he gasped in huge breaths, and looked to his right where the others were, but could see little through the spray. Then another wave would lift him and he would duck under the whitewater, endure its tumbling, come up again. Efforts to swim sideways to Birsay were useless, and getting to Garth and the swimmer unthinkable: and yet she was only ninety feet away.

He could only concentrate on getting under each wave with a full breath, and on staying upright in his float. The night fell into an endless pattern of rising, ducking under whitewater, holding on with lungs bursting, popping back out into the shrieking wind, resting against the float's restraint. Then again. And again. It went on until at one point he got so tired it seemed he couldn't go on, and he considered cutting the rope and floating off to the south on the groundswell. But then a sort of second wind came to him, a stubbornness suffusing every cell of his muscles and lungs, and he worked to make each forced plunge as streamlined and efficient as he could, grimly trying to relax and be at ease as the broken water threw him about, as loose as a rag on a clothesline in a stiff wind. He fell into a rhythm. Nothing marked the passing of time, it seemed he had been breathing in a pattern of submergence in the sea for years. The water began to feel cool, then cold. His head and arms were frigid in the wind's rip.

Then as he floated, waiting for the next rise, lightning forked down to his left. By the fey snap of light he glimpsed dots on the water, heads and floats – and then he was under again. The lightning struck again when he was underwater, he saw the flash and opened his closed eyes and saw a field of bubbles, white in green – then black. Three or four more times lightning struck, but always when he was submerged. He wondered if they would be electrocuted.

Then one wave thumped him down onto rock. The air burst from his lungs and he nearly blacked out before resurfacing. It was still dark night up there, the storm raging, rain coming down harder than ever: he could get a refreshing swallow of fresh water merely by turning his open mouth to the northwest. Submerged again, he kept his feet down and hit the rock bottom more gently. But it got harder as the tide ebbed, and the broken waves swept across the brough more wildly; often they knocked him down against the bottom and thumped him against it repeatedly, until he ached with the battering, and it seemed that after all the night's labors he might be killed by his landing.

Eventually he stood chest high in the waves' troughs, then waist high; but it was too much work to stand, and too cold. He crouched down in the water and let the float and rope hold him, peering through the blackness for the next onrushing wall of whitewater.

Finally the broken waves themselves were low enough that he could float over them, his head clear; and in the troughs the whitewater only sluiced over his knees. He hauled himself up the rope toward the knob, where it was shallower still; he could sit, and turn his back to the waves and the wind. Relaxing his stomach muscles made him retch. When he had gathered some strength he hauled himself up onto the knob, and found the other anchors, and slogged down the length of Garth's rope; out in the murk he could see Garth bobbing.

But it was only his float. 'No,' Thel said. Rather than return to the knob he just swung on his rope sideways, and bumped into Birsay unexpectedly; but Birsay hung in his float, head back, mouth and eyes wide open to the waves. He had drowned.

Stomach spasming, Thel swung back the other way, stepping on sharp rock. No sign of the swimmer. Back, forth, up, back; nothing. He had to walk back to the knob and find her anchor. The rope hung loose in the water, trailing out to sea, and he hauled it in feeling like Death the Fisherman, afraid and sick at heart. Its end came to him, frayed. In the first predawn blue he peered at the ends of the fibers; it looked like she had chewed through the rope, bitten her way free. The swimmer. He kneeled on the rock, collapsing around his cramped stomach. The swimmer. She had freed herself but kept the float, smart woman. Perhaps she had swum over and pulled Garth from his float, yes. Took them both off the bar, off to where the groundswell would pose no challenge to her swimming powers. Yes. She would come back. Or else swim to the cape in the west.

When dawn illuminated the seascape the tide had ebbed and the brough had returned, though it was often overrun by the storm surf. Everything today was green, the sea a light jade color, the clouds a heavy dark gray tinged with green, the bar brown, but greenish as if with algae.

Thel untied the float from his chest and tossed it aside. Angrily he kicked Birsay's anchor, left him bobbing in the waves. He put his bags over his shoulder, the mirror like a heavy plate in its wet sack. He took off along the bar, squish squish.

It was hard to walk. Often he got off Birsay's path and fell in knee-deep transverse crevices, cracking his shins so hard that the world itself burst with pain, as it had when he was shoved through the mirror. The wind keened across the brough, in his ear and cold. It rained intermittently and clouds rushed overhead like the horses of the facewomen. Several times he heard the swimmer and Garth calling to him from the surf to his left, but he never saw them. The current in the southern sea was running swiftly toward the cape to the west, which now appeared as a dark hill in the clouds. A good sign, it would help them along. He drank sea water, he was so thirsty; he drank the blood from his shins for food, cupping it in a palm and getting a good mouthful after every fall. Its taste reminded him of Garth's fruit. Blindly he kicked on, and then the brough was sand. He ate some of it. The mirror was heavy on his back, he wanted to toss it aside but didn't.

He lay on the cape beach, in wet sand. Sand crabs hopped around him, tried to eat him and he ate them in return. Along the southern side of the cape, that was where they would land. A beach stream, fresh water cutting through the shingle. He lay in it and drank. When he woke again he was stronger, and could bury himself in the sand and sleep properly. The next day he found abalone studding a beach reef like geodes, and he broke them with rocks and ate the mussels after pounding them tender. That and the beach stream infused him with strength, and he began walking the cape's broad southern beach, under the steep green prow of the reemerging peninsula. The beach was studded with pools of water blue as the sky, and with driftwood logs from what had been immense trees, and with shell fragments that were sometimes big enough to sit in. All kinds of debris, on fine tawny sand, loose underfoot so that he often stumbled, and sometimes fell.

All kinds of debris: and yet when he came across one piece of driftwood, he knew it instantly. It was the remains of a shrub, stripped of leaves and bark – a thin trunk dividing into thinner branches, their broken ends rounded and smooth as if rolled in the waves for years. Just a sand-colored piece of driftwood, a splay of branches like a hand reaching out. He sat on the sand and wept.

CHAPTER 15
Submergence

He wandered the beaches on the southern side of the cape, and during each low tide ventured back out on the brough, looking for signs of the swimmer. In the evenings he grubbed on a beach of oval flat stones for crabs, and cracked more abalone, and felt a traitor to Garth and the swimmer every time he swallowed. He hated his hunger then, the way it drove him, the way he was its slave. The days were so long. During one he sat in the sand at the tip of the cape, on the edge of the prow that rose out of the sea to a grassy peak some five hundred feet above; and each part of that day passed like a year of grieving.

The next day he climbed the grassy peak. When he reached the top he could see far over the brough, a dark swath in the sea studded with whitecaps. It was an overcast day, the sun a white smeary blob and the sky like the inside of an abalone shell, arched over a sea of lead. The brough seemed to disappear out at the horizon, with no sign of the peninsula on the other side, as if the peninsula were sinking as he passed, sinking and disappearing forever, so that even if he walked around the world he would only someday come to a final cape, with the empty sea beyond and the land he stood on sinking.

71

CHAPTER 16

Walking Every Day

As blank and bleached as a fragment of driftwood, he sat and let waves break on his head. He drank the salty tide until he could drink no more, threw it up, crawled to the beach stream to drink. One afternoon it occurred to him that the currents could have shifted, she could have come ashore on the north beaches, or been swept by currents far down the peninsula to the west, past him. Those small white teeth chewing away at the rope – surely such pure will had lived! Surely the will to survive had something to do with survival!

Next morning he walked west on the spine, investigating every cove beach tucked out of the view of the crest trail. Days passed like that, he no longer remembered much of the night of the storm, it was too much like the memory of a dream, vague, incoherent, illuminated in flashes, intensely disturbing. We forget dreams, he thought, because they are too vivid to face. He sometimes had trouble remembering what had happened to him on the peninsula before the storm; once he couldn't recall what he was looking for, it was just something he did, climb up and down rocks step after step, looking closely at the margin of sea and shore, searching for patterns in the sand. Clouds rolled overhead, west to east in their own frilly groundswell, wave after wave of fronts, the masses of warm air wedging under the cold air and then rising like bubbles up through that drafty emptiness, clouds burgeoning into existence as the warm air expressed its watery milk.

For a week the sunsets were purest pink. Why in perfectly clear air some sunsets were pink, others bronze, others purple: he pondered that through many dusks, tending fires of driftwood started with a lens of clear glass he had found beachcombing.

Through the long days he hiked westward and westward, roving from shore to shore. It was a task, a filling of the hours, a compulsion, a destiny. Kicking the rocks with the toe of his boot he heard chants come from his own mouth, wordless grunts, howls of pain, broken phrases: 'And that. And that. And that. And that. And . . .'

Off to the right was a narrow ridge like a knife of rock, extending perpendicularly from the larger peninsula into the northern sea, disappearing over the horizon. It was so regular that it looked artificial, an impossibly long drawbridge connecting something over the horizon to the peninsula's great mass.

Where this ridge connected to the peninsula there stood the grass-covered walls of an old hill fort, which had perhaps served to defend this end of the drawbridge, who could say. Around the old grassy mounds were a cluster of driftwood crofts, their roofs made of sod. The people he found there were tiny, thin and brown. At their bidding he entered the largest croft and sat and ate with them, around the smoke of a peat fire. The east wall had two small windows, and shafts of sunlight shone mottley through the reek.

Later he went back outside to escape the smoke. An old woman joined him and he saw that she cast no shadow except on her body. The sun was directly overhead, at least in this season, at midday. He thought about it for a while.

'Is there a trail over the ridge?' he asked the old woman.

'It is a trail narrow as virtue,' she recited.

'What lies at the far end?'

'A temple, they say.'

'How far away is it?'

She didn't know.

Driven by a bleached, dispassionate curiosity, he found the peninsular end of the ridge trail, and hiked out onto it. The trail was a ragged row of squarish marble stones, set in the edge of the splintered ridge. Sometimes it led over arches like literal drawbridges, spanning blocky debris-choked seas.

He hiked in shifts, timing himself by the sun's slow flight, hoping to get some kind of regular 'day's march' to measure the distance he traveled. The trail never got as narrow as the old woman had claimed it was. He hiked for ten days, then came to an enormous geometrical cone of dirt, overgrown with thick green grass and cut by the staircase that the trail here became. He hurried up these stone stairs and stepped onto a flagged circular terrace at the top, with the breath whooshing in his lungs and his blood pounding through him. Behind him the knife edge was a slender thread dropped over the sea, a kind of stone pier extending all the way to the watery horizon, which gave no clue of the peninsula. It was a frightening view.

But it was midday, so he took a straight stick from his pack and stuck it between two flagstones, so that it would cast its shadow to the north, over a square of yellow marble. A straight stick, straight up. Its shadow looked like the black dirt under a fingernail.

He sucked in his breath, measured the shadow with another stick he had brought, finely notched for the purpose. It was impossible to be very accurate with the shadow so miniscule, but he tried.

The stick was something like a thousand times longer than its shadow!

He sat down and thought it over, aware that this was not his idea, that somewhere in his blank past he had heard of the method, and admired it. But the details, the details ... A spasm of pain as he felt the presence of his lost past, a world in which one could stand on the accumulated knowledge of all those who came before, a world in which one could feel one knew something more than what blazed in the senses ... Think, think. If the shadow were the same length as the stick, then he would be halfway to the pole (discounting the curvature of the planet), and the world would be eight times his hike in circumference, or eighty marches around. Right? It seemed so.

But the shadow was only the thousandth part of the stick in length, and it had taken ten days to get here; so it would take ten thousand days to make it halfway to the pole; and therefore eighty thousand days to circumnavigate the globe. Was that right? Garth had once said that the years here were four hundred days long. So to walk around the world would take ... two hundred years.

CHAPTER 17

The Past

On the way back to the peninsula it rained, and then even snowed a bit, a cold wet slushy snow, heavy flakes swirling down and filling the air with white clots. Clouds gusted onto him so that he could seldom see more than a few feet of the knife edge, and perhaps gray waves thrashing themselves to foam on rocks below. The wind keened over the ridge's obstruction, and he couldn't escape it without huddling below the ridge on the lee side, where the lack of movement made him just as cold as the wind would have. He had run out of the food the crofters had given him, and every night was a miserable eternity, so long he lost every hope. He could free himself to sleep through only a quarter or a third of those endless nights, and the dawns were a deep stabbing relief, not only physically but in his feelings.

Through the days in the snowy fog he hiked as long and hard as he could. There was a kind of moss that was a startling, unreal green, and it grew in a mixed pattern with a silvery gray bracken, and olive and yellow lichen; the colors made a quilt over the fresh white granite and distracted his eye as he walked, even to the point of making him unsteady. He began to sleep through midday and the early afternoon, and crawl along the path through much of the night, to generate warmth. He began to eat the moss.

One day, staggering along thinking about his days on the peninsula, he realized that even if his lost past before the night beach were suddenly to return to him, it would no longer matter in the slightest. Compared to what had happened to him since, any more distant past would seem no more than news of a previous incarnation – news of someone else.

That occurred to him in the late morning; and in the afternoon, after hours of tramping through slush and watching snowflakes swirl up the ridge and down the other side, it further occurred to him that if that were true, if the return of a forgotten past would mean nothing to his feelings, then it might also be true that the past's continuous and uninterrupted presence in his mind would not have made any difference in the situation. It might be that events more than a few months gone would always be nothing more than broken and fleeting images, images like those that fled from the mind each morning upon waking, fragments of dreams too powerful to face. The past was a dream.

CHAPTER 18
The Queen of Desire

Rising up over the horizon, the peninsula looked like the tall edge of a world-wrapping continent; there was no indication at all that the ocean stood just on the other side of that long wall of rock.

When he stood on the peninsula again, it felt like home, and he turned west with relief. On the southern slope it felt warm even under a steady blanket of cloud, so warm that he arched his shoulders and lay on rocks just to feel it. Then one day as he passed a small cove the sun broke out, and he ran down into the water, and rolled naked in the sand until a coat of it stuck everywhere to his skin, and he fell asleep on the beach baking in that layer of crushed rock and shell. He slept all day.

In the later afternoon he foraged for beach food, and that evening he walked easily along the southern slope, reveling in the warm air and his full belly. Just to be alive and thoughtless, an animal in its moment of pure duration, that was happiness enough. The flood of stars spilled across the sky, providing light enough to see the wide trail on the bluff above the southern beaches. Up and down over grassy hills he walked, until ahead of him he saw a cluster of lights, as if a constellation of yellow stars had fallen onto the spine.

Torches.

He approached carelessly because he was careless, and found himself in the outskirts of what once must have been a considerable town, sprawling over a plateau in the spine from north beach to south. Now many of the stone buildings were in ruins, big quartz blocks tumbled about the maze of streets, shattered in a way that suggested earthquake; many of the walls were only waist high. But in the center of town was a plaza flagged by turquoise and coral, smoothed to a sheen by centuries of wear, and around it several small buildings remained standing, lit by torches that flickered in the breeze atop short fat pillars.

Many people were gathered in this plaza, laughing and eating from long tables piled high with food: they greeted Thel cordially and without surprise, and bid him eat, watching his face and nudging each other with elbows. They wore feather capes over plain brown pants and skirts; various birds' most colorful plumage had been sewn together, so that there were capes of solid emerald or sapphire, others striped like metallic rainbows, yet others spotted with enormous eyes.

A tall black-haired woman wrapped in a full-length cape of ruby feathers emerged from the largest building, and approached Thel. She commanded the attention of all, and when she turned and gave instructions under her breath to a retinue of young women in blue, they hurried giggling back into the building.

The woman then smiled at Thel, and welcomed him in a commanding voice. 'This is Olimbos, and I am Khora, its queen. Tonight we celebrate our new year, and the arrival of a stranger after sunset is a good sign. Will you join our celebration?'

Thel nodded and said he would.

The queen smiled, laughed; the citizens of Olimbos laughed with her, then chattered among themselves. Musicians playing hand drums and mandolins struck up a long flowing melody, which never seemed to end. More torches burned and the quartz blocks sparked all shot with light.

The queen sat at a table and ate. Some women gave Thel a plate of pungent cooked meat, and a tall glass of a fiery liquor that tasted of dune grass; it burned all the way to his stomach, and made his vision jump.

The young women serving the queen emerged with a long yellow cape, which they cast over Thel's shoulders as if throwing a net. Everyone cheered and the music picked up its tempo, the hand drums quick and insistent, the mandolins sweet and swaying. Thel had seen a small bird whose chest feathers were the color of his cape, a bird that flashed above streams as it struck the surface, a kind of kingfisher, its breast a glittering yellow in the shadows under the banks. It had taken a lot of them to make a cape so large. Thel drank more of the grass liquor and pulled the cape about him, pleased at its brightness. They gave him a chair to sit in, and he sat and watched.

When the tables of food were considerably emptier people stood and danced in the plaza, turning in groups of two, three and four, small steps punctuated by spins that swirled their capes in the air. The queen stood and walked among the dancers. She threw her cape back over her shoulders and Thel saw that she was naked under it. Her body was long and smoothly muscled, dramatic in the torchlight: as she walked among the dancers her hipbones jutted and swayed, flanking the long curve of her belly, which led the eye down to a tall mass of glossy black pubic hair. As Thel looked at this triangle of hair it bulged out and down like the tail of a panther, waving before the queen; then the cord of fur extended forward and grew into a cat's body and hind legs, which touched the ground as the forelegs and head bloomed out of the body's front end. A small black cat, yes, walking before the queen with its tail a sort of long leash, stretching back up and into the queen's pubic fur.

Thel swallowed heavily, and his pulse raced. He could not shift his gaze from the cat, and saw the queen's laughter only peripherally. She walked around the plaza toward him, and the black cat ranged from side to side ahead of her, its eyes two reflective dots of green torchlight. The dancers swirled in circles about the queen and Thel in his chair, shedding the clothes under their capes. Some kissed each other hungrily as they danced, others watched the queen approaching Thel.

She stood before him. The cat padded forward and rubbed itself against his ankles, purring loudly. The queen smiled. Her ribs moved with her quick breath. The small smile stayed on her lips, and her gaze wouldn't leave him.

The black cat jumped neatly into his lap, curled up there. The queen leaned forward, put her hands on his shoulders, kissed him. He felt the kiss, and then the blood pouring down into his penis, stiffening it under the cat's body.

The queen caught up his arms and pulled him to his feet, and he had to catch the cat in his hands. He could feel the little ribcage cradled in his palm, feel the vibration of its purr. The queen reached down and unfastened his pants, and they dropped around his ankles; as he stepped free each hard knock of his heart lifted his cock another notch, until it stood upright before his belly, feeling taut and live and full. Just to walk felt good with such an erection. The queen led him across the plaza to her residence, and dimly he heard the cheers of the dancers, mixed with the hand drums and mandolins.

Inside the building rugs and tapestries warmed one central room, which was lit by a score of small torches. A big square bed against one wall was piled high with quilted blankets, and the queen pulled Thel onto them, kissing him passionately. As they kissed the cat purred and licked at him, its little tongue rough against his skin. Thel thrust with his cock at the cat's head, and the long tail pulled back up into the queen until cat and cock disappeared in her, in one fluid purring motion. Then they were joined and the queen was laughing at his expression, rolling over onto him and riding his thrusts. She rolled sideways and Thel buried his face in her tangled hair and plunged away, and they rocked in rhythm to the hand drums for as long as he could hold on, until his spine shot great bolts of electric pleasure down and around and up, the pleasure radiating sideways in him until he felt it tingling in his arms, his hands, his face, all his skin.

Later as he lay beside her the black cat returned, purring and licking him back to life. The queen twisted so that she could lick at him along with the cat, and he was instantly stiff again. And so it went, through the night. Thel scarcely noticed the faces in the doorway to the chamber, and when he did, he didn't care.

In the blue just before sunrise he crawled past the guttering torches to his clothes and bags, left in the doorway by some thoughtful celebrant. The mirror was still in its bag, and on a whim he took it from its cloth sack and looked into it.

It was the queen's face – the male version of the queen's face, coarser and bearded, but recognizably hers. The queen stirred in her sleep on the bed, and he put the flat gold plate back in the bag. It fell heavily against his legs.

He returned to the bed, looked down at the sleeping queen. His head was cold. If only he could warm his ears; it seemed never once on this endless peninsula had he gotten his ears warm.

He got back under the blankets and snuggled next to her, put his ear against her ribs and heard her heart, beating quietly. She stirred and rolled toward him, pulled him to her; feeling her warmth triggered a wash of pure desire in him, and he melted again.

CHAPTER 19

The Theater of Ghosts

Days passed, and it stayed like that. Nothing seemed to warm him but Khora's touch. Otherwise he felt empty and cold. He swam under the sun, lay asleep on the beach, fished; and always cold.

Khora's people wandered the ruins of quartz, furtive by day and lascivious in the dusk, stroking each other, kissing, reaching inside each others' clothes. Nights were much darker and quieter than the festival night of Thel's arrival: the evenings punctuated by soft laughter and the gleam of one central torch, breaking its light in the big chipped blocks of quartz that lay around the plaza; and the long nights strange voyages of pleasure in the queen's big bedroom. The cat never again flowed out of her pubic mound, but the memory of it – the idea of it – inflamed Thel's imagination, at the same time that he was repulsed by it. In the bed she pushed him about, brought her maids in to watch, told him what to do, even slapped him hard in the face; and he began to find this more and more exciting, even though he hated her for it. He only seemed truly to live when he was in contact with her body. Everything changed then, the chamber seemed charged with color, and the stars in the doorway sparked as if engendered by a blow to the head.

Then one night – he had lost track of time, it seemed he had been in this life for weeks and weeks – the routine changed, and they lit four torches and set them at the corners of the plaza, and sat at the center among their crossed shadows. The queen walked among them, naked under her long red cape.

'You wonder how this world came to be,' she said to Thel.

He shrugged, surprised. In fact he had stopped wondering long before. He didn't know what to say.

The queen laughed at his expression. 'You talk in your sleep, you see. Now listen. Everything is full of gods. And in the beginning the sea god filled the universe. The sea's ideas were bubbles, and one bubble idea she called love, and all the water in the universe fell into that bubble, taking all the other gods with it. Most drowned, but two learned to swim, and these were the gods rock and dragon. These two loved the sea goddess, and for ages they swam in her and the three were lovers, and all was well until dragon went away, and came back and found rock plunged to ocean's very center, an embrace dragon could never know, for rock did not need to breathe, and dragon did. And in a rage dragon flew away and grew as big as the sky, and reached back with one bony hand and clenched it around the two lovers, cutting through ocean's body to grasp rock and strangle him. And rock died; and the sea goddess, cut in half, died; and seeing his two lovers dead, dragon died. And the bubble burst, leaving nothing but a theater of ghosts. And the lovers' bodies rotted, until nothing of dragon was left but his skeleton; nothing of rock but his heart; nothing of ocean but her salty blood. And ages later dragon's skeleton broke away and flew off through the empty sky, scattering its bones that are the stars. Only the bones of the hand which had strangled the lovers remained here, wrapping the round drop of ocean's blood, cutting it down to rock. All who live on the remains of these three are accidental vermin, walking an edge of bone, which is highest at the old wristbones, and nearly submerged where forefinger once met thumb. We live by drinking ocean, eating rock, and standing on the dragon's bones.'

And Khora laughed bitterly, and walked toward Thel with a stalking, vengeful lust.

CHAPTER 20

The Crucible of Souls

Cold days on the beach, warm nights in the queen's bed. In the evenings sometimes she stripped him bare, aroused him and then led him out among her subjects, tugging on his erection as if it were a leash. He would flush with shame and an intense arousal, and back on her bed he felt his orgasms as if a too-large spine were erupting out of him; his life; she would take one more portion of it from him, laughing and gasping, her long supple torso contracting across the stomach while she came herself.

It was horrible, and each time he hoped it would last forever. During the days he could hardly wait for the next night, and he spent some part of each afternoon lying on the sand, dreaming of the moment when he would be led through the crowd, tugged this way and that by his imperious queen.

When one of her people told her that he owned the mirror, she laughed and made him show his reflection to the night's gathering. Her face, her masculine face, stared out of the smooth gold surface, surrounded by a halo of torchlight, and when Thel rubbed his hand over his jaw trying to feel if there were an actual correspondence with the image, the villagers howled.

Afterward the queen showed no more interest in the mirror. This was a relief to him, because now it seemed that the mirror was his only friend, and sometimes he would take the bag on walks down the beach and let the mirror out and set it flat on the sand, the wet round gold surface indigo with reflected sky, and turning it every way but at himself and his traitor's face, he saw in it the beach he had been born on, the cliffs he had first climbed to get up on the crest, the spine king's bloody camp, the horse meadows, all a past that felt as remote to him as a life among the stars. Grains of sand on a circle of golden indigo, the limpid sky marred by a small fluttering dot, a kestrel hanging on the wind . . .

When he looked up and saw the little hawk was real, he rolled off his belly surprised, and sat up to watch it. It stood feathering on its column of air, falcon's beak pointed down at the sea as it darted down and held itself back, darted and held back, then sideslipped and carved the wind with a splay of strong wings, before settling again in the invisible current. A windhover.

CHAPTER 21

A Face

He trod home through soft sand, the image of the hawk fixed in his mind. That night Khora's dominion seemed more sad and degraded than ever, a tired performance of a play whose audience had long since gone away, the mating automatic, the torch gleam on the quartz a tawdry effect of colored light, nothing more. And yet he behaved just as always.

Stirring in the queen's disordered bed, then driven out into the silent night by his thoughts, Thel stared up at the stars, feeling himself draining out of his body with his wine-scented piss. The torchlight snagged in the cracks in the quartz, and he stood for long moments, mindless.

By the ruddy light he saw a face rise over a broken wall. He stepped toward it and she stood up from behind the wall – the swimmer, gesturing for silence.

He fell running to her, but when he stood she was still there, hopping the wall to come to him, finger crossing lips as she whispered 'Shh, shh, shh,' and he was holding her, holding that strong hard body and then he pushed her back to look at her. Still her: it made him weep and laugh at once in the same hot convulsion of his face, it was her, no doubt of it, standing right before him as real as his living hand. 'I thought you were dead,' he whispered.

'And I you.' Her voice. 'Come on, get your things. Clothes, sandals, some food.'

'They'll stop us.'

She looked around. 'They're asleep. Drunk sleep.'

Irrational fear spiked through him. 'She'll stop us.' And explained: 'Their queen, she has . . . powers.'

'Don't wake her, then. Be quick about it, and quiet.'

So he tiptoed back into the queen's chamber, over the crumpled tapestries and her snoring courtiers, and picked up pants and boots and the mirror in its bag, averting his head so that he would not see Khora's sleeping face, never see it again, and the pain of that was completely flooded in a rising elation, he skipped out the broad arched doorway into the plaza where a false dawn streaked the eastern horizon and made the guttering torchlight pale and ghastly. There the swimmer took his hand and led him out of the ruins west and up a tumbled boulderslope to the crest of the spine, where they could see the light pool of the sea split by the dark peninsula, and the sky darkly luminous and semi-transparent, revealing for an instant the world behind the sky, and he could always have done this, could always have just walked on westward, but the swimmer had shown him the way; still astounded by her presence he started to run, pulled her along in her clumsy swimmer's gait and they ran along the spine trail.

CHAPTER 21

Exfoliation

It was like being born again. They hiked through the long days napping only briefly at midday, and wandered the long dusks hunting for food on the beaches, swimming and then sleeping in sand. In the midnights Thel rose and walked about looking at stars till he chilled, then returned to the swimmer and her blanket.

One night when he returned to the swimmer, lying against her back with an arm over her and feeling her bottom shift back into his belly, he noticed the wind pouring over them. They were sleeping on the very edge of a beach cliff, just for the fun of the views at sunset and dawn, tucked into a hollow scooped at the cliff's edge, and wind was tearing down and out to sea; but as he had walked around the central plateau of the peninsula the night had been perfectly still, he had noticed it particularly. He got up and walked back out onto the hills, and again it was still; and at the cliff's edge, windy. He roused the swimmer and moved them inland a bit for the second half of the night. 'The weight of the air keeps me awake,' he told her. 'It's falling over the edge.'

He found out what had happened to her in the time since the storm on the brough, but only in snatches, in response to his questions. She had bitten her way free of the rope, as he had guessed. She had swum for a long time, she couldn't say how long, but from the way she spoke of it (or didn't), he thought it might have been very long indeed; days, certainly. She had landed on the southern side, and assuming they had all survived and made it to the cape, she had walked back to it and searched for them, but found nothing. She waited there for a long time, regaining her strength and assuming she would see Birsay, escorting other travelers across; but no one ever appeared, and so finally she started west again. Groups traveling east to west passed her, and she had hidden from them, afraid that they might be the spine kings or the sorcerers. And then one night she had come on him in the ruins.

'We may have been wandering on the opposites sides of that cape at around the same time,' Thel said. 'And even along the peninsula.' It was painful to think that he could have avoided the whole episode at Khora's, simply by making an arbitrary change of direction that would have resulted in running into the swimmer earlier. 'Ah, but then I spent a long time out on the drawbridge, as I called it. Did you see that?' He described it; she had, but had passed by it without stopping.

'We're lucky we ever met again at all,' she said. 'It's a big world.'

'But narrow.' The thought of never meeting her again made him shiver. 'As long as we both continued westward . . .'

'We were lucky. We've always been lucky.'

One night after lying down and talking for a while they rolled together and kissed, then mated, and at first he was frightened, but it was such an affirmation, such a gesture of liking, that it was hard for him to believe it was the same act he had performed with Khora. It wasn't, really, and the difference was such that he began to find it hard to remember those nights in the queen's chamber; they slipped away, except in certain dreams that woke him trembling.

As they continued westward the peninsula rose in elevation again, the backbone of pure granite breaking up out of the sea and sand and climbing like the edge of some enormous battered scimitar. They walked without urgency, merely to walk, to create a good space between themselves and Khora and all that lay behind, and each day was spent watching where each step went, climbing the shattered staircase of stone, becoming intimate with the local granite, an ever-modulating mixture of feldspars pink or orange or yellow, big clear grains of quartz, flecks of black hornblende. These three types of rock, jumbled and melded, forming the hard cracked fin of granite lifting out of the sea: it was hard for Thel not to be mesmerized by such a thing, to

89

imagine it amelt and flowing like candle wax under the immense pressures inside the earth.

They came to a long straight stretch of the spine, where the feldspar was white and the hornblende just freckled the mix, making it the whitest granite possible. Here the southern side of the spine became a perfectly vertical drop to the sea, while the northern flank offered a gentle rocky slope to a wide white beach. The trail stayed well away from the southern cliff, but at midday or dusk they sometimes walked up to the edge to take a look down, and one evening in a dulcet sunset they looked over the edge and found that the whole cliff was a single gigantic overhang, as if the spine had been tipped to the south. They looked straight down at the sea, and could see nothing of the upper third of the cliff under them.

Quickly they stepped back, then lay flat and crawled forward, to stick their heads over the edge and have another look. The two or three thousand feet of the cliff looked like the curved inner wall of a shallow cave; they lay on an immense overhang. Thel could feel his stomach trying to reach through his skin and clamp onto the rock, like an abalone mussel; the drop was such that he and the swimmer laughed, in an instinctive attempt to ward off the fear of it. Thel crawled back and grabbed a loose rock that was as heavy as he cared to play with in that area, and shoved it over the edge. They watched it fall until it was a speck that disappeared, but the splash was bigger, a brief burst of white in the flat plate of blue, a *long* distance offshore from the cliff's bottom. They exclaimed at the sight, and did it again, and then they lay there until the light was almost gone, hypnotized by the lascivious false sense of danger, the sublimity. Mid-dusk a flock of seabirds rose up from the water in spiraling gyres, big white birds like cormorants that apparently nested in cracks or arches in the exfoliated cliff under them, out of their sight – for the birds rose and rose, tilting together on updrafts, flapping and banking, growing bigger, shifting this way and that like bubbles rising in water.

CHAPTER 23

Nautilus Universe

A week or so later the spine twisted south and dropped again, fanning out into a big broken rockfield, granite hills and knobs faulted with long grabens that had become skinny ponds or rectangular pools, or thin meadows that cut the rock from beach to beach. Up and down they walked over this terrain, sometimes on the trail which continued to snake its way along the path of least action, or else rambling over the rock, down into a meadow, up ledges, over the rock, down into another grassy swale. It was good land, dotted with trees that clung to the steep jumbles of rock and soil that walled the meadows: foxtail pines, no taller than the two travelers but with thick riven trunks, and bare dead branches spiking out of them in every direction. Steep bluffs stood over the white bay beaches, and many of the bluff tops were rimmed by a tuck of these foxtails, growing crabbed and horizontal in the winds.

They crossed this land for many days, and one afternoon when they were foraging on the southern beach for food, they came upon a shallow bay, a perfect arc of a circle. The bluffs backing the bay were cut by sandy ravines, and between bluff and beach there was a crescent of dunes covered with olive and silver grass.

Scattered over the dunes in irregular rows were sea shells as big as houses. They resembled nautilus shells in which the smaller segments have been pulled a bit out to the side, but they stood about three or four times Thel's height. Their thick curved walls were colored in complex spiraling patterns of brown or deep purple trapezoids, which turned with the shape of the shells and grew smaller and smaller as they twisted around to an invisible center point, like the eyefaces of the facewomen.

Thel and the swimmer walked among these specimens in awe,

91

observing how they gleamed in the late afternoon light, for each one appeared to have been polished as smooth as glass; and there were even, they saw, windows of some clear material replacing some of the brown and purple trapezoids, high in the curved sides.

They were just looking under the bottom edge of one shell when a short brown woman ducked out and regarded them suspiciously. 'Who are you?' she demanded, touching the thick edge of her shell, looking as though she might bolt back under at any second. 'What are you doing?'

'I am a swimmer,' the swimmer said gently. 'This is Thel. We are travelers from east of the brough. We seek nothing of you, and will leave if our presence makes you unhappy.'

'No, no,' the woman said. 'Not necessary.' As she spoke, others ducked out from their shell cottages, people small like the woman, and with leathery skin of brown or purplish cast. They were a nervous crowd, and as they shuffled about the two they moved away reflexively each time the swimmer gestured. But in the end they welcomed the two cordially enough, and invited them to eat with them, a varied meal of fish and seaweed bits, washed down by a sparkling liquor that made the two instantly drunk. The shell people offered them a shell of their own to spend the night in, and they agreed, dropping to hands and knees to get under the edge of one really large brown-flecked specimen.

Once inside it much resembled other beach cottages, or so the swimmer said. Cut plank floors had been set flat in each chamber, with plank staircases leading through holes cut from one chamber to the next. In each chamber driftwood furniture was covered with padded cloth made of fine seaweed hair, on which simple striped patterns had been printed with shell dyes. There were knick-knacks from the sea on the curved walls, and in an upper chamber a small bed was tucked under a window, across from a brick fireplace cut into the central wall. Each chamber had a window cut in its outer wall, the trapezoids filled with a clear fibrous material in the lower chambers where the windows were big, with mosaics of colored driftglass upstairs where the windows were small.

The swimmer observed it all with a delighted, little girl's smile, unlike any Thel had seen on her face. 'It's just like my aunt and uncle's,' she kept saying. 'I used to love visiting them.'

So they spent the night dry and warm, cuddled together in a narrow bed, and in the morning the shell people were out working the beach or the ravines or the meadows up above the bluffs. Their next door neighbor said to them, 'If you will collect puka shells for us, you can stay in that house for as long as you care to. It hasn't been used in ages.'

Collecting puka shells, they found, was a simple business, so simple that the shell people found it tedious; all of them but the children had more interesting or important things to do. Nevertheless they loved having the jewelry made from these shells. On the steep strand of the bay a vicious shorebreak sluiced the coarse blond sand back and forth, and as it did it ground up all the shells and coral bits and rocks that had found their way there, turning them into more of the coarse sand. Their next door neighbor showed the two travelers that among the shell fragments being washed up and down were many specimens of a small fat cone-shaped shell, all of which were being worn down until only the thick caps at the base of the cone remained, round and usually holed in the middle, at the centerpoint of the shell's whorl where it had been quite thin to begin with. So at a certain point in their disintegration these round flat holed pieces made perfect necklace beads, ready to be strung and worn; and a tiny percentage of them were a rich, deep blue, the color of the sky in mid-twilight. These blue pieces the shell folk treasured, and the most important members of the community wore many necklaces and bracelets and anklets of the blue buttons, and every shell person owned at least one big necklace of them.

The easiest method of finding them was simple, they were told. Stand in the shorebreak facing the shore, and as the waves sluiced back down over the coarse sand, one saw thousands of fragments of pastel shell color. Once every dozen or score of waves one saw a flash of the blue, a flash that somehow suggested it was not a jagged tiny fragment but a complete cap; and then with a quick pounce and some luck one could snatch it up, in a streaming handful of wet sand.

So Thel and the swimmer spent a day hunting puka shells, and at sunset they each had a small belt bag filled with the little blue circles. The shell folk were tremendously pleased, and fed them a feast of squid, shark, seaweed salad, and corn. And the day had passed pleasantly enough and the swimmer remained delighted with their curved shell home; and so they decided to stay a while.

Soon enough they found that all was not peaceful among the shell folk. In fact they were all involved in ceaseless conflicts with one another, and alliances and social wars among them were quick, constant and volatile. The division among them between brown skin and purple seemed part of the conflict, but in some original sense that had been long since lost in subsequent permutations; now purple-skinned folk were likely to refer to themselves as brown, and vice versa, and they all wore clothing and shell jewelry in color codes, to indicate where their loyalties stood on any given day. The important shifts in alliances and enemies were marked by the physical moving of their shell homes. The inhabitants, never more than one or two to a shell, would enlist friends and drag their home over the sand to a new neighborhood, sent on their way by bursts of violent cursing from their old neighbors, and leaving a swath through the sand to mark the dramatic event. The bay beach was crisscrossed by these trails, which wind and tide erased quickly enough; but there were always new tracks to replace the old. Psara, a lithe graceful man with purple skin that was the darkest in the village, explained to them that this was a fundamental part of their nature, and with a broad white smile he offered an explanation: 'There are too few of us to reproduce properly if there is anything short of a total mixture. We cannot afford tribes or even families of any extent. Besides – ' he grinned – 'we are descended from crabs, and inclined to be solitary and feisty. An argument a day and you live forever, we say.'

Thel and the swimmer found this a bit much, and one day they decided to take advantage of the mobility of residence, and they got Psara and some others to help them drag their shell out to the edge of the village, just inside the broad eastern point of the bay, beside a stream, behind a dune, and all by themselves. Their old neighbors shouted abuse at them as they left, but in a friendly tone, and they dropped by later to help return all the furniture to its proper place, and to trade for the previous day's catch of blue puka shells.

CHAPTER 24

Pure Duration

And so they fell into the rhythm of the bay, into their own rhythm. They had their home, isolated from the battles and out under the eastern point's bluff. That whole stretch of beach they had to themselves, especially in the mornings; and the point was washed by the tides, and was an especially rich source of the blue shells.

Each strangely long day became a sort of eternity in itself. In the mornings the air was cool and clear and salty, the sea calm and the sun blazing over it. They stood calf-deep in the tumbling waves, facing the beach and the granite bluff behind, watching the water and sand mix wildly in the water, tiny shell fragments of pink and brown and yellow and purple and red tumbling over each other among the clear and white and tan grains of sand, all a tumble and a rush of wet brilliant color with the clear foam-flecked water pouring over it, and once in a while a flash of blue like a dark sky would reveal itself among the rest and they would dive, scoop up handfuls of sand, let it sift through fingers until the blue fragment was there to be plucked out and put in a bag. If they proved to have missed it, they groaned and started again. And it seemed it would be morning forever.

At midday they sat on the beach and ate something, and slept on the sand or talked, and it seemed the midday would last forever, a warm lazy eternal nap; and then in the afternoons they would walk the beach in search of food or the rare overlooked blue button poking out of the dry sand, or get in the surf and hunt again, and it seemed the afternoon would never end, the sun white and stationary in the broad western sky. Only at sunset did it seem time passed; slow, stately, the sun dropped and slowed as it dropped, it seemed, until it stood on the horizon chopped into orange slices by the layering of the atmosphere, and they had time to climb the bluffs and watch the mallow sea go indigo and the air become visible and the pared sun turn to a yellow sliver, then an emerald green dot, the green flash that ended the sunset. And then they were in the endless dusk, all its dark grainy colors filling with blackness as the eternal night came on. And this was just one day in an eternal round of unchanging days, until Thel felt that they lived forever every couple of weeks; and beyond that, in the unimaginable fullness of whole years, lay the touch of pure duration.

CHAPTER 25

Castaway

Most of these endless days they spent alone, but sometimes one or more of the shell folk would drop by, especially the children, who were delighted to see them do something as childish as recover pukas. Their most frequent adult companion was Psara, who occasionally joined them in the surf, laughing at the sport but incredibly fluid and quick-eyed and quick-handed at it; he could collect more blue shells in a morning than Thel could in a couple of days. As he dove and spluttered in the shorebreak he regaled them with the village gossip, which was consistently lurid and melodramatic, a never-ending extravaganza of petty feuds and sordid sexual affairs. He also invited them in to the rare festival nights, when everyone came out to a driftwood fire by the biggest stream and drank the clear liquor until they were all maudlin with drunken affection for one another, their feuds forgotten in the brilliant yellow light of festival reality. They would dance in rings around the fire, holding hands and crashing left and right, embracing their partners and declaring them wonderful browns or purples.

During one of these parties, late, when the fire was a pile of pulsing embers and the shell folk were comatose with liquor and neighborly feeling, Psara regarded the two beachcombers with his quick ironic smile, and slipped over to them and put a sensuous hand on the swimmer's broad shoulder, and on Thel's. 'Would you like to hear a story?'

The two nodded easily.

'Paros,' Psara said loudly, and the oldest person there jerked upright, peered around sleepily. 'Tell us the story of the castaways, Paros!' and several children said, 'Yes please, please!'

Old Paros nodded and stood precariously. 'This is a story from

98

the world's beginning, when ocean never equalled gleamed in the dark, perfect and white and empty. Across her white body sailed a raft, not our ship of fools but an orderly and good society, the brown and the purple having little to do with each other but coexisting in peace.' Some of the villagers laughed at that.

'But one day a brown man and a purple woman met at the mast, and talked, and later they did it again, and again, and when the browns and the purples bathed over the side they dove under the raft and swam together for a time; and they fell in love.

'Now both of them were married, and their partners were prominent in the societies of brown and purple. So when the two were finally discovered, all the browns and purples were outraged, and there were calls to drown the two lovers.

'But the raft sailed by an island in the white sea, the smallest speck of land – a rock, a tree, a shell and a stream. And the browns and purples decided to maroon the two lovers, and threw them overboard, and the two swam to the island. And as they swam, ocean never equalled seeped into their minds and took all memory of the raft away from them, so that they would not despair.

'And they landed on the island, and the raft sailed away and would never come back. The woman gave birth to many children, and the children quarreled and would have killed each other. So ocean never equalled made the island longer, so that there would be room for the children and grandchildren of the two lovers to live without mortal strife between them. But they fought and multiplied at such a rate that ocean never equalled had to stretch the island all the way around her, to give them room to chase each other endlessly; and the white sea turned blue with the blood and tears shed.'

Silence. Paros sat down. Gray film fluttered on the dull coals of the fire. Thel felt as though he were falling, he had to clasp the swimmer's arm to steady himself, even though they were sitting.

Later as they walked back home he stumbled once or twice, though he had not drunk that much. And several times he started to speak, and stopped; and he noticed the swimmer did the same. And that night in their narrow bed they hugged each other like two frightened children, lost at night in the woods.

CHAPTER 26

We Are Clouds

Days passed. In the summer the shallows got so hot that they had to swim offshore to get any refreshment from the sea, and they searched for shells naked, as brown as the brown shellfolk. In the winter the water was so cold that it hurt their ankles as it rushed over their feet, and each day their skin turned as purple as the purple shellfolk, teeth chattering so that the fire in their bedroom was a lovely warmth. They spent storm days sitting in the bed watching the fire and talking and making love, while wind and rain lashed at their streaming window. Days like that were wonderful to Thel, but better yet were the long summer days, knee deep in surf under the sun, the intense rays pulsing on his neck in what felt like discrete little pushes of light and heat. He would look up from the sand tumbling in the whitewater and see the swimmer make some graceful move, her naked brown body twisting as she dove for a blue fragment, or streaming with water as she stood up after a dive; or the muscles of her arms rippling like backwash hitting an oncoming wave; or the sight of her legs and bottom and back as she walked away down the beach; or the tilt of her head as she walked toward him, looking down at the whitewater; and his heart would swell like an erection inside him and he would run through the broken surf and tackle her, kissing her neck and face until she laughed at him and they would make love there, with water and sand running over them. And sometimes she would run up and tackle him and they would do the same. And afterwards they would play grunion in the surf, lying in the shorebreak and rolling up and down with the broken waves, taking the sea in and spurting it out like fountains, not thinking a thing. Every part of the day eternal, on summer days like that.

But the sun moved, and time passed nevertheless. Sitting in the shorebreak and watching his lover roll back and forth like beautifully rounded driftwood, Thel couldn't help thinking of that, from time to time; of time passing: and he wished he could be a man of bronze, unchanging, living the same day over and over. He would have chosen that day.

Looking across the bay, he saw clouds rushing over the granite boulders of the point. Both granite and cloud had deeply complex textured surfaces, but it was startling to think how different they were in their mutability. Each moment the clouds changed and would never be the same; while the point rocks would remain much as they were now, ages after he and the swimmer were forever gone. Reflecting on this he was surprised when she rolled into him on a wave and said, 'We are clouds.' And even more surprised when he heard himself reply, 'But mountains are clouds, too.'

101

CHAPTER 27

An Old Coin

Another day, in late autumn, Thel was standing in the surf, hunting pukas in the colorful tumbling retreat of a wave, when he saw a bright flash – something metallic – and his pounce, trained now to a fine accuracy, brought it up in his sand-streaming hands: an old coin, worn almost smooth but still bright, a color between the gold of the mirror's surface and the bronze of a bronze sunset. One side held the profile of a head, and holding it up to see it better, Thel caught sight of his swimmer with her close-cropped head in profile some yards away; and it was exactly her profile on the coin. The same strong nose, full mouth, distinct jaw, high forehead: as exact an image as a black paper silhouette cut by a sidewalk artist, in some life he could not otherwise remember. It had to be her. And yet the coin was obviously ancient, the remnant of a long dead civilization.

Thel pocketed the coin, and that night in their shell cottage he put it on the brick mantle of their chimney, next to the spot where light occasionally pulsed through the wall, from the mirror hung in the next chamber. He said to the swimmer, 'Were you ever the queen of an ancient kingdom?'

'Yes,' she muttered sleepily. 'And I still am.'

But this, he supposed, was another of their misunderstandings. Thel had first noticed this phenomenon when he had seen a windhover, hunting over the meadows inland. 'Look,' he had said, 'a kestrel.' But the swimmer had thought him crazy for pointing into the sky, for that to her was the name of a kind of fish. And later he found that when he said *loyalty* she understood it to mean *stubbornness*, and when she said *arbitrary* she meant *beautiful*, and that when she said *melancholy* she did not mean that sadness we enjoy feeling, but rather *mendacity*; and when she said *actually* she meant *currently*; and when he said 'I love you,' she thought he was saying 'I will leave you.' They had slowly worked up quite a list of these false cognates, Thel could recite scores and scores of them, and he had come to understand that they did not share a language so much as the illusion of a language; they spoke strong idiolects, and lived in worlds of meaning distinct and isolated from the other. So that she no doubt understood *queen of an ancient kingdom* to mean something like *a swimmer in the deep sea*; and the mystery of the ancient alloy coin was never explained and, he realized, never would be. It gave him a shiver of fear, thinking about it – it seemed to him that nothing would ever be explained, and that all of a sudden each day was slipping away, that time was flying by and they were getting old and nothing would ever come clear. He sat on the beach watching the clouds tumble overhead and letting handfuls of sand run through his fingers, the little clear grains of quartz, flecks of black mica, pieces of coral, shell fragments like small bits of hard ceramic, and he saw that a substantial portion of the sand was made of shells, that living things had labored all their lives to create ceramic shelters, homes, the most permanent parts of themselves; which had then been pummelled into shards just big enough to see, millions upon millions of lives ground up and strewn under him, the beach made out of the wreckage of generations. And before long he and the swimmer too would become no more than sand on a beach; and they would never really have understood anything.

CHAPTER 28
Festival

One evening in early spring, after a long day on the hot tawny beach, Thel and the swimmer walked homeward, between great logs of driftwood that had washed ashore in the winter. In the blue twilight the logs looked like the bodies of fallen giants after a titanic battle, and above them in the sky a black star was fluttering, a bird high in the air. The swimmer clasped Thel's arm: 'Look,' she said, and pointed down the beach. 'We have visitors.' Torchlight glimmered around their shell home, a dozen points of yellow weaving in the dusk.

It was a group of the shellfolk, drinking liquor from curved shells and laughing as they danced in a circle around their home.

'Is it New Year's already?' the swimmer asked.

'Something else,' Thel said.

They walked into the circle of light, and the shellfolk greeted them and explained it was Paros's birthday, and, as had happened once or twice before, they had decided to celebrate out at Thel and the swimmer's home, because they had not been able to agree whether brown or purple should host. So Thel and the swimmer joined the party, and ate and danced around the bonfire, and drank the liquor until everything was bright with the colors of fire and night, and the faces of the shellfolk were like crude masks of their daytime selves. Thel stumbled as he swung his feet out in dance, and a face the brown nearest black appeared before him, harsh with laughter and some shouted curse he didn't understand. Then someone the purple nearest black darted from the side, trying to trip him; Thel looked up and it seemed that people were not quite themselves, so that when Psara came out of their house holding the mirror overhead, Thel saw immediately that it was not Psara but Tinou. Tinou's black skin was now purplish in tint, and his face was twisted into Psara's visage, but with Tinou's big grin on it, and Tinou's shouting laugh.

As the transformed shellfolk seized Thel and the swimmer by the arms and dragged them to Tinou, a part of Thel was distracted, wondering if Psara had been Tinou all along, waiting all these years for whatever unimaginable reason to reveal himself – or if he had recently arrived in the village, and for reasons equally beyond comprehension had taken over Psara's form. In any case the voice was the same, and as Tinou placed the mirror in the wooden frame familiar from Oia, he laughed and said, 'All life is a case of *déjà vu*, don't you think? And here we are again. Let us put the woman through first, so Thel can see what it looks like.'

Thel struggled against the hands holding him down, but there were too many of them; all his neighbors, faces gleaming yellow and their eyes big and hungry as they watched the other group lift the struggling swimmer and force her feet into the bright liquid surface of the mirror. Tinou laughed and began his litany of questions, face inches from hers, spittle flying over her as he shouted in a gross parody of solicitousness, 'Pinching? pressing? gnawing? cramping? crushing? wrenching? scalding? searing?' Thel was proud of her, the way she could hold her face rigid in a mask of stoic disgust, staring Tinou in the eye; but his stomach was flip-flopping inside him as he saw the flesh of her legs and torso jerk at the contact with the mirror. Her body remained visible on the other side, flesh pale and inert yet still there among them. But remembering his own voyage on the other side, Thel feared they would be separated again, separated for good, and as her head popped through and she tumbled unconscious to the ground behind the mirror, Thel ripped convulsively away from the hands holding him and leaped forward to dive head first through the mirror and after her. The last thing he saw was Tinou's face, bright with torchlight and astonishment, as big a round as the mirror itself.

CHAPTER 29

The Pursuit

It was early morning, sun bright in his eyes. The swimmer lay next to him, sleeping or unconscious, and the world smelled as fresh as the shadows under trees. It hurt to move – to raise his head, to sit up – each joint a stab of pain when he moved it. Nevertheless he was happy to be with her still.

And yet it hurt, it hurt to move. This was an aspect of pain he noticed at once: it was hard to see through it to anything else. It took a discipline that would have to be learned.

Groaning, he rolled to her side and shook her awake. She woke with a gasp and held her left arm to her side. They sat up, looked around at a cold windy hillside – the spine, in fact, near the crest, on a prominence overlooking the sea. There was no sign of the shellfolk's bay. 'The sun,' the swimmer said. 'It's moving east. It will set in the east.'

Thel ignored the conundrum of how she could orient herself by something other than the sun in the sky, and merely nodded. 'It's the mirror world,' he said. 'Everything's backwards.'

They would need clothes, having been thrust into this world nearly naked. Even something like the leaf capes that the treefolk had worn would help shelter them from the wind.

Then the swimmer pointed. 'Look, it's him. The thing that took over our Psara.' Far to the east, on the crest of the spine, a figure was walking away from them. It had a lump on its back. 'He's carrying the mirror,' the swimmer said. She had a hand shading her eyes, and was squinting. 'It's Tinou, isn't it.'

'Yes.' Thel peered after the tiny figure speculatively. 'If we could get the mirror from him, and push through it again . . .'

It might end the pain. It might return them to their hot tawny

106

beach. It might ... They looked each other in the eyes, stood with some difficulty, followed the figure east.

It was hard going, even on the trail. At sunset each day they descended to the beach, the sun sinking into the eastern sea. Over time they wove capes of palm and fan seaweed; and each night they foraged for food, and the swimmer found a mollusk that when eaten dulled the pain of her arm, and Thel's joints. But the spine was getting higher and higher as they moved farther to the mirror east, and the trail stayed right on the crest of the spine, and the descent to the beaches became more difficult. Tinou stayed about the same distance ahead of them, so perhaps he was descending to water each night as well; but finally one sunset it was impossible, and the next, possible but too strenuous to contemplate. Besides, in the dusk the swimmer caught sight of Tinou, sitting next to the trail far above them; so they slept tucked in a fault to get out of the wind, and it was cold but they found birds' nests, and were able to raid them for food. Holes and dips in the granite held rainwater for their thirst, and the swimmer had dried a collection of the mollusks for their pain. But they ran out quickly enough.

Because the spine continued to rise they caught sight of Tinou several times a day, always most of a day's walk ahead of them, a speck against the pinkish broken granite of the spine's bony edge. The peninsula here resembled the precipitous blade of rock that Thel had traversed with the treefolk, a knife edge of scarcely weathered granite slicing the world ocean into two halves, so many thousands of feet high that the waves were no more than the faintest pattern of curves on the sea; and yet if the peninsula had been nothing but dunes, it would have been only a morning's walk to cross it from sea to sea. Higher and higher this great ridge arched into the sky, in irregular swoops, with many small ridge peaks, and an unhappily large number of sudden drops in the ridge line that they were forced to climb down, and then up again. As they made their way they sometimes saw broken bird nests scattered down the cliffs to right and left, the precious meat of eggs burst and dried over the rocks and sticks: Tinou had been kicking them apart as he passed, and so must have known they were following.

When the swimmer's mollusks were gone, they hiked on in pain; her arm never healed, and Thel's joints creaked as if filled with grit, and each day's march added to their scrapes, bruises, sprains: and none of these ever seemed to heal. In the mirror world their bodies had lost that ability. Hunger plagued them as well, but not thirst; some of the ponds they passed had Tinou's feces floating in them, but there were more of the little granite pools than he could find to foul, and they drank as deeply as if they might be able to get their sustenance from water alone. They ate mice, and birds, and eggs, and once a whole glorious patch of blueberries; then later, the bright green moss that Thel had found on the drawbridge. There was a lot of this moss as they climbed higher – moss, and blotchy lichen, and junipers and foxtail pines that up here were nothing but little wind-tortured bushes, tucked between boulders and down in cracks. They slept under these piney shrubs, and tried eating their cones but couldn't.

One evening in the indigo twilight Thel looked at the swimmer's bright pain-filled eyes. It was hard to remember the world on the other side of the mirror, their life on the hot tawny beach – a blur, a moment like the snapping of fingers, a dream. He said, 'We never gain on him, and we're going slower every day. My joints – ' he stopped, wanting to cry. 'I'm hungry,' he said instead.

She gave him a handful of the moss. He noticed that her fingers were narrower and longer, with full webs of skin between them, and a dusting of blond fur over the backs of the hands. She said, 'Whatever happens, you must accept it.'

He ate, considering what that implied. His own hands were gnarled and his thumbs were longer and less opposed to the fingers than they used to be. Flickering, pulsing, throbbing, shooting, lancing, cutting, rasping, splitting, yes. All of these. 'Maybe,' he said, feeling his face and the enlarged jaw, 'maybe if we made an extraordinary effort. If we hiked all night – if we kept hiking till we caught him, you know. He's sleeping at night like we are, or we'd never be keeping pace with him. If we dispensed with that, and hiked all night . . .'

'Tomorrow,' she said, sleepy. Her nose was smaller, and it

108

twitched at the end. 'One last night of rest, and we'll start tomorrow.'

So the next sunset they stopped and foraged hard, collecting for their waist bags a bit of everything that was not granite itself, and they kept walking as the sun's light dimmed in the eastern sky, until only a few clouds high over the eastern sea caught a dim red glow in the deep indigo; and then by the light of the million stars they stumbled on.

Even in these remote heights the trail continued to wind its way along the spine crest, weaving to north or south depending on the shape of the rock and the cliffs on each side. The trail was in poor repair and had not been used, it appeared, in years. Sometimes, because it was the only flatness in a vertical land-scape, and had been crushed to sand over the centuries, it was the only foothold for the green moss, so that a mossy path extended through the white rock, a highly visible black sidewalk in the starry night. Elsewhere the trail was just a slightly less obstacle-filled track of blasted rock, and nearly impossible to see. They kept losing it and coming on it again, and each time they rediscovered it Thel felt a tiny bit of satisfaction, of communion across time with whoever had built the trail; they had both picked the same route as best. And now it was essential that they keep to that route, if they were not to come to some impassable drop-off or rise; so in places they moved on hands and knees, feeling for sand and the intangible traces of earlier feet. At times they could move their head to the side and stare straight down to the obsidian sea, flat and glossy some thousands of feet below; then they crawled, happy to hug the rock, long past talk, merely panting, gasping, from time to time whimpering or cursing under their breath, or simply groaning.

It was a long night. When dawn came and light leaked back into the world, in the hour when everything was made of translucent slabs of gray, Thel looked at the swimmer and observed that her whole shape was changing; torso longer, feet longer, ribs visible but not quite human, she was making a slow transformation back to something clearly aquatic – as she had always been, but now it was more pronounced, obvious that her race had descended from some fluid water mammal. She would be forced to crawl all the time if the transformation continued. And if her joints felt anything like his ... he exerted the discipline, peered through the black haze of pain, saw that his own legs were thicker and his arms longer and heavier: it was a comfortable prospect to walk on all fours, and climbing the endless granite staircase of the spine was in some senses a happy challenge. Tree ancestor, he thought, and the image of a quick beautiful creature came into his mind, with the word *baboon*.

When the sun rose behind them, he looked at the ridge ahead carefully. This was the time of day when Tinou, looking back into the western dawn, would have trouble spotting them; while they looked up the ridge for him with the blaze of a nearby star as their spotlight. And eventually Thel's patience was rewarded. A head popped over the rock, just above and beyond them, a few minutes' walk only, and Tinou emerged, looked back blindly into the sun, and then hiked east up the ridge trail.

All that day they hunted him, hiding when he looked back, and so losing some ground on him. In pain as they were they could not keep pace with him in any case. But after sunset they caught sight of him, settling for the night at a flat spot in the trail.

There was still a trace of dusk in the sky when they crawled silently over the granite knobs to his camp. He was sleeping in the trail's sand, rolled in a blanket, or so they thought; but as they crept toward him his eyes opened, the whites reflecting starlight so that it seemed two glittery little jewels had popped into being, and with a laugh he said, 'What persistent little things, crawling around in the night! Come out in the open, my little ones!'

He was standing over them. 'My, my.' Amusement made his beautiful voice bounce musically, a low fast burble. 'A monkey and a water rat, it seems! Following me all this way, whatever for?' He loomed over Thel, and anger threaded into the amusement: 'What kind of creature jumps through the mirror, eh? What kind of thing?'

But Thel and the swimmer were long past the snare of language, long past even much hearing Tinou's beautiful voice. He seemed to recognize this, for when they stood and approached him, spreading out to come at him from two sides, he retreated to the flat spot and his blanket.

'We want the mirror,' Thel croaked, shuffling in toward him, sidling at angles in the hope of getting close more quickly than Tinou could notice. 'Give it to us and we'll call it quits.'

Tinou laughed and reached down into his blankets, pulled out the mirror bag. He held it out, then swung it around to throw it over the cliff into the southern sea – but he had not reckoned on Thel's new animal swiftness, and the bag crashed into Thel's upper arm as Thel rushed forward, and quicker than Thel could react or plan his numbed arm had caught Tinou by the throat and the claws of his other hand were raking Tinou's face and knocking aside the flailing arms and then with tremendous force he caught up the sorcerer's head in both hands and threw the man's whole body to the ground. The swimmer dove and bit the bent and exposed neck, and awkwardly she got to her feet and they stood watching Tinou's blood drain out of him. Mortality, how strange: that Tinou, who had given them so much, was now gone! That he had left no more behind than this! It was hard to grasp.

Thel recovered the mirror bag and checked inside it; the mirror was unbroken, its surface the color of the sky some hour or two before. Meanwhile the swimmer had taken a knife from Tinou's bag, then found a firestone and clapper. The skeleton of a dead juniper stood twisted in the lee of boulders protecting the flat, and they broke it apart right down to the ground, bashing it with rocks they could barely lift. Thel started a fire while the swimmer cut away the skin over Tinou's thighs and buttocks, and hacked out big steaks that they roasted on sticks of juniper. When they were full they slept all the way through to dawn, warmed by the coals of the fire, and their first real meal in weeks.

CHAPTER 30

The Green Flash

They woke in the late morning and hiked on, continuing eastward without discussion; it seemed clear to Thel that it was necessary, that they could not recross the mirror's smooth barrier on the site of Tinou's murder. That, in fact, there was a specific moment when it would be possible, a time and a place of which he knew nothing. They would have to watch. Without speaking of it he knew the swimmer had come to the same conclusion.

So they hiked on. The spine continued to rise, a granite wall splitting the sea, curving sinuously left and right, its top edge shattered over the eons into a broken split serrated knife edge of a ridge, rising unevenly as they crawled ant-like along it. Often they crawled in the literal sense, as it was too painful and precipitous to walk. The moss grew less frequently here and they were often hungry, they often recalled the delicious meal of Tinou and regretted bitterly not staying to eat all of him, or at least not taking with them his heart and liver, they drooled thinking of it. 'But livers make you mad,' Thel said, 'someone told me. Livers and life.'

Hunger made them light and they found they could almost float up smaller arêtes, just a touch here and there on the rough grainy rock, something to keep them from blowing away – to keep their shells from blowing away – everything inside having danced off on the wind. Once Thel tried to tell the swimmer how he felt about that, and he couldn't find the words to express it. He listened to the thin slow trickle of his thoughts and was surprised to hear how simple it had become: *I am climbing. I will always climb. The ocean is far below. That is a rock. I hope we find some moss*. These were his thoughts. And all that great whirling maelstrom of feeling and significance, of meaning: on the other side of the mirror, back down the peninsula among his forgotten friends, adventures, hopes, loves, dreams. All the dreams forgotten in the moment of waking, the flight that mattered so much ... it was strange to no longer desire his desires, to look at the swimmer and see a broken ancient animal, to understand that all their love had been a way of fixing time, each embrace a moment's touch of the eternal, because the caress preserves. And yet here he crawled, something like a baboon, long knuckled hairy claws at the end of furred forearms, next to something like an otter, and only her eyes remained hers, the face he remembered mostly gone, but all of it evoked by those calm black eyes unfogged by the pain that crippled her gait, clear and calm and looking around, still capable of that small ironic amused squint, as when she laid her forearm next to his and said, 'Now you see why we never had children.'

They had come from different worlds. They spoke different languages. What they had shared had been at least partly illusion. And yet, and yet, and yet ... He took comfort in limping along the trail beside her, before her, behind her, thumping shoulders together or sharing moss they found. Beauty is only the beginning of terror, but just to have company, to share the news: there is a block of pink quartz. The seas look high. The wind is strong. And so the terror is staved off. Through black haze, beauty still perceived.

The ridge became deeply serrated, peaks like the teeth of a crude saw, making progress nearly impossible. Why go on? Thel thought one morning, but then the swimmer started off, scrambling up a broken cliff, using all fours, and he followed. Why was one of the questions that had gone away. Pain clouded his vision. A bird's nest gave them a feast. A storm left them soaked and cold. Near its end lightning shattered the peak above them, leaving their ears blasted, their nerves tingling, the strong smell of ozone in the wind. The shock of it seemed to invigorate the swimmer and she led all the next day with a will, over peak after peak, and down into deep cols. Their bodies were continuing to devolve, and only this allowed them to continue; now she could slither up rock, and how he could cling!

Then late one afternoon they made their way slowly over a

hump of granite, and on the other side of it the peninsula dropped off into the sea, and came to an end.

It did so in a sheer clean prow, so smooth that it had to have been crafted. Also there was a smoothed waist-high wall to each side, bowing in and meeting at an angle, at the final point of the ridge. They walked out to the meeting of the two walls and leaned out to look. Clearly in some past age some civilisation had come here and cut the granite capesmooth, creating two polished curving walls that came together in a straight edge which dropped to the sea in a single swoop, a clean crease like the bowline of a great ship. It was a drop, Thel estimated, of about ten thousand feet.

They walked around on this last forecastle, south to north and back again, looking down at the workmanship of the two cliffsides. The polished granite was a flecked color, an infinitely dense mix of feldspar, quartz, and hornblende, so that just below them it appeared speckled like a trout, while farther down it seemed only a pinkish brown, like a kind of marble. Stones that Thel dropped over the walls skipped down and disappeared, and he never even saw them mar the dark blue of the sea.

It was nearly sunset. The swimmer wandered about, collecting rocks and laying them on the triangular block where the two walls met, the outermost point. Thel asked what she was doing and she smiled, gesturing at the mirror bag. 'This must be the place, yes?'

Thel shivered, looked around. They could see for many, many miles, and the horizon was a clear sharp line between sea and sky; but the air was somehow thick, the sunlight in it dark. He took the mirror from the bag and put it on the final tip of the wall, held it in place with the rocks the swimmer had gathered. The eastern sky was full of the setting sun's yellow, and the mirror's surface glowed like a lens, as if scooping up all the beautiful sunlight in the world and flinging it westward, in a single coherent beam. 'But what will we do?' Thel asked.

The swimmer stretched and stood on her hind legs, pointing with one foreleg at the glass. 'At the last moment of sunset we will leap through,' she said happily. But she was a sea creature, and this was, perhaps, a return to the sea; while he was a tree

114

creature, in a land without trees, and he was afraid. And yet, and yet . . .

They sat on the wall and watched the sunset, the light leaking out of the sky, the wind rustling the great space of dusk and the sea. The incredible furnace of the sun fountained light even as it sank into the ocean, which gleamed like a cut polished stone. Overhead a windhover fluttered in place, slicing the wind and sideslipping, and seeing it Thel was calmed. Whatever happened, yes, but more than that there was a kind of glory in it, to fling themselves out into the spaces they breathed, if only for one last dive or flight. The sun pared to a yellow line on the sea, and the sky darkened still; the mirror surface, still a kind of lens gathering sunlight, glowed a rich yellow that greened and greened as the sun's rays bent around the curve of the globe, prisming under gravity's pull. Out on the horizon the brilliant yellow line contracted in from both sides, greening all the while, until at last it was nothing but a single point of the most intense emerald light: the green flash, the sun's farewell, and the mirror's surface was flush with green light, the whole circle a pool of glowing green, and the swimmer's paw caught Thel by the arm and pulled him to his feet. Overhead the kestrel tipped and dove, down in a curving stoop, shooting by them and falling faster until it burst to white, like a meteor streaking over the sea; and with a cry the swimmer leaped forward and jumped through the mirror, and Thel followed fast on her heels.

The Blind Geometer

A. When you are born blind, your development is different from that of sighted infants. (I was born blind, I know.) The reasons for this are fairly obvious. Much normal early infant development, both physical and mental, is linked to vision, which coordinates all sense and action. Without vision reality is ... (it's hard to describe) a sort of void, in which transitory things come to existence when grasped and mouthed and heard – then when the things fall silent or are dropped, they melt away, they *cease to exist*. (I wonder if I have not kept a bit of that feeling with me always.) It can be shown that this sense of object permanence must be learned by sighted infants as well – move a toy behind a screen and very young babies will assume the toy has ceased to exist – but vision (seeing part of a toy [or a person] behind the screen, etc.) makes their construction of a sense of object permanence fairly rapid and easy. With the blind child it is a much harder task, it takes months, sometimes years. And with no sense of an object world, there can be no complementary concept of self; without this concept, all phenomena can be experienced as part of an extended 'body.' (Haptic space [or tactile space, the space of the body] expanding to fill visual space ...) Every blind infant is in danger of autism.

'But we also have and know that we have, the capacity of complete freedom to transform, in thought and phantasy, our human historical existence ... '

– Edmund Husserl, *The Origin of Geometry*

C. *Mark point A. Then mark point B. Only one line, AB, can be drawn through these two points.* Say that events, happening hadon by hadon in the unimaginably brief slice of reality that is the present, are points. Connecting these points would then create lines, and the lines figures – figures that would give a shape to our lives, our world. If the world were a Euclidean space, this would make the shapes of our lives comprehensible to us. But the world is not a Euclidean space. And so all our understanding is no more than a reductive mathematics for the world. Language as a kind of geometry.

AB. My first memories are of the Christmas morning when I was some three and a half years old, when one of my gifts was a bag of marbles. I was fascinated by the way the handfuls of marbles felt in my fingers: heavy glass spheres, all so smooth and clickety, all so much the same. I was equally impressed by the leather bag that had contained them. It was so pliable, had such a baggy shape, could be drawn up by such a leathery draw string. (I must tell you, from the viewpoint of tactual aesthetics, there is nothing quite so beautiful as well-oiled leather. My favorite toy was my father's boot.) Anyway, I was rolling on my belly over the marbles spread on the floor (more contact) when I came against the Christmas tree, all prickly and piney. Reaching up to break off some needles to rub between my fingers, I touched an ornament that felt to me, in my excitement, like a lost marble. I yanked on it (and on the branch, no doubt) and – down came the tree.

The alarum afterward is only a blur in my memory, as if it all were on tape, and parts of it forever fast-forwarded to squeaks and trills. Little unspliced snippets of tape: my memory. (My story.)

BA. How often have I searched for snippets before that one, from the long years of my coming to consciousness? How did I first discover the world beyond my body, beyond my searching hands? It was one of my greatest intellectual feats – perhaps the greatest – and yet it is lost to me.

So I read, and learned how other blind infants accomplished the task. I understood better how important my mother had to have been in this process, I began to understand why I felt about her the way I did, why I missed her so.

My own life, known to me through words – the world become a text – this happens to me all the time. It is what T. D. Cutsforth called entering the world of 'verbal unreality,' and it is part of the fate of the curious blind person.

O. I never did like Jeremy Blasingame. He had been a colleague for a few years, and his office was six doors down from mine. It seemed to me that he was one of those people who are fundamentally uncomfortable around the blind; and it's always the blind person's job to put these people at their ease, which gets to be a pain in the ass. (In fact, I usually ignore the problem.) Jeremy always watched me closely (you can tell this by voice), and it was clear that he found it hard to believe that I was one of the co-editors of *Topological Geometry*, a journal he submitted to occasionally. But he was a good mathematician, and a fair topologist, and we had published some of his submissions, so that he and I remained superficially friendly.

Still, he was always probing, always picking my brains. At this time I was working hard on the geometry of n-dimensional manifolds, and some of the latest results from CERN and SLAC and the big new accelerator on Oahu were fitting into the work in an interesting way: it appeared that certain sub-atomic particles were moving as if in a multi-dimensional manifold, and I had Sullivan and Wu and some of the other physicists from these places asking questions about my work in multi-dimensional geometries. With them I was happy to talk, but with Jeremy I couldn't see the point. Certain speculations I once made in conversation with him later showed up in one of his papers; and it just seemed to me that he was looking for help without actually saying so.

And there was the matter of his image. In the sun I perceived him as a shifting, flecked brightness. It's unusual I can see people at all, and as I couldn't really account for this (was it vision, or something else?) it made me uncomfortable.

But no doubt in retrospect I have somewhat exaggerated this uneasiness.

AC. The first event of my life that I recall that has any emotion attached to it (the earlier ones being mere snips of tape that could have come from anyone's life, given how much feeling is associated with them) comes from my eighth year, and has to do, emblematically enough, with maths. I was adding columns with my Braille punch, and excited at my new power, I took the bumpy sheet of figures to show my father. He puzzled over it for a while. 'Hmm,' he said. 'Here, you have to make very sure that the columns are in straight vertical rows.' His long fingers guided mine down a column. 'Twenty-two is off to the left, feel that? You have to keep them all straight.'

Impatiently I pulled my hand away, and the flood of frustration began its tidal wash through me (most familiar of sensations, felt scores of times a day); my voice tightened to a high whine: 'But *why*? It doesn't *matter* – '

'Yes it does.' My father wasn't one for unnecessary neatness, as I already knew well from tripping over his misplaced briefcase, ice skates, shoes ... 'Let's see.' He had my fingers again. 'You know how numbers work. Here's twenty-two. Now what that means, is two twos, and two tens. This two marks the twenty, this two marks the two, even though they're both just two characters, right? Well, when you're adding, the column to the far right is the column of ones. Next over is the column of tens, and next over is the column of hundreds. Here you've got three hundreds, right? Now if you have the twenty-two over to the left too far, you'll add the twenty in the hundreds column, as if the number were two hundred twenty rather than twenty-two. And that'll be wrong, So you have to keep the columns really straight – '

Understanding, ringing me as if I were a big old church bell, and it the clapper. It's the first time I remember feeling that sensation that has remained one of the enduring joys of my life: *to understand*.

And understanding mathematical concepts quickly led to power (and how I craved that!), power not only in the abstract world of maths, but in the real world of father and school. I remember jumping up and down, my dad laughing cheerily, me dashing to my room to stamp out columns as straight as the ruler's edge, to add column after column of figures.

A. Oh yes: Carlos Oleg Nevsky, here. Mother Mexican, father Russian (military advisor). Born in Mexico City in 2018, three months premature, after my mother suffered a bout of German measles during the pregnancy. Result: almost total blindness (I can tell dark from [bright] light.) Lived in Mexico City until father was transferred to Soviet embassy in Washington, DC, when I was five. Lived in Washington almost continuously since then. My parents divorced when I was ten, and my mother returned to Mexico City when I was thirteen. I never understood that; their whole relationship took place out of earshot, it seemed. But from then on I was wary.

Mathematics professor at George Washington University since 2043.

OA. One cold spring afternoon I encountered Jeremy Blasingame in the faculty lounge as I went to get a coffee refill – in the lounge, where nobody ever hangs out. 'Hello, Carlos, how's it going?'

'Fine,' I said, reaching about the table for the sugar. 'And you?'

'Pretty good. I've got a kind of an interesting problem over at my consulting job, though. It's giving me fits.'

Jeremy worked for the Pentagon in military intelligence or something, but he seldom talked about what he did there, and I certainly never asked. 'Oh yes?' I said as I found the sugar and spooned some in.

'Yes. They've got a coding problem that I bet would interest you.'

'I'm not much for cryptography.' Spy games – the math involved is really very limited. Sweet smell of sugar, dissolving in the lounge's bad coffee.

'Yes, I know,' Jeremy said. 'But – ' An edge of frustration in his voice; it's hard to tell when I'm paying attention, I know. (A form of control.) 'But this may be a geometer's code. We have a subject, you see, drawing diagrams.'

A subject. 'Hmph,' I said. Some poor spy scribbling away in a cell somewhere . . .

'So – I've got one of the drawings here. It reminds me of the theorem in your last article. Some projection, perhaps.'

'Yes?' Now what spy would draw something like that?

'Yeah, and it seems to have something to do with her speech, too. Her verbal sequencing is all dislocated – words in strange order, sometimes.'

'Yes? What happened to her?'

'Well . . . Here, check out the drawing.'

I put out a hand. 'I'll take a look.'

'And next time you want coffee, come ask me. I do a proper job of it in my office.'

'All right.'

AB. I suppose I have wondered all my life what it would be like to see. And all my work, no doubt, is an effort to envision things

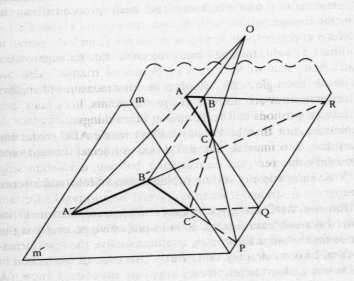

Figure 1

in the inward theater. 'I see it *feelingly*.' In language, in music, most of all in the laws of geometry, I find the best ways I can to see: by analogy to touch, and to sound, and to abstractions. Understand: to know the geometries fully is to comprehend exactly the physical world that light reveals; in a way one is then perceiving something like the Platonic ideal forms underlying the visible phenomena of the world. Sometimes the great ringing of comprehension fills me so entirely that I feel I *must* be seeing; what more could it be? I believe that I see.

Then comes the problem of crossing the street, of finding my misplaced keys. Geometry is little help; it's back to the hands and ears as eyes, at that point. And then I know that I do not see at all.

BC. Let me put it another way. Projective geometry began in the Renaissance, as an aid to painters newly interested in perspective, in the problems of representing the three-dimensional world on a canvas; it quickly became a mathematics of great power and elegance. The basic procedure can be illustrated quickly.

Here a geometrical figure is *projected* from one plane to another (as light, they tell me, projects a slide's image onto a wall). Note that while certain properties of triangle ABC are changed in triangle A′B′C′ (lengths of sides, measures of angles), other properties are not: points are still points, lines lines, and certain proportions still hold, among other things.

Now imagine that the visual world is triangle ABC (reduction ...). But then imagine that it has been projected inward onto something different, not onto a plane, but onto a Moebius strip or a Klein bottle say, or really, onto a manifold much more complex and strange than those (you'd be surprised.) Certain features of ABC are gone for good (color, for instance), but other essential features remain. And projective geometry is the art of finding what features or qualities survive the transformations of projection ...

Do you understand me?

A way into the world, a mode of consciousness, a philosophy, a type of being. A vision. A geometry for the self. Non-

Euclidean, of course; in fact, strictly Nevskyan, as it has to be to help me, as I make my projections from visual space to auditive space, to haptic space, to the world inside.

OA. The next time I met Blasingame he was anxious to hear what I thought of his diagram. (There could be an acoustics of emotion, thus a mathematics of emotion; meanwhile the ears of the blind do these calculations every day.)

'One drawing isn't much to go on, Jeremy. I mean, you're right, it looks like a simple projective drawing, but with some odd lines crossing it. Who knows what they mean? The whole thing might be something scribbled by a kid.'

'She's not that young. Want to see more?'

'Well . . . ' This woman he kept mentioning, some sort of Mata Hari prisoner in the Pentagon, drawing geometrical figures and refusing to speak except in riddles . . . naturally I was intrigued.

'Here, take these anyway. There seems to be a sort of progression.'

'It would help if I could talk to this *subject* who's doing all these.'

'Actually, I don't think so. But' – (seeing my irritation) – 'I can bring her by, I think, if these interest you.'

'I'll check them out.'

'Good, good.' Peculiar edge of excitement in his voice, tension, triumph, fear, the anticipation of . . . something. Frowning, I took the papers from him.

That afternoon I shuffled them into my special xerox machine, and the stiff reproductions rolled out of it heavily ridged. I ran my hands over the raised lines and letters slowly.

Here I must confess to you that most geometrical drawings are almost useless to me. If you consider it you will quickly see why: most drawings are two-dimensional representations of what a three-dimensional construction *looks* like. This does me no good, and in fact is extremely confusing. Say I feel a trapezoid on the page; is that meant to be a trapezoid, or is it rather a representation of a rectangle not co-terminous with the page it lies on? Or the conventional representation of a plane? Only a *description* of the drawing will tell me that. Without a description

I can only deduce what the figure appears to mean. Much easier to have 3-D models to explore with my hands.

But in this case, not possible. So I swept over the mishmash of ridges with both hands, redrew it with my ridging pen several times over, located the two triangles in it, and the lines connecting the two triangles' corners, and the lines made by extending the triangles' sides in one direction. I tried to make from my Taylor collection a 3-D model that accounted for the drawing – try that sometimes, and understand how difficult this kind of intellectual feat can be. Projective imagination . . .

Certainly it seemed to be a rough sketch of Desargues's Theorem.

C. Desargues's Theorem was one of the first theorems clearly concerned with projective geometry; it was proposed by Girard Desargues in the mid-seventeenth century, in between his architectural and engineering efforts, his books on music, etc. It is a relatively simple theorem, in fact in three dimensions it is completely banal. Figure 1 describes it, refer back to it if you want; the theorem states that given the relationships shown in the diagram, points P, Q, and R will be collinear. The proof is simple indeed. By definition P, Q, and R lie on the same plane *m* as triangle ABC, and they lie on the same plane *m'* as A'B'C'. Two planes can only intersect in a line, and as P, Q, and R lie on both *m* and *m'* they must lie on that line of intersection. Therefore P, Q, and R are collinear, as was to be proved.

Obvious, you say, and it is true. But you would be surprised to learn how many proofs in geometry, when taken step by step and reduced to their constituent parts, are just as obvious. With a language so pure, things become clear. Would we had such a language for the heart.

It is also true, by the way, that this theorem is reciprocal: that is, if you postulate two triangles whose extensions of the sides meet at three collinear points, then it is possible to show that lines AA', BB', and CC' meet in a single point. As they say in the textbooks, I leave the proof of this as an exercise for the reader.

AC. But so what? I mean, it is a beautiful theorem, with the sort of purity and elegance characteristic of Renaissance math – but what was it doing in a drawing made by some poor prisoner of the Pentagon?

I considered this as I walked to my health club, Warren's Spa (considered it secondarily, anyway, and no doubt subconsciously; my primary concerns were the streets and the traffic. Washington's streets bear a certain resemblance to one of those confusing geometrical diagrams I described [the state streets crossing diagonally the regular gridwork, creating a variety of inter-sections]; happily one doesn't have to comprehend all the city at once to walk in it. But it is easy to become lost. So as I walked I concentrated on distances, on the sounds of the streets that tended to remain constant, on smells [the dirt of the park at M and New Hampshire, the hot-dog vendor on Twenty-first and K]; meanwhile my cane established the world directly before my feet, my sonar shades whistled rising or falling notes as objects approached or receded ... It takes some work just to get from point A to point B without getting disoriented [at which point one has to grind one's teeth and ask for directions] but it can be done, it is one of those small tasks/accomplishments [one chooses which, every time] that the blind cannot escape) – still, I did consider the matter of the drawing as I walked.

On H Street and Twenty-first I was pleased to smell the pretzel cart of my friend Ramon, who is also blind. His cart is the only one where the hot plate hasn't roasted several pretzels to that metallic burnt odor that all the other carts put off; Ramon prefers the clean smell of freshly baked dough, and he claims it brings him more customers, which I certainly believe. 'Change only please,' he was saying to someone briskly, 'there's a change machine on the other side of the cart for your convenience, thanks. Hot pretzels! Hot pretzels, one dollar!'

'Hey there, Superblink!' I called as I approached him.

'Hey yourself, Professor Superblink,' he replied. (*Superblink* is a mildly derogatory name used by irritated sighted social service people to describe those of their blind colleagues who are aggressively or ostentatiously competent in getting around, etc., who make a *display* of their competence. Naturally we have appropriated the term for our own use; sometimes it means the same thing for us – when used in the third person, usually – but in the second person it's a term of affection.) 'Want a pretzel?'

'Sure.'

'You off to the gym?'

'Yeah, I'm going to throw. Next time we play you're in trouble.'

'That'll be the day, when my main mark starts beating me!'

I put four quarters in his callused hand and he gave me a pretzel. 'Here's a puzzle for you,' I said. 'Why would someone try to convey a message by geometrical diagram?'

He laughed. 'Don't ask me, that's your department!'

'But the message isn't for me.'

'Are you sure about that?'

I frowned.

BC. At the health club I greeted Warren and Amanda at the front desk. They were laughing over a headline in the tabloid newspaper Amanda was shaking; they devoured those things, and pasted the best headlines all over the gym.

'What's the gem of the day?' I asked.

'How about "Gay Bigfoot Molests Young Boys"?' Warren suggested.

'Or "Woman Found Guilty of Turning Husband into Bank President." ' Amanda said, giggling. 'She drugged him and did bemod to him until he went from teller to president.'

Warren said, 'I'll have to do that for you, eh Amanda?'

'Make me something better than a bank president.'

Warren clicked his tongue. 'Entirely too many designer drugs, these days. Come on, Carlos, I'll get the range turned on.' I went to the locker room and changed, and when I got to the target room Warren was just done setting it up. 'Ready to go,' he said cheerily as he rolled past me.

I stepped in, closed the door, and walked out to the center of the room, where a waist-high wire column was filled with baseballs. I pulled out a baseball, hefted it, felt the stitching. A baseball is a beautiful object: nicely flared curves of the seams over the surface of a perfect sphere, an ideal object, exactly the right weight for throwing.

I turned on the range with a flick of a switch, and stepped away from the feeder, a ball in each hand. Now it was quite silent, only the slightest whirr faintly breathing through the soundproofed walls. I did what I could to reduce the sound of my own breathing, heard my heartbeat in my ears.

Then a *beep* behind me to my left, and low; I swirled and threw. Dull thud. 'Right . . . low,' said the machine voice from above, softly. *Beep* I threw again: 'Right . . . high,' it said louder, meaning I had missed by more. 'Shit,' I said as I got another two balls. 'Bad start.'

Beep – a hard throw to my left – *clang!* 'Yeah!' There is very little in life more satisfying than the bell-like clanging of the target circle when hit square. It rings at about middle C with several overtones, like a small thick church bell hit with a hammer. The sound of success.

Seven more throws, four more hits. 'Five for ten,' the machine voice said. 'Average strike time, one-point-three-five seconds. Fastest strike time, point-eight-four seconds.'

Ramon sometimes hit the target in half a second or less, but I needed to hear the full beep to keep my average up. I set up for another round, pushed the button, got quiet, *beep* throw, *beep* throw, working to shift my feet faster, to follow through, to use the information from my misses to correct for the next time the target was near the floor, or the ceiling, or behind me (my weakness is the low ones, I can't seem to throw down accurately). And as I warmed up I threw harder and harder. Just throwing a baseball as hard as you can is a joy in itself. And then to set that bell ringing! *Clang!* It chimes every cell of you.

But when I quit and took a shower, and stood before my locker and reached in to free my shirt from a snag on the top of the door, my fingers brushed a small metal buttonlike thing stuck to an upper inside corner, where the door would usually conceal it from both me and my sighted companions; it came away when I pulled on it. I fingered it. The world is full of peculiar things. The cold touch of the unknown, so often felt . . . I am wary, I am always wary, I have to be wary.

I couldn't be certain what it was, but I had my suspicions, so I took it to my friend James Gold, who works in acoustics in the engineering department, and had him take a confidential look at it.

'It's a little remote microphone, all right,' he said, and then joked: 'Who's bugging you, Carlos?'

He got serious when I asked him where I could get a system like that for myself.

AB. 'John Metcalf – "Blind Jack of Knaresborough" – (1717-1810). At six he lost his sight through small-pox, at nine he could get on pretty well unaided, at fourteen he announced his intention of disregarding his affliction thence forward and of behaving in every respect as a normal human being. It is true that immediately on this brave resolve he fell into a gravel pit and received a serious hurt while escaping, under pursuit, from an orchard he was robbing ... fortunately this did not affect his self-reliance. At twenty he had made a reputation as a pugilist.'(!)
      – Ernest Bramah, Introduction,
                The Eyes of Max Carrados

I have to fight, do you understand? The world wasn't made for me. Every day is fifteen rounds, a scramble to avoid being knocked flat, a counterpunch at every threatening sound.

When I was young I loved to read Ernest Bramah's stories about Max Carrados, the blind detective. Carrados could hear, smell, and feel with incredible sensitivity, and his ingenious deductions were never short of brilliant; he was fearless in a pinch; also, he was rich, and had a mansion, and a secretary, manservant, and chauffeur who acted as his eyes. All great stuff for the imaginative young reader, as certainly I was. I read every book I could get my hands on; the voice of my reading machine was more familiar to me than any human voice that I knew. Between that reading and my mathematical work, I could have easily withdrawn from the world of my own experience into Cutsforth's 'verbal unreality,' and babbled on like Helen Keller about the shapes of clouds and the colors of flowers and the like. The world become nothing but a series of texts; sounds kind of

131

like deconstructionism, doesn't it? And of course at an older age I was enamored of the deconstructionists of the last century. The world as text. Husserl's *The Origin of Geometry* is twenty-two pages long, Derrida's *Introduction to the Origin of Geometry* is a hundred and fifty-three pages long – you can see why it would have appealed to me. If, as the deconstructionists seemed to say, the world is nothing but a collection of texts, and I can read, then I am not missing anything by being blind, am I?

The young can be very stubborn, very stupid.

AO. 'All right, Jeremy,' I said. 'Let me meet this mysterious *subject* of yours who draws all this stuff.'

'You want to?' he said, trying to conceal his excitement.

'Sure,' I replied. 'I'm not going to find out any more about all this until I do.' My own subtext, yes; but I am better at hiding such things than Jeremy is.

'What have you found out? Do the diagrams mean anything to you?'

'Not much. You know me, Jeremy, drawings are my weakness. I'd rather have her do it in models, or writing, or verbally. You'll have to bring her by if you want me to continue.'

'Well, okay. I'll see what I can do. She's not much help, though. You'll find out.' But he was pleased.

BA. One time in high school I was walking out of the gym after PE, and I heard one of my coaches (one of the best teachers I have ever had) in his office, speaking to someone (he must have had his back to me) – he said, 'You know, it's not the physical handicaps that will be the problem for most of these kids. It's the emotional problems that tend to come with the handicaps that will be the real burden for most of them.'

OAA'. I was in my office listening to my reading machine. Its flat, uninflected mechanical voice (almost unintelligible to some of my colleagues) had over the years become a sort of helpless, stupid friend. I called it George, and was always programming into it another pronunciation rule to try to aid its poor speech, but to no avail; George always found new ways to butcher the language. I put the book face-down on the glass; 'Finding first line,' croaked George as the scanner inside the machine thumped around. Then it read from Roberto Torretti, a philosopher of geometry, quoting and discussing Ernst Mach. (Hear this spoken in the most stilted, awkward, syllable-by-syllable mispronunciation that you can imagine.)

'Mach says that our notions of space are rooted in our *physiological* constitution, and that geometric concepts are the product of the idealization of *physical* experiences of space.' (George raises his voice in pitch to indicate italics, which also slow him down considerably.) 'But physiological space is quite different from the infinite, isotropic, metric space of classical geometry and physics. It can, at most, be structured as a topological space. When viewed in this way, it naturally falls into several components: visual or optic space, tactile or haptic space, auditive space, etc. Optic space is anisotropic, finite, limited. Haptic space or the space of our skin, Mach says, corresponds to a two-dimensional, finite, unlimited (closed) Riemannian space. This is nonsense, for R-spaces are metric while haptic space is not. I take it that Mach means to say that haptic space can naturally be regarded as a two-dimensional compact connected topological space. But Mach does not emphasize enough the disconnectedness of haptic from optic space – '

There came four quick knocks at my door. I pressed the button on George that stopped him, and said, 'Come in!'

The door opened. 'Carlos!'

'Jeremy,' I said. 'How are you.'

'Fine. I've brought Mary Unser with me – you know – the one who drew – '

I stood, feeling/hearing the presence of the other in the room. And there are times (like this one) when you *know* the other is in some odd, undefinable way, *different*, or . . . (Our language is not made for the experience of the blind. No words for this feeling, this apprehension.)

'I'm glad to meet you,' I said.

I have said that I can tell dark from light, and I can, to an extent, though it is seldom very useful information. In this case, however, I was startled to have my attention drawn to my 'sight'

– for this woman was darker than other people, she was a sort of bundle of darkness in the room, her face distinctly lighter than the rest of her (or was that her face, exactly?).

A long pause. Then: 'On border stand we n-dimensional space the,' she said. Coming just after George's reading, I was struck by a certain similarity: the mechanical lilt from word to word; the basic incomprehension of a reading machine ... Goose bumps rose on my forearms.

Her voice itself, on the other hand, had George beat hands down. Fundamentally vibrant under the odd intonation, it was a voice with a very thick timbre, a bassoon or a hurdy-gurdy of a voice, with the buzz of someone who habitually speaks partly through the sinuses; this combined with overrelaxed vocal cords, what speech pathologists call *glottal fry*. Usually nasal voices are not pleasant, but pitch them low enough ...

She spoke again, more slowly (definitely glottal fry): 'We stand on the border of n-dimensional space.'

'Hey,' Jeremy said. 'Pretty good!' He exclaimed: 'Her word order isn't usually as ... ordinary as that.'

'So I gathered,' I said. 'Mary, what do you mean by that?'

'I – *oh* – ' A kazoo squeak of distress, pain. I approached her, put out a hand. She took it as if to shake: a hand about the size of mine, narrow, strong fat muscle at base of thumb; trembling distinctly.

'I work on the geometries of topologically complex spaces,' I said. 'I am more likely than most to understand what you say.'

'Are within never see we points us.'

'That's true.' But there was something wrong here, something I didn't like, though I couldn't tell exactly what it was. Had she spoken toward Jeremy? Speaking to me while she looked at him? The cold touch ... a bundle of darkness in the dark ... 'But why are your sentences so disordered, Mary? Your words don't come out in the order you thought them. You must know that, since you understand us.'

'Folded – *oh*!' Again the double-reed squeak, and suddenly she was weeping, trembling hard; we sat her down on my visitor's couch and Jeremy got her a glass of water, while she quaked in my hands. I stroked her hair (short, loosely curled, wild) and took the opportunity for a quick phrenological check: skull regular and as far as I could tell, undamaged; temples wide, distinct; same for eye sockets; nose a fairly ordinary pyramidal segment, no bridge to speak of; narrow cheeks, wet with tears. She reached up and took my right hand, and her little finger squeezed it hard, three times fast, three times slow, while she sobbed and sort of hiccuped words: 'Pain it, station, I, or, hold end, bright, light, space fold, oh, ohhh ...'

Well, the direct question is not always the best way. Jeremy returned with a glass of water, and drinking some seemed to calm her. Jeremy said, 'Perhaps we could try again later. Although – ' He didn't seem very surprised.

'Sure,' I said. 'Listen, Mary, I'll talk to you again when you're feeling better.'

But the language of touch, reduced to a simple code. SO ... S?

OA. After Jeremy got her out of the office and disposed of her (how? with whom?) he returned to the seventh floor.

'So what the hell happened to her?' I asked angrily. 'Why is she like that?'

'We aren't completely sure,' he said slowly. 'Here's why. She was one of the scientists staffing Tsiolkovsky Base Five, up in the mountains on the back side of the moon, you know. She's an astronomer and cosmologist. Well – I have to ask you to keep this quiet – one day Base Five stopped all broadcasting, and when they went over to see what was wrong, they found only her, wandering the station alone in a sort of catatonic state. No sign of the other scientists or station crew – eighteen people gone without a trace. And nothing much different to explain what had happened, either.'

I *hmphed*. 'What do they think happened?'

'They're still not sure. Apparently no one else was in the area, or could have been, et cetera. It's been suggested by the Russians, who had ten people there, that this could be first contact – you know, that aliens took the missing ones, and somehow disarranged Mary's thought processes, leaving her

135

behind as a messenger that isn't working. Her brain scans are bizarre. I mean, it doesn't sound very likely – '

'No.'

'But it's the only theory that explains everything they found there. Some of which they won't tell me about. So, we're doing what we can to get Mary's testimony, but as you can see, it's hard. She seems most comfortable drawing diagrams.'

'Next time we'll start with that.'

'Okay. Any other ideas?'

'No,' I lied. 'When can you bring her back again?'

AO. As if because I was blind I couldn't tell I was being duped!

Alone again, I struck fist into palm angrily. Oh, they were making a mistake, all right. They didn't know how much the voice reveals. The voice's secret expressivity reveals *so much*! – the language really is not adequate to tell it, we need that mathematics of emotion . . . In the high school for the blind that I briefly attended for some of my classes, it often happened that a new teacher was instantly disliked, for some falseness in his or her voice, some quality of condescension or pity or self-congratulation that the teacher (and his or her superiors) thought completely concealed, if they knew of it at all. But it was entirely obvious to the students, because the voice is so utterly revealing, much more so I think than facial expressions; certainly it is less under our control. This is what makes most acting performances unsatisfactory to me; the vocal qualities are so stylized, so removed from those of real life . . .

And here, I thought, I was witnessing a performance.

There is a moment in Olivier Messiaen's *Visions de l'Amen* when one piano is playing a progression of major chords, very traditionally harmonic, while on another piano high pairs of notes plonk down across the other's chords, ruining their harmony, crying out, Something's wrong! Something's wrong!

I sat at my desk and swayed side to side, living just such a moment. Something was wrong. Jeremy and this woman were lying, their voices said it in every intonation.

When I collected myself I called the department secretary,

who had a view of the hall to the elevator. 'Delphina, did Jeremy just leave?'

'Yes, Carlos. Do you want me to try and catch him?'

'No, I only need a book he left in his office. Can I borrow the master key and get it?'

'Okay.'

I got the key, entered Jeremy's office, closed the door. One of the tiny pickups that James Gold had gotten for me fit right under the snap-in plug of the telephone cord. Then a microphone under the desk, behind a drawer. And out. (I have to be bold every day, you see, just to get by. I have to be wary, I have to be *bold*. But they didn't know that.)

Back in my office I closed and locked the door, and began to search. My office is big: two couches, several tall bookcases, my desk, a file cabinet, a coffee table ... When the partitions on the seventh floor of the Gelman Library were moved around to make more room, Delphina and George Hampton, who was chairman that year, had approached me nervously: 'Carlos, you wouldn't mind an office with no windows, would you?'

I laughed. All of the full professors had offices on the outer perimeter of the floor, with windows.

'You see,' George said, 'since none of the windows in the building opens anyway, you won't be missing out on any breezes. And if you take this room in the inner core of the building, then we'll have enough space for a good faculty lounge.'

'Fine,' I said, not mentioning that I could see sunlight, distinguish light and dark. It made me angry that they hadn't remembered that, hadn't thought to ask. So I nicknamed my office 'The Vault,' and I had a lot of room, but no windows. The halls had no windows either, so I was really without sun, but I didn't complain.

Now I got down on hands and knees and continued searching, feeling like it was hopeless. But I found one, on the bottom of the couch. And there was another in the phone. Bugged. I left them in position and went home.

Home was a small top-floor apartment up near Twenty-first and N streets, and I supposed it was bugged too. I turned up Stockhausen's *Telemusik* as loud as I could stand it, hoping to drive my listeners into a suicidal fugal state, or at least give them a headache. Then I slapped together a sandwich, downed it angrily.

I imagined I was captain of a naval sailing ship (like Horatio Hornblower), and that because of my sharp awareness of the wind I was the best captain afloat. They had had to evacuate the city and all the people I knew were aboard, depending on me to save them. But we were caught against a lee shore by two large ships of the line, and in the ensuing broadsides (roar of cannon, smell of gunpowder and blood, screams of wounded like shrieking sea gulls), everyone I knew fell – chopped in half, speared by giant splinters, heads removed by cannon-ball, you name it. Then when they were all corpses on the sand-strewn splintered decking, I felt a final broadside discharge, every ball converging on me as if I were point O in figure 1. Instant dissolution and death.

I came out of it feeling faintly disgusted with myself. But Cutsforth says that because this type of fantasy in the blind subject actively defends the ego by eradicating those who attack its self-esteem, it is a healthy thing. (At least in fourteen-year-olds.) So be it. Here's to health. Fuck all of you.

C. Geometry is a language, with a vocabulary and syntax as clear and precise as humans can make them. In many cases definitions of terms and operations are explicitly spelled out, to help achieve this clarity. For instance, one could say:

Let (parentheses) designate additional information.
Let [brackets] designate secret causes.
Let {braces} designate . . .
But would it be true, in this other language of the heart?

AB. Next afternoon I played beepball with my team. Sun hot on my face and arms, spring smell of pollen and wet grass. Ramon got six runs in the at-bat before mine (beepball is a sort of cricket/softball mix, played with softball equipment ['It shows you can play cricket blind' one Anglophobe {she was Irish} said to me once]), and when I got up I scratched out two and then struck out. Swinging *too* hard. I decided I liked outfield better.

The beepball off in the distance, lofted up in a short arc, smack of bat, follow the ball up and up – out toward me! – drift in its direction, the rush of fear, glove before face as it approaches, stab for it, off after it as it rolls by – pick it up – Ramon's voice calling clearly, 'Right here! Right here!' – and letting loose with a throw – really putting everything into it – and then, sometimes, hearing that beepball lance off into the distance and smack into Ramon's glove. It was great. Nothing like outfield.

And next inning I hit one *hard*, and that's great too. A counterpunch. That feeling goes right up your arms and all through you.

Walking home I brooded over Max Carrados, blind detective, and over Horatio Hornblower, sighted naval captain. Over Thomas Gore, blind senator from Oklahoma. As a boy his fantasy was to become a senator. He read the *Congressional Record*, joined the debate team, organized his whole life around the project. And he became senator. I knew that sort of fantasy as well as I knew the vengeful adolescent daydreams: all through my youth I dreamed of being a mathematician. And here I was. So one could do it. One could imagine doing something, and then do it.

But that meant that one had, by definition, imagined something *possible*. And one couldn't always say ahead of the attempt whether one had imagined the possible or the impossible. And even if one had imagined something possible, that didn't guarantee a successful execution of the plan.

The team we had played was called 'Helen Keller Jokes' (there are some good ones, too [they come {of course} from Australia] but I won't go into that). It's sad that such an intelligent woman was so miseducated – not so much by Sullivan as by her whole era: all that treacly Victorian sentimentality poured into her, 'The fishing villages of Cornwall are very picturesque, seen either from the beaches or the hilltops, with all their boats riding to their moorings or sailing about in the harbor – When the moon, large and serene, floats up the sky, leaving in the water a long track of brightness like a plow breaking up a soil of silver, I can only sigh my ecstasy,' come on, Helen. Get off it. Now that is living in a world of texts.

But didn't I live most (all?) of my life in texts at least as unreal to me as moonlight on water was to Helen Keller? These *n*-dimensional manifolds I had explored for so long . . . I suppose the basis for my abilities in them was the lived reality of haptic space, but still, it was many removes from my actual experience. And so was the situation I found myself confronted with now, Jeremy and Mary acting out some drama I did not comprehend. And so was my plan to deal with it. Verbalism, words versus reality . . .

I caressed my glove, refelt the shiver of bat against beepball. Brooded anxiously over my plan. Under attack, disoriented, frightened. For months after my mother left I made plans to get her back. I invented ailments, I injured myself, I tried to slip away and fly to Mexico. Why had she gone? It was inconceivable. Father didn't want to speak of it. They didn't love each other anymore, he said once. It was hard for her, she didn't speak the language. They wouldn't let her stay as a single person. She couldn't take care of me in Mexico, she had family burdens, things were bad there, and besides he didn't want me to leave, he was my principal teacher now, my caretaker. None of it meant anything to me. I barely even heard him. A whole language of hands, lost. I began to forget and clasped my own hands together and made the words, forefingers for food, the outdoor squeeze, the wanting sweep, the pressure that said I love you. No one heard.

OAA′. The next time Jeremy brought Mary Unser by my office, I said very little. I got out my visitor's supply of paper and pencils, and set her down at the coffee table. I brought over my models: subatomic particles breaking up in a spray of wire lines, like water out of a shower head; strawlike Taylor sticks for model making; polyhedric blocks of every kind. I sat down with the ridged sheets made from her earlier drawings, and the models I had attempted to make of them, and I started asking very limited questions. 'What does this line mean? Does it go before or behind? Is this R or R'? Have I got this right?'

And she would honk a sort of laugh, or say 'No, no, no, no,' (no problem with sequencing there) and draw furiously. I took the pages as she finished them and put them in my xerox, took out the ridged, bumpy sheets and had her guide my fingers over them. Even so they were difficult, and with a squeak of frustration she went to the straw models, clicking together triangles, parallels, etc. This was easier, but eventually she reached a limit here, too. 'Need drawing beyond,' she said.

'Fine. Write down whatever you want.'

She wrote, and then read aloud to me, or I put it through my xerox machine marked 'translation to Braille.' And we forged on, with Jeremy looking over our shoulders the whole time.

And eventually we came very close to the edge of my work. (The cold touch.) Following subatomic particles down into the microdimensions where they appeared to make their 'jumps.' I had proposed an n-dimensional topological manifold, where $1 < n <$ infinity, so that the continuum being mapped fluctuated between one and some finite number of dimensions, going from a curving line to a sort of n-dimensional Swiss cheese, if you like, depending on the amounts of energy displayed in the area in any of the four forms, electromagnetism, gravity, or the strong and weak interactions. The geometry for this manifold pattern (so close to the experience of haptic space) had, as I have said, attracted the attention of physicists at CERN and SLAC – but there were still unexplained areas, as far as I could tell, and the truth was *I had not published this work.*

So here I was 'conversing' with a young woman who in ordinary conversations could not order her words correctly – who in this realm spoke with perfect coherence – who was in fact speaking about (inquiring about?) the edges of my own private work.

The kind of work that Jeremy Blasingame used to ask me about so curiously.

I sighed. We had been going on for two or three hours, and I sat back on the couch. My hand was taken up in Mary's, given a reassuring squeeze. I didn't know what to make of it. 'I'm tired,' I said.

'I feel better,' she said. 'Easier to talk way – this way.'

'Ah,' I said. I took up the model of a positron hitting a 'stationary' muon: a wire tree, trunk suddenly bursting in to a mass of curling branches . . . So it was here: one set of events, a whole scattering of explanations. Still, the bulk of the particles shot out in a single general direction (the truths of haptic space).

She let go of my hand to make one last diagram. Then she xeroxed it for me, and guided my hands over the ridged copy.

Once again it was Desargues's Theorem: triangles ABC and A'B'C', projected from point O. Only this time the two triangles were in the same plane, and AB and A'B' were parellel, as were BC and B'C', and AC and A'C'. P, Q, and R had become ideal points; and she put my finger in the areas marking these ideal points, time after time.

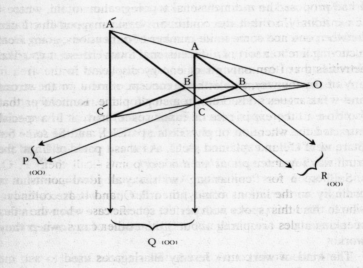

Figure 2

C. Perhaps I should explain a little further, for now we leave the Euclidean world behind.

The geometry of ordinary points and lines (Euclidean geometry) is greatly complicated by the fact that a pair of parallel lines do not meet in a point. Why should this be so? Altering

Euclid's fifth axiom concerning parallels led to the first non-Euclidean geometries of Lobachevski and Bolyai and Riemann. To enter this altered world we only need to add to the ordinary points on each line a single 'ideal' point. This point belongs to all lines parallel to the given line. Now every pair of lines in the plane will intersect in a single point; lines not parallel will intersect in an ordinary point, and lines parallel will intersect in the ideal point common to the two lines. For intuitive reasons the ideal point is called the *point at infinity* on the line.

(This notion of ideality can be extended to other geometrical figures: all the points at infinity in a plane lie on a *line at infinity*; all the lines at infinity lie on the plane at infinity, the ideal plane in space, out beyond the rest; and all ideal planes lie in the *space at infinity*, in the next dimension over; and so on, unto *n* dimensions. [In the haptic space of Nevskyan geometry I can feel the presence of these ideal realms, for beyond certain ideal planes {membranes just beyond my touch} there are ideal activities that I can only imagine, can only yearn for ...])

Note, by the way, that with the concept of ideal points we can prove Desargues's Theorem in a single plane. Remember that to prove a theorem in general it suffices to prove it in a special case, as here, where AB and A'B' are parallel, and the same for BC and B'C', and AC and A'C'. As these pairs of lines are parallel, they intersect at their ideal points – call them P, Q, and R again for familiarity. And since all ideal points in a plane lie on the line at infinity, then P, Q, and R are collinear. Simple. And this proves not only the specific case when the sides of the triangles are parallel, but all the other cases, when they are not.

If only the world conformed to this rigorous logic!

A'AO. At this point Mary said, 'Mr Blasingame, I need a drink of water.' He went out to the hall water dispenser, and she quickly took my forefinger between her finger and thumb (pads flattening with an inappropriate pressure, until my finger ached) – squeezed twice, and jabbed my finger first onto her leg, then onto the diagram, tracing out one of the triangles. She repeated the movements, then poked my leg and traced out the other triangle. Fine; she was one, I was the other. We were parallel, and in projection from point O, which was . . .

But she only traced the lines to point O, over and over. What did she mean?

Jeremy returned, and she let my hand go. Then in a while, after the amenities (hard handshake, quivering hand) Jeremy whisked her off.

When he returned, I said, 'Jeremy, is there any chance I can talk to her alone? I think she's made nervous by your presence – the associations, you know. She really does have an interesting perspective on the *n*-dimensional manifold, but she gets confused when she stops and interacts with you. I'd just like to take her for a walk, you know – down by the canal, or the Tidal Basin, perhaps, and talk things over with her. It might get the results you want.'

'I'll see what they say,' Jeremy said in an expressionless voice.

That night I put on a pair of earplugs, and played the tape of Jeremy's phone conversations. In one when the phone was picked up he said:

'He wants to talk with her alone now.'

'Fine,' said a tenor voice. 'She's prepared for that.'

'This weekend?'

'If he agrees.' *Click.*

BA. I listen to music. I listen to twentieth-century composers the most, because many of them made their music out of the sounds of the world we live in now, the world of jets and sirens and industrial machinery, as well as bird song and wood block and the human voice. Messiaen, Partch, Reich, Glass, Shapiro, Subotnik, Nigeti, Penderecki – these first explorers away from the orchestra and the classical tradition remain for me the voices of our age. They speak to me. In fact they speak for me; in their dissonance and confusion and anger I hear myself being expressed, I hear the loss and feel its transformation into something else, into something less painful. And so I listen to their difficult, complex music because I understand it, which gives me pleasure, and because while doing so I am participating fully, I am excelling. No one can bring more to the act than I. I am *in control*.

I listened to music.

O. You see, these n-dimensional manifolds ... if we understood them well enough to manipulate them, to tap their energy ... well, there is a tremendous amount of energy contained there. That kind of energy means power, and power ... draws the powerful. Or those seeking power, fighting for it. I began to feel the extent of the danger.

BB'. She was quiet as we walked across the Mall toward the Lincoln Monument. I think she would have stopped me if I had spoken about anything important. But I knew enough to say nothing, and I think she guessed I knew she was bugged. I held the back of her upper arm loosely in my left hand, and let her guide us. A sunny, windy day, with occasional clouds obscuring the sun for a minute or two. Down by the Mall's lake the slightly stagnant smell of wet algae tinged all the other scents: grass, dust, the double strand of lighter fluid and cooking meat ... The sink of darkness swirling around the Vietnam Memorial. Pigeons cooed their weird, larger-than-life coos, and flapped away noisily as we walked through their affairs. We sat on grass that had been recently cut, and I brushed a hand over the stiff blades.

A curious procedure, this conversation. No visuals, for me; and perhaps we were being watched, as well. (Such a common anxiety of the blind, the fear of being watched – and here it was true.) And we couldn't talk freely, even though at the same time we had to say something, to keep Blasingame and friends from thinking I was aware of anything wrong. 'Nice day.' 'Yeah. I'd love to be out on the water on a day like this.' 'Really?' 'Yeah.'

And all the while two fingers held one finger. My hands are my eyes, and always have been. Now they were as expressive as voice, as receptive as ever touch can be, and into haptic space we projected a conversation of rare urgency. Are you okay? I'm okay. Do you know what's going on? Not entirely, can't explain.

'Let's walk down to the paddle boats and go out on the Basin, then.'

I said, 'Your speech is much better today.'

She squeezed my hand thrice, hard. False information? 'I . . .

had ... electroshock.' Her voice slid, slurred; it wasn't entirely under control.

'It seems to have helped.'

'Yes. Sometimes.'

'And the ordering of your mathematical thought?'

Buzzing laugh, hurdy-gurdy voice: 'I don't know – more disarranged, perhaps – complementary procedure? You'll have to tell me.'

'As a cosmologist did you work in this area?'

'The topology of the microdimensions apparently determines both gravity and the weak interaction, wouldn't you agree?'

'I couldn't say. I'm not much of a physicist.'

Three squeezes again. 'But you must have an idea or two about it?'

'Not really? You?'

'Perhaps ... once. But it seems to me your work is directly concerned with it.'

'Not that I know of.'

Stalemate. Was that right? I was becoming more and more curious about this woman, whose signals to me were so mixed ... Once again she seemed a bundling of darkness in the day, a whirlpool where all lightness disappeared, except for around her head. (I suppose I imagine all that I 'see,' I suppose they are always haptic visions.)

'Are you wearing dark clothes?'

'Not really. Red, beige ...'

As we walked I held her arm more tightly. She was about my height. Her arm muscles were distinct, and her lats pushed out from her ribs. 'You must swim.'

'Weight lifting, I'm afraid. They made us on Luna.'

'On Luna,' I repeated.

'Yes,' and she fell silent.

This really was impossible. I didn't think she was completely an ally – in fact I thought she was lying – but I felt an underlying sympathy from her, and a sense of conspiracy with her, that grew more powerful the longer we were together. The problem was, what did that feeling mean? Without the ability to converse freely, I was stymied in my attempts to learn more; pushed this way and that in the cross-currents of her behavior, I could only wonder what she was thinking. And what our listeners made of this mostly silent day in the sun.

So we paddled out onto the Tidal Basin, and talked from time to time about the scene around us. I love the feel of being on water – the gentle rocking over other boats' wakes, the wet stale smell . . . 'Are the cherry trees blossoming still?'

'Oh yes. Not quite at the peak, but just past. It's beautiful. Here – ' she leaned out – 'here's one about to drown.' She put it in my hand. I sniffed at it. 'Do they smell?'

'No, not much,' I said. 'The prettier people say flowers are, the less scent they seem to have. Did you ever notice that?'

'I guess. I like the scent of roses.'

'It's faint, though. These blossoms must be very beautiful – they smell hardly at all.'

'En masse they are lovely. I wish you could see them.'

I shrugged. 'And I wish you could touch their petals, or feel us bouncing about as I do. I have enough sense data to keep entertained.'

'Yes . . . I suppose you do.' She left her hand covering mine. 'I suppose we're out quite a ways,' I said. So that we couldn't be seen well from the shore, I meant.

'From the dock, anyway. We're actually almost across the Basin.'

I moved my hand from under hers, and held her shoulder. Deep hollow behind her collarbone. This contact, this conversation of touch . . . it was most expressive hand to hand, and so I took her hand again, and our fingers made random entanglements, explorations. Children shouting, then laughing in boats to our left, voices charged with excitement. How to speak in this language of touch?

Well, we all know that. Fingertips, brushing lines of the palm; ruffling the fine hair at the back of the wrist; fingers pressing each other back: these are sentences, certainly. And it is a difficult language to lie in. That catlike sensuous stretch, under my stroking fingertips . . .

'We've got a clear run ahead of us,' she said after a time, voice charged with humming overtones.

147

'Stoke the furnaces,' I cried. 'Damn the torpedoes!' And with a gurgling *clug-clug-clug-clug* we paddle-wheeled over the Basin into the fresh wet wind, sun on our faces, laughing at the release from tension (bassoon and baritone), crying out 'Mark twain!' or 'Snag dead ahead' in jocular tones, entwined hands crushing the other as we pedaled harder and harder ... 'Down the Potomac!' 'Across the sea!' and the spray cold on the breeze –

She stopped pedaling, and we swerved left.

'We're almost back,' she said quietly.

We let the boat drift in, without a word.

OA. My bugs told me that my office had been broken into, by two, possibly three people, only one of whom spoke – a man, in an undertone: 'Try the file cabinet.' The cabinet drawers were rolled out (familiar clicking of the runners over the ball bearings), and the desk drawers, too, and then there was the sound of paper shuffling, of things being knocked about.

I also got an interesting phone conversation over Jeremy's phone. The call was incoming; Jeremy said 'Yes?' and a male voice – the same one Jeremy had called earlier – said, 'She says he's unwilling to go into any detail.'

'That doesn't surprise me,' Jeremy said. 'But I'm sure he's got – '

'Yes, I know. Go ahead and try what we discussed.'

The break-in, I supposed.

'Okay.' *Click.*

AO. No doubt it never even occurred to them that I might turn the tables on them, or act against them in any way, or even figure out that something was strange. It made me furious.

OA. At the same time I was frightened. You feel the lines of force, living in Washington, DC; feel the struggle for power among the shadowy manifolds surrounding the official government space; read of the unsolved murders, of shadowy people whose jobs are not made clear ... As a blind person one feels apart from that nebulous world of intrigue and hidden force, on the edge by reason of disability. ('No one harms a blind man.')

Now I knew I was part of it, pulled in, on my own. It was frightening.

But they didn't know how much I knew. Snuffle of an approaching boxer, counterpunch right in the face. I have to be bold just to cross the street!

AA'. One night I was immersed in Harry Partch's *Cloud Chamber Music*, floating in those big glassy notes, when my doorbell rang. I picked up the phone. 'Hello?'

'It's Mary Unser. May I come up?'

'Sure.' I pushed the button and walked onto the landing.

She came up the stairs alone. 'Sorry to bother you at home,' she buzzed, out of breath. Such a voice. 'I looked up your address in the phone book. I'm not supposed . . .'

She stood before me, touched my right arm. I lifted my hand and held her elbow. 'Yes?'

Nervous, resonant laugh. 'I'm not supposed to be here.'

Then you'll soon be in trouble, I wanted to say. But surely she knew my apartment would be bugged? Surely she *was* supposed to be here? She was trembling violently, enough so that I put up my other hand and held her by the shoulders. 'Are you all right?'

'Yes. No.' Falling oboe tones, laugh that was not a laugh . . . She seemed frightened, very frightened. I thought, if she is acting she is *very* good.

'Come on in,' I said, and led her inside. I went to the stereo and turned down the Partch – then reconsidered, and turned it back up. 'Have a seat – the couch is nice.' I was nervous myself. 'Would you like something to drink?' Quite suddenly it all seemed unreal, a dream, one of my fantasies. Phantasmagoric cloud chamber ringing to things, how did I know what was real? Those membranes. Beyond the plane at infinity, what?

'No. Or yes.' She laughed again, that laugh that was not a laugh.

'I've got some beer.' I went to the refrigerator, got a couple of bottles, opened them.

'So what's going on?' I said as I sat down beside her. As she spoke I drank from my beer, and she stopped from time to time to take long swallows.

'Well, I feel that the more I understand what you're saying about the transfer of energies between n-dimensional manifolds, the better I understand what . . . happened to me.' But now there was a different sound to her voice – an overtone was gone, it was less resonant, less nasal.

I said, 'I don't know what I can tell you. It's not something I can talk about, or even write down. What I can express, I have, you know. In papers.' This a bit louder, for the benefit of our audience. (If there was one?)

'Well . . .' and her hand, under mine, began to tremble again.

We sat there for a very long time, and all during that time we conversed through those two hands, saying things I can scarcely recall now, because we have no language for that sort of thing. But they were important things nevertheless, and after a while I said, 'Here. Come with me. I'm on the top floor, so I have a sort of a porch on the roof. Finish your beer. It's a pleasant night out, you'll feel better outside.' I led her through the kitchen to the pantry, where the door to the backstairs was. 'Go on up.' I went back to the stereo and put on Jarrett's *Köln Concert*, loud enough so we'd be able to hear it. Then I went up the stairs onto the roof, and crunched over the tarred gravel.

This was one of my favorite places. The sides of the building came up to the chest around the edge of the roof, and on two sides large willows draped their branches over it, making it a sort of haven. I had set a big old wreck of a couch out there, and on certain nights when the wind was up and the air was cool, I would lie back on it with a bumpy Braille planisphere in my hands, listening to Scholz's *Starcharts* and feeling that with those projections I knew what it was to see the night sky.

'This is nice,' she said.

'Isn't it?' I pulled the plastic sheet from the couch, and we sat.

'Carlos?'

'Yes?'

'I – I – ' That double-reed squeak –

I put an arm around her. 'Please,' I said, suddenly upset myself. 'Not now. Not now. Just relax. Please.' And she turned into me, her head rested on my shoulder; she trembled. I dug my fingers into her hair and slowly pulled them through the tangles.

Shoulder length, no more. I cupped her ears, stroked her neck. She calmed.

Time passed, and I only caressed. No other thought, no other perception. How long this went on I couldn't say – perhaps a half hour? Perhaps longer. She made a sort of purring kazoo sound, and I leaned forward and kissed her. Jarrett's voice, crying out briefly over a fluid run of piano notes. She pulled me to her, her breath caught, rushed out of her. The kiss became intense, tongues dancing together in a whole intercourse of their own, which I felt all through me in that *chakra* way, neck, spine, belly, groin, nothing but kiss. And without the slightest bit of either intention or resistance, I fell into it.

I remember a college friend once asked me, hesitantly, if I didn't have trouble with my love life. 'Isn't it hard to tell when they ... want to?' I had laughed. The whole process, I had wanted to say, was amazingly easy. The blind's dependence on touch puts them in an advance position, so to speak: using hands to see faces, being led by the hand (being dependent), one has already crossed what Russ calls the border between the world of not-sex and the world of sex; once over that border (with an other feeling protective) ...

My hands explored her body, discovering it then and there for the first time: as intensely exciting a moment as there is, in the whole process. I suppose I expect narrow-cheeked people to be narrow-hipped (it's mostly true, you'll find), but it wasn't so, in this case – her hips flared in those feminine curves that one can only hold, without ever getting used to (without ever [the otherness of the other] quite believing). On their own my fingers slipped under clothes, between buttons, as adroit as little mice, clever lusty little creatures, unbuttoning blouse, reaching behind to undo bra with a twist. She shrugged out of them both and I felt the softness of her breasts while she tugged at my belt. I shifted, rolled, put my ear to her hard sternum, kissing the inside of one breast as it pressed against my face, feeling that quick heartbeat speak to me ... She moved me back, got me unzipped, we paused for a speedy moment and got the rest of our clothes off, fumbling at our own and each other's until they were clear. Then it was flesh to flesh, skin to skin, in a single haptic space jumping with energy, with the insistent *yes* of caresses, mouth to mouth, four hands full, body to body, with breasts and erect penis crushed, as it were, between two pulsing walls of muscle.

The skin is the ultimate voice.

So we made love. As we did (my feet jabbing the end of the couch, which was quite broad enough, but a little too short) I arched up and let the breeze between us (cool on our sweat), leaned down and sucked on first one nipple and then the other –

(thus becoming helpless in a sense, a needy infant, completely dependent [because for the blind from birth, mother love is even more crucial than for the rest of us – the blind depend on their mothers for almost *everything*, for the sense of object permanence, for the education that makes the distinction between self and world, for the beginning of language, and also for the establishment of a private language that compensates for the lack of sight {if your mother doesn't know that a sweeping hand means '*I want*'} and bridges the way to the common tongue – without all that, which only a mother can give, the blind infant is lost – without mother love beyond mother love, the blind child will very likely go mad] so that [for any of us] to suck on a lover's nipple brings back that primal world of trust and need, I am sure of it)

– I was sure of it even then, as I made love to this strange other Mary Unser, a woman as unknown to me as any I had ever spoken with. At least until now. Now with each plunge into her (cylinder capped by cone, sliding through cylinder into rough sphere, neuron to neuron, millions of them fusing across, so that I could not tell where I stopped and she began) I learned more about her, the shape of her, her rhythms, her whole nerve-reality, spoken to me in movement and touch (spread hands holding my back, flanks, bottom) and in those broken bassoon tones that were like someone humming, briefly, involuntarily. 'Ah,' I said happily at all this sensation, all this new knowledge, feeling all my skin and all my nerves swirl up like a gust of wind into my spine, the back of my balls, to pitch into her all my self –

When we were done (oboe squeaks) I slid down, bending my

knees so my feet stuck up in the air. I wiggled my toes in the breeze. Faint traffic noises played a sort of city music to accompany the piano in the apartment. From the airshaft came the sound of a chorus of pigeons, sounding like monkeys with their jaws wired shut, trying to chatter. Mary's skin was damp and I licked it, loving the salt. Patch of darkness in my blur of vision, darkness bundling in it . . . She rolled onto her side and my hands played over her. Her biceps made a smooth hard bulge. There were several moles on her back, like little raisins half-buried in her skin. I pushed them down, fingered the knobs of her spine. The muscles of her back put her spine in a deep trough of flesh. Women are so bifurcated that way: between the shoulder blades the spine drops into a valley between two ridges of muscle, then dives even deeper between the halves of the butt, past the curl of the coccyx, past anus and vagina and the split nest of pubic hair and over the pubic bone, a sort of low pass; then on most women the valley begins again, as a broad depression up to belly button and up to sternum, and between breasts, and all the way up to the hollow between the collarbones, so that their whole torso is divided this way, into left and right. I explored this valley in Mary's body and she shifted, threw her top leg over mine. My head rested on her biceps, snuggled against her side.

I remembered a day my blind science class was taken to a museum, where we were allowed to feel a skeleton. All those hard bones, in just the right places; it made perfect sense, it was exactly as it felt under skin, really – there were no big surprises. But I remember being so upset by the experience of feeling the skeleton that I had to go outside and sit down on the museum steps. I don't know to this day exactly why I was so shaken, but I suppose (all those hard things left behind) it was something like this: it was frightening to know how *real* we were!

Now I tugged at her, gently. 'Who are you, then.'

'Not now.' And as I started to speak again she put a finger to my mouth (scent of us): 'A friend.' Buzzing nasal whisper, like a tuning fork, like a voice I was beginning (and this scared me, for I knew I did not know her) to love: 'A friend . . .'

* * *

C. At a certain point in geometrical thinking vision becomes only an obstruction. Those used to visualizing theorems (as in Euclidean geometry) reach a point, in the *n*-dimensional manifolds or elsewhere, where the concepts simply *can't* be visualized; and the attempt to do so only leads to confusion and misunderstanding. Beyond that point an interior geometry, a haptic geometry, guided by a kinetic aesthetics, is probably the best sensory analogy we have; and so I have my advantage.

But in the real world, in the geometries of the heart, do I ever have any comparable advantage? Are there things we feel that can never be seen?

OA. The central problem for everyone concerned with the relationship between geometry and the real world is the question of how one moves from the incommunicable impressions of the sensory world (vague fields of force, of danger), to the generally agreed-upon abstractions of the math (the explanation). Or, as Edmund Husserl puts it in *The Origin of Geometry* (and on this particular morning George was enunciating this passage for me with the utmost awkwardness): 'How does geometrical ideality (just like that of all the sciences) proceed from its primary intrapersonal origin, where it is a structure within the conscious space of the first inventor's soul, to its ideal objectivity?'

At this point Jeremy knocked at my door: four quick raps. 'Come in, Jeremy,' I said, my pulse quickening.

He opened the door and looked in. 'I have a pot of coffee just ready to go,' he said. 'Come on down and have some.'

So I joined him in his office, which smelled wonderfully of strong French roast. I sat in one of the plush armchairs that circled Jeremy's desk, accepted a small glazed cup, sipped from it. Jeremy moved about the room restlessly as he chattered about one minor matter after another, obviously avoiding the topic of Mary, and all that she represented. The coffee sent a warm flush through me – even the flesh of my feet buzzed with heat, though in the blast of air-conditioned air from the ceiling vent I didn't start to sweat. At first it was a comfortable, even pleasant sensation. The bitter, murky taste of the coffee washed over my palate, through the roof of my mouth into my sinuses, from there up behind my eyes, through my brain, all the way down my throat, into my lungs: I breathed coffee, my blood singing with warmth.

... I had been talking about something. Jeremy's voice came from directly above and before me, and it had a crackly, tinny quality to it, as if made by an old carbon microphone: 'And what would happen if the Q energy from this manifold were directed through these vectored dimensions into the macrodimensional manifold?'

Happily I babbled, 'Well, provide each point P of an n-dimensional differentiable manifold M with the analogue of a tangent plane, an n-dimensional vector space Tp(M), called the tangent space at P. Now we can define a *path* in manifold M as a differentiable mapping of an open interval of R into M. And along this path we can fit the *whole* of the forces defining K the submanifold of M, a lot of energy to be sure,' oh, yes, a lot of energy, and I was writing it all down, when the somatic effect of the drug caught up with the mental effect, and I recognized what was happening. ('Entirely too many new designer drugs these days ...')

Jeremy's breathing snagged as he looked up to see what had stopped me; meanwhile I struggled with a slight wave of nausea, caused more by the realization that I had been drugged than by the chemicals themselves, which had very little noise. What had I told him? And why, for God's sake, did it matter so much?

'Sorry,' I muttered through the roar of the ventilator. 'Bit of a headache.'

'Sorry to hear that,' Jeremy said, in a voice exactly like George's. 'You look a little pale.'

'Yes,' I said, trying to conceal my anger. (Later, listening to the tape of the conversation, I thought I only sounded confused.) (And I hadn't said much about my work, either – mostly definitions.) 'Sorry to run out on you, but it really is bothering me.'

I stood, and for a moment I panicked; the location of the room's door – the most fundamental point of orientation, remembered without effort in every circumstance – wouldn't come to me. I was damned if I would ask Jeremy Blasingame about such a thing, or stumble about in front of him. I consciously fought to remember: desk faces door, chair faces desk, door therefore behind you . . .

'Let me walk you to your office,' Jeremy said, taking me by the arm. 'Listen, maybe I can give you a lift home?'

'That's all right,' I said, shrugging him off. I found the door by accident, it seemed, and left him. Down to my office, wondering if I would get the right door. My blood was hot Turkish coffee. My head spun. The key worked, so I had found the right door. Locked in I went to my couch and lay down. I was as dizzy there as standing, but found I couldn't move again. I spun in place helplessly. I had read that the drugs used for such purposes had almost no somatic effect, but perhaps this was true only for subjects less sensitive to their kinetic reality – otherwise, why was I reacting so? Fear. Or Jeremy had put something beyond the truth drug in me. A warning? Against? Suddenly I was aware of the tight boundaries of my comprehension, beyond it the wide manifold of action I did not understand – and the latter threatened to completely flood the former, so that there would be left nothing at all that I understood about this matter. Drowned in the unknown, ah, God, such a prospect terrified me!

Sometime later – perhaps as much as an hour – I felt I had to get home. Physically I felt much better, and it was only when I got outside in the wind that I realized that the psychological effects of the drug were still having their way with me. Rare, heavy waft of diesel exhaust, a person wearing clothes rank with old sweat: these smells overwhelmed any chance I had of locating Ramon's cart by nose. My cane felt unusually long, and the rising and falling whistles of my sonar glasses made a musical composition like something out of Messiaen's *Catalogue d'Oiseaux*. I stood entranced by the effect. Cars zoomed past with their electric whirrs, the wind made more sound than I could process. I couldn't find Ramon and decided to give up trying; it would be bad to get him mixed up in any of this anyway. Ramon was my best friend. All those hours at Warren's throwing together, and when we played beeper Ping-Pong at his apartment we sometimes got to laughing so hard we couldn't stand – and what else is friendship than that, after all?

Distracted by thoughts such as these, and by the bizarre music of wind and traffic, I lost track of which street I was crossing. The *whoosh* of a car nearly brushing me as I stepped up from a curb. Lost! 'Excuse me, is this Pennsylvania or K?' Fuckyouverymuch. Threading my way fearfully between broken bottles, punji-stick nails poking up out of boards on the sidewalk, low-hanging wires holding up tree branch or street sign, dogshit on the curb waiting like banana peel to skid me into the street under a bus, speeding cars with completely silent electric motors careening around the corner, muggers who didn't care if I was blind or paraplegic or whatever, open manholes in the crosswalks, rabid dogs with their toothy jaws stuck out between the rails of a fence, ready to bite ... Oh yes, I fought off all these dangers and more, and I must have looked mad tiptoeing down the sidewalk, whapping my cane about like a man beating off devils.

AO. By the time I got into my apartment I was shaking with fury. I turned on Steve Reich's *Come Out* (in which the phrase 'Come out to show them' is looped countless times) as loud as I could stand it, and barged around my place alternately cursing and crying (that stinging of the eyes), all under the sound of the music. I formulated a hundred impossible plans of revenge against Jeremy Blasingame and his shadowy employers, brushed my teeth for fifteen minutes to get the taste of coffee out of my mouth.

By the next morning I had a plan: it was time for some confrontation. It was a Saturday and I was able to work in my office without interruption. I entered the office and unlocked a briefcase, opened my file cabinet and made sounds of moving papers from briefcase to cabinet. Much more silently I got out a big mousetrap that I had bought that morning. On the back of it I wrote, *You're caught. The next trap kills.* I set the trap and placed it carefully behind the new file I had added to the cabinet. This was straight out of one of my adolescent rage fantasies, of course, but I didn't care, it was the best way I could think of to both punish them and warn them from a distance. When the file was pulled from the cabinet, the trap would release onto the hand pulling the file out, and it would also break tape set in a pattern only I would be able to feel. So if the trap went off, I would know.

The first step was ready.

CA. In Penderecki's *Threnody for the Victims of Hiroshima*, a moment of deadly stillness, strings humming dissonant strokes as the whole world waits.

Cut shaving; the smell of blood.

Across the road, a carpenter hammering nails on a roof, each set of seven strokes a crescendo: *tap-tap-tap-tap-tap-tap-TAP! Tap-tap-tap-tap-tap-tap-TAP!*

In that mathematics of emotion, stress calculations to measure one's tension: already there for us to use. Perhaps all of math already charts states of consciousness, moments of being.

CC'. She came to me again late at night, with the wind swirling by her through the doorway. It was late, the wind was chill and blustery, the barometer was falling. Storm coming.

'I wanted to see you,' she said.

I felt a great thrill of fear, and another of pleasure, and I could not tell which was stronger or, after a time, which was which.

'Good.' We entered the kitchen, I served her water, circled her unsteadily, my voice calm as we discussed trivia in fits and starts. After many minutes of this I very firmly took her by the hand. 'Come along.' I led her into the pantry, up the narrow musty stairs, out the roof door into the wind. A spattering of big raindrops hit us. 'Carlos – ' 'Never mind that!' The *whoosh* of the wind was accompanied by the rain smell of wet dust and hot asphalt, and a certain electricity in the air. Off in the distance, to the south, a low rumble of thunder shook the air.

'It's going to rain,' she ventured, shouting a bit over the wind.

'Quiet,' I told her, and kept her hand crushed in mine. The wind gusted through our clothes, and mixed with my anger and my fear I felt rising the electric elation that storms evoke in me. Face to the wind, hair pulled back from my scalp, I held her hand and waited: 'Listen,' I said, 'watch, feel the storm.' And after a time I felt – no, I saw, I *saw* the sudden jerk of lightness that marked lightning. 'Ah,' I said aloud, counting to myself. The thunder pushed us about ten seconds later. Just a couple of miles away.

'Tell me what you see,' I commanded, and heard in my own voice a vibrancy that could not be denied. Punching through the membranes . . .

'It's – it's a thunderstorm,' she replied, uncertain of me in this new mood. 'The clouds are very dark, and fairly low at their bottoms, but broken up in places by some largish gaps. Kind of like immense boulders rolling overhead. The lightning – there! You noticed that?' I had jumped. 'I can see lightning,' I said, grinning. 'I have a basic perception of light and darkness, and everything flashes to lightness for a moment. As if the sun had turned on and then off.'

'Yes. It's sort of like that, only the light is shaped in jagged white lines, extending from cloud to ground. Like that model you have of subatomic particles breaking up – a sort of broken wire sculpture, white as the sun, forking the earth for just an instant, as bright as the thunder is loud.' Her voice rasped with an excitement that had sparked across our hands – also with apprehension, curiosity, I didn't know what. *Light . . . Blam*, the thunder struck us like a fist and she jumped. I laughed. 'That was off to the side!' she said fearfully. 'We're in the middle of it!'

I couldn't control a laugh. 'More!' I shouted. 'Pick up the pace!' And as if I were a weather-monger the lightning snapped away the darkness around us, flash-*blam* . . . flash-*blam* . . . flash-*BLAM*!

'We should get down!' Mary shouted over the wind's ripping, over the reverberating crashes of thunder. I shook my head back and forth and back and forth, gripped her by the arm so hard it must have hurt.

'*No!* This is *my* visual world, do you understand? This is as beautiful as it ever – ' flash-*crack-blam*.

'*Carlos* – '

'No! Shut up!' Flash-flash-flash-*BOOM*! Rolling thunder, now, hollow casks the size of mountains, rolling across a concrete floor.

'I'm afraid,' she said miserably, tugging away from me.

'You feel the exposure, eh?' I shouted at her, as lightning

flashed and the wind tore at us, and rain drops pummeled the roof, throwing up a tarry smell to mix with the lightning's ozone. 'You feel what it's like to stand helpless before a power that can kill you, is that right?'

Between thunderclaps she said, desperately, 'Yes!'

'Now you know how I've felt around you people!' I shouted. *BLAM! BLAM!* 'God damn it,' I said, pain searing my voice as the lightning seared the air, 'I can go sit in the corner park with the drug dealers and the bums and the crazies and I *know* I'll be safe, because even those people still have the idea that it isn't right to hurt a blind man. But you people!' I couldn't go on. I shoved her away from me and staggered back, remembering it all. Flash-*blam*! Flash-*blam*!

'Carlos – ' Hands pulling me around.

'What.'

'I didn't – '

'The hell you didn't! You came in and gave me that story about the moon, and talked backward, and drew stuff, and all to steal my work – how could you do it? How could you do it.'

'I *didn't*, Carlos, I didn't!' I batted her hands away, but it was as if a dam had burst, as if only now, charged to it in the storm, was she able to speak and it all came pouring out of her, '*Listen to me*!' Flash-*blam*. '*I'm just like you*. They made me do it. They took me because I have some math background, I guess, and they ran me through more memory implants than I can even count!' Now the charged buzzing timbre of her desperate voice scraped directly across my nervous system: 'You know what they can do with those drugs and implants. They can program you just like a machine. You walk through your paces and watch yourself and can't do a thing about it.' *Blam*. 'And they programmed me and I went in there and spouted it all off to you on cue. But you *know*' – *blam* – 'was trying, you know there's the parts of the mind they can't touch – I fought them as hard as I could, don't you see?'

Flash-*blam*. Sizzle of scorched air, ozone, ringing eardrums. That one was close.

'I took TNPP-50,' she said, calmer now. 'That and MDMA. I

160

just *made* myself duck into a pharmacy on my way to meet you alone, and I used a blank prescription pad I keep, and got them. I was so drugged up when we went to the Tidal Basin that I could barely walk. But it helped me to speak, helped me to fight the programming.'

'You were drugged?' I said, amazed. (I know – Max Carrados would have figured it out. But me –)

'Yes!' *Boom.* 'Every time I saw you after that time. And it's worked better every time. But I've had to pretend I was still working on you, to protect us both. The last time we were up here' – *boom* – 'you *know* I'm with you, Carlos, do you think I would have faked that?'

Bassoon voice, hoarse with pain. Low rumble of thunder, in the distance. Flickers in the darkness, no longer as distinct as before: my moments of vision were coming to an end. 'But what do they *want*?' I cried.

'Blasingame thinks your work will solve the problems they're having getting sufficient power into a particle-beam weapon. They think they can channel energy out of the microdimensions you've been studying.' *Blam.* 'Or so I guess, from what I've overheard.'

'Those fools.' Although to an extent there might be something to the idea. I had almost guessed it, in fact. So much energy ... 'Blasingame is such a *fool*. He and his stupid Pentagon bosses – '

'*Pentagon!*' Mary exclaimed. 'Carlos, these people are *not* with the Pentagon! I don't know who they are – a group from West Germany, I think. But they kidnapped me right out of my apartment, and I'm a statistician for the Defense Department! The Pentagon has nothing to do with it!'

Blam. 'But Jeremy ...' My stomach was falling.

'I don't know how he got into it. But whoever they are, they're dangerous. I've been afraid they'll kill us both. I know they've discussed killing you, I've heard them. They think you're onto them. Ever since the Tidal Basin I've been injecting myself with Fifty and MDMA, a lot of it, and telling them you don't know a thing, that you just haven't *got* the formula yet. But if they were to find out you know about them ...'

161

'God I hate this spy shit!' I exclaimed bitterly. And the oh-so-clever trap in my office, warning Jeremy off . . .

It started to rain hard. I let Mary lead me down into my apartment. No time to lose, I thought. I had to get to my office and remove the trap. But I didn't want her at risk, I was suddenly frightened more for this newly revealed ally than for myself –

'Listen, Mary,' I said when we were inside. Then I remembered, and whispered in her ear. 'Is this room bugged?'

'No.'

'For God's sake' – all those silences – she must have thought me deranged! 'All right. I want to make some calls, and I'm sure my phones are bugged. I'm going to go out for a bit, but I want you to stay right here. All right?' She started to protest and I stopped her. 'Please! *Stay right here*, I'll be right back. Just stay here and wait for me, *please.*'

'Okay, okay. I'll stay.'

'You promise?'

'I promise.'

OA. Down on the street I turned left and took off for my offices. Rain struck my face and I automatically thought to return for an umbrella, then angrily shook the thought away. Thunder still rumbled overhead from time to time, but the brilliant ('brilliant!' I say – meaning I saw a certain lightness in the midst of a certain darkness) – the brilliant flashes that had given me a momentary taste of vision were gone.

Repeatedly I cursed myself, my stupidity, my presumption. I had made axioms out of theorems (humanity's most common logical-syntactic flaw?), never pausing to consider that my whole edifice of subsequent reasoning rested on them. And now, having presumed to challenge a force I didn't understand, I was in real danger, no doubt about it; and no doubt (as corollary) Mary was as well. The more I thought of it the more frightened I became, until finally I was as scared as I should have been all along.

The rain shifted to an irregular drizzle. The air was cooled, the wind had dropped to an occasional gust. Cars hissed by over wet Twenty-first Street, humming like Mary's voice, and everywhere water sounded, squishing and splashing and dripping. I passed Twenty-first and K, where Ramon usually set up his cart; I was glad that he wouldn't be there, that I wouldn't have to walk by him in silence, perhaps ignoring his cheerful invitation to buy, or even his specific hello. I would have hated to fool him so. Yet if I had wanted to, how easy it would have been! Just walk on by, he would have had no way of knowing.

A sickening sensation of my disability swept over me, all the small frustrations and occasional hard-learned limits of my entire life balling up and washing through me in a great wave of fear and apprehension, like the flash-*boom* of the lightning and thunder, the drenching of the downpour: where was I, where was I going, how could I take even one step more?

It is important to split the great fear into component parts, because if ever they all coalesce – paralysis. I was paralyzed by fear, I felt as though I had never come down from the drugs Jeremy had given me, as though I struggled under their hallucinatory influence still. I literally had to stop walking, had to lean on my cane.

And so I heard their footsteps. Henry Cowell's *The Banshee* begins with fingernails scraping repeatedly up the high wires of an open piano; the same music played my nervous system. Behind me three or four sets of footsteps had come to a halt, just a moment after I myself had stopped.

For a while my heart hammered so hard within me that I could hear nothing else. I forced it to slow, took a deep breath. Of course I was being followed. It made perfect sense. And ahead, at my office ...

I started walking again. The rain picked up on a gust of wind, and silently I cursed it; it is difficult to hear well when rain is pouring down everywhere, so that one stands at the center of a universal *puh-puh-puh-puh*. But attuned now to their presence, I could hear them behind me, three or four (likely three) people walking, walking at just my pace.

Detour time. Instead of continuing down Twenty-first Street I decided to go west on Pennsylvania, and see what they did. No sound of nearby cars as I stood still; I crossed swiftly, nearly losing my cane as it struck the curb. As casually, as 'accidentally' as I could, I turned and faced the street; the sonar glasses whistled up at me, and I knew people were approaching, though I could not hear their footsteps in the rain. More fervently than ever before I blessed the glasses, turned and struck off again, hurrying as much as seemed natural.

Wind and rain, the electric hum and tire hiss of a passing car. Washington late on a stormy spring night, unusually quiet and empty. Behind me the wet footsteps were audible again. I forced myself to keep a steady pace, to avoid giving away the fact that I was aware of their presence. Just a late-night stroll to the office . . .

At Twenty-second I turned south again. Ordinarily no one would have backtracked on Pennsylvania like that, but these people followed me. Now we approached the university hospital, and there was a bit more activity, people passing to left and right, voices across the street discussing a movie, an umbrella being shaken out and folded, cars passing . . . still the footsteps were back there, farther away now, almost out of earshot.

As I approached Gelman Library my pulse picked up again, my mind raced through a network of plans, all unsatisfactory in different ways . . . Outdoors I couldn't evade pursuit. Given. In the building –

My sonar whistled up as Gelman loomed over me, and I hurried down the steps from the sidewalk to the foyer containing the elevator to the sixth and seventh floors. I missed the door and adrenaline flooded me, then there it was just to my left. The footsteps behind me hurried down the sidewalk steps as I slipped inside and stepped left into the single elevator, punched the button for the seventh floor. The doors stood open, waiting . . . then mercifully they slid together, and I was off alone.

A curious feature of Gelman Library is that there are no stairways to the sixth and seventh floors (the offices above the library proper) that are not fire escapes, locked on the outside. To get to the offices you are forced to take the single elevator, a fact I had complained about many times before – I liked to walk. Now I was thankful, as the arrangement would give me some time. When the elevator opened at the seventh floor, I stepped out, reached back in and punched the buttons for all seven floors. Only when the door closed did it occur to me that

I could have tried to find and hit the emergency-stop button, putting the elevator out of action. 'Damn!' I cried. Biting my lip, I ran for my office. I started jangling through my keys for the right one, rattled by a mistake as foolish as that.

I couldn't find the key.

I slowed down. Went through them one by one. I found the key, opened my door, propped it wide with the stopper at its base. Over to the file cabinet, where I opened the middle drawer and very carefully slid one hand down the side of the correct file.

The mousetrap was gone. They knew that I knew.

AO. I don't know how long I stood there thinking; it couldn't have been long, though my thoughts spun madly through scores of plans. Then I went to my desk and got the scissors from the top drawer. I followed the power cord of the desk computer to its wall socket beside the file cabinet. I pulled out the plugs there, opened the scissors wide, fitted one point into a socket, jammed it in and twisted it hard.

Crack. The current held me cramped down for a moment – intense pain pulsed through me – I was knocked away, found myself on my knees, slumping against the file cabinets.

(For a while when I was young I fancied I was allergic to novocaine, and my dentist drilled my teeth without anesthetic. It was horribly uncomfortable, but tangent to normal pain: pain beyond pain. So it was with the shock that coursed through me. Later I asked my brother, who is an electrician, about it, and he said that the nervous system was indeed capable of feeling the sixty cycles per second of the alternating current: 'When you get bit, you always feel it pumping like that, very fast but distinct.' He also said that with my wet shoes I could have been killed. 'The current cramps the muscles down so that you're latched on to the source, and that can kill you. You were lucky. Did you find blisters on the bottoms of your feet?' I had.)

Now I struggled up, with my left arm aching fiercely, and a loud hum in my ears. I went to my couch end table, turned on a desk lamp left there for guests, put my face to it. Light. The lights were still working, it seemed; jamming scissors into the wall socket had done nothing but destroy my hearing. Feeling panicky I ran around the corner and down to Delphina's office, remembering a day long before when the lights on the floor had gone out and I had had an opportunity to superblink around for a while, the blind leading the sightless. Somewhere behind her desk, a panel – flush with the wall, how to get it open – a wire handle, open the panel. Circuit breakers in a long vertical row. I clacked them all from left to right and ran back to my office. Face in the lamp. No sensation of light. Heat receding from the bulb. Lights out on the seventh floor.

I took a big breath. Stopped to listen. My glasses beeped fairly loudly, so I took them off and put them on a bookshelf facing the door. I tested the radio, still unsure if the floor had lost all power or not. No sound from the radio. I went into the hall briefly to look into a ceiling light. Nothing, but would I have been able to see if it were on?

Had to assume all power was gone. Back at my desk I took stapler and water tumbler, put them beside the file cabinet. I went to the bookshelves and gathered all the plastic polyhedral shapes (the sphere was just like a big cue ball), and took them to the file cabinet as well. Then I relocated the scissors on the floor.

Out in the hall the elevator doors opened.

'It's dark – '

'Shh.'

Hesitant steps, into the hall.

I tiptoed to the doorway. Here it was possible to tell for sure that there were only three of them. There would be light from the elevator, I recalled suddenly, and stepped back into my room.

(Once Max Carrados was caught in a situation similar to mine, and he simply announced to his assailants that he had a gun on them, and would shoot the first person to move. In his case it had worked. But now I saw clearly that the plan was insanely risky. More verbal unreality . . .)

'Down here,' one whispered. 'Spread out, and be quiet.'

Rustling, quiet footsteps, three small clicks (gun safeties?).

I retreated into the office, behind the side of the file cabinet. Stilled my breathing, and was silent in a way they'd never be able to achieve. If they heard anything, it would be my glasses . . .

'It's here,' the first voice whispered. 'Door's open, watch it.' Their breathing was quick. They were bunched up outside the door, and one said, 'Hey, I've got a lighter,' so I threw the pulled-open scissors overhand.

'*Ah!* Ah – ' Clatter, hard bump against the hall wall, voices clashing, 'What' – 'threw a knife' – '*ah*' –

I threw the stapler as hard as I could, *wham* – the wall above, I guessed, and threw the dodecahedron as they leaped back. I don't know what I hit. I jumped almost to the doorway, and heard a voice whisper, 'Hey.' I threw the cue-ball sphere right at the voice. *Ponk*. It sounded like – like nothing else I have ever heard. (Although every once in a while some outfielder takes a beepball in the head, and it sounded something like that, wooden and hollow). The victim fell right to the hall floor, making a heavy sound like a car door closing; a metallic clatter marked his gun skidding across the floor. Then CRACK! CRACK! CRACK! another of them shot into the office. I cowered on the floor and crawled swiftly back to the file cabinet, ears ringing painfully, hearing wiped out, fear filling me like the smell of cordite leaking into the room. No way of telling what they were doing. The floor was carpet on concrete, with no vibrations to speak of. I hung my mouth open, trying to focus my hearing on the sound of my glasses. They would whistle up if people entered the room quickly, perhaps (again) more loudly than the people would be on their own. The glasses were still emitting their little beep, now heard through the pulsing wash of noise the gunshots had set off in my ears.

I hefted the water tumbler – it was a fat glass cylinder, with a heavy bottom. A rising whistle – and then, in the hall, the rasp of a lighter flint being sparked –

I threw the tumbler. *Crash*, tinkle of glass falling. A man entered the office. I picked up the pentahedron and threw it. Thump of it against the far wall. I couldn't find any of the other polyhedrons, somehow they weren't there beside the cabinet. I crouched and pulled off a shoe –

He swept my glasses aside and I threw the shoe. I think it hit him, but nothing happened. And there I was, without a weapon, utterly vulnerable, curled over waiting to be killed, revealed in the glow of a damned cigarette lighter ...

When the shots came I thought they had missed, or that I was hit and couldn't feel it. Then I realized some of the shots had come from the doorway, others from the bookcase. Sounds of bodies hit, staggering, exhaling, falling, writhing – and all the while I cowered in my corner, trembling.

Then I heard a nasal groan from the hall, a groan like a viola bowed by a rasp. 'Mary,' I cried, and ran into the hallway to her, tripped on her. She was sitting against the wall – 'Mary!' Blood on her – 'Carlos,' she squeaked painfully, sounding surprised.

A′. Endless moments of fear beyond fear. I had never felt anything like it. Ears ringing, hands exploring her, saying her name over and over, feeling the blood seep out of her shoulder. Feeling her harsh breath. I was bent over my stomach, sick with fear. Under my hands lay the only person I had been bold enough to love in years and years and years, and she was hurt beyond speech, barely conscious, her blood ran over my hands. If she were to die! If I were to lose her, after all that time ...

I know, I know. That I could be so selfish in such a moment as that. The first axiom. But I barely knew her, I only knew us, I only knew what I felt. We only know what we feel.

There are eons in every hadon, when you are afraid enough. I learned that then.

Finally I gathered the courage to leave her long enough to make a call. Phones still working. 911, our number code for a scream of fear, a desperate cry for help.

And then I waited, in darkness so far beyond my daily darkness I was shocked to awareness of it. Suddenly aware that in ordinary life I walked sightless in sunlight.

And then help came.

AA′. Fortunately, it turned out that she had only been wounded. The bullet had entered just beside the shoulder, wrecking it for a long time after. But no fatal damage.

I learned this later, at the hospital. More than an hour after our arrival a doctor came out and told me, and the sickening knot of tension in my diaphragm untied all at once, making me feel sick in another way, dizzy and nauseous with relief. Unbelievably intense relief. Time lurched back to its ordinary rate of speed.

After that I went through a session with the police. Later Mary talked a lot with her employers, and we both answered a lot of questions from the FBI. (In fact, that process took days.) Two of our assailants were dead (one shot, another hit in the temple with a sphere) and the third had been stabbed: what had happened? I stayed up all through that first night explaining, retrieving and playing my tapes, and so on, and still they didn't go for Jeremy until dawn; by that time he was nowhere to be found.

Eventually I got a moment alone with Mary, about ten the following morning.

'You didn't stay at my place,' I said.

'No. I thought you were headed for Blasingame's apartment, and I drove there, but it was empty. So I drove to your office and came upstairs. The elevator opened just as shots were being fired, so I hit the deck and crawled right over a gun. But then I had a hell of a time figuring out who was where. I don't know how you do it.'

'Ah.'

'So I broke my promise.'

'I'm glad.'

'Me too.'

Our hands found each other and embraced, and I leaned forward until my forehead touched her shoulder (the good one), and rested.

CC'. A couple of days later I said to her, 'But what were all those diagrams of Desargues's Theorem about?'

She laughed, and the rich timbre of it cut through me like a miniature of the current from my wall socket. 'Well, they programmed me, with all those geometrical questions for you, and I was roboting through all that, you know, and struggling underneath it all to understand what was going on, what they wanted. And later, how I could alert you. And really, Desargues's Theorem was the only geometry of my own that I could remember from school. I'm a statistician, you know, most of my training is in that and analysis ... So I kept drawing it to try to get your attention to *me*. I had a message in it, you see. You were the triangle in the first plane, and I was the triangle in the second plane, but we were both controlled by the point of projection – '

'But I knew that already!' I exclaimed.

'Did you? But also I marked a little *J* with my thumbnail by the point of projection, so you would know Jeremy was doing it. Did you feel that?'

'No. I xeroxed your drawings, and an impression like that wouldn't show up.' So my indented copy had not included the crucial indentation ...

'I know, but I was hoping you would brush it or something. Stupid. Well, anyway, between us all we were making the three collinear points off to the side, which is what they were after, you see.'

I laughed. 'It never occurred to me,' I said, and laughed again, 'but I sure do like your way of thinking!'

C. I saw, however, that the diagram had a clearer symbolism than that. Points (events) determine what we are. The essential self, the disabilities, the compensations: isosceles characters projecting onto each other, distorting some features, clarifying others ... Ah yes. A fantastically complex topology, reduced to stark Euclidean triangles. Lovely.

CBA. When I told Ramon about it, he laughed too. 'Here you're the mathematician and you never got it! It was too simple for you!'

'I don't know if I'd call it *too simple* – '

'And wait – wait – you say you told this here girlfriend of yours to stay behind at your house, when you knew you were going to run into those thugs at your office?'

'Well, I didn't *know* they'd be there right then. But ...'

'Now *that* was superblink.'

'Yeah.'

I had to admit it; I had been stupid. I had gone too far. And it occurred to me then that in the realm of thought, of analysis and planning – in the realm where I might be most expected to deal competently with the problem – I had consistently and spectacularly failed. Whereas in the physical continuum of action, I had (up to a point) (a point that I didn't like to remember [*ponk* of sphere breaking skull, cowering revealed in a lighter glare]) done pretty well. Though it was disturbing, in the end this reflection pleased me. For a while there, anyway, I had been almost free of the world of texts.

PQR. *Take two parallel lines*, and slide down them to their intersection, to the point at infinity. To a new haptic space:

Naturally it took a while for Mary to regain her health. The kidnapping, the behavior programming, the shooting, and most of all the repeated druggings her captors and she had subjected herself to, had left her quite sick, and she was in the hospital for some weeks. I visited every day; we talked for hours.

And naturally, it took quite a while for us to sort things out. Not only with the authorities, but with each other. What was real and permanent between us, and what was a product of the strange circumstances of our meeting – no one could say for sure which was which, there.

And maybe we never did disentangle those strands. The start of a relationship remains a part of it forever; and in our case, we had seen things in each other that we might never have otherwise, to our own great good. I know that years later, sometimes, when her hand touched mine I would feel that primal thrill of fear and exhilaration that her first touches had caused in me, and I would shiver again under the mysterious impact of the unknown other ... And sometimes, arm in arm, the feeling floods me that we are teamed together in an immense storm of trouble that cracks and thunders all around us, threatening every moment of our lives. So that it seems clear to me, now, that loves forged in the smithy of intense and dangerous circumstances are surely the strongest loves of all.

I leave the proof of this as an exercise for the reader.

171

The Lunatics

They were very near the center of the moon, Jakob told them. He was the newest member of the bullpen, but already their leader.

'How do you know?' Solly challenged him. It was stifling, the hot air thick with the reek of their sweat, and a pungent stink from the waste bucket in the corner. In the pure black, under the blanket of the rock's basalt silence, their shifting and snuffling loomed large, defined the size of the pen. 'I suppose you see it with your third eye.'

Jakob had a laugh as big as his hands. He was a big man, never a doubt of that. 'Of course not, Solly. The third eye is for seeing in the black. It's a natural sense just like the others. It takes all the data from the rest of the senses, and processes them into a visual image transmitted by the third optic nerve, which runs from the forehead to the sight centers at the back of the brain. But you can only focus it by an act of the will – same as with all the other senses. It's not magic. We just never needed it till now.'

'So how do you know?'

'It's a problem in spherical geometry, and I solved it. Oliver and I solved it. This big vein of blue runs right down into the core, I believe, down into the moon's molten heart where we can never go. But we'll follow it as far as we can. Note how light we're getting. There's less gravity near the center of things.'

'I feel heavier than ever.'

'You are heavy, Solly. Heavy with disbelief.'

'Where's Freeman?' Hester said in her crow's rasp.

No one replied.

175

Oliver stirred uneasily over the rough basalt of the pen's floor. First Naomi, then mute Elijah, now Freeman. Somewhere out in the shafts and caverns, tunnels and corridors – somewhere in the dark maze of mines, people were disappearing. Their pen was emptying, it seemed. And the other pens?

'Free at last,' Jakob murmured.

'There's something out there,' Hester said, fear edging her harsh voice, so that it scraped Oliver's nerves like the screech of an ore car's wheels over a too-sharp bend in the tracks. 'Something out there!'

The rumor had spread through the bullpens already, whispered mouth to ear or in huddled groups of bodies. There were thousands of shafts bored through the rock, hundreds of chambers and caverns. Lots of these were closed off, but many more were left open, and there was room to hide – miles and miles of it. First some of their cows had disappeared. Now it was people too. And Oliver had heard a miner jabbering at the low edge of hysteria, about a giant foreman gone mad after an accident took both his arms at the shoulder – the arms had been replaced by prostheses, and the foreman had escaped into the black, where he preyed on miners off by themselves, ripping them up, feeding on them –

They all heard the steely squeak of a car's wheel. Up to the mother shaft, past across tunnel Forty; had to be foremen at this time of shift. Would the car turn at the fork to their concourse? Their hypersensitive ears focused on the distant sound; no one breathed. The wheels squeaked, turned their way. Oliver, who was already shivering, began to shake hard.

The car stopped before their pen. The door opened, all in darkness. Not a sound from the quaking miners.

Fierce white light blasted them and they cried out, leaped back against the cage bars vainly. Blinded, Oliver cringed at the clawing of a foreman's hands, searching under his shirt and pants. Through pupils like pinholes he glimpsed brief black-and-white snapshots of gaunt bodies undergoing similar searches, then blows. Shouts, cries of pain, smack of flesh on flesh, an electric buzzing. Shaving their heads, could it be that time again already? He was struck in the stomach, choked around the neck. Hester's long wiry brown arms, wrapped around her head. Scalp burned, *buzzz*, all chopped up. Thrown to the rock.

'Where's the twelfth?' In the foremen's staccato language.

No one answered.

The foremen left, light receding with them until it was black again, the pure dense black that was their own. Except now it was swimming with bright red bars, washing around in painful tears. Oliver's third eye opened a little, which calmed him, because it was still a new experience; he could make out his companions, dim redblack shapes in the black, huddled over themselves, gasping.

Jakob moved among them, checking for hurts, comforting. He cupped Oliver's forehead and Oliver said, 'It's seeing already.'

'Good work.' On his knees Jakob clumped to their shit bucket, took off the lid, reached in. He pulled something out. Oliver marveled at how clearly he was able to see all this. Before, floating blobs of color had drifted in the black; but he had always assumed they were afterimages, or hallucinations. Only with Jakob's instruction had he been able to perceive the patterns they made, the vision that they constituted. It was an act of will. That was the key.

Now, as Jakob cleaned the object with his urine and spit, Oliver found that the eye in his forehead saw even more, in sharp blood etchings. Jakob held the lump overhead, and it seemed it was a little lamp, pouring light over them in a wavelength they had always been able to see, but had never needed before. By its faint ghostly radiance the whole pen was made clear, a structure etched in blood, redblack on black. 'Promethium,' Jakob breathed. The miners crowded around him, faces lifted to it. Solly had a little pug nose, and squinched his face terribly in the effort to focus. Hester had a face to go with her voice, stark bones under skin scored with lines. 'The most precious element. On Earth our masters rule by it. All their civilization is based on it, on the movement inside it, electrons escaping their shells and crashing into neutrons, giving off heat and more blue as well. So they condemn us to a life of pulling it out of the moon for them.'

He chipped at the chunk with a thumbnail. They all knew

precisely its clayey texture, its heaviness, the dull silvery gray of it, which pulsed green under some lasers, blue under others. Jakob gave each of them a sliver of it. 'Take it between two molars and crush hard. Then swallow.'

'It's poison, isn't it?' said Solly.

'After years and years.' The big laugh, filling the black. 'We don't have years and years, you know that. And in the short run it helps your vision in the black. It strengthens the will.'

Oliver put the soft heavy silver between his teeth, chomped down, felt the metallic jolt, swallowed. It throbbed in him. He could see the others' faces, the mesh of the pen walls, the pens farther down the concourse, the robot tracks – all in the lightless black.

'Promethium is the moon's living substance,' Jakob said quietly. 'We walk in the nerves of the moon, tearing them out under the lash of the foremen. The shafts are a map of where the neurons used to be. As they drag the moon's mind out by its roots, to take it back to Earth and use it for their own enrichment, the lunar consciousness fills us and we become its mind ourselves, to save it from extinction.'

They joined hands: Solly, Hester, Jakob, and Oliver. The surge of energy passed through them, leaving a sweet afterglow.

Then they lay down on their rock bed, and Jakob told them tales of his home, of the Pacific dockyards, of the cliffs and wind and waves, and the way the sun's light lay on it all. Of the jazz in the bars, and how trumpet and clarinet could cross each other. 'How do you remember?' Solly asked plaintively. 'They burned me blank.'

Jakob laughed hard. 'I fell on my mother's knitting needles when I was a boy, and one went right up my nose. Chopped the hippocampus in two. So all my life my brain has been storing what memories it can somewhere else. They burned a dead part of me, and left the living memory intact.'

'Did it hurt?' Hester croaked.

'The needles? You bet. A flash like the foremen's prods, right there in the center of me. I suppose the moon feels the same pain, when we mine her. But I'm grateful now, because it opened my third eye right at that moment. Ever since then I've seen with it. And down here, without our third eye it's nothing but the black.'

Oliver nodded, remembering.

'And something out there,' croaked Hester.

Next shift start Oliver was keyed by a foreman, then made his way through the dark to the end of the long, slender vein of blue he was working. Oliver was a tall youth, and some of the shaft was low; no time had been wasted smoothing out the vein's irregular shape. He had to crawl between the narrow tracks bolted to the rocky uneven floor, scraping through some gaps as if working through a great twisted intestine.

At the shaft head he turned on the robot, a long low-slung metal box on wheels. He activated the laser drill, which faintly lit the exposed surface of the blue, blinding him for some time. When he regained a certain visual equilibrium – mostly by ignoring the weird illumination of the drill beam – he typed instructions into the robot, and went to work drilling into the face, then guiding the robot's scoop and hoist to the broken pieces of blue. When the big chunks were in the ore cars behind the robot, he jackhammered loose any fragments of the ore that adhered to the basalt walls, and added them to the cars before sending them off.

This vein was tapering down, becoming a mere tendril in the lunar body, and there was less and less room to work in. Soon the robot would be too big for the shaft, and they would have to bore through basalt; they would follow the tendril to its very end, hoping for a bole or a fan.

At first Oliver didn't much mind the shift's work. But IR-directed cameras on the robot surveyed him as well as the shaft face, and occasional shocks from its prod reminded him to keep hustling. And in the heat and bad air, as he grew ever more famished, it soon enough became the usual desperate, painful struggle to keep to the required pace.

Time disappeared into that zone of endless agony that was the latter part of a shift. Then he heard the distant klaxon of shift's end, echoing down the shaft like a cry in a dream. He turned the key in the robot and was plunged into noiseless black, the

179

pure absolute of Nonbeing. Too tired to try opening his third
eye, Oliver started back up the shaft by feel, following the last
ore car of the shift. It rolled quickly ahead of him and was gone.

In the new silence distant mechanical noises were like creaks
in the rock. He measured out the shift's work, having marked
its beginning on the shaft floor: eighty-nine lengths of his body.
Average.

It took a long time to get back to the junction with the shaft
above his. Here there was a confluence of veins and the room
opened out, into an odd chamber some seven feet high, but wider
than Oliver could determine in every direction. When he
snapped his fingers there was no rebound at all. The usual light
at the far end of the low chamber was absent. Feeling sandwiched
between two endless rough planes of rock, Oliver experienced
a sudden claustrophobia; there was a whole world overhead, he
was buried alive . . . He crouched and every few steps tapped
one rail with his ankle, navigating blindly, a hand held forward
to discover any dips in the ceiling.

He was somewhere in the middle of this space when he heard
a noise behind him. He froze. Air pushed at his face. It was
completely dark, completely silent. The noise squeaked behind
him again: a sound like a fingernail, brushed along the banded
metal of piano wire. It ran right up his spine, and he felt the hair
on his forearms pull away from the dried sweat and stick straight
out. He was holding his breath. Very slow footsteps were placed
softly behind him, perhaps forty feet away . . . an airy snuffle,
like a big nostril sniffing. For the footsteps to be so spaced out
it would have to be . . .

Oliver loosened his joints, held one arm out and the other
forward, tiptoed away from the rail, at right angles to it, for
twelve feathery steps. In the lunar gravity he felt he might even
float. Then he sank to his knees, breathed through his nose as
slowly as he could stand to. His heart knocked at the back of his
throat, he was sure it was louder than his breath by far. Over
that noise and the roar of blood in his ears he concentrated his
hearing to the utmost pitch. Now he could hear the faint sounds
of ore cars and perhaps miners and foremen, far down the tunnel
that led from the far side of this chamber back to the pens. Even

as faint as they were, they obscured further his chances of hearing whatever it was in the cavern with him.

The footsteps had stopped. Then came another metallic *scrick* over the rail, heard against a light sniff. Oliver cowered, held his arms hard against his sides, knowing he smelled of sweat and fear. Far down the distant shaft a foreman spoke sharply. If he could reach that voice . . . he resisted the urge to run for it, feeling sure somehow that whatever was in there with him was fast.

Another *scrick*. Oliver cringed, trying to reduce his echo profile. There was a chip of rock under his hand. He fingered it, hand shaking. His forehead throbbed and he understood it was his third eye, straining to pierce the black silence and *see* . . .

A shape with pillar-thick legs, all in blocks of redblack. It was some sort of . . .

Scrick. Sniff. It was turning his way. A flick of the wrist, the chip of rock skittered, hitting ceiling and then floor, back in the direction he had come from.

Very slow soft footsteps, as if the legs were somehow . . . they were coming in his direction.

He straightened and reached above him, hands scrabbling over the rough basalt. He felt a deep groove in the rock, and next to it a vertical hole. He jammed a hand in the hole, made a fist; put the fingers of the other hand along the side of the groove, and pulled himself up. The toes of his boot fit the groove, and he flattened up against the ceiling. In the lunar gravity he could stay there forever. Holding his breath.

Step . . . step . . . snuffle, fairly near the floor, which had given him the idea for this move. He couldn't turn to look. He felt something scrape the hip pocket of his pants and thought he was dead, but fear kept him frozen; and the sounds moved off into the distance of the vast chamber, without a pause.

He dropped to the ground and bolted doubled over for the far tunnel, which loomed before him redblack in the black, exuding air and faint noise. He plunged right in it, feeling one wall nick a knuckle. He took the sharp right he knew was there and threw himself down to the intersection of floor and wall. Footsteps padded by him, apparently running on the rails.

When he couldn't hold his breath any longer he breathed.

Three or four minutes passed and he couldn't bear to stay still. He hurried to the intersection, turned left and slunk to the bullpen. At the check point the monitor's horn squawked and a foreman blasted him with a searchlight, pawed him roughly. 'Hey!' The foreman held a big chunk of blue, taken from Oliver's hip pocket. What was this?

'Sorry, boss,' Oliver said jerkily, trying to see it properly, remembering the thing brushing him as it passed under. 'Must've fallen in.' He ignored the foreman's curse and blow, and fell into the pen tearful with the pain of the light, with relief at being back among the others. Every muscle in him was shaking.

But Hester never came back from that shift.

Sometime later the foremen came back into their bullpen, wielding the lights and the prods to line them up against one mesh wall. Through pinprick pupils Oliver saw just the grossest slabs of shapes, all grainy black-and-gray: Jakob was a big stout man, with a short black beard under the shaved head, and eyes that popped out, glittering even in Oliver's silhouette world.

'Miners are disappearing from your pen,' the foreman said, in the miner's language. His voice was like the quartz they tunneled through occasionally: hard, and sparkly with cracks and stresses, as if it might break at any moment into a laugh or a scream.

No one answered.

Finally Jakob said, 'We know.'

The foreman stood before him. 'They started disappearing when you arrived.'

Jakob shrugged. 'Not what I hear.'

The foreman's searchlight was right on Jakob's face, which stood out brilliantly, as if two of the searchlights were pointed at each other. Oliver's third eye suddenly opened and gave the face substance: brown skin, heavy brows, scarred scalp. Not at all the white cut-out blazing from the black shadows. 'You'd better be careful, miner.'

Loudly enough to be heard from neighboring pens, Jakob said, 'Not my fault if something out there is eating us, boss.'

The foreman struck him. Lights bounced and they all dropped to the floor for protection, presenting their backs to the boots.

Rain of blows, pain of blows. Still, several pens had to have heard him.

Foremen gone. White blindness returned to black blindness, to the death velvet of their pure darkness. For a long time they lay in their own private worlds, hugging the warm rock of the floor, feeling the bruises blush. Then Jakob crawled around and squatted by each of them, placing his hands on their foreheads. 'Oh yeah,' he would say. 'You're okay. Wake up now. Look around you.' And in the afterblack they stretched and stretched, quivering like dogs on a scent. The bulks in the black, the shapes they made as they moved and ground . . . eyes, it came to Oliver again, and he rubbed his face and looked around, eyes shut to help him see. 'I ran into it on the way back in,' he said.

They all went still. He told them what had happened.

'The blue in your pocket?'

They considered his story in silence. No one understood it.

No one spoke of Hester. Oliver found he couldn't. She had been his friend. To live without that gaunt crow's voice . . .

Some time later the side door slid up, and they hurried into the barn to eat. The chickens squawked as they took the eggs, the cows mooed as they milked them. The stove plates turned the slightest bit luminous – redblack, again – and by their light his three eyes saw all. Solly cracked and fried eggs. Oliver went to work on his vats of cheese, pulled out a round of it that was ready. Jakob sat at the rear of one cow and laughed as it turned to butt his knee. Splish splish! Splish splish! When he was done he picked up the cow and put it down in front of its hay, where it chomped happily. Animal stink of them all, the many fine smells of food cutting through it. Jakob laughed at his cow, which butted his knee again as if objecting to the ridicule. 'Little pig of a cow, little piglet. Mexican cows. They bred for this size, you know. On Earth the ordinary cow is as tall as Oliver, and about as big as this whole pen.'

They laughed at the idea, not believing him. The buzzer cut them off, and the meal was over. Back into their pen, to lay their bodies down.

Still no talk of Hester, and Oliver found his skin crawling again as he recalled his encounter with whatever it was that sniffed through the mines. Jakob came over and asked him about it, sounding puzzled. Then he handed Oliver a rock. 'Imagine this is a perfect sphere, like a baseball.'

'Baseball?'

'Like a ball bearing, perfectly round and smooth, you know.'

Ah yes. Spherical geometry again. Trigonometry too. Oliver groaned, resisting the work. Then Jakob got him interested despite himself, in the intricacy of it all, the way it all fell together in a complex but comprehensible pattern. Sine and cosine, so clear! And the clearer it got the more he could see: the mesh of the bullpen, the network of shafts and tunnels and caverns piercing the jumbled fabric of the moon's body . . . all clear lines of redblack on black, like the metal of the stove plate as it just came visible, and all from Jakob's clear, patiently fingered, perfectly balanced equations. He could see through rock.

'Good work,' Jakob said when Oliver got tired. They lay there among the others, shifting around to find hollows for their hips.

Silence of the off shift. Muffled clanks downshaft, floor trembling at a detonation miles of rock away; ears popped as air smashed into the dead end of their tunnel, compressed to something nearly liquid for just an instant. Must have been a Boesman. Ringing silence again.

'So what is it, Jakob?' Solly asked when they could hear each other again.

'It's an element,' Jakob said sleepily. 'A strange kind of element, nothing else like it. Promethium. Number 61 on the periodic table. A rare earth, a lanthanide, an inner transition metal. We're finding it in veins of an ore called monazite, and in pure grains and nuggets scattered in the ore.'

Impatient, almost pleading: 'But what makes it so special?'

For a long time Jakob didn't answer. They could hear him thinking. Then he said, 'Atoms have a nucleus, made of protons and neutrons bound together. Around this nucleus, shells of electrons spin, and each shell is either full or trying to get full, to balance with the number of protons – to balance the positive and negative charges. An atom is like a human heart, you see.

'Now promethium is radioactive, which means it's out of balance, and parts of it are breaking free. But promethium never reaches its balance, because it radiates in a manner that increases its instability rather than the reverse. Promethium atoms release energy in the form of positrons, flying free when neutrons are hit by electrons. But during that impact more neutrons appear in the nucleus. Seems they're coming from nowhere. Some people say that they're little white holes, every single atom of them. Burning forever at nine hundred and forty curies per gram. So each atom of the blue is a power loop in itself, giving off energy perpetually. Bringing energy into our universe from somewhere else. Little gateways.'

Solly's sigh filled the black, expressing incomprehension for all of them. 'So it's poisonous?'

'It's dangerous, sure, because the positrons breaking away from it fly right through flesh like ours. Mostly they never touch a thing in us, because that's how close to phantoms we are – mostly blood, which is almost light. That's why we can see each other so well. But sometimes a beta particle will hit something small on its way through. Could mean nothing or it could kill you on the spot. Eventually it'll get us all.'

Oliver fell asleep dreaming of threads of light like concentrations of the foremen's fierce flashes, passing right through him. Shifts passed in their timeless round. They ached when they woke on the warm basalt floor, they ached when they finished the long work shifts. They were hungry and often injured. None of them could say how long they had been there. None of them could say how old they were. Sometimes they lived without light other than the robots' lasers and the stove plates. Sometimes the foremen visited with their scorching lighthouse beams every off shift, shouting questions and beating them. Apparently cows were disappearing, cylinders of air and oxygen, supplies of all sorts. None of it mattered to Oliver but the spherical geometry. He knew where he was, he could see it. The three dimensional map in his head grew more extensive every shift. But everything else was fading away . . .

'So it's the most powerful substance in the world,' Solly said. 'But why us? Why are we here?'

'You don't know?' Jakob said.

'They blanked us, remember? All that's gone.'

185

But because of Jakob, they knew what was up there: the domed palaces on the lunar surface, the fantastic luxuries of Earth ... when he spoke of it, in fact, a lot of Earth came back to them, and they babbled and chattered at the unexpected upwellings. Memories that deep couldn't be blanked without killing, Jakob said. And so they prevailed after all, in a way.

But there was much that had been burnt forever. And so Jakob sighed. 'Yeah, yeah, I remember. I just thought – well. We're here for different reasons. Some were criminals. Some complained.'

'Like Hester!' They laughed.

'Yeah, I suppose that's what got her here. But a lot of us were just in the wrong place at the wrong time. Wrong politics or skin or whatever. Wrong look on your face.'

'That was me, I bet,' Solly said, and the others laughed at him. 'Well, I got a funny face, I know I do! I can feel it.'

Jakob was silent for a long time. 'What about you?' Oliver asked.

More silence. The rumble of a distant detonation, like muted thunder.

'I wish I knew. But I'm like you in that. I don't remember the actual arrest. They must have hit me on the head. Given me a concussion. I must have said something against the mines, I guess. And the wrong people heard me.'

'Bad luck.'

'Yeah. Bad luck.'

More shifts passed. Oliver rigged a timepiece with two rocks, a length of detonation cord and a set of pulleys, and confirmed over time what he had come to suspect; the work shifts were getting longer. It was more and more difficult to get all the way through one, harder to stay awake for the meals and the geometry lessons during the off-shifts. The foremen came every off-shift now, blasting in with their searchlights and shouts and kicks, leaving in a swirl of afterimages and pain. Solly went out one shift cursing them under his breath, and never came back. Disappeared. The foremen beat them for it and Oliver shouted with rage, 'It's not our fault! There's something out there, I saw it! It's killing us!'

Then next shift his little tendril of a vein bloomed, he couldn't find any rock around the blue: a big bole. He would have to tell the foremen, start working in a crew. He dismantled his clock.

On the way back he heard the footsteps again, shuffling along slowly behind him. This time he was at the entrance to the last tunnel, the pens close behind him. He turned to stare into the darkness with his third eye, willing himself to see the thing. Whoosh of air, a sniff, a footfall on the rail . . . far across the thin wedge of air a beam of light flashed, making a long narrow cone of white talc. Steel tracks gleamed where the wheels of the car burnished them. Pupils shrinking like a snail's antennae, he stared back at the footsteps, saw nothing. Then, just barely, two points of red: retinas, reflecting the distant lance of light. They blinked. He bolted and ran again, reached the foremen at the checkpoint in seconds. They blinded him as he panted, passed him through and into the bullpen.

After the meal on that shift Oliver lay trembling on the floor of the bullpen and told Jakob about it. 'I'm scared, Jakob. Solly, Hester, Freeman, mute Lije, Naomi – they're all gone. Everyone I know here is gone but us.'

'Free at last,' Jakob said shortly. 'Here, let's do your problems for tonight.'

'I don't care about them.'

'You have to care about them. Nothing matters unless you do. That blue is the mind of the moon being torn away, and the moon knows it. If we learn what the network says in its shapes, then the moon knows that too, and we're suffered to live.'

'Not if that thing finds us!'

'You don't know. Anyway nothing to be done about it. Come on, let's do the lesson. We need it.'

So they worked on equations in the dark. Both were distracted and the work went slowly; they fell asleep in the middle of it, right there on their faces.

Shifts passed. Oliver pulled a muscle in his back, and excavating the bole he had found was an agony of discomfort. When the bole was cleared it left a space like the interior of an egg, ivory and black and quite smooth, punctuated only by the bluish spots of other tendrils of monazite extending away through the basalt. They left a catwalk across the central space, with decks cut into the rock on each side, and ramps leading to each of the veins of blue; and began drilling on their own again, one man and robot team to each vein. At each shift's end Oliver rushed to get to the egg-chamber at the same time as all the others, so that he could return the rest of the way to the bullpen in a crowd. This worked well until one shift came to an end with the hoist chock full of the ore. It took him some time to dump it into the ore car and shut down.

So he had to cross the catwalk alone, and he would be alone all the way back to the pens. Surely it was past time to move the pens closer to the shaft heads! He didn't want to do this . . .

Halfway across the catwalk he heard a faint noise ahead of him. *Scrick; scriiiiiick.* He jerked to a stop, held the rail hard. Couldn't reach the ceiling here. Back stabbing its protest, he started to climb over the railing. He could hang from the underside.

He was right on the top of the railing when he was seized up by a number of strong cold hands. He opened his mouth to scream and his mouth was filled with wet clay. The blue. His head was held steady and his ears filled with the same stuff, so that the sounds of his own terrified sharp nasal exhalations were suddenly cut off. Promethium; it would kill him. It hurt his back to struggle on. He was being carried horizontally, ankles whipped, arms tied against his body. Then plugs of the clay were shoved up his nose and in the middle of a final paroxysm of resistance his mind fell away into the black.

The lowest whisper in the world said, 'Oliver Pen Twelve.' He heard the voice with his stomach. He was astonished to be alive.

'You will never be given anything again. Do you accept the charge?'

He struggled to nod. I never wanted anything! he tried to say. I only wanted a life like anyone else.

'You will have to fight for every scrap of food, every swallow of water, every breath of air. Do you accept the charge?'

I accept the charge. I welcome it.

'In the eternal night you will steal from the foremen, kill the foremen, oppose their work in every way. Do you accept the charge?'

I welcome it.

'You will live free in the mind of the moon. Will you take up this charge!'

He sat up. His mouth was clear, filled only with the sharp electric aftertaste of the blue. He saw the shapes around him: there were five of them, five people there. And suddenly he understood. Joy ballooned in him and he said, 'I will. Oh, I will!'

A light appeared. Accustomed as he was either to no light or to intense blasts of it, Oliver at first didn't comprehend. He thought his third eye was rapidly gaining power. As perhaps it was. But there was also a laser drill from one of the A robots, shot at low power through a cylindrical ceramic electronic element, in a way that made the cylinder glow yellow. Blind like a fish, open-mouthed, weak eyes gaping and watering floods, he saw around him Solly, Hester, Freeman, mute Elijah, Naomi. 'Yes,' he said, and tried to embrace them all at once. 'Oh, yes.'

They were in one of the long abandoned caverns, a flat-bottomed bole with only three tendrils extending away from it. The chamber was filled with objects Oliver was more used to identifying by feel or sound or smell: pens of cows and hens, a stack of air cylinders and suits, three ore cars, two B robots, an A robot, a pile of tracks and miscellaneous gear. He walked through it all slowly, Hester at his side. She was gaunt as ever, her skin as dark as the shadows; it sucked up the weak light from the ceramic tube and gave it back only in little points and lines. 'Why didn't you tell me?'

'It was the same for all of us. This is the way.'

'And Naomi?'

'The same for her too; but when she agreed to it, she found herself alone.'

Then it was Jakob, he thought suddenly. 'Where's Jakob?'

Rasped: 'He's coming, we think.'

Oliver nodded, thought about it. 'Was it you, then, following me those times? Why didn't you speak?'

'That wasn't us,' Hester said when he explained what had

happened. She cawed a laugh. 'That was something else, still out there . . .'

Then Jakob stood before them, making them both jump. They shouted and the others all came running, pressed into a mass together. Jakob laughed. 'All here now,' he said. 'Turn that light off. We don't need it.'

And they didn't. Laser shut down, ceramic cooled, they could still see: they could see right into each other, red shapes in the black, radiating joy. Everything in the little chamber was quite distinct, quite *visible*.

'We are the mind of the moon.'

Without shifts to mark the passage of time Oliver found he could not judge it at all. They worked hard, and they were constantly on the move: always up, through level after level of the mine. 'Like shells of the atom, and we're that particle, busted loose and on its way out.' They ate when they were famished, slept when they had to. Most of the time they worked, either bringing down shafts behind them, or dismantling depots and stealing everything Jakob designated theirs. A few times they ambushed gangs of foremen, killing them with laser cutters and stripping them of valuables; but on Jakob's orders they avoided contact with foremen when they could. He wanted only material. After a long time – twenty sleeps at least – they had six ore cars of it, all trailing an A robot up long abandoned and empty shafts, where they had to lay the track ahead of them and pull it out behind, as fast as they could move. Among other items Jakob had an insatiable hunger for explosives; he couldn't get enough of them.

It got harder to avoid the foremen, who were now heavily armed, and on their guard. Perhaps even searching for them, it was hard to tell. But they searched with their lighthouse beams on full power, to stay out of ambush: it was easy to see them at a distance, draw them off, lose them in dead ends, detonate mines under them. All the while the little band moved up, rising by infinitely long detours toward the front side of the moon. The rock around them cooled. The air circulated more strongly, until it was a constant wind. Through the seismometers they could hear from far below the rumbling of cars, heavy machinery, detonations. 'Oh they're after us all right,' Jakob said. 'They're running scared.'

He was happy with the booty they had accumulated, which included a great number of cylinders of compressed air and pure oxygen. Also vacuum suits for all of them, and a lot more explosives, including ten Boesmans, which were much too big for any ordinary mining. 'We're getting close,' Jakob said as they ate and drank, then tended the cows and hens. As they lay down to sleep by the cars he would talk to them about their work. Each of them had various jobs: mute Elijah was in charge of their supplies, Solly of the robot, Hester of the seismography. Naomi and Freeman were learning demolition, and were in some undefined sense Jakob's lieutenants. Oliver kept working at his navigation. They had found charts of the tunnel systems in their area, and Oliver was memorizing them, so that he would know at each moment exactly where they were. He found he could do it remarkably well; each time they ventured on he knew where the forks would come, where they would lead. Always upward.

But the pursuit was getting hotter. It seemed there were foremen everywhere, patrolling the shafts in search of them. 'Soon they'll mine some passages and try to drive us into them,' Jakob said. 'It's about time we left.'

'Left?' Oliver repeated.

'Left the system. Struck out on our own.'

'Dig our own tunnel,' Naomi said happily.

'Yes.'

'To where?' Hester croaked.

Then they were rocked by an explosion that almost broke their eardrums, and the air rushed away. The rock around them trembled, creaked, groaned, cracked, and down the tunnel the ceiling collapsed, shoving dust towards them in a roaring *whoosh*!' 'A Boesman!' Solly cried.

Jakob laughed out loud. They were all scrambling into their vacuum suits as fast as they could. 'Time to leave!' he cried, maneuvering their A robot against the side of the chamber. He put one of their Boesmans against the wall and set the timer.

191

'Okay,' he said over the suit's intercom. 'Now we got to mine like we never mined before. To the surface!'

The first task was to get far enough away from the Boesman that they wouldn't be killed when it went off. They were now drilling a narrow tunnel and moving the loosened rock behind them to fill up the hole as they passed through it; this loose fill would fly like bullets down a rifle barrel when the Boesman went off. So they made three abrupt turns at acute angles to stop the fill's movement, and then drilled away from the area as fast as they could. Naomi and Jakob were confident that the explosion of the Boesman would shatter the surrounding rock to such an extent that it would never be possible for anyone to locate the starting point for their tunnel.

'Hopefully they'll think we did ourselves in,' Naomi said, 'either on purpose or by accident.' Oliver enjoyed hearing her light laugh, her clear voice that was so pure and musical compared to Hester's croaking. He had never known Naomi well before, but now he admired her grace and power, her pulsing energy; she worked harder than Jakob, even. Harder than any of them.

A few shifts into their new life Naomi checked the detonator timer she kept on a cord around her neck. 'It should be going off soon. Someone go try and keep the cows and chickens calmed down.' But Solly had just reached the cows' pen when the Boesman went off. They were all sledge-hammered by the blast, which was louder than a mere explosion, something more basic and fundamental: the violent smash of a whole world shutting the door on them. Deafened, bruised, they staggered up and checked each other for serious injuries, then pacified the cows, whose terrified moos they felt in their hands rather than actually heard. The structural integrity of their tunnel seemed okay; they were in an old flow of the mantle's convection current, now cooled to stasis, and it was plastic enough to take such a blast without shattering. Perfect miner's rock, protecting them like a mother. They lifted up the cows and set them upright on the bottom of the ore car that had been made into the barn. Freeman hurried back down the tunnel to see how the rear of it looked.

When he came back their hearing was returning, and through the ringing that would persist for several shifts he shouted, 'It's walled off good! Fused!'

So they were in a little tunnel of their own. They fell together in a clump, hugging each other and shouting. 'Free at last!' Jakob roared, booming out a laugh louder than anything Oliver had ever heard from him. Then they settled down to the task of turning on an air cylinder and recycler, and regulating their gas exchange.

They soon settled into a routine that moved their tunnel forward as quickly and quietly as possible. One of them operated the robot, digging as narrow a shaft as they could possibly work in. This person used only laser drills unless confronted with extremely hard rock, when it was judged worth the risk to set off small explosions, timed by seismometer to follow closely other detonations back in the mines; Jakob and Naomi hoped that the complex interior of the moon would prevent any listeners from noticing that their explosion was anything more than an echo of the mining blast.

Three of them dealt with the rock freed by the robot's drilling, moving it from the front of the tunnel to its rear, and at intervals pulling up the cars' tracks and bringing them forward. The placement of the loose rock was a serious matter, because if it displaced much more volume than it had at the front of the tunnel, they would eventually fill in all the open space they had; this was the classic problem of the 'creeping worm' tunnel. It was necessary to pack the blocks into the space at the rear with an absolute minimum of gaps, in exactly the way they had been cut, like pieces of a puzzle; they all got very good at the craft of this, losing only a few inches of open space in every mile they dug. This work was the hardest both physically and mentally, and each shift of it left Oliver more tired than he had ever been while mining. Because the truth was all of them were working at full speed, and for the middle team it meant almost running, back and forth, back and forth, back and forth ... Their little bit of open tunnel was only some sixty yards long, but after a while on the midshift it seemed like five hundred.

The three people not working on the rock tended the air and the livestock, ate, helped out with large blocks and the like, and snatched some sleep. They rotated one at a time through the three stations, and worked one shift (timed by detonator timer) at each post. It made for a routine so mesmerizing in its exhaustiveness that Oliver found it very hard to do his calculations of their position in his shift off. 'You've got to keep at it,' Jakob told him as he ran back from the robot to help with the calculating. 'It's not just anywhere we want to come up, but right under the domed city of Selene, next to the rocket rails. To do that we'll need some good navigation. We get that and we'll come up right in the middle of the masters who have gotten rich from selling the blue to Earth, and that will be a very gratifying thing I assure you.'

So Oliver would work on it until he slept. Actually it was relatively easy; he knew where they had been in the moon when they struck out on their own, and Jakob had given him the surface co-ordinates for Selene: so it was just a matter of dead reckoning.

It was even possible to calculate their average speed, and therefore when they could expect to reach the surface. That could be checked against the rate of depletion of their fixed resources – air, water lost in the recycler, and food for the livestock. It took a few shifts of consultation with mute Elijah to determine all the factors reliably, and after that it was a simple matter of arithmetic.

When Oliver and Elijah completed these calculations they called Jakob over and explained what they had done.

'Good work,' Jakob said. 'I should have thought of that.'

'But look,' Oliver said, 'we've got enough air and water, and the robot's power pack is ten times what we'll need – same with explosives – it's only food is a problem. I don't know if we've got enough hay for the cows.'

Jakob nodded as he looked over Oliver's shoulder and examined their figures. 'We'll have to kill and eat the cows one by one. That'll feed us and cut down on the amount of hay we need, at the same time.'

'Eat the cows?' Oliver was stunned.

'Sure! They're meat! People on Earth eat them all the time!'

'Well . . .' Oliver was doubtful, but under the lash of Hester's bitter laughter he didn't say any more.

Still, Jakob and Freeman and Naomi decided it would be best if they stepped up the pace a little bit, to provide them with more of a margin for error. They shifted two people to the shaft face and supplemented the robot's continuous drilling with hand drill work around the sides of the tunnel, and ate on the run while moving blocks to the back, and slept as little as they could. They were making miles on every shift.

The rock they wormed through began to change in character. The hard, dark, unbroken basalt gave way to lighter rock that was sometimes dangerously fractured. 'Anorthosite,' Jakob said. 'We're reaching the crust.' After that every shift brought them through a new zone of rock. Once they tunneled through great layers of calcium feldspar striped with basalt intrusions, so that it looked like badly made brick. Another time they blasted their way through a wall of jasper as hard as steel. Only once did they pass through a vein of the blue; when they did it occurred to Oliver that his whole conception of the moon's composition had been warped by their mining. He had thought the moon was bursting with promethium, but as they dug across the narrow vein he realized it was uncommon, a loose net of threads in the great lunar body.

As they left the vein behind Solly picked up a piece of the ore and stared at it curiously, lower eyes shut, face contorted as he struggled to focus his third eye. Suddenly he dashed the chunk to the ground, turned and marched to the head of their tunnel, attacked it with a drill. 'I've given my whole life to the blue,' he said, voice thick. 'And what is it but a God-damned rock.'

Jakob laughed shortly. They tunneled on, away from the precious metal that now represented to them only a softer material to dig through. 'Pick up the pace!' Jakob cried, slapping Solly on the back and leaping over the blocks beside the robot. 'This rock has melted and melted again, changing over eons to the stones we see. Metamorphosis,' he chanted, stretching the word out, lingering on the syllable *mor* until the word became a kind of song. 'Meta*mor*phosis. Meta-*mor*-pho-sis.' Naomi and Hester took up the chant, and mute Elijah tapped his drill against the robot in double time. Jakob chanted over it. 'Soon we will come to the city of the masters, the domes of Xanadu with their glass and fruit and steaming pools, and their vases and sports and their fine aged wines. And then there will be a – '

'Meta*mor*phosis.'

And they tunneled ever faster.

Sitting in the sleeping car, chewing on some cheese, Oliver regarded the bulk of Jakob lying beside him. Jakob breathed deeply, very tired, almost asleep. 'How do you know about the domes?' Oliver asked him softly. 'How do you know all the things that you know?'

'Don't know,' Jakob muttered. 'Everyone knows. Less they burn your brain. Put you in a hole to live out your life. I don't know much, boy. Make most of it up. Love of a moon. Whatever we need . . .' and he slept.

They came up through a layer of marble – white marble all laced with quartz, so that it gleamed and sparkled in their lightless sight, and made them feel as though they dug through stone made of their cows' good milk, mixed with water like diamonds. This went on for a long time, until it filled them up and they became intoxicated with its smooth muscly texture, with the sparks of light lazing out of it. 'I remember once we went to see a jazz band,' Jakob said to all of them. Puffing as he ran the white rock along the cars to the rear, stacked it ever so carefully. 'It was in Richmond among all the docks and refineries and giant oil tanks and we were so drunk we kept getting lost. But finally we found it – huh! – and it was just this broken down trumpeter and a back line. He played sitting in a chair and you could just see in his face that his life had been a tough scuffle. His hat covered his whole household. And trumpet is a young man's instrument, too, it tears your lip to tatters. So we sat down to drink not expecting a thing, and they started up the last song of a set. "Bucket's Got a Hole In It." Four bar blues, as simple as a song can get.'

'Meta*mor*phosis,' rasped Hester.

'Yeah! Like that. And this trumpeter started to play it. And they went through it over and over and over. Huh! They must have done it a hundred times. Two hundred times. And sure enough this trumpeter was playing low and half the time in his hat, using all the tricks a broken-down trumpeter uses to save his lip, to hide the fact that it went west thirty years before. But after a while that didn't matter, because he was playing. He was playing! Everything he had learned in all his life, all the music and all the sorry rest of it, all that was jammed into the poor old "Bucket" and by God it was mind over matter time, because that old song began to *roll*.' And still on the run he broke into it:

'Oh the buck-et's got a hole in it – Yeah the buck-et's got a hole in it

Say the buck-et's got a hole in it – Can't buy no beer!'

And over again. Oliver, Solly, Freeman, Hester, Naomi – they couldn't help laughing. What Jakob came up with out of his unburnt past! Mute Elijah banged a car wall happily, then squeezed the udder of a cow between one verse and the next – 'Can't buy, no beer – *Moo!*'

They all joined in, breathing or singing it. It fit the pace of their work perfectly; fast but not too fast, regular, repetitive, simple, endless. All the syllables got the same length, a bit syncopated, except 'hole,' which was stretched out, and 'can't buy no beer,' which was high and all stretched out, stretched into a great shout of triumph, which was crazy since what it was saying was bad news, or should have been. But the song made it a cry of joy, and every time it rolled around they sang it louder, more stretched out. Jakob scatted up and down and around the tune, and Hester found all kinds of higher harmonics in a voice like a saw cutting steel, and the old tune rocked over and over and over and over and over and over and over and over and over and over, in a great passacaglia, in the crucible where all poverty is wrenched to delight: the blues. Met*amor*phosis. They sang it

197

continuously for two shifts running, until they were all completely hypnotized by it; and then frequently, for long spells, for the rest of their time together.

It was sheer bad luck that they broke into a shaft from below, and that the shaft was filled with armed foremen; and worse luck that Jakob was working the robot, so that he was the first to leap out firing his hand drill like a weapon, and the only one to get struck by return fire before Naomi threw a knotchopper past him and blew the foremen to shreds. They got him on a car and rolled the robot back and pulled up the track and cut off in a new direction, leaving another Boesman behind to destroy evidence of their passing.

So they were all racing around with the blood and stuff still covering them and the cows mooing in distress and Jakob breathing through clenched teeth in double time, and only Hester and Oliver could sit in the car with him and try to tend him, ripping away the pants from a leg that was all cut up. Hester took a hand drill to cauterize the wounds that were bleeding hard, but Jakob shook his head at her, neck muscles bulging out. 'Got the big artery inside of the thigh,' he said through his teeth.

Hester hissed. 'Come here,' she croaked at Solly and the rest. 'Stop that and come here!'

They were in a mass of broken quartz, the fractured clear crystals all pink with oxidation. The robot continued drilling away, the air cylinder hissed, the cows mooed. Jakob's breathing was harsh and somehow all of them were also breathing in the same way, irregularly, too fast; so that as his breathing slowed and calmed, theirs did too. He was lying back in the sleeping car, on a bed of hay, staring up at the fractured sparkly quartz ceiling of their tunnel, as if he could see far into it. 'All these different kinds of rock,' he said, his voice filled with wonder and pain. 'You see, the moon itself was the world, once upon a time, and the earth its moon; but there was an impact, and everything changed.'

They cut a small side passage in the quartz and left Jakob there, so that when they filled in their tunnel as they moved on he was left behind, in his own deep crypt. And from then on the moon for them was only his big tomb, rolling through space till the sun itself died, as he had said it someday would.

Oliver got them back on a course, feeling radically uncertain of his navigational calculations now that Jakob was not there to nod over his shoulder, to approve them. Dully he gave Naomi and Freeman the co-ordinates for Selene. 'But what will we do when we get there?' Jakob had never actually made that clear. Find the leaders of the city, demand justice for the miners? Kill them. Get to the rockets of the great magnetic rail accelerators, and hijack one to Earth? Try to slip unnoticed into the populace?

'You leave that to us,' Naomi said. 'Just get us there.' And he saw a light in Naomi and Freeman's eyes that hadn't been there before. It reminded him of the thing that had chased him in the dark, the thing that even Jakob hadn't been able to explain; it frightened him.

So he set the course and they tunneled on as fast as they ever had. They never sang and they rarely talked; they threw themselves at the rock, hurt themselves in the effort, returned to attack it more fiercely than before. When he could not stave off sleep Oliver lay down on Jakob's dried blood, and bitterness filled him like a block of the anorthosite they wrestled with.

They were running out of hay. They killed a cow, ate its roasted flesh. The water recycler's filters were clogging, and their water smelled of urine. Hester listened to the seismometer as often as she could now, and she thought they were being pursued. But she also thought they were approaching Selene's underside.

Naomi laughed, but it wasn't like her old laugh. 'You got us there, Oliver. Good work.'

Oliver bit back a cry.

'Is it big?' Solly asked.

Hester shook her head. 'Doesn't sound like it. Maybe twice the diameter of the Great Bole, not more.'

'Good,' Freeman said, looking at Naomi.

'But what will we do?' Oliver said.

Hester and Naomi and Freeman and Solly all turned to look at him, eyes blazing like twelve chunks of pure promethium. 'We've got eight Boesmans left,' Freeman said in a low voice.

199

'All the rest of the explosives add up to a couple more. I'm going to set them just right. It'll be my best work ever, my masterpiece. And we'll blow Selene right off into space.'

It took them ten shifts to get all the Boesmans placed to Freeman and Naomi's satisfaction, and then another three to get far enough down and to one side to be protected from the shock of the blast, which luckily for them was directly upward against something that would give, and therefore would have less recoil.

Finally they were set, and they sat in the sleeping car in a circle of six, around the pile of components that sat under the master detonator. For a long time they just sat there crosslegged, breathing slowly and staring at it. Staring at each other, in the dark, in perfect redblack clarity. Then Naomi put both arms out, placed her hands carefully on the detonator's button. Mute Elijah put his hands on hers – then Freeman, Hester, Solly, finally Oliver – just in the order that Jakob had taken them. Oliver hesitated, feeling the flesh and bone under his hands, the warmth of his companions. He felt they should say something but he didn't know what it was.

'Seven,' Hester croaked suddenly.

'Six,' Freeman said.

Elijah blew air through his teeth, hard.

'Four,' said Naomi.

'Three!' Solly cried.

'Two,' Oliver said.

And they all waited a beat, swallowing hard, waiting for the moon and the man in the moon to speak to them. Then they pressed down on the button. They smashed at it with their fists, hit it so violently they scarcely felt the shock of the explosion.

They had put on vacuum suits and were breathing pure oxygen as they came up the last tunnel, clearing it of rubble. A great number of other shafts were revealed as they moved into the huge conical cavity left by the Boesmans; tunnels snaked away from the cavity in all directions, so that they had sudden long vistas of blasted tubes extending off into the depths of the moon they had come out of. And at the top of the cavity, struggling over its broken edge, over the rounded wall of a new crater . . .

It was black. It was not like rock. Spread across it was a spill of white points, some bright, some so faint that they disappeared into the black if you looked straight at them. There were thousands of these white points, scattered over a black dome that was not a dome . . .

And there in the middle, almost directly overhead: a blue and white ball. Big, bright, blue, distant, rounded; half of it bright as a foreman's flash, the other half just a shadow . . . it was clearly round, a big ball in the . . . sky. In the sky.

Wordlessly they stood on the great pile of rubble ringing the edge of their hole. Half buried in the broken anorthosite were shards of clear plastic, steel struts, patches of green glass, fragments of metal, an arm, broken branches, a bit of orange ceramic. Heads back to stare at the ball in the sky, at the astonishing fact of the void, they scarcely noticed these things.

A long time passed, and none of them moved except to look round. Past the jumble of dark trash that had mostly been thrown off in a single direction, the surface of the moon was an immense expanse of white hills, as strange and glorious as the stars above. The size of it all! Oliver had never dreamed that everything could be so big.

'The blue must be promethium,' Solly said, pointing up at the Earth. 'They've covered the whole Earth with the blue we mined.'

Their mouths hung open as they stared at it. 'How far away is it?' Freeman asked. No one answered.

'There they all are,' Solly said. He laughed harshly. 'I wish I could blow up the Earth too!'

He walked in circles on the rubble of the crater's rim. The rocket rails, Oliver thought suddenly, must have been in the direction Freeman had sent the debris. Bad luck. The final upward sweep of them poked up out of the dark dirt and glass. Solly pointed at them. His voice was loud in Oliver's ears, it strained the intercom: 'Too bad we can't fly to the Earth, and blow it up too! I wish we could!'

And mute Elijah took a few steps, leaped off the mount into the sky, took a swipe with one hand at the blue ball. They laughed at him. 'Almost got it, didn't you!' Freeman and Solly tried themselves, and then they all did: taking quick runs, leaping, flying slowly up through space, for five or six or seven seconds, making a grab at the sky overhead, floating back down as if in a dream, to land in a tumble, and try it again . . . It felt wonderful to hang up there at the top of the leap, free in the vacuum, free of gravity and everything else, for just that instant.

After a while they sat down on the new crater's rim, covered with white dust and black dirt. Oliver sat on the very edge of the crater, legs over the edge, so that he could see back down into their sublunar world, at the same time that he looked up into the sky. Three eyes were not enough to judge such immensities. His heart pounded, he felt too intoxicated to move anymore. Tired, drunk. The intercom rasped with the sounds of their breathing, which slowly calmed, fell into a rhythm together. Hester buzzed one phrase of 'Bucket' and they laughed softly. They lay back on the rubble, all but Oliver, and stared up into the dizzy reaches of the universe, the velvet black of infinity. Oliver sat with elbows on knees, watched the white hills glowing under the black sky. They were lit by earthlight – earthlight and starlight. The white mountains on the horizon were as sharp-edged as the shards of dome glass sticking out of the rock. And all the time the Earth looked down at him. It was all too fantastic to believe. He drank it in like oxygen, felt it filling him up, expanding in his chest.

'What do you think they'll do with us when they get here?' Solly asked.

'Kill us,' Hester croaked.

'Or put us back to work,' Naomi added.

Oliver laughed. Whatever happened, it was impossible in that moment to care. For above them a milky spill of stars lay thrown across the infinite black sky, lighting a million better worlds; while just over their heads the Earth glowed like a fine blue lamp; and under their feet rolled the hills of the happy moon, holed like a great cheese.

A Transect

for Thabo Daniel K. Moeti

After he had secured a window seat in the Amtrak coach, he set his dark brown leather briefcase in his lap and unlocked it. *Clunk. Clunk.* He liked the way the gold-plated hasps snapped open. About fifty times more power in the springs than was necessary. Sign of a well-tooled briefcase: big, heavy, powerful. Expensive. Something for clients to note with approval. Part of their confidence in him.

Riffling through his account files was depressing. Nothing in there but bad news. No one was buying fine paper in quantity these days; he had to bust a gut just to stay even. North-east Section Marketing and Sales Vice President, forever and ever amen. He sighed; at times like this he felt utterly stuck. No chance of advancement whatsoever. Stuck at forty-five thousand a year for good, and with wife and kids throwing it away faster than he could make it. Lucky his credit was good, he could spend his future right up to his death and beyond, no doubt. Ah, the end of a long, hard trip: he needed a drink.

The train came out of its hole and he looked into the industrial yards of Montreal. Beyond them was the city center where he had spent the day selling. Sun setting behind it. Funny how much Canada looked like the States (he always thought that). He let his files accordion back into the briefcase and pulled out his copy of the day's *Wall Street Journal*. Up and down the train car, other copies of the same paper were blooming over the plush maroon seats, covering the businessmen behind them. A young punk wearing earphones sat in the aisle seat beside him, cramping his reading. Faint whispers of percussive music joined the rustling of newspapers in the strangely hushed car.

Nothing in the day's *Journal* was of interest. He folded it and put it in his lap. They were out of the industrial district, in the trees between suburbs. Too late in the fall: the half-bare trees looked bedraggled, the leaf-matted ground wet and boggy. He folded his suit jacket over twice and used it as a pillow against the inner window. It would have to be dry-cleaned anyway; he had spilled a few drops of Burgundy on it at lunch, right on the top of the right cuff, where clients would see it when he signed things.

'*Hei broer!* Watch out where you going when you walking backwards like that! Here, you need a hand with those?'

'Thanks, I got them.' He heaved up on the straps tied around his two boxes and pulled them past the old man down the center of the train. The benches on both sides were crowded with migrant workers going home, jammed together hip to hip. Their boxes and bags were stacked on the wooden floor, leaving him just enough room to maneuver to the end of the car. There, because it was the last car on the train, he could set his two boxes in the middle of the aisle and sit on them, as several other men had already done. He greeted them with a lift of his chin.

'Where you from, *broer*?'

'Mzimhlope Hostels. I did my eleven months there – now I going home. Home to Kwa-Xhosa.'

'Home,' said a thin colored man bitterly. 'Just how is Kwa-Xhosa Bantustan your home?'

'My folks is there,' he said with a shrug.

'Your folks is there because the government moved them there,' the man said. 'Me, my home is Robben Island. It been my home nine years, and all because of one night's ANC meeting at my house. They gave me two and a half years for taking subscriptions, one and a half years for meeting, and five years for distributing pamphlets. All the same night!' He laughed harshly. 'Now I'm out, and they ban me! Clearly I must be meeting a whole bunch of Communists in those nine years, for they ban me the moment I out! Ban me to Kwa-Xhosa, where I never been in my whole life, where I can never see my family, for five long years.'

The others laughed their sympathy. 'That too bad, Pieter!'

'You got to watch all those bad phone calls you make from the island, man!'

The conversation focused on the newcomer. 'What your name?'

'Norman.'

'What did you do in Soweto?'

'Bricklayer,' Norman said.

The train jerked twice and they rolled out of Park Station.

'That against the law, you know,' Pieter said. 'If they pay attention to their own law, you could not have that job. *Nie kaffir* bricklayers, *nie!*' – this with the heavy Afrikaaner tone. The men laughed. Several in the car turned on transistor radios, and the hard rhythms clashed. The train cleared the outskirts of Johannesburg and clattered through the outlying townships.

Norman looked out the window and saw three women sitting on a step, leaning in on each other in a stupor. Empty bottles. Blank faces under the streetlight. He recognized in the slump of their shoulders that moment of exhaustion and peace, and felt his own shoulders relax with it. He was on his way home.

The train swayed as it took a sharp turn. One last view of Montreal. He put his suit jacket on the chair arm and pulled a Sherman cigarette from the box in his briefcase. The punk next to him appeared to be asleep, although faint music still whispered from his earphones. He lit the Sherman with the gold lighter his boss had given him, and felt a certain uneasiness leave him, breath by breath. Hard to sleep on a train. Another station stop. The people in his car were mostly commuters. Briefcases, cuff links, polished shoes. The *swish-swish* of nyloned legs rubbing together; his head shifted so he could see the tight dress between the two seat backs in front of him. She sat two seats ahead. A man with a cough sat behind him. Muted voices came from the car behind theirs, until a door hissed shut.

When the Sherman was finished, he took a last look at the night lights of Montreal. The company's awards dinner had been in Montreal, just a month earlier, in the fashionable district downtown. He had expected to win the regional sales award for the year, because things were tough everywhere and he did have some big regular clientele. He took his wife along. All that backslapping and joking about the awards at the cocktail party before, as if no one cared about them, as if they were bowling trophies or something – when everyone knew they were a strong indicator of what the upper echelon thought of your prospects. So that in that sense they represented thousands of dollars – careers, even. So that looking around the room there was a part of him that hated all his colleagues, his competitors. Even more so afterwards, when he had to do like all the rest and go up to congratulate the winner, George Dulak, head of the Midwestern Section (which in itself was an advantage): beaming winner surrounded by envious admirers, shiny gold pen set cradled in one hand . . . Finally he had gone away to get a drink. It was just like management to make the work a contest like this, to get them all at each other's throats. Competition more productive than teamwork: the American way!

'On Robben Island,' Pieter said, 'the *agter-nyer* is the one the warden uses to control the rest – he the guard inside, and gets the little extras you know, tobacco and such. But our *agter-nyer* was not a bad man, he help to get us food sometimes. And one night we was entertaining one another, Solly, he acting out the various guards and the wardens – all without one word, you see, but just watching him we knew exactly who he mean. And we giggling and brushing – we never clapped, you see, for fear of the guards' attentions, so to applaud we rubbed our hands together like so.' They heard nothing of Pieter's prison applause over the talk and the radios. 'And we in such a state we never in the world hear the guard coming, but for the *agter-nyer* sitting on the cement at the door watching for them. He been standing watch for us all those nights, and never let us know till he had to.' He laughed. 'A good man!'

'I been living in a prison, too, these last eleven months,' Norman said suddenly, surprising them all, including himself. 'A prison called the Mzimhlophe Hostels.'

Most of them had been living around Soweto in the men's dormitories that house the migrant laborers from the bantustans, and some said, 'We hear that, *broer*!' But Pieter quickly disagreed – 'nothing's prison but prison, man' – and continued telling stories of Robben Island. Norman was not listening to Pieter anymore, however; he was back in the hostels, looking over row after row of low gray brick dorms, their chimneys jutting out of asbestos roofs into the sky. One morning after a Friday night's drinking, he had gotten up and stumbled out of the dorm to the toilets in the next building – in the door, past the cement troughs for washing dishes and clothes, to the open toilet basins, there to retch miserably. As he returned to his dorm, he felt so sick he was sure he would die before his eleven months' stint of work in Soweto was up. That certainty gave him new eyes as he entered the dorm and crossed the dusty concrete floor, past the low concrete slabs on metal struts that were their tables, past the benches also made of concrete slabs to the sleeping cubicles, where men slept on the door-like lids of the brick trunks that held all their possessions. In the gloom it seemed they slept on coffins. Beyond in the kitchen cubicle, men were still playing guitars connected to little amplifiers, and the low electric twangs were the only signs that the men sitting around the small stove were still awake, still alive – a single candle on the slab beside them, shadows everywhere in the dim air, drying shirts hung overhead – and bitterly he thought, what a place to die in.

Perhaps he would get a drink. The restaurant car was only two ahead, and he was thirsty and needed to wash down some aspirin. He needed a drink. He stood and managed to step over the sleeping punk; debated taking the briefcase with him, but after all it was locked and no one was going anywhere anyway. Hopefully by his presence the punk would guard it.

Down the car. His balance was shaky; something wrong with him this night. He should have gotten a sleeper. Too much pride in his endurance as a traveler. Out of the sound-proofed compartment and into the cold, jouncing passageway between cars. Here you could believe the train was really moving. Back into the hush of the next car. Only half the overhead lights were still on here, and most of the occupants were asleep. Some read or listened to earphones. Half their heads were shaved or tinted green or purple, it seemed. Craziness. His daughter, only fourteen years old, had brought one of those home once. He hadn't known how to express his disgust; he left it to Vicki, tried to forget about it.

There was a line at the little bar in the restaurant car. The two black bartenders went about their work casually, chatting to each other about vacationing in Jamaica, just as if there weren't a line. When one of them asked him what he wanted, he curtly ordered a gin and tonic and a foil bag of nuts, but his disapproval didn't seem to register. He sipped the gin and tonic – a weak one – to give himself some room for jiggling while he walked, then saw that the woman in the tight dress was sitting at one of the little tables. He sat at another and watched her as he drank. Not actually very good-looking. When he finished the drink, it felt like a million miles separated him from everyone else there. He stood and returned to his seat. Should have gotten a sleeper. Something wrong with him, some kind of tension somehow ... had to avoid that kind of thing, or it was back to the Tagamet for him.

Back in his seat he stared through his reflection in the window at the world outside. Clanking red lights at railroad crossings, time after time. A sleeping town, even the neon off. Loading docks, laundromat, Village Video Rental. You saw a lot of those video places these days, even in the little backwoods towns. 'Movies in the privacy of your own home!' and then it was gone. The drink began to go to his head, and the repeated hoot of the train's horn – so distant, so muted – was like the cry of some mournful beast, lulling him toward sleep and then calling him back, time after time.

The beauty of the Witwatersrand took his breath away. He had forgotten that such open, clean land existed in South Africa, and at the sight of it something in his chest hurt. White clouds sprawled across a cobalt sky, and there in the yellowwoods and Camdeboo stinkwoods dotting the sere grass of the veldt flew loeris, doves, hoepoe, and drongos, with small white hawks circling far above. Wild gardenia growing by the tracks. It affected all the men similarly, and they threw open the windows and laughed and shouted at the sky, aware suddenly that they really were going home. They danced in the aisle to the fast mbaqanga beat and sang American spirituals. 'Swing Low, Sweet Chariot,' accompanied by a fifteen-year-old boy playing harmonica for all he was worth – it was grand.

210

Then the train pulled into Vereeninging Station. Still in a celebratory mood, the men stuck their heads out the train window and shouted for the platform hawkers. 'Dresses and aprons for your loved ones at only five rand, *broers*!' 'Not a chance, *suster*, you bore me with your dresses, let that *bierman* through to us.' They bought dumpies of beer at an extortionate price, and downed most of them before the train rattled off again. Then through the outskirts of town: corrugated iron, donkeys, pigs, children, Indian corner groceries, paw-paw trees, women with washtubs, prickly pears, and scraps of paper everywhere, all over the hard-packed earth of the streets. 'Oh, how I hate this town, the most hateful town in the world to me,' one man cried. 'My wife got off the train at this station and I never saw her again up to this very day.' The men whooped their sympathy. 'Wasn't that Georgina the hippo left you, man?' 'She found you were undermining her interest with that girl in Joburg, didn't she? You lucky you didn't see snake's butt that day instead!' And the man laughed 'hee, hee, hee,' as he shook his head to deny them.

The man in the seat behind him could not stop coughing. A couple minutes' labored breathing, the strained efforts to control it – then *kar! karugh! urrkhkraugh!* He couldn't believe it. Next time, he thought, I'll drive. To hell with this. His throat was beginning to tickle a little, right there below his Adam's apple, and briefly he glanced over his shoulder in irritation. Old pasty-faced man with dark rings under his eyes, in a shabby gray suit. Italian-looking. Incredibly inconsiderate of him to travel sick and infect everyone else on the train. He really was coming down with it! He swallowed over and over. There was only a single light on in the car – some insomniac businessman reading *In Search of Excellence*, still looking fresh and unruffled at 2 A.M. Yeah, you'll win the award, he thought angrily, and me, I'll just catch a cold. And all because of the luck of seating availability. He hated being sick. You couldn't possibly make a good impression with a cold. Sales out of the question. Might as well stay at home and watch Vicki take care of things. More coughs; it was enough to make him envy the sleeping punk his earphones. Although that would still be no protection for his throat.

Abruptly he stood and took a walk toward the restaurant car. It was closed for the night. Back between cars, in the cold passageway, he noticed that the train was moving very slowly. He looked through the thick little window in the passageway door. They were over water; Lake Champlain, he guessed. The railroad bridge was so old and rickety that the train had to cross at about ten miles an hour. Looking down he couldn't even see the bridge, it was so narrow. White mist lay over the water, swirling eerily under the half-moon. He shivered convulsively: something *odd* about this night, the hush too quiet, the distances too great . . . he must be getting ill. Or . . . something. For the last few years he had gotten his life into such a groove, such a routine of day to day activities, each day resembling its predecessor from the week before, Mondays all alike, Fridays all alike, Saturdays . . . that he had found himself with time on his hands. It seemed he could live his life on a sort of automatic pilot, leaving him all sorts of time to just . . . think. Like he really never had before. And once or twice in this new thinking he had wondered what it (*it* being his life, the world, everything) was all about. No great answer had jumped immediately to mind; often he was left with just this sort of uneasy feeling. Out there, was that another train? No, just mist. A lake of white cotton . . .

Nothing for it but to return to his seat. As the night progressed he fell in and out of a half-sleep that resembled a trance. Several times they stopped at stations briefly, and once he woke completely when the police boarded to check everyone's pass-books. Two big white security police, making an old black ticket taker do most of the work. The migrants dug through their possessions for their reference books. Tins, boxes, old water drums bound with straps, all heavily loaded with basic groceries to help out the families on the bantustans. Norman's boxes were full of sugar, salt, and tea, all packed under his extra shirt and pants. His passbook was in the spare shirt's pocket; he pulled it out and bent the corners back down. All his stamps were in order, and he gave the ticket taker the book without looking up. Out the window Cape fig trees shaded the tiny veldt station, flanking the tracks like a hedge. Signs marked the entrances to the station house: BLANKES. NIE-BLANKES.

One of the security police took Pieter's passbook from the ticket taker's hand and inspected it closely. Suddenly no one in the car was talking. The radios babbled in Zulu and Xhosa. Then the policeman showed it to his companion and laughed. '*Robben vir Kwa-Xhosa! Die lewe is swaar né, Pieter!*'

'*Ja, my baas*,' Pieter said, looking at the floor of the corridor. 'Life is hard, all right.'

'Listen to me, *seuntjie*,' the policeman said, and gave Pieter a little lecture: more God, *volk* and trek, as someone said when they were gone. Pieter resolutely stared at the floor. When the policeman finished, Pieter looked up at him, the hatred clear in his eyes. 'My stamps are good, *ja baas*?'

'*Ja, seuntjie*,' the big man said easily, and tossed Pieter his passbook. The two police led the ticket taker out of the car, laughing over something, the pass check already forgotten. 'Cape Town whores are best.' 'Moering kaffirs will kill you in bed, though!'

Then they were gone, and everyone started breathing properly again. Only now could they be sure that all the passbooks were really in order; often they were not, and so one didn't discuss the matter. There had been a good chance someone on the car would be dragged off to jail. But they were all legal this time, and the talk began again. 'They stick him on the tenth floor by the open window, you know, but he refuse the jump and so he in jail and his kids is starving with hungry –'

' – you ever try sharing a bed with such a hippo? You got to sleep like a flea, ready to jump quick. And the fatter she got the worse her temper! Man I kissed Mother Earth daily living with her. Ha! Ha! She ransack me good sometime –'

' – *ja*, and if you get out, it's to the labor bureau like me, to sell yourself off to the coal mines of Witbank a thousand miles from home. We had a bad one at our labor bureau – he says, which of you boys wants a job, and of course we all jumping up and down like dogs, pick me *baas*, pick me, and he pick one after another to tell them no, they not good enough. Then he pick and look through my workbook, won't your wife sleep around while you gone, boy, I bet she sleep with me for giving you this job, until he tire of the game and give me the joy of eleven months work away from my folks.'

'And that better still than prison,' Pieter took it up; but Norman turned from Pieter's bitter comedies and looked out the window. Train nosing out of the station with hard jerks, as if the engine were yanking on it. An old man sitting in the dirt by a wheelbarrow stacked with baskets; too late in the day to sell anymore, but still he sat, in that twilight moment ... SLEGS BLANKES.

He got up to go to the bathroom, feeling distant, disoriented. Stepping over the punk was getting easy – the kid was slumped lower every time. Once again, trouble with balance. Something wrong. Everything too hushed, almost silent. Like cotton in his ear. Everything a great distance away.

The bathroom at the front of the car was occupied. He turned and went to the car behind, the last one of the train. Maneuvered through all the tight turns and heavy narrow doors between cars, found an empty bathroom. For the disabled, but he used it anyway. Not *exclusively* for the disabled, right? Down the iron toilet he could see the track ties flashing beneath the train. When he was done he looked at himself in the cracked coppery mirror: hair mussed, face stubbly, some odd disquiet in his eyes ...

The beer wanted out of him, and he stood up to use the lavatory at the end of the next car up. By now the travelers were drowsy with beer and fatigue, and he had to step over men sleeping in the aisles. Somehow they sprawled in a way that always left footing just where it was needed. Outside in the dusk the hillocks bordering the Orange River were etched against a moonless blue sky. Igqili River, he said to himself, mother of my country Azania. He stepped through the doorway into the connecting corridor, over the shifting joints of the iron floor. The joints squealed loudly and looking down at them he almost ran into the man coming his way. A white, from one of the first-class cars: confused, he said, 'Sorry, *baas*.'

The black kid muttered something under his breath, so sullenly that he was suddenly afraid he might be mugged right there between the two cars. The wheels rolling over the track were loud, no one would hear him: 'Sorry about that,' he said hastily, feeling dizzy, and yielded to the right. The train jerked and they bumped together hard; the black man reached out a hand to

214

hold him steady, then withdrew as if shocked, his frightened eyes round and white in the gloom. Their gazes met and held.

The look.

Dark brown iris, the whites a bit yellowed; pale blue iris, the whites a bit bloodshot. And the pupils identical round black holes, the windows of the soul, through which one can fall, spinning dizzily, to land cut, confused, stunned, in a new place; and all with a look –

. . . He wasn't sure how long the kid's feral stare had held him still, when he jerked free and pulled himself, staggering slightly, away. The doors were heavy and had to be pulled into the walls to right and left. Back in his car the hush seemed more pronounced than ever. Unsteadily he stepped back over the sleeping punk, feeling utterly shaken. The plush maroon velvet of his seat arm. Silvery ashtray, sliding in and out of the arm. Long brown cigarette butts wasted inside. Looking around: such incredible, excessive luxury – and this was just a train! He stared . . .

The migrants swayed with the train like luggage as he made his way in some confusion back to his boxes. Smell of sweat, beer, the hot veldt night. He ended his *dwaal* on his boxes and looked at his companions. Their clothes were frayed and dirty. Their shoes were broken and full of holes. They slept, or slumped in stupors of non-thought; and suddenly it seemed he could read what pain had chiseled in each worn face. The boy still hummed thoughtfully into his harmonica – bleak falling chords –

Finally they slid into the labyrinth of Penn Station. Darkness, trains passing by, their lit windows making them look like submarines. Then track lights everywhere. The punk woke and stood up. Everyone standing, stretching. He put his coat on in the aisle, feeling its smooth texture. The sick man was struggling to get his suitcase off the overhead racks, and awkwardly he helped him get it down. A haggard smile for thanks; he nodded quickly, embarrassed. A press of people (he held his briefcase close by his side), and he was out of the train, onto the long, crowded platform. Up a set of stairs, turn and follow everyone else to the next set. Up again. Into the light and glare of Penn Station's big central waiting area, with the businessmen and the

students and the cops and the cleaning men and the bums. And
then suddenly his wife was upon him, with a quick hug and kiss.
Strong scent of perfume. She laughed at his exhaustion and held
his arm as they made their way up to the street, chattering over
something or other and pleased that she had found a legal spot
to park their car. She drove, and he sat back in the deep seat
and looked at the bright dashboard, at her: glossy cap of blonde
hair, blush on her cheeks like two bruises, upper eyelids blue,
purple, lashes spiky black. He thought: she's mine. This is mine.
I'm safe. At a red light she glanced over at him and laughed
again, lips dark red, teeth perfectly white, and quickly leaned
over to steady themselves as the old train clattered up the grade
and out of the hills. Night passed, dawn arrived, they were in
Kwa-Xhosa now and it was as if S.A. Railways had been a time
machine, taking them a century into the past overnight. Women
they passed wore white turbans and led donkeys on dirt paths.
On the plains before the blue mountains on the horizon were
villages of circular thatched rondewels, whitewashed under the
thatch and around the doors. Finally the train clanked into
e'Ncgobo, past some men on donkeys and around the last curve
to the small wooden building and platform that served as the
train station. As the train rolled in, all the men stuck their heads
out the windows on the right to look; but under the harsh
morning light they saw that the station platform stood deserted,
white splintered dusty planks utterly empty in the sun. Not a
single soul was there to greet them. *And Thabo said to me, 'So
many had gone and come back, and so many had gone and never
come back again, that no one waited anymore.'*

Down and Out in the Year 2000

Down and Out in the Year 2000

He walked down 34th Street, with its curious alternation of solid fortresses and dilapidated buildings, to the Mall. There, the khaki tents illuminated by broad field of fire and makeshift tents and the odd patch of grass. Most of the prisoners were still asleep in their scattered tent villages, but there was no active erped around the Washington Monument.

It was going to be hot again. Summer in Washington, DC – Leroy Robinson woke and rolled on his mattress, broke into a sweat. That kind of a day. He got up and kneeled over the other mattress in the small room. Debra shifted as he shaded her from the sun angling in the open window. The corners of her mouth were caked white and her forehead was still hot and dry, but her breathing was regular and she appeared to be sleeping well. Quietly Leroy slipped on his jeans and walked down the hall to the bathroom. Locked. He waited; Ramon came out wet and groggy. 'Morning, Robbie.' Into the bathroom, where he hung his pants on the hook and did his morning ritual. One bloodshot eye, staring back at him from the splinter of mirror still in the frame. The dirt around the toilet base. The shower curtain blotched with black algae, as if it had a fatal disease. That kind of morning.

Out of the shower he dried off with his jeans and started to sweat again. Back in his room Debra was still sleeping. Worried, he watched her for a while, then filled his pockets and went into the hall to put on sneakers and tank-top. Debra slept light these days, and the strangest things would rouse her. He jogged down the four flights of stairs to the street, and sweating freely stepped out into the steamy air.

He walked down 16th Street, with its curious alternation of condo fortresses and abandoned buildings, to the Mall. There, big khaki tanks dominated the broad field of dirt and trash and tents and the odd patch of grass. Most of the protesters were still asleep in their scattered tent villages, but there was an active crowd around the Washington Monument,

219

and Leroy walked on over, ignoring the soldiers by the tanks.

The crowd surrounded a slingshot as tall as a man, made of a forked tree branch. Inner tubes formed the sling, and the base was buried in the ground. Excited protesters placed balloons filled with red paint into the sling, and fired them up at the monument. If a balloon hit above the red that already covered the tower, splashing clean white – a rare event, as the monument was pure red up a good third of it – the protesters cheered crazily. Leroy watched them as they danced around the sling after a successful shot. He approached some of the calmer seated spectators.

'Want to buy a joint?'

'How much?'

'Five dollars.'

'Too much, man! You must be kidding! How about a dollar?' Leroy walked on.

'Hey, wait! One joint, then. Five dollars ... shit.'

'Going rate, man.'

The protester pushed long blond hair out of his eyes and pulled a five from a thick clip of bills. Leroy got the battered Marlboro box from his pocket and took the smallest joint from it. 'Here you go. Have fun. Why don't you fire one of them paint bombs at those tanks, huh?'

The kids on the ground laughed. 'We will when you get them stoned!'

He walked on. Only five joints left. It took him less than an hour to sell them. That meant thirty dollars, but that was it. Nothing left to sell. As he left the Mall he looked back at the monument; under its wash of paint it looked like a bone sticking out of raw flesh.

Anxious about coming to the end of his supply, Leroy hoofed it up to Dupon Circle and sat on the perimeter bench in the shade of one of the big trees, footsore and hot. In the muggy air it was hard to catch his breath. He ran the water from the drinking fountain over his hands until someone got in line for a drink. He crossed the circle, giving a wide berth to a bunch of lawyers in long-sleeved shirts and loosened ties, lunching on wine and cheese under the watchful eye of their bodyguard. On the other side of the park Delmont Briggs sat by his cup, almost asleep, his sign propped on his lap. The wasted man. Delmont's sign – and a little side business – provided him with just enough money to get by on the street. The sign, a battered square of cardboard, said PLEASE HELP – HUNGRY. People still looked through Delmont like he wasn't there, but every once in a while it got to somebody. Leroy shook his head distastefully at the idea.

'Delmont, you know any weed I can buy? I need a finger baggie for twenty.'

'Not so easy to do, Robbie.' Delmont hemmed and hawed and they dickered for a while, then he sent Leroy over to Jim Johnson, who made the sale under a cheery exchange of the day's news, over by the chess tables. After that Leroy bought a pack of cigarettes in a liquor store, and went up to the little triangular park between 17th, S, and New Hampshire, where no police or strangers ever came. They called it Fish Park for the incongruous cement whale sitting by one of the trash cans. He sat down on the long broken bench, among his acquaintances who were hanging out there, and fended them off while he carefully emptied the Marlboros, cut some tobacco into the weed, and refilled the cigarette papers with the new mix. With their ends twisted he had a dozen more joints. They smoked one and he sold two more for a dollar each before he got out of the park.

But he was still anxious, and since it was the hottest part of the day and few people were about, he decided to visit his plants. He knew it would be at least a week till harvest, but he wanted to see them. Anyway it was about watering day.

East between 16th and 15th he hit no-man's land. The mixed neighborhood of fortress apartments and burned-out hulks gave way to a block or two of entirely abandoned buildings. Here the police had been at work, and looters had finished the job. The buildings were battered and burnt out, their ground floors blasted wide open, some of them collapsed entirely, into heaps of rubble. No one walked the broken sidewalk, sirens a few blocks off, and the distant hum of traffic, were the only signs that the whole city wasn't just like this. Little jumps in the corner of his eye were no more than that; nothing there when he looked directly. The first time, Leroy had found walking down the abandoned street nerve-racking; now he was reassured by the silence, the stillness, the no-man's land smell of torn asphalt and wet charcoal, the wavering streetscape empty under a sour milk sky.

His first building was a corner brownstone, blackened on the street sides, all its windows and doors gone, but otherwise sound. He walked past it without stopping, turned and surveyed the neighborhood. No movement anywhere. He stepped up the steps and through the doorway, being careful to make no footprints in the mud behind the doorjamb. Another glance outside, then up the broken stairs to the second floor. The second floor was a jumble of beams and busted furniture, and Leroy waited a minute to let his sight adjust to the gloom. The staircase to the third floor had collapsed, which was the reason he had chosen this building: no easy way up. But he had a route worked out, and with a leap he grabbed a beam hanging from the stairwell and hoisted himself onto it. Some crawling up the beam and he could swing onto the third floor, and from there a careful walk up gapped stairs brought him to the fourth floor.

The room surrounding the stairwell was dim, and he had jammed the door to the next room, so that he had to crawl through a hole in the wall to get through. Then he was there.

Sweating profusely, he blinked in the sudden sunlight, and stepped to his plants, all lined out in plastic pots on the far wall. Eleven medium-sized female marijuana plants, their splayed green leaves drooping for lack of water. He took the rain funnel from one of the gallon jugs and watered the plants. The buds were just longer than his thumbnail; if he could wait another week or two at least, they would be the size of his thumb or more, and worth fifty bucks apiece. He twisted off some water leaves and put them in a baggie.

He found a patch of shade and sat with the plants for a while, watched them soak up the water. Wonderful green they had, lighter than most leaves in DC. Little red threads in the buds. The white sky lowered over the big break in the roof, huffing little gasps of muggy air onto them all.

*   *   *

His next spot was several blocks north, on the roof of a burned-out hulk that had no interior floors left. Access was by way of a tree growing next to the wall. Climbing it was a challenge, but he had a route here he took, and he liked the way leaves concealed him even from passersby directly beneath him once he got above the lowest branches.

The plants here were younger – in fact one had sprouted seeds since he last saw them, and he pulled the plant out and put it in the baggie. After watering them and adjusting the aluminum foil rain funnels on the jug tops, he climbed down the tree and walked back down 14th.

He stopped to rest in Charlie's Baseball Club. Charlie sponsored a city team with the profits from his bar, and old members of the team welcomed Leroy, who hadn't been by in a while. Leroy had played left field and batted fifth a year or two before, until his job with the park service had been cut. After that he had had to pawn his glove and cleats, and he had missed Charlie's minimal membership charge three seasons running, and so he had quit. And then it had been too painful to go by the club, and drink with the guys and look at all the trophies on the wall, a couple of which he had helped to win. But on this day he enjoyed the fan blowing, and the dark, and the fries that Charlie and Fisher shared with him.

Break over, he went to the spot closest to home, where the new plants were struggling through the soil, on the top floor of an empty stone husk on 15th and Caroline. The first floor was a drinking place for derelicts, and old Thunderbird and whiskey bottles, half still in bags, littered the dark room, which smelled of alcohol, urine, and rotting wood. All the better: few people would be foolish enough to enter such an obviously dangerous hole. And the stairs were as near gone as made no difference. He climbed over the holes to the second floor, turned and climbed to the third.

The baby plants were fine, bursting out of the soil and up to the sun, the two leaves covered by four, up into four again . . . he watered them and headed home.

*   *   *

223

On the way he stopped at the little market that the Vietnamese family ran, and bought three cans of soup, a box of crackers and some Coke. 'Twenty-two oh five tonight, Robbie,' old Huang said with a four-toothed grin.

The neighbors were out on the sidewalk, the women sitting on the stoop, the men kicking a soccer ball about aimlessly as they watched Sam sand down an old table, the kids running around. Too hot to stay inside this evening, although it wasn't much better on the street. Leroy helloed through them and walked up the flights of stairs slowly, feeling the day's travels in his feet and legs.

In his room Debra was awake, and sitting up against her pillows. 'I'm hungry, Leroy.' She looked hot, bored; he shuddered to think of her day.

'That's a good sign, that means you're feeling better. I've got some soup here should be real good for you.' He touched her cheek, smiling.

'It's too hot for soup.'

'Yeah, that's true, but we'll let it cool down after it cooks, it'll still taste good.' He sat on the floor and turned on the hot plate, poured water from the plastic jug into the pot, opened the can of soup, mixed it in. While they were spooning it out Rochelle Jackson knocked on the door and came in.

'Feeling better, I see.' Rochelle had been a nurse before her hospital closed, and Leroy had enlisted her help when Debra fell sick. 'We'll have to take your temperature later.'

Leroy wolfed down crackers while he watched Rochelle fuss over Debra. Eventually she took a temperature and Leroy walked her out.

'It's still pretty high, Leroy.'

'What's she *got*?' he asked, as he always did. Frustration . . .

'I don't know any more than yesterday. Some kind of flu I guess.'

'Would a flu hang on this long?'

'Some of them do. Just keep her sleeping and drinking as much as you can, and feed her when she's hungry. – Don't be scared, Leroy.'

'I can't help it! I'm afraid she'll get sicker ... And there ain't nothing I can do!'

'Yeah, I know. Just keep her fed. You're doing just what I would do.'

After cleaning up he left Debra to sleep and went back down to the street, to join the men on the picnic tables and benches in the park tucked into the intersection. This was the 'living room' on summer evenings, and all the regulars were there in their usual spots, sitting on tables or bench backs. 'Hey there, Robbie! What's happening?'

'Not much, not much. No man, don't kick that soccer ball at me, I can't kick no soccer ball tonight.'

'You been walking the streets, hey?'

'How else we going to find her to bring her home to you.'

'Hey lookee here, Ghost is bringing out his TV.'

'It's Tuesday night at the movies, y'all!' Ghost called out as he approached and plunked a little hologram TV and a Honda generator on the picnic table. They laughed and watched Ghost's pale skin glow in the dusk as he hooked the system up.

'Where'd you get this one, Ghost? You been sniffing around the funeral parlors again?'

'You bet I have!' Ghost grinned. 'This one's picture is all fucked up, but it still works – I think – '

He turned the set on and blurry three-dee figures swam into shape in a cube above the box – all in dark shades of blue.

'Man, we *must* have the blues tonight,' Ramon remarked. 'Look at that!'

'They all look like Ghost,' said Leroy.

'Hey, it works, don't it?' Ghost said. Hoots of derision. 'And dig the sound! The sound works – '

'Turn it up then.'

'It's up all the way.'

'What's this?' Leroy laughed. 'We got to watch frozen midgets whispering, is that it Ghost? What do midgets say on a cold night?'

'Who the fuck is this?' said Ramon.

Johnnie said, 'That be Sam Spade, the greatest computer spy in the world.'

225

'How come he live in that shack, then?' Ramon asked.

'That's to show it's a rough scuffle making it as a computer spy, real tough.'

'How come he got four million dollars worth of computers right there in the shack, then?' Ramon asked, and the others commenced giggling, Leroy loudest of all. Johnnie and Ramon could be killer sometimes. A bottle of rum started around, and Steve broke in to bounce the soccer ball on the TV, smashing the blue figures repeatedly.

'Watch out now, Sam about to go plug his brains in to try and find out who he is.'

'And then he gonna be told of some stolen *wetware* he got to find.'

'I got some wetware myself, only I call it a shirt.'

Steve dropped the ball and kicked it against the side of the picnic table, and a few of the watchers joined in a game of pepper. Some men in a stopped van shouted a conversation with the guys on the corner. Those watching the show leaned forward. 'Where's he gonna go?' said Ramon. 'Hong Kong? Monaco? He gonna take the bus on over to Monaco?'

Johnnie shook his head. 'Rio, man. Fucking Rio de Janeiro.'

Sure enough, Sam was off to Rio. Ghost choked out an objection: 'Johnnie – ha! – you must have seen this one before.'

Johnnie shook his head, though he winked at Leroy. 'No man, that's just where all the good stolen wetware ends up.'

A series of commercials interrupted their fun: deodorant, burglarkillers, cars. The men in the van drove off. Then the show was back, in Rio, and Johnnie said, 'He's about to meet a slinky Afro-Asian spy.'

When Sam was approached by a beautiful black Asian woman the men couldn't stand it. 'Y'all *have* seen this one before!' Ghost cried.

Johnnie sputtered over the bottle, struggled to swallow. 'No way! Experience counts, man, that's all.'

'And Johnnie has watched one hell of a lot of Sam Spade,' Ramon added.

Leroy said, 'I wonder why they're always Afro-Asian.'

Steve burst in, laughed. 'So they can fuck all of us at once, man!' He dribbled on the image, changed the channel. '– *army command in Los Angeles reports that the rioting killed at least* – ' He punched the channel again. 'What else we got here – man! – what's *this*?'

'Cyborgs Versus Androids,' Johnnie said after a quick glance at the blue shadows. 'Lots of fighting.'

'Yeah!' Steve exclaimed. Distracted, some of the watchers wandered off. 'I'm a cyborg myself, see, I got these false teeth!'

'Shit.'

Leroy went for a walk around the block with Ramon, who was feeling good. 'Sometimes I feel so good, Robbie! So strong! I walk around this city and I say, the city is falling apart, it can't last much longer like this. And here I am like some kind of animal, you know, living day to day by my wits and figuring out all the little ways to get by ... you know there are people living up in Rock Creek Park like Indians or something, hunting and fishing and all. And it's just the same in here, you know. The buildings don't make it no different. Just hunting and scrapping to get by, and man I feel so *alive* – ' he waved the rum bottle at the sky.

Leroy sighed. 'Yeah.' Still, Ramon was one of the biggest fences in the area. It was really a steady job. For the rest ... They finished their walk, and Leroy went back up to his room. Debra was sleeping fitfully. He went to the bathroom, soaked his shirt in the sink, wrung it out. In the room it was stifling, and not even a waft of a breeze came in the window. Lying on his mattress sweating, figuring out how long he could make their money last, it took him a long time to fall asleep.

The next day he returned to Charlie's Baseball Club to see if Charlie could give him any piecework, as he had one or two times in the past. But Charlie only said no, very shortly, and he and everyone else in the bar looked at him oddly, so that Leroy felt uncomfortable enough to leave without a drink. After that he returned to the Mall, where the protesters were facing the troops ranked in front of the Capitol, dancing and jeering and throwing stuff. With all the police out it took him a good part of the afternoon to sell all the joints left, and when he had he walked back up 17th Street feeling tired and worried. Perhaps another purchase from Delmont could string them along a few more days ...

At 17th and Q a tall skinny kid ran out into the street and tried to open the door of a car stopped for a red light. But it was a protected car despite its cheap look, and the kid shrieked as the handle shocked him. He was still stuck by the hand to it when the car roared off, so that he was launched through the air and rolled over the asphalt. Cars drove on by. A crowd gathered around the bleeding kid. Leroy walked on, his jaw clenched. At least the kid would live. He had seen bodyguards gun thieves down in the street, kill them dead and walk away.

Passing Fish Park he saw a man sitting on a corner bench looking around. The guy was white, young; his hair was blond and short, he wore wire-rimmed glasses, his clothes were casual but new, like the protesters' down on the Mall. He had money. Leroy snarled as the sharp-faced stranger, approached him.

'What you doing here?'

'Sitting!' The man was startled, nervous. 'Just sitting in a park!'

'This ain't no *park*, man. This is our front yard. You see any front yard to these apartment buildings here? No. This here is our front yard, and we don't like people just coming into it and sitting down anywhere!'

The man stood and walked away, looked back once, his expression angry and frightened. The other men sitting on the park benches looked at Leroy curiously.

Two days later he was nearly out of money. He walked over to Connecticut Avenue, where his old friend Victor played harmonica for coins, when he couldn't find other work. Today he was there, belting out 'Amazing Grace.' He cut it off when he saw Leroy. 'Robbie! What's happening?'

'Not much. You?'

Victor gestured at his empty hat, on the sidewalk before him. 'You see it. Don't even have seed coin for the cap, man.'

'So you ain't been getting any gardening work lately?'

228

'No, no. Not lately. I do all right here, though. People still pay for music, man, some of them. Music's the angle.' He looked at Leroy, face twisted up against the sun. They had worked together for the park service, in times past. Every morning through the summers they had gone out and run the truck down the streets, stopping at every tree to hoist each other up in slings. The one hoisted had to stand out from trunk or branches like an acrobat, moving around to cut off every branch below twelve feet, and it took careful handling of the chain saw to avoid chopping into legs and such. Those were good times. But now the park service was gone, and Victor gazed at Leroy with a stoic squint, sitting behind an empty hat.

'Do you ever look up at the trees anymore, Robbie?'

'Not much.'

'I do. They're growing wild, man! Growing like fucking weeds! Every summer they go like crazy. Pretty soon people are gonna have to drive their cars through the branches. The streets'll be tunnels. And with half the buildings in this area falling down ... I like the idea that the forest is taking this city back again. Running over it like kudzu, till maybe it just be forest again at last.'

That evening Leroy and Debra ate tortillas and refries, purchased with the last of their money. Debra had a restless night, and her temperature stayed high. Rochelle's forehead wrinkled as she watched her.

Leroy decided he would have to harvest a couple of the biggest plants prematurely. He could dry them over the hot plate and be in business by the following day.

The next afternoon he walked east into no-man's land, right at twilight. Big thunderheads loomed to the east, lit by the sun, but it had not rained that day and the muggy heat was like an invisible blanket, choking each breath with moisture. Leroy came to his abandoned building, looked around. Again the complete stillness of an empty city. He recalled Ramon's tales of the people who lived forever in the no-man's land, channeling rain into basement pools, growing vegetables in empty lots, and existing entirely on their own with no need for money ...

He entered the building, ascended the stairs, climbed the beam, struggled sweating up to the fourth floor and through the hole into his room.

The plants were gone.

'Wha ...' He kneeled, feeling like he had been punched in the stomach. The plastic pots were knocked over, and fans of soil lay spread over the old wood flooring.

Sick with anxiety he hurried downstairs and jogged north to his second hideaway. Sweat spilled into his eye and it stung fiercely. He lost his breath and had to walk. Climbing the tree was a struggle.

The second crop was gone too.

Now he was stunned, shocked almost beyond thought. Someone must have followed him ... It was nearly dark, and the mottled sky lowered over him, empty but somehow, now, watchful. He descended the tree and ran south again, catching his breath in a sort of sobbing. It was dark by the time he reached 16th and Caroline, and he made his way up the busted stairs using a cigarette for illumination. Once on the fourth floor the lighter revealed broken pots, dirt strewn everywhere, the young plants gone. That small they hadn't been worth anything. Even the aluminum foil rain funnels on his plastic jugs had been ripped up and thrown around.

He sat down, soaking wet with sweat, and leaned back against the scored, moldy wall. Leaned his head back and looked up at the orange-white clouds, lit by the city.

After a while he stumbled downstairs to the first floor and stood on the filthy concrete, among the shadows and the discarded bottles. He went and picked up a whiskey bottle, sniffed it. Going from bottle to bottle he poured whatever drops remained in them into the whiskey bottle. When he was done he had a finger or so of liquor, which he downed in one long pull. He coughed. Threw the bottle against the wall. Picked up each bottle and threw it against the wall. Then he went outside and sat on the curb, and watched the traffic pass by.

He decided that some of his old teammates from Charlie's Baseball Club must have followed him around and discovered

230

his spots, which would explain why they had looked at him so funny the other day. He went over to check it out immediately. But when he got there he found the place closed, shut down, a big new padlock on the door.

'What happened?' he asked one of the men hanging out on the corner, someone from this year's team.

'They busted Charlie this morning. Got him for selling speed, first thing this morning. Now the club be gone for good, and the team too.'

When he got back to the apartment building it was late, after midnight. He went to Rochelle's door and tapped lightly.

'Who is it?'

'Leroy.' Rochelle opened the door and looked out. Leroy explained what had happened. 'Can I borrow a can of soup for Debra for tonight? I'll get it back to you.'

'Okay. But I want one back soon, you hear?'

Back in his room Debra was awake. 'Where you been, Leroy?' she asked weakly. 'I was worried about you.'

He sat down at the hot plate, exhausted.

'I'm hungry.'

'That's a good sign. Some cream of mushroom soup, coming right up.' He began to cook, feeling dizzy and sick. When Debra finished eating he had to force the remaining soup down him.

Clearly, he realized, someone he knew had ripped him off – one of his neighbors, or a park acquaintance. They must have guessed his source of weed, then followed him as he made his rounds. Someone he knew. One of his friends.

Early the next day he fished a newspaper out of a trashcan and looked through the short column of want ads for dishwashing work and the like. There was a busboy job at the Dupont Hotel and he walked over and asked about it. The man turned him away after a single look: 'Sorry, man, we looking for people who can walk out into the restaurant, you know.' Staring in one of the big silvered windows as he walked up New Hampshire, Leroy saw what the man saw: his hair spiked out everywhere as if he

231

would be a Rasta in five or ten years, his clothes were torn and dirty, his eyes wild ... With a deep stab of fear he realized he was too poor to be able to get any job – beyond the point where he could turn it around.

He walked the shimmery black streets, checking phone booths for change. He walked down to M Street and over to 12th, stopping at all the grills and little Asian restaurants, he went up to Pill Park and tried to get some of his old buddies to front him, he kept looking in pay phones and puzzling through blown scraps of newspaper, desperately hoping that one of them might list a job for him ... and with each footsore step the fear spiked up in him like the pain lancing up his legs, until it soared into a thoughtless panic. Around noon he got so shaky and sick-feeling he had to stop, and despite his fear he slept flat on his back in Dupont Circle park through the hottest hours of the day.

In the late afternoon he picked it up again, wandering almost aimlessly. He stuck his fingers in every phone booth for blocks around, but other fingers had been there before his. The change boxes of the old farecard machines in the Metro would have yielded more, but with the subway system closed, all those holes into the earth were gated off, and slowly filling with trash. Nothing but big trash pits.

Back at Dupont Circle he tried a pay phone coin return and got a dime. 'Yeah,' he said aloud; that got him over a dollar. He looked up and saw that a man had stopped to watch him: one of the fucking lawyers, in loosened tie and long-sleeved shirt and slacks and leather shoes, staring at him open-mouthed as his group and its bodyguard crossed the street. Leroy held up the coin between thumb and forefinger and glared at the man, trying to impress on him the reality of a dime.

He stopped at the Vietnamese market. 'Huang, can I buy some soup from you and pay you tomorrow?'

The old man shook his head sadly. 'I can't do that, Robbie. I do that even once, and – ' he wiggled his hands – 'the whole house come down. You know that.'

'Yeah. Listen, what can I get for – ' he pulled the day's change from his pocket and counted it again. 'A dollar ten.'

232

Huang shrugged. 'Candy bar? No?' He studied Leroy. 'Potatoes. Here, two potatoes from the back. Dollar ten.'

'I didn't think you had any potatoes.'

'Keep them for family, you see. But I sell these to you.'

'Thanks, Huang.' Leroy took the potatoes and left. There was a trash dumpster behind the store; he considered it, opened it, looked in. There was a half-eaten hot dog – but the stench overwhelmed him, and he remembered the poisonous taste of the discarded liquor he had punished himself with. He let the lid of the dumpster slam down and went home.

After the potatoes were boiled and mashed and Debra was fed, he went to the bathroom and showered until someone hammered on the door. Back in his room he still felt hot, and he had trouble catching his breath. Debra rolled from side to side, moaning. Sometimes he was sure she was getting sicker, and at the thought his fear spiked up and through him again, he got so scared he couldn't breathe at all ... 'I'm hungry, Leroy. Can't I have nothing more to eat?'

'Tomorrow, Deb, tomorrow. We ain't got nothing now.'

She fell into an uneasy sleep. Leroy sat on his mattress and stared out the window. White-orange clouds sat overhead, unmoving. He felt a bit dizzy, even feverish, as if he was coming down with whatever Debra had. He remembered how poor he had felt even back when he had had his crops to sell, when each month ended with such a desperate push to make rent. But now ... He sat and watched the shadowy figure of Debra, the walls, the hotplate and utensils in the corner, the clouds out the window. Nothing changed. It was only an hour or two before dawn when he fell asleep, still sitting against the wall.

Next day he battled fever to seek out potato money from the pay phones and the gutters, but he only had thirty-five cents when he had to quit. He drank as much water as he could hold, slept in the park, and then went to see Victor.

'Vic, let me borrow your harmonica tonight.'

Victor's face squinted with distress. 'I can't, Robbie. I need it myself. You know – ' pleading with him to understand.

'I know,' Leroy said, staring off into space. He tried to think. The two friends looked at each other.

'Hey, man, you can use my kazoo.'

'What?'

'Yeah, man, I got a good kazoo here, I mean a big metal one with a good buzz to it. It sounds kind of like a harmonica, and it's easier to play it. You just hum notes.' Leroy tried it. 'No, hum, man. Hum in it.'

Leroy tried again, and the kazoo buzzed a long crazy note.

'See? Hum a tune, now.'

Leroy hummed around for a bit.

'And then you can practice on my harmonica till you get good on it, and get your own. You ain't going to make anything with a harmonica till you can play it, anyway.'

'But this – ' Leroy said, looking at the kazoo.

Victor shrugged. 'Worth a try.'

Leroy nodded. 'Yeah.' He clapped Victor on the shoulder, squeezed it. Pointed at Victor's sign, which said *Help a musician!* 'You think that helps?'

Victor shrugged. 'Yeah.'

'Okay. I'm going to get far enough away so's I don't cut into your business.'

'You do that. Come back and tell me how you do.'

'I will.'

So Leroy walked south to Connecticut and M, where the sidewalks were wide and there were lots of banks and restaurants. It was just after sunset, the heat as oppressive as at midday. He had a piece of cardboard taken from a trashcan, and now he tore it straight, took his ballpoint from his pocket and copied Delmont's message. PLEASE HELP – HUNGRY. He had always admired its economy, how it cut right to the main point.

But when he got to what appeared to be a good corner, he couldn't make himself sit down. He stood there, started to leave, returned. He pounded his fist against his thigh, stared about wildly, walked to the curb and sat on it to think things over.

Finally he stepped to a bank pillar mid-sidewalk and leaned

back against it. He put the sign against the pillar face-out, and put his old baseball cap upside-down on the ground in front of him. Put his thirty-five cents in it as seed money. He took the kazoo from his pocket, fingered it. 'Goddamn it,' he said at the sidewalk between clenched teeth. 'If you're going to make me live this way, you're going to have to pay for it.' And he started to play.

He blew so hard that the kazoo squealed, and his face puffed up till it hurt. *Columbia, the Gem of the Ocean* blasted into all the passing faces, louder and louder –

When he had blown his fury out he stopped to consider it. He wasn't going to make any money that way. The loose-ties and the career women in dresses and running shoes were staring at him and moving out toward the curb as they passed, huddling closer together in their little flocks as their bodyguards got between him and them. No money in that.

He took a deep breath, started again. *Swing Low, Sweet Chariot*. It really was like singing. And what a song. How you could put your heart into that one, your whole body. Just like singing.

One of the flocks had paused off to the side; they had a red light to wait for. It was as he had observed with Delmont: the lawyers looked right through beggars, they didn't want to think about them. He played louder, and one young man glanced over briefly. Sharp face, wire-rims – with a start Leroy recognized the man as the one he had harrassed out of Fish Park a couple days before. The guy wouldn't look at Leroy directly, and so he didn't recognize him back. Maybe he wouldn't have anyway. But he was hearing the kazoo. He turned to his companions, student types gathered to the lawyer flock for the temporary protection of the bodyguard. He said something to them – 'I love street music,' or something like that – and took a dollar from his pocket. He hurried over and put the folded bill in Leroy's baseball cap, without looking up at Leroy. The *Walk* light came on, they all scurried away. Leroy played on.

* * *

That night after feeding Debra her potato, and eating two himself, he washed the pot in the bathroom sink, and then took a can of mushroom soup up to Rochelle, who gave him a big smile.

Walking down the stairs he beeped the kazoo, listening to the stairwell's echoes. Ramon passed him and grinned. 'Just call you Robinson Caruso,' he said, and cackled.

'Yeah.'

Leroy returned to his room. He and Debra talked for a while, and then she fell into a half-sleep, and fretted as if in a dream.

'No, that's all right,' Leroy said softly. He was sitting on his mattress, leaning back against the wall. The cardboard sign was face down on the floor. The kazoo was in his mouth, and it half buzzed with his words. 'We'll be all right. I'll get some seeds from Delmont, and take the pots to new hideouts, better ones.' It occurred to him that rent would be due in a couple of weeks; he banished the thought. 'Maybe start some gardens in no-man's land. And I'll practice on Vic's harmonica, and buy one from the pawn shop later.' He took the kazoo from his mouth, stared at it. 'It's strange what will make money.'

He kneeled at the window, stuck his head out, hummed through the kazoo. Tune after tune buzzed the still, hot air. From the floor below Ramon stuck his head out his window to object: 'Hey, Robinson Caruso! Ha! Ha! Shut the fuck up, I'm trying to sleep!' But Leroy only played quieter. *Columbia, the Gem of the Ocean –*

236

Our Town

I found my friend Desmond Kean at the northeast corner of the penthouse viewing terrace, assembling a telescope with which to look at the world below. He took a metal cylinder holding a lens and screwed it into the side of the telescope, then put his eye to the lens, the picture of concentrated absorption. How often I had found him like this in recent months! It made me shiver a little; this new obsession of his, so much more intense than the hand-made clocks, or the stuffed birds, or the geometric proofs, seemed to me a serious malady.

Clearing my throat did nothing to get his attention, so I ventured to say, 'Desmond, you're wanted inside.'

'Look at this,' he replied. 'Just look at it!' He stepped back, and I put my eye to his device.

I have never understood how looking through two pieces of curved glass can bring close distant sights; doesn't the same amount of light hit the first lens as would hit a plain circle of glass? And if so, what then could possibly be done to that amount of light within two lenses, to make it reveal so much more? Mystified, I looked down at the lush greenery of Tunisia. There in the shimmery circle of glass was a jumble of wood and thatch in a rice paddy, pale browns on light green. 'Amazing,' I said.

I directed the telescope to the north. On certain days, as Desmond once explained to me, when the temperature gradients layer the atmosphere in the right way, light is curved through the air (and tell me how that works!) so that we can see farther over the horizon than usual. This was one of those strange days, and in the lens wavered a black dot, resting on top of a silver pin that stuck up over the horizon. The black dot was Rome, the silver pin was the top of the graceful spire that holds the Eternal

239

City aloft. My heart leaped to know that I gazed from Carthage to Rome.

'It's beautiful,' I said.

'No, no,' Desmond exclaimed angrily. 'Look down! Look what's below!'

I did as he directed, even leaning a tiny bit over the railing to do so. Our new Carthage has a spire of its own, one every bit the equal of Rome's, or that of any other of the great cities of the world. The spire seemed to the naked eye a silver rope, a thread, a strand of gossamer. But through the telescope I saw the massy base of the spire, a concrete block like an immense blind fortress.

'Stunning,' I said.

'No!' he seized the spyglass from me. 'Look at the people camped there on the base! Look what they're doing!'

I looked through the glass where he had aimed it. Smoky fires, huts of cardboard, ribs perfectly delineated under taut brown skin. 'See,' Desmond hissed. 'There where the bonfires are set. They keep the fires going for days, then pour water on the concrete. To crack it, do you see?'

I saw, there in the curved glass surface; it was just as he had said.

'At that pace it will take them ten thousand years,' Desmond said bitterly.

I stood back from the railing. 'Please, Desmond. The world has gotten itself into a sorry state, and it's very distressing, but what can any one person do?'

He took the telescope, looked through it again. For a while I thought he wouldn't answer. But then he said, 'I . . . I'm not so sure, friend Roarick. It's a good question, isn't it. But I feel that someone with knowledge, with expertise, could make a bit of a difference. Heal the sick, or . . . give advice about agricultural practices. I've been studying up on that pretty hard. They're wrecking their soil. Or . . . or just put one more shoulder to the wheel! Add one more hand to tend that fire! . . . I don't know. I don't know! Do we ever know, until we act?'

'But Desmond,' I said. 'Do you mean down there?'

He looked up at me. 'Of course.'

I shivered again. Up at our altitude the air stays pretty chill all the time, even in the sun. 'Come back inside, Desmond,' I said, feeling sorry for him. These obsessions . . . . 'The exhibition is about to open, and if you're not there for it Cleo will press for the full set of sanctions.'

'Now there's something to fear,' he said nastily.

'Come on inside. Don't give Cleo the chance. You can return here another day.'

With a grimace he put the telescope in the big duffel bag, picked it up and followed me in.

Inside the glass wall, jacaranda trees showered the giant curved greenhouse-gallery with purple flowers. All the tableaux of the exhibit were still covered by saffron sheets, but soon after we entered the sheets were raised, all at once. The human form was revealed in all its variety and beauty, frozen in place yet still pulsing with life. I noted a man loping, a pair of women fighting, a diver launched in air, four drunks playing cards, a couple stopped forever at orgasm. I felt the familiar opening night quiver of excitement, caused partly by the force fields of the tableaux as they kept the living ectogenes stopped in place, but mostly by rapture, by a physical response to art and natural beauty. 'At first glance it seems a good year,' I said. 'I already see three or four pieces of merit.'

'Obscene travesties,' said Desmond.

'Now, now, it isn't as bad as all that. Some imitation of last year, yes, but no more than usual.'

We walked down the hall to see how my entry had been placed. Like Desmond, before he quit sculpting, I was chiefly interested in finding and isolating moments of dance that revealed, by themselves, all the grace of the whole act. This year I had stopped a pair of ballet dancers at the end of a *pas de deux*, the ballerina just off the base of the display as her partner firmly but deliberately returned her to the boards. How long I had worked with the breeders, to get ectogenes with these lean dancers' bodies! How many hours I had spent, programing their unconscious education, and training and choreographing them in their brief waking hours! And then at the end, how very often

I had had them dance on the tableaux base, and stopped them in the force field, before I caught them in the exact moment that I had envisioned! Yes, I had spent a great deal of time in my sculpting chamber, this year; and now my statue stood before us like the epitome of all that is graceful in the human spirit. At a proper angle to the viewers, I was pleased to see, and under tolerable lighting, too. On the two faces were expressions which said that for these two, nothing existed but dance; and in this case it was almost literally true. Yes, it was satisfactory.

Desmond only shook his head. 'No, Roarick. You don't understand. We can't keep doing this – '

'Desmond!' cried Cleo, flowing through the crowd of sculptors and their guests. Her smile was wide, her eyes bright with malice. 'Come see my latest, dear absent one!'

Wordlessly Desmond followed her, his face so blank of expression that all his thoughts showed clear. A whole crew followed us discreetly, for Desmond and Cleo's antipathy was legendary. How it had started none remembered, although some said they had once been lovers. If so, it was before I knew them. Others said Desmond hated Cleo for her success in the sculpture competitions, and some of the more sharp-tongued gossips said that this envy explained Desmond's new, morbid interest in the world below – sour grapes, you know. But Desmond had always been interested in things no one else cared about – rediscovering little scientific truths and the like – and to me it was clear that his fascination was simply the result of his temperament, and of what his telescope had newly revealed to him. No, his and Cleo's was a more fundamental hatred, a clash of contrary natures.

Now Desmond stared at Cleo's new statue. It is undeniable that Cleo is a superb artist, especially in facial expressions, those utterly complex projections of unique emotional states; and this work displayed her usual brilliance in that most difficult medium. It was a solo piece: a red-haired young woman looked back over one shoulder with an expression of intense vulnerability and confusion, pierced by a sharp melancholy. It was exquisite.

The sight of this sculpture snapped some final restraint in Desmond Kean; I saw it happen. His eye filled with pity and disgust; his lip curled, and he said loudly, 'How did you do it,

Cleo? What did you do to her in your little bubble world to get that expression out of her?'

Now, this was a question one simply didn't ask. Each artist's arcology was his or her own sovereign ground, a physical projection of the artist's creative unconscious, an entirely private cosmos. What one did to one's material there was one's own business.

But the truth was no one had forgotten the unfortunate Arthur Magister, who had exhibited increasingly strange and morbid statues over a period of years, ending with one of a maiden who had had on her face such an expression that no one could bear to look at it. Though the rule of privacy was maintained, there were of course questions muttered; but no one would ever have found out the answers, if Arthur had not blown up himself and his arcology, revealing in the wreckage, among other things, a number of unpleasantly dismembered ectogenes.

So it was a sensitive issue; and when Desmond asked Cleo his brazen question, with its dark implication, she blanched, then reddened with anger. Disdainfully (though I sensed she was afraid, too) she refused to reply. Desmond stared fiercely at us all; were he an ectogene, I would have stopped him at just that instant.

'Little gods,' he snarled, and left the room.

That would cost him, in reputation if not in actual sanctions. But the rest of us forgot his distemper, relieved that we could now begin the exhibit's opening reception in earnest. Down at the drink tables champagne corks were already bringing down a fresh shower of jacaranda blooms.

It was just a few hours later, when the reception was a riotous party, that I heard the news, passed from group to group instantly, that someone had broken the locks on the tableaux (this was supposed to be impossible) and turned their force fields off, letting most of the statues free. And it was while we rushed to the far end of the greenhouse-gallery, around the great curve of the perimeter of the penthouse, that I heard that Desmond Kean had been seen, leaving the gallery with Cleo's red-headed ectogene.

Utter scandal. This would cost Desmond more than money; they would exile him to some tedious sector of the city, to scrub walls with robots or teach children or the like: they would make him pay in time. And Cleo! I groaned; he would never live to see the end of her wrath.

Well, a friend can only do so much, but while the rest were rounding up and pacifying the disoriented ectogents (which included, alas, my two dancers, who were huddled in each others' arms) I went in search of Desmond, to warn him that he had been seen. I knew his haunts well, having shared most of them, and I hurried to them through the uncrowded, vaguely Parisian boulevards of the penthouse's northern quarter.

My first try was the broken planetaria near the baths; I opened the door with the key we had quietly reproduced years before. An indiscretion! Desmond and the young ectogene were making love on the dais in the middle of the chamber, Desmond on his back, the woman straddling him, arced as if all the energy of the great spire were flowing up into her ... he was breaking all the taboos this night. Immediately I shut the door, but given the situation saw fit to pound loudly on it. 'Desmond! It's Roarick! They saw you with the girl, you've got to leave!'

Silence. What to do in such a situation? I had no precedent. After a good thirty seconds had passed I opened the door again. No Desmond, no girl.

I, however, was one of those who with Desmond had first discovered the other exit from the planetaria, and I hurried to the central ball of optical fibers which even he could not fix, and pulled up the trap door beside it. Down the stairs and along the passageway, into one of the penthouse's other infrastructures I ran.

I will not detail my long search, nor my desperate and ludicrous attempts to evade rival search parties. Despite my knowledge of Desmond's ways and my anxious thoroughness, I did not find him until I thought of the place that should have occurred to me first. I returned to the northeast corner of the viewing terrace, right there outside the glass wall of the greenhouse-gallery, where (as it was now dusk) if the artists inside could have seen through their own reflections, they would have looked right at him.

He and the redhead were standing next to Desmond's telescope, their elbows on the railing as they looked over the edge side by side. Desmond had his duffel bag at his feet. Something in their stance kept me from emerging from the shadows. They looked as though they had just finished the most casual and intimate of conversations – a talk about trivial, inessential things, the kind of talk lovers have together after years of companionship. Such calmness, such resignation ... I could only look, at what seemed to me then an unbreakable, eternal tableau.

Desmond sighed and turned to look at her. He took a red curl of her hair between his fingers, watched the gold in it gleam in a band across the middle of the curl. 'There are three kinds of red hair,' he said sadly. 'Red black, red brown, and red gold. And the greatest of these is ...'

'Black,' said the girl.

'Gold,' said Desmond. He fingered the curl ...

The woman pointed. 'What's all that down there?'

Dusky world below, long since in night: vast dark Africa, the foliage like black fur, sparking with the sooty flares of a thousand bonfires, little pricks of light like yellow stars. 'That's the world,' Desmond said, voice tightened to a burr. 'I suppose you don't know a thing about it. Around those fires down there are people. They are slaves, they live lives even worse than yours, almost.'

But his words didn't appear to touch the woman. She turned away, and lifted an empty glass left on the railing. On her face was an expression so ... lost – a sudden echo of her expression as statue – that I shivered in the cold wind. She didn't have the slightest idea what was going on.

'Damn,' she said. 'I wish I'd remembered to bring another drink.'

A conversation from another world, resumed here. I saw Desmond Kean's face then, and I know that I did right to interrupt at that moment. 'Desmond!' I rushed forward and grasped his arm. 'There's no time, you really must get to one of our private rooms and hide! You don't want to find out what sort of sentence they might hand down for this sort of thing!'

245

A long moment: I shudder to think of the tableaux we three made. The world is a cruel sculptor.

'All right,' Desmond said at last. 'Here, Roarick, take her and get her out of here.' He bent over to fumble in his bag. 'They'll put her down after all this if they catch her.'

'But – but where should I go?' I stammered.

'You know this city as well as I! Try the gallery's service elevator, and get on the underfloor – you know,' he insisted, and yet he was about to give me further directions when the far greenhouse door burst open and a whole mob poured out. We were forced to run for it; I took the woman by the hand and sprinted for the closer greenhouse door. The last I saw of Desmond Kean, he was climbing over the railing. *My God*, I thought, *he's going to kill himself!* – but then I saw the purposefully rectangular package strapped to his back.

The Return From Rainbow Bridge

The Return From Rainbow Bridge

When I was fifteen years old I visited the Navaho reservation north of Flagstaff, Arizona, to help the Indians celebrate the Fourth of July. Even before I arrived I thought that was kind of a strange thing to do. But something much stranger than that happened to me out there, before I left; something so strange that I have never been able to forget even the slightest detail of it, from that day to this.

On arrival late one Sunday afternoon I got out of my cousin Luke's blue VW, followed by my young brother David. My great-aunt Miriam, a tall gray-haired woman in a cotton print dress, greeted us with a sweet girlish smile, holding our hands in hers. I walked around the car to stretch my legs and survey the grounds.

As it happened our arrival coincided with the onset of a summer storm. Overhead clouds like great dark lobes of marble filled the western sky. The setting sun leaked under the edge of this front, and glazed everything with a harsh orange glare. We stood on a broad, high, bare tableland; the horizon was an immense distance away. The blacktop road merged with the dark land to east and west, one shadow ribbon among many.

Small at the center of all this space, Inscription House Mission stood before us: a church, a house, and some rough outbuildings, all whitewashed, all glowing now in the fan of stormlight, the walls' whites tinged the color of the earth, and striped with solid black shadows, but intensely bright in the surrounding gloom, like lamps at dusk. Before these sun-colored walls my cousin's car, a brilliant metallic blue even in ordinary light, gleamed like the shell of a glittering scarab, a visitor from another world.

We carried our bags into my great-aunt's house just as muddy dark splotches began starring the dusty earth around us. As we entered the house I looked back, and under the gray sheets of the squall I saw a figure, standing on a bare rise to the north, near the horizon. Silhouetted, solitary, somehow more heraldic than real, it raised both arms as if to encourage the coming downpour. My first Indian, I thought, and wondered if I had seen a sort of raindance. I closed the door.

'That guy out there'll get wet,' I said wisely.

'Who's that?' Luke asked, surprised.

'That Indian, out there under the storm.'

He shook his head. 'No one out there, far as I saw.'

I opened the door again and looked out. There was nothing under the squall, no one out there on that whole broad plateau. And nowhere to hide. 'What ... ?' A gust of wind pushed at the door, as if something was trying to get in; I shivered.

That was the start of it.

While the rain drummed on the shingles of Aunt Miriam's house the four of us talked; I didn't mention again the figure I had seen. Aunt Miriam served us powdered milk. It was the first time I had drunk it, and I didn't like the taste. 'It tastes funny,' I said, surprised.

Aunt Miriam smiled. 'It's all we've got out here.'

'You get used to it,' Luke said with a laugh.

The rain stopped after about half an hour, and as it was Sunday we walked over to the church to join the evening service. Yellow light from the church windows streaked the puddles in the yard, under a low black sky. The church's interior was one medium-sized room, filled with Navahos sitting in folding chairs. There were about forty of them, in rows facing a narrow lectern and a piano at the front of the room. I was surprised to see so many people; I hadn't thought very many Indians would be Christian. David and I sat in chairs set against the side wall, near the front.

An older Navaho man spoke to them in Navaho from the lectern; while he did I looked through a Bible and hymnal that had been on my chair. I saw that the Navaho language had an incredible frequency of vowels; there were words like *aanapalaooaa, liineaupoonaa, kreeaiioo* . . . it reminded me of an infant's babbling.

When the old man was done they sang hymns, Aunt Miriam accompanying them on the piano. They used the old tunes of Luther, Wesley, and Watt, but had translated the lyrics, and with all those vowels, and a wild warble in the women's voice, the familiar hymns – *A Mighty Fortress Is Our God, Onward Christian Soldiers* – were transformed, made utterly strange, unlike any music I had ever heard. Their beauty took me by surprise, and my cheeks flushed as I listened. Up at the front Aunt Miriam sang along, an expression of pure bliss on her upraised face. She had played the flute in the Chicago Symphony, I recalled; but that could never have made her look as she did now.

While they sang these weird hymns I stared at their faces. I was a bookish youth, and I had lived all my life in a southern California suburb, a white middle-class town that couldn't have been more homogeneous if it had been legislated that way. The truth was, in my entire life I had never seen faces like these before me: dark-skinned, sun-wrinkled, hawk-nosed, heavy-lidded, life-battered faces, each the map of a world, each framed and made beautiful by sleek straight black hair, and jewelry of silver and turquoise . . . extraordinary faces: visions out of my book lore, but real. Suddenly I experienced a convulsive blush, as with the music but stronger – because I realized, right then and there, that it went beyond mere stories in books: the world was real. *The world was real.* Man, I thought, not understanding what I felt – these are really Indians!

The next morning I went outside early to walk around a bit.

The great plateau of the Navaho reservation stands over six thousand feet above sea level; I suppose that is part of the reason everything looked different to me that morning. The sky was a dark, pure blue, and in this blue the feathering of a cirrus cloud was a startling white. The cool air was hard and clear, like a glass that sharpened vision. The rainstorm had washed the land, and the earth was dark red, or the color of wet sand. Sagebrush and an occasional pine tree were scattered across the land. The sage was a shifting silvery color, like olive leaves, a shade that fit the earth tones; but the pines appeared to burst with green, as if more color had been pumped into them than they could actually hold: every pine needle poked the air, distinct in itself, dark with greenness flowing outward. I walked over to one of these pines, a juniper, I thought, feeling that I was swimming in color: red earth, green trees, blacktop road, white clouds, cobalt sky . . .

I had been collecting the small, tight green cones of my tree for several minutes – just for something to do – when I looked up and saw that an Indian was watching me from no more than ten feet away. I jumped back, frightened; I hadn't heard him approach.

He was about my height, and somewhere in his forties or fifties, I guessed; it was hard to tell. He wore old blue jeans, a plaid cotton shirt, and a cowboy hat. His face was like those of the people in church the night before (though I hadn't seen his there): broad, impassive, masklike. 'Hello!' I said nervously, afraid that I was stealing his pine cones or something.

'Hello.' And he stared at me, calmly. Finally, after a long pause: 'Do you like pine cones?'

'Well . . . sure! I mean they're . . . interesting!'

He looked at me. Later I became painfully familiar with that look . . .

My nervousness increased. Finally, to break the silence, I said, 'Do you live around here?'

'North some.' He gestured briefly at the road. After that, silence again. He didn't seem to mind, but I was getting more uncomfortable by the second.

Perhaps he saw this. He cocked his head, watching me. 'Do you play basketball?'

'Yeah!' I said, surprised. I told him about my ninth-grade team. He nodded without expression. 'Come on.'

I followed him back toward the mission, confused and uncertain. Then we rounded one of the rough outbuildings, and I saw that the far end of the yard was a big basketball court. A group of Navaho men and boys were crowded under one basket, milling around in a tussle for the ball.

The man stopped beside me. 'It's twenty-one. You can play if you want.'

So he and I joined the game. Everyone struggled for rebounds, and when you got one the whole group was your opponent; if you managed to score anyway, you went to the free throw line and shot till you missed. Points were scored as in regular basketball, and the first person to reach twenty-one won.

It was a wild game, a free-for-all really, and I dashed around the outskirts of it somewhat at a loss. The court's surface was wet dirt sprinkled with loose gravel; not the most level of surfaces. A skinny tree trunk held up a backboard that was not quite square to the court, and the basket itself seemed unusually high, say eleven feet; perhaps it only looked that way because the backboard was so small. All in all it was not what I was used to, and when a rebound came my way I lost it dribbling. Frustrated, I got into the crowd and was elbowed and pushed with the rest of the boys as we scrambled around the men for loose balls. Impossible to hold on with six or seven hands slapping the ball; discouraged, I moved back outside, and was mostly watching when my new acquaintance took a rebound and drove into the crowd. When he was blocked off he fired a pass back over one shoulder, right at me. I got my hands up just in time to catch it, had an open moment, shot; incredibly, the ball caromed off the backboard and through the net.

At the free throw line looking up, I knew that I would miss. Even back home I couldn't make free throws, and here the basket looked twice as far away. I only hoped I would avoid an air ball.

No such luck. The ball missed everything by two feet. Involuntarily I cried out: 'Aaaa!' The men and boys laughed, but in a friendly way; I had amused them by expressing aloud what everyone felt when they missed. I laughed, too, and felt more at ease. Then some men arrived and there were enough to start a real game; the boys were kicked off the court. My Indian walked over to his team without even a glance in my direction, as if he had forgotten my existence.

* * *

I sat and watched the game, and Luke joined me. 'They like basketball,' I said.

He cracked up. 'That's right. In fact they love basketball. Basketball and pickup trucks – those are the white man's things that the Navaho have really taken to.' He laughed again. 'These men – they've all got kids enough that the kids can take care of the sheep during the day. Dad can come down here and play ball with his friends, for an hour or two anyway. They play almost every day.'

I pointed out my acquaintance and asked who he was.

'That's Paul. Why do you ask?'

'He brought me over here and got me in the twenty-one game.'

Luke smiled. 'He's a good man. He's the one I'm trying to get to hike with us to Rainbow Bridge, after the Fourth. A good man.' He frowned, tossed a few pieces of gravel back onto the court. 'Paul's got a son about your age. But he moved to Flagstaff.'

'That's good, isn't it?' Get out there in the modern world . . .

Luke shook his head. 'Alcohol's illegal on the reservation, see. It's just too much of a problem for them. So people who are . . . who want alcohol, they generally move down to Flagstaff. And then they're in trouble, because they can get it so easily.'

'But he's only my age, you said!'

'That's right.'

I didn't understand. He wasn't even old enough to *buy* alcohol . . .

'Come on,' Luke said, standing. 'Let's go find your brother and go for a ride. I've got to go to the trading post.'

Luke was one of those people whose internal dynamo is pitched several thousand r.p.m. higher than anyone else's. This was his vacation, he was just visiting Aunt Miriam (his great-aunt too, from a different direction), but every day he had a long list of things to do, and he hustled around doing them until everyone with him dropped from exhaustion. Loading pickups with supplies, giving people rides up dirt tracks into the back country, building houses or fences, hunting for lost sheep: it was all great fun to him. I would have thought that Luke would be resented for all this help, but it wasn't so. In fact he had a real knack for pleasing the Navaho, for drawing them out. That afternoon, for instance, three times we passed solitary Navaho men walking down the road toward the trading post, some six miles away. Each time Luke stopped by them, even though after the first got in the VW was full. 'Want a ride? Where you going?' And they all got in, so that after the third one David and I were crushed into a corner of the backseat. The men were forbidding in their silence, and apparently Luke didn't know any of them; it made me nervous. But Luke laughed at the crowding, and started asking them questions, where do you live, how many sheep have you got, how many kids, do you go to that VISTA place, aren't those folks strange (they grinned), did you get caught out in that storm yesterday ... and by the time we got to the trading post the Navaho were talking away, both to Luke and among themselves, but always in English so we would be included, and they all took up his offer to load the VW and drive back to their homes (how are *we* going to fit in, I wanted to say), and while we were stuffing the Beetle with heavy boxes something Luke said struck them funny, I'm not sure what, and their stoic faces tilted up at the sky and broke into a million laugh lines as they cackled away. Luke just grinned, having a great time as usual. I envied him that ease, that skill.

That night at Aunt Miriam's we had mutton and bread. I had noticed the Navaho ate the same thing, every meal: bread and coffee for breakfast, mutton, bread, and coffee for lunch, and mutton, bread, and coffee for dinner. 'Boy,' I said, 'these Navaho must sure like mutton bread and coffee!'

From the strain in my aunt's beautiful smile I knew I had said something stupid, but I didn't know what. Over the next few bites I worked it out. 'They don't have anything else?'

My aunt shook her head, the smile gone.

'They have some canned stuff,' Luke said. 'But mutton bread and coffee, those are the staples.'

I continued eating, and imagined having the meal before me, every day; it tasted different, somehow.

The Fourth of July came. In the cool morning Paul came by in his pickup. Luke introduced him to David and me; he nodded, smiling a little smile at me. We drove out to a gravel pit in a dry streambed, took giant shovels and filled the bed of the truck with gravel. Then we drove back to the mission and shoveled the gravel onto the basketball court.

A fresh coat for the big day. As I spread gravel evenly over the long court I puzzled over the idea of Indians celebrating the Fourth of July. Shouldn't they hate this day, shouldn't they be lighting bonfires and burning flags, or maybe the stray white man or two?

Apparently they didn't feel that way about it. Family after family drove up in pickup trucks. The women set big hampers of food on the picnic tables flanking the yard. They roasted big sides of sheep over fires set in brick pits; fragrant white plumes of smoke rose into the sunny blue sky. The Navaho chatted cheerfully with the large group of white missionaries there for the day. The food was set out beside paper plates, and we filed past and loaded up: mutton, bread, and coffee – and also chili, watermelon, and Cokes. A real celebration. There must have been a hundred people there, maybe two hundred. I wandered around eating and watching, enjoying myself.

Only when the missionaries imposed a sequence of games on the group did the Navaho show the slightest sign that all was not perfect on that day. As these games began they withdrew into themselves, and went along with it all impassively. A missionary friend of my aunt's called me over to him. 'Come here, we need you for this one!' I was into it before I understood what the game was; when I did, I groaned. The game was this: one of the missionaries stood with his back to a group of us, and threw wrapped pieces of candy over his head in our direction, and then we scrambled to pick up as many pieces as we could.

I couldn't believe it. No wonder all the kids around me were between five and ten years old, no wonder all the Navaho boys my age had refused to join, and were now standing in the circle of observers, watching me. So *undignified* . . . Then the man threw the candy, and I gritted my teeth and went after some; damned if I could get my hands on a single piece. Those little kids were *serious* about this game, and they were fast as squirrels, and the bits of candy all disappeared almost before they hit the ground. Near the end of the ordeal I straightened up, after managing to wrestle a piece of toffee out of the clenched fist of a six-year-old, and saw the stares of all the boys my age. I felt myself flush scarlet with humiliation. And there was Paul, too, on the edge of the group, watching without expression. He said something in Navaho, and the crowd dispersed; the kids left to tally their prizes; there was no one left for the missionary to inflict the game on. Paul walked off, and I stared after him gratefully, wondering what he could have said.

Immediately I was called by the missionaries into a volleyball game, with the boys my own age. Ah-ha, I thought; I'll get back some lost face, here. I had played quite a bit of volleyball at home, and I jumped about making hits as often as I could. Once I got an opportunity to spike the ball over the low net, and showing off a bit I leaped up and hit it hard. It bounced off across the yard, a clean point for our side. Then I saw the way all the other boys were looking at me, faces impassive but perfectly contemptuous, and I understood in a flash that they played the game differently here; it was like that beach paddle game, where you try to keep the ball in play for as long as possible. Humiliated again, I got my brother to take my place, and left the game. And I saw that once more Paul had been watching, from some distance away, standing there with his arms folded across his chest. I gritted my teeth unhappily.

Then it was time for the basketball game, and all the Navaho men perked up. Here was a real game, a proper way to celebrate the holiday.

They started the game before two in the afternoon, and it didn't end till after five, and the entire game was played in the most manic fast-break style I had ever seen. After a shot or rebound was made, everyone broke for the other basket, gravel spraying, the ball passed as if shot from cannons: a pass or two, a quick shot gunned, a tussle for the rebound, and off they flew the other way. Back and forth without letup, all afternoon long. I sat on the end of one bench, openmouthed at the pace of this wonderful game, and hid from the missionaries. I tried to forget the humiliations they had just caused me, but they kept coming back to mind.

Then about an hour into the game Paul jogged by and said, 'Want to play?'

I jumped up and took the place of one of Paul's teammates. I was the only white man out there, and I felt keenly the eyes of the game's audience. My team seemed most comfortable ignoring me, but Paul passed me the ball once or twice, and I managed to dribble and pass it off without mishap. Once I took it and drove for the basket, then passed it out to Paul, just as he had to me in the game of twenty-one: he caught it without a hitch and pumped it through for two.

Like the rest of the men, Paul was an incorrigible gunner. He would take passes on a little rise near half-court, and fire two-handed shots straight for the sky. The ball flew two or three times as high as the basket, it seemed, then swooped down and practically ripped the net off the hoop. No fooling with the backboard for Paul. If he missed and the ball hit the rim, it made an iron crash like the hoop was breaking off, and bounced so far out or up that the rebounders were confused. But I would say he hit about sixty percent of these bombs, and many of the other men were almost as accurate. It made for a high-scoring game; although to tell the truth, I don't think they were keeping score.

I played for about twenty minutes, and left the game so beat I could hardly walk. After some rest and a couple of Cokes I recovered, and I chatted with Luke and David and Aunt Miriam while we watched the rest of the game. 'These guys could beat any team in the NBA!' I said, excited. Luke grinned and added, 'If it weren't for the fact that the tallest one out there is five eleven.' I laughed; I was pleased; the earlier embarrassments were forgotten. The Fourth of July was turning out all right after all.

Only late that night in bed, did it occur to me whose doing that had been.

A day or two later Luke and I drove north to Paul's home, to fix the date of our hike to Rainbow Bridge, 'the biggest natural arch in the world!' – also to make sure Paul would come. Luke was a little vague about it: 'Well, Paul's got a lot of responsibilities, we have to see if he's still free ...' Up a bumpy dirt track, rocky and pink in the surrounding tans, into the wash of a flat-bottomed canyon, past tall delicate white-barked trees, their broad green leaves translucent in the sunlight ...

Tucked up against the canyon wall were fences, Paul's pickup, a low oval hut. We stopped in the yard and got out. Red chickens scattered before us. There were five-gallon plastic jugs lined against one wall of the hut, which seemed *woven*, sort of: wood and wicker and perhaps *mud*, in a complex pattern. The place was quite clearly *handmade*.

Luke knocked on the wooden door and was called in: I stood in the doorway and stared into the gloom, uncertain about following. Paul was getting up from an old stuffed armchair; some others sat around a table, near a fat black stove. Paul greeted us politely, shook both our hands – because we were visiting his home, I guessed. Luke said something and they all laughed. The two men talked, and the eyes around the stove watched me. The interior walls were hung with boldly patterned rugs, earth tones cut by bright white zigzags. There were some sort of masks in the corner, it looked like. Paul and Luke were busy talking and I backed out the door, confused and uncomfortable under the gaze of Paul's family.

Penned against the little house by the fences were sheep – or goats, actually. Goats. They looked dirty, and had an awful smell. The whole place was so shabby, so small ... Poverty, I thought: this is what poverty looks like. Maybe I would have gone to Flagstaff too ...

Luke ducked out. 'We're all set,' he said. 'He wants to take off tomorrow. Some folks on the Hopi reservation need his help in a few days, so the sooner the better for the trip.'

On the drive back I had a hard time collecting myself. Luke noticed; he said, 'That's a *hogan* they live in, the traditional Navaho home. You're lucky to have seen one.'

I couldn't help myself: 'But it was so small! And ... dirty!'

'Not dirty. They're actually quite clean. Small, true. But it's easier to heat them that way.'

'But this is the desert!' We were sweating even with the windows down.

'Yes, but in the winter it snows. Blizzards like you can't believe. Hot in the summer and cold in the winter, that's the high desert for you. It's hard to make housing that will keep you comfortable in both extremes, especially without electricity. A lot of Paul's friends are building new houses, regular framing and walls of stuccoed plasterboard . . . They look like the houses down in Flagstaff, you probably would think they were nicer, but they freeze in the winter, and bake in the summer, and fall apart in ten years. The hogans are actually better homes.'

This was interesting, and I found it comforting to an extent; but the sight of the hogan, home of the man I had thought powerful and influential – so small, dark, *primitive* – had shocked me, and that shock was more powerful than Luke's calm reasoning.

The next morning Luke woke us in the dark, and while the sky bent from indigo to the rich velvet sky blue of predawn, we drove north. David slept on the backseat, and I watched the headlight beams light the asphalt road against the dusty blond shadows of the land. Paul followed us in his truck. We drove uphill, and the low gnarled pine trees, scattered here and there like black boulders, proliferated until we drove through a kind of rocky low forest.

We parked in a gravel lot next to the Navaho Mountain Trading Post, a single wooden building, closed. The lot was empty except for us. Luke was pleased: 'We'll have the whole trail to ourselves, I bet.' In the morning chill we ate apples, and their cidery smell mixed with the piney odor of the trees.

Paul and Luke had packs, and David and I carried our cotton sleeping bags in rolls strapped to our shoulders. We started walking on the trail, a level white swath through the thick network of trees.

The trees shifted from black to green. The sun rose to our right, and shadows jumped down the slope to the west. Above us the east rugged sandstone ramparts alternated with steep pine-filled ravines; Navaho Mountain, Luke told us, was above and beyond the cliffs we could see. The trees were scattered everywhere now, for as far as we could see. 'Piñon pines,'

Luke said. 'Biggest stand of piñon pines in the whole world.'

The broad trail was marked every mile by a metal pole, cemented in the dirt and painted bright red. Milestones, I thought. Luke laughed at them. It was fifteen miles to Rainbow Bridge.

The trail turned left, down to the west. The land began to fall away so rapidly that the trail switchbacked; here the tableland fell down into the canyons surrounding the Colorado River. We could see a long way down to the west, over tawny ridges, knobs, shadowed canyon walls. We passed milepole number five.

The trail brought us around the head of a deep canyon that snaked out to the west. 'Look down there!' Luke said, pointing. 'There's the trail in the canyon bottom, see it?'

There it was, far below, a white line across tan rocks. Between us and it was an immense slope like the inside of a bowl, all jumbled by stratification and erosion. 'How will we get down there?' David asked.

I had been wondering that myself; I couldn't see the trail anywhere on the canyon walls. Luke started walking again, to the right rather than down. 'The north side is less steep, the trail goes down there.' We traversed most of a mile around the head of the canyon, then left the trees and descended the wall by following hundreds of wide switchbacks in the trail. It was fun swinging around each hairpin turn, changing directions and views as we dropped deeper and deeper into the rocky canyon world . . .

More than an hour later we reached the canyon floor. The perspective was different down there; the broad prospect we had enjoyed up on the forested mountainside plateaux was gone, and now our view was confined to the walls of the canyon we were in. Above, white-blue sky. The canyon was a deep flat-bottomed river gorge, and the trail followed the shallow pebbly stream at the bottom. Green reeds, silvery shrubs, and small cottonwoods banked this meager stream. 'Cliff Canyon,' Luke told us. 'We'll stay in this one for a long time.'

We followed the stream in its descent, milepole after milepole. I sang *Onward, Christian Soldiers* to myself as a marching song, and discovered that if I took one step for every quarter note, the hymn took me exactly one hundred steps. This seemed to me clever planning on the part of the composer. I counted steps from one red pole to the next; 1,962 steps for a mile. Four more steps and I would have hit the year. I tried to step just a little bit smaller.

We stopped and had lunch at the pool where Cliff Canyon met Redbud Pass gorge. The surface of the pool had a perfect blue sheen to it, while under it polished pebbles gleamed pink and chocolate; and the two colors, satin blue and mottled pebblestone, coexisted without mixing, both completely filling the same surface. I stared at the impossible sight, entranced.

We made the abrupt right turn and hiked up Redbud Pass gorge, and it was unexpectedly tiring to go uphill at even that slight angle. But we came to a section of the canyon that was so narrow that we had to twist to get through some parts; for almost a mile we could touch both walls at once, and they rose straight up on each side for over four hundred feet, Luke said. The sky was no more than a blue ribbon atop these endless rock walls. It was such an extraordinary thing that we were all excited: Luke sang, 'Fat man's misereee!' and David and I laughed helplessly as we slipped along. We forgot we were tired, and hiked heads up until our necks hurt. Paul, bringing up the rear, had a big smile on his face: white teeth, brown skin in a million laugh lines: wild hawk face, enjoying the canyon once again, enjoying our first-time amazement.

The gorge of the pass opened up into Redbud Creek Canyon; we took a left turn and started down again. This canyon's stream made many big twists and turns, and the canyon walls S'ed with it, exposing hundreds of fluted sandstone columns, balancing boulders, smooth overhung curves, knobs like elephant heads.

I was getting a little too tired to really enjoy them, however, and poor David was beginning to drag indeed, when the canyon took a big oxbow bend to the left, and there in the outside wall of this bend was a bulge, a narrow horseshoe-shaped extension of the canyon into the cliffside. The cliff surrounding this bulge was a tall, curved, overhanging wall of rust-colored sandstone; the floor of it was flat, and just higher than the canyon floor proper. Underneath the great curving overhang was a stand of big old trees, a pool fed by a cold spring, several old picnic tables, a brick fireplace with a blackened grill on top, a stack of firewood, and scattered about, six old bedstands, stripped to metal.

'Here's camp!' Luke said, seeing our confused looks.

'But what about Rainbow Bridge?' I asked.

'It's just a little way down the canyon. Let's leave our stuff here and go have a look.'

Rainbow Bridge was less than a quarter mile away; we could see it for most of the walk there. A broad arch of sandstone, it began not up atop the canyon walls as I had expected, but down at their bases, to left and right as we approached. The canyon opened up quite a bit here, so the bridge was very wide, and it rose perhaps sixty feet over us. It was flat-sided, rounded on top and bottom, streaked with brown watermarks, and sure enough, it had a broad rainbow shape to it.

Though it was no later than five or six it was gloomy down in the canyon, the sun long gone and only shining on the very tops of the walls. The light tans and yellows of the sandstone around us were now brown, black, blood red. I stared up at the arch. Compared to the Golden Gate Bridge, for instance, it wasn't very big. And all day I had been walking under the most fantastic contortions of sandstone that wind and water could carve ... compared to that mad sculpture, the bridge was pretty basic stuff. But it *was* unusual; and pretty big; and when you considered that it had just *happened* out here, accidental-like ... and the way it loomed in the too-bright strip of evening sky, dark as stone – a stone rainbow, the reverse of an ordinary rainbow: slab-sided, massive, permanent ...

Luke walked around it in a fever of energy, snapping pictures with his little camera. 'I wish the light was better,' he said. 'We won't get much on film.' Paul was sitting on a rock, watching him with his eyelids crinkled, amused. 'This will probably be the last chance I get to photograph it in its natural state.'

'What's that?' I said.

'The lake. You remember? This canyon leads down to the Colorado River, about three or four miles away. But it's Lake

Powell now, you know, because of the Glen Canyon Dam. And the lake is still rising. This canyon is flooding, and they say you'll be able to boat right under the bridge in a couple of years.'

'You're kidding!'

'Nope. This'll be water, right here where we stand. It might even flood the whole bridge, although they say it won't.' Luke was matter-of-fact about it; that was just the way it was, nothing to get upset over, not when there was nothing to be done.

I glanced over at Paul. No expression on his face, none at all. The Navaho mask . . . he was looking up at the streaked sides of the arch. I walked under it again, on solid ground, and stared up at it. Massive rust band against the sky . . . it looked different, somehow.

That evening, as night fell and the stars appeared in the arc of sky standing over the cliffs, we started a fire in the brick fireplace and cooked hot dogs for dinner. The flames cast a warm, flickering yellow on the overhanging back wall. This smooth sweeping curve echoed our voices, and the crackling wood, and the low gurgle of the water leaving the spring's pool; it amplified the *whoo* of the wind flowing down-canyon.

We devoured the hot dogs, ate three or four apiece. Afterwards I walked around the camp a little. The big old trees had crumpled gray-green bark, gnarled branches, leaves as smooth and prickly-edged as holly leaves. The bare metal bedsteads gave the place the look of a ruin: giant cathedral, roof fallen in, trees growing up out of the floor, altar a fireplace, beds dragged in . . . The wind hooted and the sharp-edged leaves clattered, and feeling spooked I returned to the others.

After we had laid out our sleeping bags and gotten into them, I still felt . . . strange. I had chosen to sleep on one of the picnic tables, and was under one of the trees. Between the black leaves the stars appeared and disappeared, pricking at my sight, creating a sense of constant movement that was not necessarily in the leaves. There were a lot of little noises, echoing off the overhang. I had seldom if ever slept outdoors before, and it felt . . . exposed, somehow. Someone could just sneak right up on you! They could sneak up and murder all of us down here, and no one would know! Well, that was silly. But stuck so deep in this canyon, with the vault of the sky so far above the tree-filled black horseshoe bend, and the wind whistling over the rock, the world seemed a vast place: vast, dark, windy . . . I lay there for a long time before falling asleep.

I woke in the middle of the night, having to pee. Something in me resisted getting up: fear of the open darkness, clutching at me. But I had to go and I slid out of my sleeping bag and stepped off the picnic bench, walked down toward the bridge, out of the camp.

Once out from under the trees a great map of stars sheltered me. In their brilliance I recognized not a single constellation. It seemed the moon might be rising, or else the starlight was brighter here than I was used to; the canyon walls caught enough illumination to reveal some of their hieroglyphics of erosion. It was chill but not cold; I walked down the trail to take a brief look at the bridge in this strange light.

A man stood directly beneath the bridge, both arms raised to the sky. Paul . . . I recognized the gesture as that made by the solitary figure I had seen greeting the storm on the evening we had arrived – the figure that had disappeared! – and I understood that that had been Paul out there. He was some sort of . . . I didn't know what.

He turned around, aware of being watched, and saw me. Reluctantly I walked down the trail and joined him.

'You're up late,' I said.

'So are you.'

We stood there. As my eyes adjusted further to the dark – as the moon, perhaps, rose further in the blocked-off sky to the east – I could see his face better: crags of weathered flesh, shadowed fissures deeply scored; it looked like the sandstone around us. Water sounds, small but distinct, played between us; wind sounds, soft but large, soughed over us, as if the canyon were an immense flute that someone was breathing through . . . By moving my head a little I could make stars wink in and out of existence, there at the black edges of the arch.

'How can they flood this place?' I said quietly.

Paul shrugged. 'Build a dam ...'

'Oh, I know. I know. But ... can't you stop it?'

He shook his head.

'I wish you could ...'

'It doesn't matter.' I was about to protest that it did, when he raised a hand and held it out between us. A narrow silver ring blinked starlight, there on his little finger. 'The bridge is like the ring. Your people come to see it, on foot like you have, and soon by boat. Many people. But while the ring takes the attention like that, the rest of the hand – the rest of the body – it's all left alone.'

'You mean the reservation.'

'All the land here, all the canyons. This ring is precious, but it isn't the body. There are hundreds of canyons out here – canyons and mesas, mountains, rivers without an end to them. Arches, yes. To have all the attention on this bridge, all the visitors ... it's not such a bad thing.'

'I see. I understand.'

'Places only we know about are let be ... cliff dwellings.'

'Like the Inscription House ruin?' I said.

'Yes, like that. Only hidden. Never found, you see. Lost forever, perhaps. Let be forever.'

Then we were silent, listening to the great flute channel the wind. I thought of Rainbow Bridge as a giant stone ring, buried just a bit more than halfway into the earth. The light in the canyon grew ever stronger, though the sky to the east remained a pure black, the stars there wavering intensely in the shiver of the atmosphere.

'Do you think your son will ever come back?' I said.

He glanced at me, surprised. The wet surface of his eyes reflected tiny pinpoint stars. '... Yes,' he said finally. 'But when he does' – tapping his head with a finger – 'a part of him will be dead.'

My head felt as if he had tapped me, just over the ear. Quickened –

I woke from the dream with a start. It was dark, stars blinked in the black mesh of branches over me. The stiff, sharp-edged leaves clicked against each other. The dream hesitated on the leaf edge of oblivion – slipped back into my memory, intact. I thought about it.

I did have to pee. I got out of the sleeping bag, stepped off the picnic table, walked around the tree.

When I was done I rounded the tree and almost ran into him. 'Ah!' I leaped back, tripped, almost fell.

'Hey,' Paul said softly, helping me get to my feet. 'It's just me.' He let go of me, looked at me. In the dark I couldn't read his expression; I could barely see it. 'Still me.' He walked past me, toward his bedroll.

When I got back in my sleeping bag my heart was still thumping, as loud in my ears as snapped fingers. *Still me . . .* The side of my head tingled. I looked up at the patternless smeary white stars, sure it would take me hours to fall asleep again; but I don't recall staying awake for even so much as a minute.

The next morning we ate a breakfast of crackers and oranges, rolled our bags and packed our gear, poured water on the ashes of the fire, and took off. It was a warm morning, the cliff-rimmed patch of sky a clear pale blue. Paul didn't mention our encounter of the previous night; in fact he said hardly a word during breakfast, and led the way up the canyon without looking back. Luke, David and I followed.

It didn't take long to discover that hiking back up out of the canyons was harder than descending into them. Yesterday I hadn't even noticed how continuous the descent was; now every step up spoke to me. And at some 1,962 steps per mile . . . for fifteen miles . . . I couldn't finish the multiplication in my head, but I knew it was a lot of walking.

We had a short respite, going down the Redbud Pass gorge, and the narrow section was still wonderful; but once in Cliff Canyon it was uphill for good. The sun burst over the south wall of the canyon, and the day got hot. Frequently we stopped to drink. We stayed in the same order: Paul, me, David, Luke. I started to sing *Onward, Christian Soldiers* but looking at Paul's back before me I felt stupid doing it, and I stopped.

David was the first to give out; he sat down by a pool and

rolled onto his back. I was kind of proud of him: he had walked until he dropped, without a single word of complaint. A tough kid, my little brother.

We sat by the pool and considered it. David, nearly asleep where he lay, was clearly played out, Luke, unworried and cheerful, filled David's water cup at the pool. 'Why don't you two go on ahead,' he said to Paul and me. 'You can take Paul's truck back to the mission, and that way Aunt Miriam won't worry about us. I'll come up with David either late tonight, or tomorrow morning.'

Paul and I nodded, and after a short rest the two of us started off.

After about an hour of hiking behind Paul, watching Cliff Canyon broaden and open up, I saw the canyon's head. Before us stood a curved slope just as steep as the walls to right and left. This was where the trail had that long sequence of switchbacks, ascending the left wall, reaching the tableland above, and then skirting the canyon's rim up there, to a patch of piñon over on the top of the right wall. I could even see where the trail went, up among those tiny trees; it was so *far* above. I couldn't believe how far above it was; surely we hadn't come down from there!

Later I learned that the trailhead is three thousand feet higher than Rainbow Bridge; and a full fifteen hundred of those vertical feet are climbed right there, on the headwall of Cliff Canyon. At the time, it looked even taller than that. And the worst part of it, as far as I was concerned, was that the trail took such a gigantic detour to the left! It effectively doubled the distance we had to go to reach that patch of piñon pine on the top of the right wall. And all those dumb switchbacks, adding distance too . . . I couldn't believe it.

I was tired, I wanted an easier way. 'Listen,' I said to Paul, 'couldn't we just head straight up the right slope to where the trail goes through those trees? It isn't much steeper than the trail side, and we'd get it over with that much faster.'

Paul shook his head. 'The trail's the best way.'

But I had convinced myself, and stubbornly I argued to

convince him. 'You can see the whole slope from here to there – just dirt – no brush to walk through – nothing to it! It's just like a stairway all the way up! And then we wouldn't have to go way off the wrong way!' On and on I went.

Paul watched me without expression. No agreement with my points; no irritation that I would debate the best route with him; just an impassive gaze, staring at me. That look, becoming familiar: did it hide a laugh?

Finally, after I had repeated my points many times, he looked away, off into the distance. 'You go that way, then. I'll take the trail, and meet you up in those trees.'

'All right,' I said, happy to have my way. I thought it was an excellent plan. 'I'll see you up there.'

He turned and trudged up the dusty white trail.

It's hard for me now to believe that I could have been that stupid. To think a cross-country route would be easier than trail; to argue with a Navaho about the best way to get from one point to another, in Navaho country; to ignore Paul's judgment, and go off on my own ... incredible. But I was fifteen, and I was tired, and I wanted an easier way. I wished one into existence, and took off.

I started up the slope. The footing was good, and I made good progress. I imagined greeting Paul at the top when he finally appeared by way of the trail. I glanced over at the other side of the canyon to see how far he had gotten, but the trail followed a crease that was probably the streambed when it rained enough, and there was a bulge in the wall between my slope and that crease, so he was out of sight. I could still see the trees at the top, however; and after a short rest I pressed on.

The canyonside I ascended was sandstone. No doubt it had been formed as successive layers of some primordial beach, eons ago; in any case it was horizontally stratified, and this meant I climbed something very like an ancient staircase, weathered now almost out of existence. Stone ledges protruded from the angled slope of grainy dirt, giving me a few inches of flat surface to step up on. On the dirt itself it was harder; the angle stretched my

Achilles tendons, and there was a slight tendency to slip back that had to be resisted.

It was hot, and there was no wind. The sun blazed overhead so that a big quadrant of sky was too white to look at. I had to wipe sweat from my eyebrows to keep it from getting in my eyes and stinging. Once the dirt beneath my shoe gave way, and I went down to one knee, and got up with my sweaty hands all dirty.

Time passed. I began to zigzag a little to decrease the angle of the slope, and give my Achilles tendons a break. I was still low in the canyon. Looking up, I could no longer see all the way to the top; steep points in the slope along the way intervened, and became my temporary skyline. Luckily, the configuration of the slope itself kept me on course: I was climbing a sort of rounded ridge, and if I deviated too far to left or right, the angle of the slope became quite a bit steeper. So I was following the edge of an indistinct buttress (though I didn't know that), and thus I had a clear route.

Onward and upward. I began taking a rest every hundred steps. I had already come to the conclusion that the trail would have been easier: you could step flat on the trail, and you didn't slide backward half the time, and you didn't have to figure out which way to go every step of the way. I felt foolish, as one always does at the halfway station between innocence and experience. Blake missed that category: *Songs of Foolishness*.

The terracing of sandstone ledges began to get more distinct, and larger in scale. Instead of stairs, they were waist or chest high, as if they were stairs for giants, with vertical sections to them that were steeper than I was used to. So each ledge had to be climbed, or else I had to zigzag a route up the various dry gullies that broke through these ledges. It was hard work. Looking up I could usually only see a hundred feet or so at a time, and the view never changed; it kept on like that no matter how long I went between rests. The day got hotter.

I had no hat. I had no water. I had no food. I had no map, or compass (though they wouldn't have done me any good if I had had them). In fact, I had nothing but a cotton sleeping bag hanging from my shoulders, and its straps were really cutting into my arms. I couldn't see my destination anymore, but judging by the canyon below, and the great wall across from me, I still had a long, long way to go. And the way kept getting harder.

Slowly but surely, fear began to seep into me. What if I lost my way, and somehow missed the exact knot of piñon pines that marked where the trail was? It would be impossible to find the trail without that landmark. And then what if I couldn't go on without water, and couldn't find any? Or – I slipped hard and banged my knee on a ledge, which made me cry out with fear – what if I hurt myself so badly I couldn't walk? This slope was so immense, no one would ever find me on it.

I shoved these fears away and climbed on a bit faster, spurred by their presence, pushing in around the edges of conscious thought. But soon enough the surge of adrenaline they had caused was used up, by a hard scramble up a dry streambed. As I got more and more tired it became impossible to hold the fears out of my thoughts, and they came pouring back in. My head ached, in a tight band across the temples. My tongue was a thick, dry thing clogging my mouth; it tasted of dust, and I couldn't work up a bit of saliva. My breaths were like ragged sobs.

The sun had shifted far to the west, and the rocks threw shadows off to the left. The light had that ominous, dark brilliance that sometimes comes late in the day after a cloudless noon, with the lengthening shadows and a mare's tail or two of cloud in the sky. Above me the slope appeared to steepen, into a genuine staircase shape of horizontal, vertical, horizontal, but on a giant's scale, the little cliffs of the verticals now ten feet tall.

The time came when panic overwhelmed me. Not in a single rush, but in a growing crescendo of fear, that pushed, and pushed, and finally became *panic*, that flood of fear-beyond-fear, fear pushed up into another plane ... how to describe it? All my senses were heightened, though their input seemed malignant: I could feel tiny puffs of breeze chilling my sweat-soaked back, could see every individual pebble and sand grain, for as far as the canyons extended ... I could feel my breathing, all my muscles, my blood washing about in me, pumping hard through the heart. I knew that I could die, astonishing knowledge for a fifteen-year-old. But I also knew that I still lived, and could act.

Panic-stricken, in a sort of exuberance of fear, I climbed again, ignoring the complaints of my muscles and the niceties of the best route, scrambling hard where I had to, moving resolutely upward, attacking the obstacles furiously ... I suppose I had never been quite as alive as in those moments, ever in my life.

In fact I suppose that all my subsequent interest in the extremities of physical endurance, in the exploration of the bleak and harsh parts of the globe – the poles, the high mountains, the deserts – was born in those moments, when I felt the reality of such extremity myself. Ever afterwards I would know what it felt like to be pressed to the edge, I would remember the strange surge into that other world of panic spring ... and the memory of it creates a certain (is it morbid?) fascination ...

Unfortunately, purest panic cannot last very long, and when it washed out of me, step by weary step, I pressed on in dull misery. As I forced myself up I wondered what Paul would think when I died and never showed up.

His face, hawklike under the gleaming black hair, popped into sight over a ledge above me. 'Paul!' I cried. 'Here!'

He saw me and grinned. 'Glad to see you!'

'*You're* glad to see *me*! Wow – ' I laughed tearfully. 'I was hoping you'd look for me. I've been sort of lost down here ... .'

'There's still a way to go. Here, come up this way, up this crack.'

I followed his directions, almost giggling with relief. 'Oh, man,' I said, remembering the last hour. 'Oh, man!' I reached the ledge he was on and stood next to him. We looked at each other. Maybe this time there was the slightest expression on his face: a raised pair of eyebrows. Well, boy?

I shrugged sheepishly, looked down: 'How long did you wait for me?'

'An hour or so.'

'It – it was harder than it looked.'

'That's almost always true, around here. Get far enough away and you can't see ledges like this at all – they just look water streaks.'

'That's right! Why from below it looked like a smooth walk all the way.'

He didn't reply. We stood there. 'I think I can go on now,' I said.

He nodded. We started climbing the slope; I followed him, put my feet in his footprints, which saved me some sliding. Up and up, step after step. He stopped often so we could rest.

I was lucky he had come down to look for me, because the slope of the wall, like the inside of a bowl, got steeper as we approached the top. The vertical sections were now sometimes twelve or fifteen feet tall, while the flat ledges narrowed to little sitting platforms . . . Time after time Paul found breaks in these faces, footholds, dry streambeds, routes of one sort or another, so that using hands to pull ourselves, we could make our way up.

'Man, how did you get *down* here?' I asked during one rest.

'Same way we're going up – that's how I know the way. It's a lot easier seeing the way down. Harder to actually do it, but if you're patient it's not bad.'

On and up. We came to one cliff about fifteen or eighteen feet high – trouble. The only way up that didn't force a long detour was a sequence of knobs and notches that had to be climbed like a ladder. Paul climbed it and showed me the holds. I took a deep breath and started up after him; his head poked over the top as he watched me.

I was almost to him when my right foot slipped out of its niche. The other foot went too, and I was falling when he grabbed me by the wrist. One hand, clamped on my wrist, holding me up; I couldn't get a purchase on the sandstone I was knocking against. My hand caught his wrist, so we were twice linked.

'Be still.' I looked up; his neck muscles bulged out, his mouth was pursed. 'I pull you up to here, you grab the ledge with your other hand. Then get a knee over. Ready?'

'Yeah,' I gasped. I felt his hand crush my wrist as he prepared for the pull, and then I was scraped up the sandstone, and scrabbling for a handhold on the ledge, pulling up, left knee up and over, like high jumping – and I was on the ledge, face in the gritty dirt. Paul was sprawled back on the ground, still holding on to my wrist. He sat up, smiling a small smile.

'You okay?'

I nodded breathlessly, looking at the white finger marks on my wrist. I didn't want to start crying, so I didn't say anything.

'We'll find a better way up any others like that. Come on.'

I staggered up and followed him. True to his word, we were able to climb gulleys to make it up every vertical slab. I was thankful; by this point I was past any extra efforts. It was hard just to walk.

Then the slope tilted back, got easier. We snaked up a little gully that was like a miniature of the canyons below. And we came out of the top of it into trees – piñon pines, on flat sandy ground. The top. And there, just by the first trees, threading its way among them, was the trail, a wide whitish trough.

'Oh, good,' I said.

Paul stopped in the trail and we rested. He saw the look on my face and said, 'Cross-country can be hard.'

I nodded mutely.

'The hard way can teach you a thing or two, though. Here. You lead. Set whatever pace you're comfortable with. We still have a way to go.'

It was true, but I didn't care. We were on the trail. I walked along it zombielike. It was amazing how easy it was to walk on a trail; no decisions to make at all, no terrible stretch of foot and Achilles tendon ... wonderful thing, trail. How long had I been off it? Four hours, five? It seemed much longer than that, but the sun still shone, there was a good deal of daylight left; it couldn't have been more than five hours. What a lot of living to fit into such a small span! What a lot of appreciation for trail, to have gained in only five hours!

I was hiking along the trail through the pines, and half thinking thoughts such as these, when I rounded a corner and saw Paul lying there ahead of me, sacked out asleep under a tree, his cowboy hat shading his face.

I jerked to a stop, spun around. No Paul following me on the trail. I had heard his steps behind me just a moment before.

I turned again, confused. The Paul under the tree heard me, tipped up his cowboy hat, saw me. He sat up, calm and slow. 'You made it,' he said.

274

I felt the skin on my back crawl. I began to tremble, and for a second light-headedness washed through me, almost made me sick. My vision returned with scores of crawling clear tubes in it. 'How – how long have you been here?'

He shrugged. 'An hour or so. You get lost?'

I shook my head. 'You didn't ...' I couldn't finish.

He stood, put on his pack, came over and looked at me. He cocked his head curiously ... something in his look, there ... not complicity, but perhaps an acknowledgment that I had a right to be confused ...

'Here,' he said. 'Want me to take that sleeping bag?'

'You won't m – you won't mind?' Because my shoulders were aching fiercely under the straps.

He smiled a little – just exactly the smile he had had on his face after he pulled me up the cliff. My wrist tingled with the memory of that crushing grip, and when he touched my arm to slip the sleeping bag off, I almost cried out, I sat down right on the spot, trembling all over, my skin rippling in great shivers of nervous shock, of fear. Rippling fields of goose bumps ... 'But I ...' But I was too frightened of him to be able to ask him anything. I looked back the way I had come, thinking he might still appear; yet here he was before me, taking off his pack, tying my sleeping bag to the top of it ...

He got it secured, put the pack back on. He looked at me, concerned. 'It's okay.'

I wiped the tears from my face. Nodded, looking down, ashamed. It was emphatically not okay. But there was nothing for it but to stand, to follow him down the trail.

He stepped in front of me, caught my ashamed gaze, reached out and touched my arm with a single finger. 'It's okay, now.' Something in his voice, his eyes – as if he knew everything that had happened ...

My shivering stopped, I nodded meekly. 'Okay. Let's go.'

But all the way back I thought of it. The trailhead was a long way across the tableland, and it was a miserable hike, through the long shadows of the last part of the day, sky already darkening with the sun still up, lenticular cloud over Navaho

Mountain glowing the color of the canyons, every little wave of it a perfectly drawn French curve ... Cruelly, the Park Service had set the red milepoles farther and farther apart the closer to the trailhead you came; I hadn't noticed on the way in. I tried counting steps one to the next and lost count in the first hundred.

Maybe he had gone down to get me, then as we hiked up the trail, had snuck ahead through the trees to lie down and give me a surprise. Only he couldn't have: the trail cut through a sort of notch there, with thick forest on each side. From the time I last saw the Paul behind me until the first moment I saw the Paul under the tree, only a couple of minutes had elapsed. There just wasn't time for such a maneuver. No ... I began to shiver again. Each time I forced myself to truly confront the memory of what had happened, I was racked with electric shivers running up and down my back, then all over me, and the spasm shook my head violently, as if my spine were a branch and my head a fruit, orange or apple or pear, that someone was trying to bring down ...

In a garish desert sunset we reached the trading post, the parking lot. The trading post was open, and we went in. While Paul spoke in Navaho I went to the big cooler in the corner, one of those refrigerated metal trunks that stands waist high. I flipped the top hatch open and pulled out a Nehi Grape drink; pulled off the flip top and drank it down in two long swallows. I can still remember perfectly the strange carbonated grape flavor of that drink. When I was done I got out another can and drank it too.

Paul drove us home through the dusk, his pickup's big headlight beams bouncing about in tandem as we hit potholes in the asphalt. I was too tired to think much, but once the sight of Paul lying there under that tree, hat over his face, flashed before me, and the goose bumps rippled over me again, like the wind shooting cat's paws over the surface of a lake. My whole nervous system resonated with fear, I once again felt his hand clamped on my wrist, my knees scraping the sandstone, feet free in the air, searching for purchase ... I've never had a better demonstration of how completely our skins are linked to our minds. Then the fit passed, and I slumped in the seat again, sweating, watching the headlight beams lance the darkness.

Maybe I had gone crazy. Yeah, that was it: I had gone crazy and hallucinated Paul's presence with me on that canyonside. And I must have hallucinated that fall, too, because if I really had fallen it was certain no hallucination was going to catch me and pull me up. Sure. The whole thing, just a frightened sunstruck dream.

The only trouble was, I knew that it hadn't been. Oh, I know, you can say if you went crazy then you were crazy, and you couldn't tell what was real and what wasn't. But that isn't the way it works, not in the real world. I mean, that's the sad thing about insane people; almost all of them know perfectly well that something is seriously wrong with them; that's what makes them so scared, so depressed. They know.

And I knew, I *knew*, that I had not hallucinated that slip and fall, or the hand on my wrist. It was all a seamless whole, from the start up the slope to the finish in the trees, and no anxious half hour – not even a half hour of panic – could have made me so crazy that my senses could have been fooled that badly. Later, when the memory faded some, I could doubt that point; but there in the truck with Paul, my wrist still aching, the whole memory of it still in my body, I was certain of it.

Finally we were back at the mission. Aunt Miriam came out to greet us, and we told her about Luke and David. Paul said he'd go back up the next day to make sure they got out all right; he glanced at me as he said it. And he smiled as he said good night, that small smile I had seen before ... For a second I saw in his eyes a clear acknowledgment of what had happened. And I understood: Paul was an Indian sorcerer, he could be in two places at once. But then he was gone, and I wasn't so sure.

I found that my skin could ripple with goose bumps even immersed in the hot water of my aunt's old bathtub; all I had to do was remember that look, that smile, the moment on the cliff face, seeing Paul under that piñon ... Despite my exhaustion, I slept very poorly that night; I kept jerking awake as I slipped off the face ... and it would all come pouring in again, until I moaned at the bright fresh fear of it. Would it never ease, this fear?

* * *

The next day about noon Luke and David drove up in Luke's VW, laughing over great adventures of their own: Luke had carried David part of the way, they had slept in the trail, Luke had hiked to the trading post and back in the middle of the night, to make sure no one was waiting and worrying ... These adventures sounded quite mundane to me. Luke had already heard some of what had happened to me from Paul, and he laughed at my silence, thinking I was only embarrassed at ignoring Paul's advice and taking off cross-country. I imagine I didn't show much of a sense of humor about it.

The day after that it was time to leave. Luke was going to drive us all the way to Phoenix to catch a plane, and then come all the way back; he was looking forward to the drive.

We were out front saying our good-byes to Aunt Miriam when Paul drove up in his truck. Only later did it occur to me that he had come specifically to say good-bye to us. To me. Only later did I recall we were driving through Flagstaff, only later did I put it together, that for Paul I was ... I don't know what, exactly.

He got out, walked over. Same jeans, same shirt ... He smiled at David and me, shook our hands. I recognized the grip, recognized it exactly. He looked me in the eye, nodded once, solemnly, as if to confirm my thought: *it happened*. He tapped the side of his head with his finger. 'That was a good hike,' he said to me. 'Remember.'

We got into the VW. As we drove off, Paul and Miriam stood side by side, waving – Paul looking right at me, nowhere else – and the two of them had identical expressions on their faces, that expression you see in the faces of your older relatives, as you wave good-bye to them after an infrequent, too-short visit; they're fond of you, they love you, they look at you with an honesty only the old have, thinking this might be the last good-bye, the last time they will ever get to see you: *pleasure; sorrow; will I see that one again before I die?*

Remember. Many years have passed since that happened; my great-aunt Miriam died in 1973, and as it turned out I never did

278

see her again. And I never heard another word of my friend Paul, from that time to this.

But I've thought about him, oh believe me I have: and every single time I have brought myself to think honestly about it, to remember it truly and admit to myself that such an impossible thing happened to me, my skin has reacted with its fearful shivered rippling; just a ghost of the original fear in its power to shake me, but still most definitely there, a cold, uncanny contact with ... something *other*. Even writing this account, here in a quiet room halfway around the world, nineteen years away, I have felt that shiver – once, in fact, as strongly as any since the first time: the room disappeared, and I was back there in those pines, Paul lying there ...

Naturally I have attempted, many times, to explain to myself what happened that afternoon. I have read of the Indian shamans of the Southwest with more than the usual interest, and recalling the masks and jugs I glimpsed so briefly at Paul's hogan, I suspect he could have been one. The Navaho are a pretty secular people, but Paul had business with the Hopi, unusual for a Navaho; and you don't get any stranger than the Hopi. And the Navaho treated Paul differently, too, he had a sort of power over them ... People are skeptical of Castañeda, and I suppose they should be – I probably would be too – but sometimes when I was reading those books, that shaman spoke right to me, through a face I knew ... Yes, it could be I was befriended by a shaman, and shown a little of the world beyond.

And of course the idea has returned to me, often, that I hallucinated Paul's presence, in my fear and need calling up his image to get me up the last, most difficult part of the climb. Sure. It's the explanation that makes the most sense, the one I believe in myself most often. But ... a hallucinated figure, an imagined conversation, those are one thing; a hallucinated cliff face, an imagined fall? For me, somehow, those are in a different category; and I have never been able to believe that I was that completely disconnected from reality. Because that *hand on my wrist*! My God, how to tell it? I was hanging there in space, falling, and that hand on my wrist *pulled me up*. It pulled me up to safety, to the life I have lived since then ... And I *felt it*.

So. In the end, I always have to let it be. Something strange happened to me, out there in the desert; I don't know what.

But lately, when I think about it, I always see the look that was on Paul's face as we drove away from the mission, and out of his life. And I see him trying to jump the giant gap between our lives, to teach me a little, mostly with looks; I see him letting me hike off on my own; I feel that hand on my wrist, pulling me up ... And now when I remember that impossible moment, I have been filled with some sort of huge, cloudy feeling – call it grace: my spirit has soared at the thought of it, flying like a shaman over the surface of this world, exhilarated and intensely happy. Either way it was a gift, you see; a gift from Paul, or from the world. Because consider it: if Paul was a shaman, and out of his feeling for me sent his spirit down that canyon wall to help me up, while the rest of him slumbered there in the sun under a piñon pine – then human beings have mysterious powers that we poor civilized rational people are unaware of, and we are much greater than we know. But if, on the other hand, I imagined Paul's presence there above me, if only I was there to clasp myself as I fell, so that I pulled myself up that cliff, by the power of my mind, and by the strength of my desire to live – then we are free indeed.

The Translator

Owen Rumford had a breakfast of postage stamp glue and mineral water. Combination of a rather strict diet and the fact that it was time again to send the bills to all the citizens of Rannoch Station. Rumford himself had had the stamps printed, and now he carefully counted out payment for them and shifted the money from the tavern's register to the postmaster strongbox, kept under the bar. A bit silly using stamps at all, since Rumford was the mailman as well as the postmaster – also the town's banker, tavern and hotel keeper, judge, and mayor. So he would be delivering the bills himself. But he liked stamps. These had a nice picture of Rannoch seen from space, all gray ocean with a chunk of onyx in it. Besides, in a town as small and isolated as Rannoch Station it was important to keep up the proprieties. Good for morale. Must, however, consider upgrading the quality of the stamp glue.

A quiet morning in the empty tavern. Hotel above empty as well; nothing had come in to the spaceport in the last few days. Unusual. Rumford decided to take advantage of the rare lull and go for a walk. On with his heavy orange overcoat. Tentlike. Rumford was a big man, tall and stout. Big fleshy face, cropped black hair, big walrus moustache that he tugged at frequently, as he did now while bidding a brief farewell to his daughters. Out into the stiff cold onshore wind. Felt good.

Down the black cobblestones of Rannoch Station's steep main street. Hellos to Simon the butcher, chopping away at a flank of mutton; then to the McEvoys, who helped administer the mines. Pleasant sound of construction behind the general store, tinsmiths and stonemasons banging and clacking away. Then left at the bottom of the street where it crossed the stream, up the track of hard black mud until he was out of the town and on the low hills overlooking the sea.

All views on the planet Rannoch were a bit dark. Its sun, G104938, known locally as the Candle, cast a pale and watery light. And the hills of Rannoch Island – the planet's only continent, located in subarctic latitudes – were composed mostly of black rock, mottled with black lichen and a bit of black bracken, all overlooking a dark sea. The dirt between stones had a high component of carbon ash, and even the perpetual frost on the bracken had gray algae growing in it. In short, only the white wrack thrown onto the black sand by the black waves gave any relief to the general gloom. It was a landscape you had to learn to be fond of.

Rumford had. Sniffing at the cold wind he observed with satisfaction the waves mushing onto the beach below the town. All the dories out fishing except the spavined ones, drawn up above the high tide mark. The town sitting above them nice and cozy, tucked into the crease made by the stream's last approach to the sea, to get out of the perpetual wind. Houses and public buildings all made of round black stones, some cracked open to reveal white quartz marbling. Materials at hand. Roofs were tin, glinted nicely in the low rays of the late morning sun. Tin mined here for local use, not for export. They had found deposits of the ore next to the big manganese mines. Easy to work it. Slag heaps inland of the town just looked like more hills, fit in very nicely in fact. Helped block the wind. Bracken already growing on them.

Altogether satisfactory. 'A wild and unearthly place,' as the song said. Rumford remembered trees from his childhood on a faraway planet, name forgotten. Only thing he missed. Trees, wonderful things. Would be nice for the girls. He'd told them tales till they'd cried for trees, for picnics in a grove, even though they hadn't the slightest. Flowering ones, perhaps. Grow in the ravines the streams cut, perhaps. Out of the wind. Worth thinking about. Damned difficult to get hold of, though; none native to this star cluster, and they were something traders out here didn't usually deal in. A shame.

Rumford was still thinking of trees when the steep black waves sweeping onto the town beach burst apart, revealing a submarine craft apparently made to roll over the sea floor. Big, dull green metal, lot of wheels, a few small windows. Some of the Ba'arni again, making a visit. Rumford frowned. Bizarre creatures, the Ba'arni. Inscrutable. It was obvious to Rumford that they were as alien to Rannoch as humans were, though he'd never gotten a Ba'ar to admit it. Good traders, though. Fishing rights for plastics, metal nodules gathered off seafloor for refined product, deep sea oddities for machine parts and miscellaneous utensils. Still, what they got from Rannoch Station wasn't enough to sustain an undersea colony. And how start it?

Aliens were strange.

The sea tank rolled above the high water mark and stopped. Door on one side clanked open, becoming a ramp. Three Ba'arni trotted out, one spotted him and they veered, trundled toward him. He walked down to meet them.

Strange looking, of course. The fishermen called them sea hippos, talked about them as if they were intelligent ocean-going hippopotami, nothing more. Ludicrous. The usual fallacy when dealing with aliens: think of them as the terran species they most resemble. Let it go at that. Rumford snorted at the idea. Really only the heads looked like hippos. Bodies too of course, to a limited extent. Massive, foursquare, rounded, etc. But the analogy held up poorly when you examined the fine bluish fur, the square dextrous fingers on all four feet, and of course the row of walnut-sized excrescences that protruded from their spines. Purpose unknown. Like mushrooms growing out of their backs. Not a pleasant sight.

Then again the pictures of hippos Rumford had seen were none too beautiful. Still, in hippos' eyes, even in pictures, you could see something you could understand. Expression maybe hostile, but perfectly comprehensible. Not so with a Ba'ar. Faces quite hippo-like, sure. Giant faces, butt ugly as the fishermen said. The eyes did it – round and big as plates, and almost as flat. And with a look in them you just couldn't read. Curious, that. The fishermen claimed to see them swimming free in the depths, above seafloor mansions of great size. That was after they'd had a few, but still. Obviously alien to Rannoch, nothing more advanced than bracken here. At least on the land. Different in the planet-wide ocean, perhaps; evolutionary advances all submarine, perhaps down in tropics? Impossible to say. But probably visitors, like the humans. Urge to travel fairly wide-spread among intelligent species. Spaceships filled with seawater. Funny thought.

The three Ba'arni stopped before Rumford. The one on the left opened his voluminous mouth and made a short sequence of whistles and clicks. From experience Rumford knew this was the usual greeting given him, meaning something like 'Hello, trading co-ordinator.' Unfortunately, he usually relied on his translation box to make the actual sound of his response, and though he knew what it sounded like he didn't find it easy making the sounds himself. And the box was back at the tavern.

He gave it a try and made the first few clicks that the box emitted when he typed in his usual hello. Then he added another click-combination, meaning, he thought, 'Trade, interrogative?'

The Ba'ar on the left replied swiftly. Trade negative, he appeared to say. Something else, well, Rumford had relied too often on the box to do the exact listening, but it seemed to him they were referring to the box itself.

Rumford shrugged. Only one course. He tried the whistle for translation, added the English words 'Rannoch Station,' and pointed to the town.

Agreement clicks from the spokesBa'ar.

Sonic booms rolled over the hills. They all looked up; Rannoch's gray sky was split by white contrails. Landing craft, coming down in a very steep descent from orbit, toward the town's spaceport a couple of miles inland. Rumford identified the craft by their extreme trajectory. Iggglas.

Then an extraordinary thing happened; all three of the Ba'arni rose up on their hind legs and took swipes at the sky, roaring louder than the sonic booms.

A bad sign. One time it had taken a shotgun blast to get a pack of Iggglas off a lone Ba'ar outside the tavern. Never understood the motive; only time he had ever seen the two species together. Not a good omen. And if the Ba'arni needed translation help –

The three of them returned to all fours with a distinct thump, then more or less herded Rumford down the track to the town. Not much chance of disagreement with them; they were remarkably fast on their feet, and must have weighed a couple of tons each. Drafted.

Rumford entered his tavern and got the translation box from the shelf behind the bar. It was an old bulky thing, in many ways obsolete; you had to type in the English half of things, and it would only translate between English and the alien languages in its program – no chance of any alien-to-alien direct contact. Made for some trouble in the tavern.

Without explanation to his daughters he was out the door. Again the Ba'arni herded him up the street. Quickly they were out of town in the other direction, onto the stony windswept road leading to the spaceport and the mines beyond.

They were still hurrying up this road, the Ba'arni moving at a brisk trot and Rumford loping, when they came round a hill and ran into a party of Iggglas. A dozen or so of them, flapping about the road and squawking loudly. The Ba'arni froze in their tracks and Rumford stumbled to a halt out in front of them.

He shuddered as he always did on first sight of an Igggla. They were beyond ugly; they were . . . well, beyond words. Languages, human languages at any rate, depend a great deal on analogies. Most abstract ideas are expressed by sometimes hidden analogies to physical things and processes, and most new things are described by analogies to older things. Naturally all these analogies are to things within human ken. But analogies to the human realm largely broke down when dealing with the Iggglas, for there was simply nothing to compare them to.

Still, Rumford thought. Analogies are all we have, after all. Especially for things alien. So the Iggglas were inevitably compared to vultures, because of body configuration. Fine except that their skins were covered by a white mucus substance instead of feathers. And their wings were not so much for flying as for hitting things. And their heads were distinctly fishlike, with long underslung jaws that made them resemble gars. Vultures with gars' heads, covered in whitish mucus: fair enough, only the analogy didn't really do justice to their sickening quality. Because above all they were *alien*, weird and hideous beyond appearance alone. Not even sure they occupied the same reality as other creatures; they seemed to *flicker* a little, as if disturbing the membrane between their physical realm and ordinary space-time. Yes; disgusting. Next to them the Ba'arni seemed handsome beasts. Almost family one might say.

Rumford stepped forward to offer some kind of greeting to the Iggglas, make sure the Ba'arni didn't have to. Touchy situation. He had dealt with Iggglas before; they came from the next planet in, and used Rannoch Station as a trade center. Trade again. Remarkable what kind of thing it put you in contact with, out in this stellar group. Certainly had to get used to these creatures. Language of theirs very loud and squawky. Every once in a while they'd spit in each other's mouths for emphasis. Some kind of chemical transfer of information. Box wasn't equipped to deal with that, luckily. Their speech was enough, although it appeared to be an odd grammar. Lacked tenses, or even verbs for that matter. Another indication of different reality.

The Iggglas liked to stick out a claw and shake humans by the hand, maybe to see if they would vomit. But Rumford could do it with hardly a quiver. No worse than a cockroach in the hand, certainly. So he shook hands with the wet claw of the biggest Igggla. Hot bodies, high metabolism. It turned its head to the side to inspect him with its left eye. Foul smell, like asfoetida.

Two of the other Iggglas led a long string of little furball creatures, a bit like rabbits without legs, up to the one Rumford had shaken hands with. Rumford sighed. Probably the high metabolisms, but still. Note the others weren't doing it –

Abruptly the biggest one snapped that gar's head down and devoured the first rabbit-thing in line, swallowing it whole so that it disappeared instantly, as in a conjuring trick. The Igggla would interrupt itself to do the same throughout the rest of the interview. It made Rumford nervous.

The Igggla squawked loudly and at length. 'Croownekkk-seetrun-p!' it sounded like. Rumford turned on the translator, switched it to *Iggglas* and typed in the message, *Again, please*.

After a short interval the box made a short screech. With a loud honk and a quick drumming of its talon-like feet, the big Igggla squawked its initial message again.

A moment later a message appeared in print on the small screen of the translator box. *Hunger interrogative*.

The Iggla batted one of the worried-looking rabbit-things forward.

No thank you, Rumford typed steadily, and waited for the box to speak. Then: *Why do you come to Rannoch interrogative.*

The head Iggla listened to the box's hooting, did a quick hopping dance, struck one of the other Igglas in the head, and replied.

The box's screen eventually produced a sentence. *Warlike viciously now descendant death fat food flame death.*

A typical grammatical artifact produced by the box when dealing with the Igglas. Rumford pondered it, switched the box to *Ba'arni*, and typed in *The Igglas express a certain hostility toward the Ba'arni.*

The box whistled and clicked in the oddly high-pitched Ba'arni language. The Ba'ar on the left, which was not the same one that had spoken to Rumford at first, whistled and clicked in reply. The box's screen printed out, *Tell them we are ready to (x-click b-flat to c-sharp click sequence; see dictionary) and the hateful poison birds will die in traditional manner.*

Hmm. Problems everywhere. With the Igglas you got grammatic hash. With Ba'arni, too many trips to the dictionary. Which was a problem in itself. The box was not entirely satisfactory, and that was the truth. Needed to be seated to type on the keyboard properly, too. So, despite the fact that it might seem undignified, Rumford sat on the ground between the two parties of aliens, called up the Ba'arni dictionary function of the box, and typed in an inquiry. The definition appeared quickly:

X-click B-flat to C-sharp click sequence: 1. Fish market. 2. Fish harvest. 3. Sunspots visible from a depth of 10 meters below the surface of the ocean on a calm day. 4. Traditional festival. 5. Astrological configuration in galactic core.

Rumford sighed. The Ba'arni dictionary could be nearly useless. Never sure if it was really serious. No idea who actually wrote the thing. Basic programming provided by linguists working for the company that made the box, of course, but in the years since then (and it was a very old box), its various owners had entered new information of their own. In fact this one was jammed with languages that factory-new boxes didn't have. No other box Rumford had seen had a Ba'arni program; that was why Rumford had bought this one when it was offered by a passing spacecraft pilot. But who in fact had added the Ba'arni program? Rather puckish individual, from the look of it. Or perhaps the Ba'arni relied more than most on context. Some languages like that. Impossible to be sure. The box had worked to this point, and that was all Rumford could say about it. Trade a different matter, however. Not quite as delicate as this.

After thinking it over, Rumford typed in another question to the Ba'arni. *Clarification please. What do you mean by x-click, b-flat to c-sharp click sequence, in context of previous sentence interrogative.*

The Ba'arni listened and the one on the left replied.

Ba'arni and poison birds fight was in (z-click double sequence; see dictionary) cycle that now returns. Time for this ritual war.

Very good. Clear as a bell. Unfortunate message, of course, but at least he understood it. Must have meant definition four, perhaps tied to the timing of three, or five. Add new definition later.

Before he could convey the Ba'arni sentiments to the Igggglas, the chief Igggla ate another rabbit-thing, danced in a circle and screeched for quite some time. The box hummed a bit, and the screen flickered.

Fine fiery wonderful this land always again war's heat slag battlefield dead fat food flame death yes now.

Rumford squinted at the screen.

Finally he typed in, *Clarification please: where is location of ritual war interrogative*, and sent it to the Igggglas.

The chief Igggla replied at length, howling shrilly.

On the screen: *Fine fiery wonderful this land always again war's heat slag battlefield dead fat food flame death yes now yes.*

The Igggglas were not much on clarification.

Rumford decided to ask the same of the Ba'arni, and switched the box over. *Clarification please: where is location of ritual war interrogative.*

The box whistled, the Ba'ar on the left clicked. The screen flickered and printed out: *Clarification unnecessary as poison birds know every twelve squared years for twelve cubed years ritual dodecimation has taken place on same ritual*

290

ground. Tell them to stop wasting time. We are ready for conflict.
A small vertical line appeared between Rumford's eyebrows.
He switched back and forth from Iggglas to Ba'arni, asking questions concerning this ritual war, explaining that the questions were essential for proper translation. Every Iggglas answer a long string of violent nouns, adjectives, and so forth, with never a verb. Every Ba'arni answer a hunt through the dictionary. Slowly Rumford put together a picture of Ba'arni and Iggglas contingents battling each other. Ritual phrases from the Ba'arni concerned *Air people opposition water people destruction land*, and so on. The Iggglas concentrated on *fat food*, although obviously it was a ritual for them as well – a sort of game, from the sounds of it. The origins of such a curious conflict remained completely obscure to Rumford; some things the Ba'arni said seemed to indicate that they may have had a religious ceremony of coming out onto land in great numbers during maximum sunspot activity, and that for many cycles now the Iggglas had been there to transform this ceremony into a bloody battle. Possibly indicating that the Ba'arni were in fact not native to Rannoch, as Rumford had speculated earlier. But he couldn't be sure. No way of knowing, really. Accident, misunderstanding; no doubt they themselves didn't have the faintest anymore.

In any case ritual war well established, this was clear. And either during or after the battle – sequentiality was difficult to determine, given the lack of tenses in the Iggglas – the two belligerent forces apparently torched, in a kind of sacrifice, the profane land they fought on.

Hmm. Rumford sat cross-legged on the ground between the two groups, thinking. Rannoch Station had only been there for the past thirty years or so. All that carbon in their dirt, sign of great fires in the past. But mining geologists said no vulcanism. Tremendous heat, one said. Solar flares? Or weapons. Tremendous heat. Tin would melt. It was possible. And after all, here they were.

Rumford cleared his throat. Sticky. He hesitated for a bit, and would have hesitated more, but some thirty sets of alien eyes (counting the rabbit-things) stared fixedly at him, and impelled him to action. He tugged his moustache. Sunspots underwater, astrology ... really a shame he didn't know more about these creatures. Now where was he? Ah yes – Ba'arni had indicated readiness for conflict. We are ready for conflict. The line between his eyebrows deepened, and finally he shrugged. He clicked the box over to *Iggglas* and typed away.

Ba'arni explain that their priest-caste have performed submarine astrology which contra-indicates ritual war this time. Request war be postponed until next scheduled time twelve squared Rannoch years from now in order to achieve proper equilibrium with the stars.

The box honked that out in a series of Iggglasian words. All the Iggglas listeners snapped their big gar jaws as they heard it, then leaped in circles thrashing the dust. Several of the rabbit-things disappeared. The chief Igggla hopped toward Rumford and shrieked for a long while.

On the screen: *War heat slag death fat food exclamation. Delay impossible war as scheduled astrology stupid exclamation.*

Rumford tugged his moustache. Not gone over so well. The three Ba'arni were staring at him curiously, waiting for him to translate what the Iggglas had just so vehemently squawked. The line between his eyebrows deepened even more. Ba'arni had visited him more frequently in the last year. Now what had they been trading for?

He switched the box to Ba'arni, typed *Iggglas state that they do not want ritual war to take place this time. They note the Ba'arni are suffering famine and therefore population difficulties. Thus ritual dodecimation could lead to extinction of Ba'arni and end of beloved war for Iggglas. They suggest skipping this time and returning to war next twelve squared years.*

A lot of clicks and whistles to convey that. The Ba'arni retreated and conferred among themselves, while the Iggglas squawked derisively at them. Rumford watched anxiously. Ba'arni had been trading rather actively for foodstuffs. Brow needed wiping. He tugged on his moustache. The Ba'arni returned in a new line-up and the one on the left clicked.

On screen: *Ba'arni completely capable of sustaining their part in (x-click b-flat to c-sharp click sequence; see dictionary). Ba'arni (z-click z-click; see dictionary) insist ritual be carried out as always. Poison birds will die.*

Rumford let out a deep breath, switched the box to dictionary function and inquired about z-click z-click.

Z-click z-click: 1. (double n-1 click sequence, B-flat; see dictionary). 2. Magnetic sense located in supra-spinal nerve nodules. 3. Eggs. 4. Large bearings. 5. Sense of place or of location. 6. Money.

Nothing there seemed completely appropriate, so he tried looking up double n-1 click sequence, B-flat.

Double n-1 click sequence, B-flat: 1. (Q-click A-flat; see dictionary.) 2. Honor. 3. Pride. 4. Shame. 5. Face. 6. Molar teeth.

Bit of an infinite regress there, could have you jumping around the dictionary forever. Definitely a prankster, whoever had entered this language in the box. But assume the Ba'arni meant some kind of pride, saving face, that kind of thing. Made sense. Every species must have a version of the concept. Fine. Assume clarification on that front. Now, where was he with the Iggglas? Looking fairly ready for an answer, they were. Rumford pursed his lips so hard that his moustache tops almost met under his chin. Astrologer bit not gone over very far. Iggglas pretty aggressive types. He clicked over to Iggglas and typed away.

Ba'arni live by submarine astrologer's divine words and intend to decline ritual war. Iggglas insistence will make no difference. Ba'arni have assured this by placement of heat bombs on floor of all seas on Iggglas. Twelve squared heat of weapons used in ritual war. If Iggglas insist on ritual war Ba'arni have no choice but to escalate to total war and annihilate Iggglas seas. Apologies but astrologers insist.

While the box spoke this message in Iggglas (and how was it doing it without verbs?), Rumford pulled a handkerchief from his coat pocket and wiped his brow. Uncommonly warm. Hunger made him feel a bit weak. Have to start eating breakfasts.

The Iggglas began to squawk among themselves very vigorously, and Rumford took a quick glance down at the screen to see if the box was translating their squabble. It was, although apparently it was having problems with the fact that two or three of the Iggglas were always speaking at the same time: *Lying fat*

*food no meteor shower maybe total war then purpose ambiguous
no exclamation one miss translator liar idiot meteor shower no
explanation maybe box direct Iggglas fat food why not meteor
shower maybe*, and so on. Rumford tried to direct one eye to
the screen and the other to the hopping Iggglas. Looked like the
second-largest one might be making the comments about the
translator and the box. Yes, even pointing at him as he spat in
leader's mouth. Problem.

The Ba'arni were whistling among themselves, so Rumford
quickly typed in another message to the Iggglas:

*Ba'arni wish to deal with senior Igggla, suggest that perhaps
second-biggest Igggla is one qualified to speak for Iggglas in this
matter.*

The box squawked this out and Rumford helpfully pointed to
the Igggla he had in mind. The chief Igggla took in the import
of the message and shrieked, leaped in the air, jumped at his
lieutenant and beat him with a flurry of quick wing blows.
Knocked the squealing creature flat and faster than Rumford
could see had the lieutenant's skinny vulture-neck between his
long toothy jaws. The lieutenant squeaked something dismal and
was allowed to live; it crawled to the back of the group of Iggglas.
The leader then strode forward and spoke to Rumford and the
Ba'arni.

On the screen: *Astrology stupid war heat fat food death always
compact between Iggglas and fat food change never good annihilation of home planet outside compact realm of total war insistence
on ritual war heat fat food death.*

Rumford's brow wrinkled as he read this. Getting nowhere
with the garheads. After a moment's thought he switched the
box to Ba'arni, and typed in, very carefully, the following:

*Iggglas understand Ba'arni capable of sustaining ritual war and
intend no slur on Ba'arni (double n-1 sequence, B-flat).* Possibly
it was a mistake to try directly for Ba'arni terms to add power
to the message. Box could mess it up entirely, in context of
sentence. He typed on: *Iggglas too have sense of honor and save
face by suggestion that Ba'arni weakness is only source of problem
in ritual war, but Iggglas also have famine trouble, and demand
ritual war be postponed twelve squared years to keep both Iggglas*

and Ba'arni in sufficient numbers to sustain ritual war in perpetuity. Suggest mutual expression of honor (exclamation) by recognition of ritual promise for next time.

Clicks and whistles, the Ba'arni listening with their big hippo ears tilted down toward the box. Rumford felt the sweat trickling down the inside of his shirt. Extraordinarily hot for Rannoch. The Ba'arni were discussing the matter among themselves, and again Rumford put one eye to the box to see what it could tell him.

We must not give (z-click z-click; see dictionary) exclamation. Necessary to (Middle C to high C).

Surreptitiously he switched over to the dictionary function and looked up middle C to high C.

Middle C to high C: 1. stand still. 2. run. 3. show interest. 4. lose. 5 alternate. 6. repair. 7. replace. 8. subtend. 9. (high C to middle C; see dictionary). 10. glance through turbid water.

Useful word. Rumford gave up on it.

Finally the Ba'ar on the left, the third one to speak from that position, raised its head and spoke. *Ba'arni (z-click z-click; see dictionary) satisfied by expression of (n-1 click sequence, b-flat; see dictionary) by poison birds toward Ba'arni and sacred dodecimation ground, if agreed that ritual war should be resumed in twelve squared years at prescribed time.*

Rumford could not prevent his eyebrows from lifting a bit. One down, apparently. Now where was he with the others? Ah yes. Tricky still, the stubborn buzzards. Entirely possible they might take up his threat of total war and act on it, which would leave the Ba'arni considerably confused. And Rannoch torched. Hmm. A problem.

He thought hard and fast. Each side a different understanding of war. Ba'arni thought of it as religious event and perhaps population control, but couldn't sustain it when population already low from famine. Thus agreeable to postponement, if face saved, and quick to arrange talk when Iggglas seen approaching. Fine, clear. And Iggglas? Food source, population control, game, who could tell? Certainly didn't care what Ba'arni astrologers thought of things. Not big on religion, the Iggglas.

Need to give convincing reasons to receiver of message, not sender. Rumford blinked at this sudden realization. Senders not hearing message, after all – not even sending it in fact. Receiver all that mattered.

He switched the box to Iggglas. *Ba'arni suffer from famine and fear war would reduce them to extinction, in which case no more ritual wars, no more fat food. Want postponement only.* The Iggglas shrieked at this in derision, but the box's screen included among the printed hash the word *understanding*. Perhaps they now had a reason they could comprehend. Best to press the point. He typed another message to the Iggglas:

Dodecimation and fat food rely on population existence, as you say. If there is no population there is no dodecimation or fat food and ritual war is ended for ever. Ba'arni therefore insist on postponement of ritual war and if Iggglas attempt to wage it regardless of traditional co-operation of the Ba'arni then Ba'arni have no choice but total war and mass suicide for all parties. Suggest therefore postponement. Astrologer's decision necessary given population of Ba'arni.

The box hooted and squawked, the Iggglas leader cocked his head to one side and listened, watching Rumford carefully. When the message was completed the leader did a little dance of its own, all on one spot. Then suddenly it approached the Ba'arni directly. Rumford held his breath. The Iggglas leader shrieked at the Ba'arni, sweeping one wing at them in a ferocious gesture.

All three Ba'arni opened their immense mouths, which appeared to split their enormous heads in half, and whistled loud and high. Rumford had to hold his hands over his ears, and the Iggglas leader stepped back. Impressive sight, those three open mouths. The Igggla opened his long mouth as if to mock them; lot of teeth in there. Impressive as well. Battle of mouths. All right if it didn't lead to anything. Tense. Need to get a response in squawks from old gar face. Can't seem to intrude too much, however.

A long minute's wait as the two parties stared each other down. The Iggglas leader suddenly turned and squawked.

On screen: *Heat death fat food postponement replacement cannibalism for Iggglas assurance renewal of slag heat war fat food in twelve squared years.*

Rumford let out a long breath.

He switched to Ba'arni, typed.

Iggglas agree to acknowledge Ba'arni honor, promise renewal of honorable battle next time in twelve squared years.

Whistle, click, whistle. The Ba'ar on the left spoke quickly.

The Ba'arni accept postponement and acknowledgement of their honor.

When Rumford conveyed the news of the Iggglas leader, it too was agreeable. Appeared to like the promise that the conflict would be renewed. But then it squawked on at length:

Iggglas negative continuance until next ritual war with heat death bombs in Iggglas seas, insistance removal immediate.

Hmm. Bit of a problem, to tell the Ba'arni to remove bombs they didn't know existed. Meanwhile they were looking at Rumford to see what had been said, and to gain time Rumford switched to Ba'arni and typed, *Iggglas agree to honor Ba'arni and agree to return to ritual war next time.*

A repeat of the previous message to them, but Rumford was too busy to think of anything else, and happily the Ba'arni didn't seem to notice. They agreed again, and Rumford returned to Iggglas.

Ba'arni state weapons on Iggglas seafloor will be de-activated. All they can do as weapons cannot be relocated.

The Igggla leader shrieked, pummelled the dust. *War war war total annihilation war fat food heat death unless sea bombs removal exclamation.*

Hmm. Wouldn't do to stop a small ritual war by starting a total war even more likely to destroy Rannoch Island. Rumford quickly got the Ba'arni's assurances that they would return in twelve squared years, then returned to Iggglas:

Ba'arni state detonator will be given to Iggglas. Detonation wavelength determined by detonator and Iggglas can change this and render bombs inoperative. Demonstration of this on small scale can be arranged in Rannoch ocean. Translator agrees to convey detonator and run demonstration as ritual forbids Ba'arni speaking to Iggglas in between ritual wars.

Could get a good long-distance detonator from the manganese mines, set up an offshore explosion. Hopefully convince them.

After a long and apparently thoughtful dance, the Iggglas

leader ate two of the rabbit-things, and indicated his acceptance of this plan. The Iggglas abruptly turned and hopped back down the road to the spaceport. The meeting was over.

Owen Rumford stood up unsteadily, and feeling drained he accompanied the three Ba'arni back to the beach. As they got into their seacraft, the one on the left said something; but Rumford had his box in his coat pocket. After the Ba'arni craft rolled under the black waves, he took the box out, turned it on and tried to imitate the last set of whistles. The box printed it as, (*Y-click x-click; see dictionary*). He switched to the dictionary function and looked it up.

Y-click, x-click: 1. Ebb tide. 2. Twisted, knotted, complex. 3. The ten forefingers. 4. Elegance. 5. The part of the moon visible in a partial eclipse. 6. Tree.

'Hmm,' Rumford said.

He walked slowly up toward the town. Y-click x-click. Those big plate eyes, staring at him. Their half of the conversation had gone pretty smoothly. Very smoothly. And all his assumptions, about the famine, the rituals. Could they be . . . just a little . . . But no. Language barrier as troublesome in telepathy as in speech, after all. Maybe.

Y-click x-click. If he had gotten the whistle right. But he thought he had. Why have a word for something they'd never seen? But Ba'arni had traded with earlier passers-by, witness box. Curious.

Tin roofs glinting in the light. Black stone walls, veined with white quartz. Black cobblestones. Very neat. Fine little town. In a hundred and forty-four years, they would have to figure something out. Well, that was their problem. More warning next time. Nothing to be done about it now.

He walked into the tavern and sat down heavily. His daughters had just finished preparing the tables for lunch. 'Papa, you look exhausted,' Isabel said. 'Have you been trying to exercise again?'

'No, no.' He looked around with a satisfied expression, heaved out a long breath. 'Just a spot of translation.' He got up and went behind the bar, started drawing a beer from the tap. Suddenly the corners of his moustache lifted a little. 'Might get a bit of payment for it,' he told her. 'If so – still care for a picnic?'

Glacier

'This is Stella,' Mrs Goldberg said. She opened the cardboard box and a gray cat leaped out and streaked under the corner table.

'That's where we'll put her blanket,' Alex's mother said.

Alex got down on hands and knees to look. Stella was a skinny old cat; her fur was an odd mix of silver, black, and pinkish tan. Yellow eyes. Part tortoise-shell, Mom had said. The color of the fur over her eyes made it appear her brow was permanently furrowed. Her ears were laid flat.

'Remember she's kind of scared of boys,' Mrs Goldberg said.

'I know.' Alex sat back on his heels. Stella hissed. 'I was just looking.' He knew the cat's whole story. She had been a stray that began visiting the Goldbergs' balcony to eat their dog's food, then – as far as anyone could tell – to hang out with the dog. Remus, a stiff-legged ancient thing, seemed happy to have the company, and after a while the two animals were inseparable. The cat had learned how to behave by watching Remus, and so it would go for a walk, come when you called it, shake hands and so on. Then Remus died, and now the Goldbergs had to move. Mom had offered to take Stella in, and though Father sighed heavily when she told him about it, he hadn't refused.

Mrs Goldberg sat on the worn carpet beside Alex, and leaned forward so she could see under the table. Her face was puffy. 'It's okay, Stell-bell,' she said. 'It's okay.'

The cat stared at Mrs Goldberg with an expression that said *You've got to be kidding*. Alex grinned to see such skepticism.

Mrs Goldberg reached under the table; the cat squeaked in protest as it was pulled out, then lay in Mrs Goldberg's lap quivering like a rabbit. The two women talked about other

301

things. Then Mrs Goldberg put Stella in Alex's mother's lap. There were scars on its ears and head. It breathed fast. Finally it calmed under Mom's hands. 'Maybe we should feed her something,' Mom said. She knew how distressed animals could get in this situation: they themselves had left behind their dog Pongo, when they moved from Toronto to Boston. Alex and she had been the ones to take Pongo to the Wallaces; the dog had howled as they left, and walking away Mom had cried. Now she told Alex to get some chicken out of the fridge and put it in a bowl for Stella. He put the bowl on the couch next to the cat, who sniffed at it disdainfully and refused to look at it. Only after much calming would it nibble at the meat, nose drawn high over one sharp eyetooth. Mom talked to Mrs Goldberg, who watched Stella eat. When the cat was done it hopped off Mom's lap and walked up and down the couch. But it wouldn't let Alex near; it crouched as he approached, and with a desperate look dashed back under the table. 'Oh Stella!' Mrs Goldberg laughed. 'It'll take her a while to get used to you,' she said to Alex, and sniffed. Alex shrugged.

Outside the wind ripped at the treetops sticking above the buildings. Alex walked up Chester Street to Brighton Avenue and turned left, hurrying to counteract the cold. Soon he reached the river and could walk the path on top of the embankment. Down in its trough the river's edges were crusted with ice, but midstream was still free, the silty gray water riffled by white. He passed the construction site for the dam and came to the moraine, a long mound of dirt, rocks, lumber, and junk. He climbed it with big steps, and stood looking at the glacier.

The glacier was immense, like a range of white hills rolling in from the west and north. The Charles poured from the bottom of it and roiled through a cut in the terminal moraine; the glacier's snout loomed so large that the river looked small, like a gutter after a storm. Bright white iceberg chunks had toppled off the face of the snout, leaving fresh blue scars and clogging the river below.

Alex walked the edge of the moraine until he was above the glacier's side. To his left was the razed zone, torn streets and fresh dirt and cellars open to the sky; beyond it Allston and Brighton, still bustling with city life. Under him, the sharp-edged mound of dirt and debris. To his right, the wilderness of ice and rock. Looking straight ahead it was hard to believe that the two halves of the view came from the same world. Neat. He descended the moraine's steep loose inside slope carefully, following a path of his own.

The meeting of glacier and moraine was a curious juncture. In some places the moraine had been undercut and had spilled across the ice in wide fans; you couldn't be sure if the dirt was solid or if it concealed crevasses. In other places melting had created a gap, so that a thick cake of ice stood over empty air, and dripped into gray pools below. Once Alex had seen a car in one of these low wet caves, stripped of its paint and squashed flat.

In still other places, however, the ice sloped down and overlaid the moraine's gravel in a perfect ramp, as if fitted by carpenters. Alex walked the trough between dirt and ice until he reached one of these areas, then took a big step onto the curved white surface. He felt the usual quiver of excitement: he was on the glacier.

It was steep on the rounded side slope, but the ice was embedded with thousands of chunks of gravel. Each pebble, heated by the sun, had sunk into a little pocket of its own, and was then frozen into position in the night; this process had been repeated until most chunks were about three-quarters buried. Thus the glacier had a peculiarly pocked, rocky surface, which gripped the torn soles of Alex's shoes. A non-slip surface. No slope on the glacier was too steep for him. Crunch, crunch, crunch: tiny arabesques of ice collapsed under his feet with every step. He could change the glacier, he was part of its action. Part of it.

Where the side slope leveled out the first big crevasses appeared. These deep blue fissures were dangerous, and Alex stepped between two of them and up a narrow ramp very carefully. He picked up a fist-sized rock, tossed it in the bigger crack. *Clunk clunk . . . splash.* He shivered and walked on, ritual satisfied. He knew from these throws that at the bottom of the glacier there were pockets of air, pools of water, streams running down to form the Charles . . . a deadly subglacial world. No one who fell into it would ever escape. It made the surface ice glow with a magical danger, an internal light.

Up on the glacier proper he could walk more easily. Crunch crunch crunch, over an undulating broken debris-covered plain. Ice for miles on miles. Looking back toward the city he saw the Hancock and Prudential towers to the right, the lower MIT towers to the left, poking up at low scudding clouds. The wind was strong here and he pulled his jacket hood's drawstring tighter. Muffled hoot of wind, a million tricklings. There were little creeks running in channels cut into the ice: it was almost like an ordinary landscape, streams running in ravines over a broad rocky meadow. And yet everything was different. The streams ran into crevasses or potholes and instantly disappeared, for instance. It was wonderfully strange to look down such a rounded hole: the ice was very blue and you could see the air bubbles in it, air from some year long ago.

Broken seracs exposed fresh ice to the sun. Scores of big erratic boulders dotted the glacier, some the size of houses. He made his way from one to the next, using them as cover. There were gangs of boys from Cambridge who occasionally came up here, and they were dangerous. It was important to see them before he was seen.

A mile or more onto the glacier, ice had flowed around one big boulder, leaving a curving wall some ten feet high – another example of the glacier's whimsy, one of hundreds of strange surface formations. Alex had wedged some stray boards into the gap between rock and ice, making a seat that was tucked out of the west wind. Flat rocks made a fine floor, and in the corner he had even made a little fireplace. Every fire he lit sank the hearth of flat stones a bit deeper into the otherwise impervious ice.

This time he didn't have enough kindling, though, so he sat on his bench, hands deep in pockets, and looked back at the city. He could see for miles. Wind whistled over the boulder. Scattered shafts of sunlight broke against ice. Mostly shadowed, the jumbled expanse was faintly pink. This was because of an algae that lived on nothing but ice and dust. Pink; the blue of the seracs; gray ice; patches of white, marking snow or sunlight. In the distance dark clouds scraped the top of the blue Hancock building, making it look like a distant serac. Alex leaned back against his plank wall, whistling one of the songs of the Pirate King.

Everyone agreed the cat was crazy. Her veneer of civilization was thin, and at any loud noise – the phone's ring, the door slamming – she would jump as if shot, then stop in mid-flight as she recalled that this particular noise entailed no danger; then lick down her fur, pretending she had never jumped in the first place. A flayed sensibility.

She was also very wary about proximity to people; this despite the fact that she had learned to love being petted. So she would often get in moods where she would approach one of them and give an exploratory, half-purring mew; then, if you responded to the invitation and crouched to pet her, she would sidle just out of arm's reach, repeating the invitation but retreating with each shift you made, until she either let you get within petting distance – just – or decided it wasn't worth the risk, and scampered away. Father laughed at this intense ambivalance. 'Stella, you're too stupid to live, aren't you,' he said in a teasing voice.

'Charles,' Mom said.

'It's the best example of approach avoidance behavior I've ever seen,' Father said. Intrigued by the challenge, he would sit on the floor, back against the couch and legs stretched ahead of him, and put Stella on his thighs. She would either endure his stroking until it ended, when she could jump away without impediment – or relax, and purr. She had a rasping loud purr, it reminded Alex of a chainsaw heard across the glacier. 'Bug brain,' Father would say to her. 'Button head.'

After a few weeks, as August turned to September and the leaves began to wither and fall, Stella started to lap sit voluntarily – but always in Mom's lap. 'She likes the warmth,' Mom said.

'It's cold on the floor,' Father agreed, and played with the cat's scarred ears. 'But why do you always sit on Helen's lap, huhn, Stell? I'm the one who started you on that.' Eventually the cat would step onto his lap as well, and stretch out as if it was something she had always done. Father laughed at her.

Stella never rested on Alex's lap voluntarily, but would sometimes stay if he put her there and stroked her slowly for a long time. On the other hand she was just as likely to look back at him, go cross-eyed with horror and leap desperately away, leaving claw marks in his thighs. 'She's so weird,' he complained to Mom after one of these abrupt departures.

'It's true,' Mom said with her low laugh. 'But you have to remember that Stella was probably an abused kitty.'

'How can you abuse a stray?'

'I'm sure there are ways. And maybe she was abused at home, and ran away.'

'Who would do that?'

'Some people would.'

Alex recalled the gangs on the glacier, and knew it was true. He tried to imagine what it would be like to be at their mercy, all the time. After that he thought he understood her permanent frown of deep concentration and distrust, as she sat staring at him. 'It's just me, Stell-bells.'

Thus when the cat followed him up onto the roof, and seemed to enjoy hanging out there with him, he was pleased. Their apartment was on the top floor, and they could take the pantry stairs and use the roof as a porch. It was a flat expanse of graveled tarpaper, a terrible imitation of the glacier's non-slip surface, but it was nice on dry days to go up there and look around, toss pebbles onto other roofs, see if the glacier was visible, and so on. Once Stella pounced at a piece of string trailing from his pants, and next time he brought up a length of Father's yarn. He was astonished and delighted when Stella responded by attacking the windblown yarn enthusiastically, biting it, clawing it, wrestling it from her back when Alex twirled it around her, and generally behaving in a very kittenish way. Perhaps she had never played as a kitten, Alex thought, so that it was all coming out now that she felt safe. But the play always ended abruptly; she would come to herself in mid-bite or bat, straighten up, and look around with a forbidding expression, as if to say *What is this yarn doing draped over me?* – then lick her fur and pretend the preceding minutes hadn't happened. It made Alex laugh.

Although the glacier had overrun many towns to the west and north, Watertown and Newton most recently, there was surprisingly little evidence of that in the moraines, or in the ice. It was almost all natural: rock and dirt and wood. Perhaps the wood had come from houses, perhaps some of the gravel had once been concrete, but you couldn't tell that now. Just dirt and rock and splinters, with an occasional chunk of plastic or metal thrown in. Apparently the overrun towns had been plowed under on the spot, or moved. Mostly it looked like the glacier had just left the White Mountains.

Father and Gary Jung had once talked about the latest plan from MIT. The enormous dam they were building downstream, between Allston and Cambridge, was to hold the glacier back. They were going to heat the concrete of the inner surface of the dam, and melt the ice as it advanced. It would become a kind of frozen reservoir. The melt water would pour through a set of turbines before becoming the Charles, and the electricity generated by these turbines would help to heat the dam. Very neat.

The ice of the glacier, when you got right down to look at it, was clear for an inch or less, cracked and bubble-filled; then it turned a milky white. You could see the transition. Where the ice had been sheared vertically, however – on the side of a serac, or down in a crevasse – the clear part extended in many inches. You could see air bubbles deep inside, as if it were badly made glass. And this ice was distinctly blue. Alex didn't understand why there should be that difference, between the white ice laying flat and the blue ice cut vertically. But there it was.

Up in New Hampshire they had tried slowing the glacier – or at least stopping the abrupt 'Alaskan slides' – by setting steel rods vertically in concrete, and laying the concrete in the glacier's path. Later they had hacked out one of these installations, and found the rods bent in perfect ninety degree angles, pressed into the scored concrete.

The ice would flow right over the dam.

* * *

One day Alex was walking by Father's study when Father called out. 'Alexander! Take a look at this.'

Alex entered the dark book-lined room. Its window overlooked the weed-filled space between buildings, and green light slanted onto Father's desk. 'Here, stand beside me and look in my coffee cup. You can see the reflection of the Morgelis' window flowers on the coffee.'

'Oh yeah! Neat.'

'It gave me a shock! I looked down and there were these white and pink flowers in my cup, bobbing against a wall in a breeze, all of it tinted sepia as if it were an old-fashioned photo. It took me a while to see where it was coming from, what was being reflected.' He laughed. 'Through a looking glass.'

Alex's father had light brown eyes, and fair wispy hair brushed back from a receding hairline. Mom called him handsome, and Alex agreed: tall, thin, graceful, delicate, distinguished. His father was a great man. Now he smiled in a way Alex didn't understand, looking into his coffee cup.

Mom had friends at the street market on Memorial Drive, and she had arranged work for Alex there. Three afternoons a week he walked over the Charles to the riverside street and helped the fishmongers gut fish, the vegetable sellers strip and clean the vegetables. He also helped set up stalls and take them down, and he swept and hosed the street afterwards. He was popular because of his energy and his willingness to get his hands wet in raw weather. The sleeves of his down jacket were permanently discolored from the frequent soakings – the dark blue almost a brown – a fact that distressed his mom. But he could handle the cold better than the adults; his hands would get a splotchy bluish white and he would put them to the red cheeks of the women and they would jump and say My *God*, Alex, how can you stand it?

This afternoon was blustery and dark but without rain, and it was enlivened by an attempted theft in the pasta stands, and by the appearance of a very mangy, very fast stray dog. This dog pounced on the pile of fishheads and entrails and disappeared with his mouth stuffed, trailing slick white-and-red guts. Everyone who saw it laughed. There weren't many stray dogs left these days, it was a pleasure to see one. An hour past sunset he was done cleaning up and on his way home, hands in his pockets, stomach full, a five dollar bill clutched in one hand. He showed his pass to the National Guardsman and walked out onto Weeks Bridge. In the middle he stopped and leaned over the railing, into the wind. Below the water churned, milky with glacial silt. The sky still held a lot of light. Low curving bands of black cloud swept in from the northwest, like great ribs of slate. Above these bands the white sky was leached away by dusk. Raw wind whistled over his hood. Light water rushing below, dark clouds rushing above ... he breathed the wind deep into him, felt himself expand until he filled everything he could see.

That night his parents' friends were gathering at their apartment for their bi-weekly party. Some of them would read stories and poems and essays and broadsides they had written, and then they would argue about them; and after that they would drink and eat whatever they had brought, and argue some more. Alex enjoyed it. But tonight when he got home Mom was rushing between computer and kitchen and muttering curses as she hit command keys or the hot water faucet, and the moment she saw him she said, 'Oh Alex I'm glad you're here, could you please run down to the laundry and do just one load for me? The Talbots are staying over tonight and there aren't any clean sheets and I don't have anything to wear tomorrow either – thanks, you're a dear.' And he was back out the door with a full laundry bag hung over his shoulder and the box of soap in the other hand, stomping grumpily past a little man in a black coat, reading a newspaper on the stoop of 19 Chester.

Down to Brighton, take a right, downstairs into the brightly lit basement laundromat. He threw laundry and soap and quarters into their places, turned the machine on and sat on top of it. Glumly he watched the other people in there, sitting on the washers and dryers. The vibrations put a lot of them to sleep. Others stared dully at the wall. Back in his apartment the guests would be arriving, taking off their overcoats, slapping arms over

309

chests and talking as fast as they could. David and Sara and John
from next door, Ira and Gary and Ilene from across the street,
the Talbots, Kathryn Grimm, and Michael Wu from Father's
university, Rom from the hospital. They would settle down in
the living room, on couches and chairs and floor, and talk and
talk. Alex liked Kathryn especially, she could talk twice as fast
as anyone else, and she called everyone darling and laughed and
chattered so fast that everyone was caught up in the rhythm of
it. Or David with his jokes, or Jay Talbot and his friendly
questions. Or Gary Jung, the way he would sit in his corner like
a bear, drinking beer and challenging everything that everyone
read. 'Why abstraction, why this distortion from the real? How
does it help us, how does it speak to us? We should forget the
abstract!' Father and Ira called him a vulgar Marxist, but he
didn't mind. 'You might as well be Plekhanov, Gary!' 'Thank
you very much!' he would say with a sharp grin, rubbing his
unshaven jowls. And someone else would read. Mary Talbot
once read a fairy tale about the Thing under the glacier; Alex
had *loved* it. Once they even got Michael Wu to bring his violin
along, and he hmm'd and hawed and pulled at the skin of his
neck and refused and said he wasn't good enough, and then
shaking like a leaf he played a melody that stilled them all. And
Stella! She hated these parties, she spent them crouched deep
in her refuge, ready for any kind of atrocity.

And here he was sitting on a washer in the laundromat.

When the laundry was dry he bundled it into the bag, then
hurried around the corner and down Chester Street. Inside the
glass door of Number 21 he glanced back out, and noticed
that the man who had been reading the paper on the stoop next
door was still sitting there. Odd. It was cold to be sitting outdoors.

Upstairs the readings had ended and the group was scattered
through the apartment, most of them in the kitchen, as Mom had
lit the stove-top burners and turned the gas up high. The blue
flames roared airily under their chatter, making the kitchen
bright and warm. 'Wonderful the way white gas burns so clean.'
'And then they found the poor thing's head and intestines in the
alley – it had been butchered right on the spot.'

'Alex, you're back! Thanks for doing that. Here, get something to eat.'

Everyone greeted him and went back to their conversations. 'Gary you are so *conservative*,' Kathryn cried, hands held out over the stove. 'It's not conservative at all,' Gary replied. 'It's a radical goal and I guess it's so radical that I have to keep reminding you it exists. Art should be used to *change* things.'

'Isn't that a distortion from the real?'

Alex wandered down the narrow hall to his parents' room, which overlooked Chester Street. Father was there, saying to Ilene, 'It's one of the only streets left with trees. It really seems residential, and here we are three blocks from Comm Ave. Hi, Alex.'

'Hi, Alex. It's like a little bit of Brookline made it over to Allston.'

'Exactly.'

Alex stood in the bay window and looked down, licking the last of the carrot cake off his fingers. The man was still down there.

'Let's close off these rooms and save the heat. Alex, you coming?'

He sat on the floor in the living room. Father and Gary and David were starting a game of hearts, and they invited him to be the fourth. He nodded happily. Looking under the corner table he saw yellow eyes, blinking back at him; Stella, a frown of the deepest disapproval on her flat face. Alex laughed. 'I knew you'd be there! It's okay, Stella. It's okay.'

They left in a group, as usual, stamping their boots and diving deep into coats and scarves and gloves and exclaiming at the cold of the stairwell. Gary gave Mom a brief hug. 'Only warm spot left in Boston,' he said, and opened the glass door. The rest followed him out, and Alex joined them. The man in the black coat was just turning right onto Brighton Avenue, toward the university and downtown.

Sometimes clouds took on just the mottled gray of the glacier, low dark points stippling a lighter gray surface as cold showers

311

draped down. At these times he felt he stood between two planes of some larger structure, two halves: icy tongue, icy roof of mouth . . .

He stood under such a sky, throwing stones. His target was an erratic some forty yards away. He hit the boulder with most of his throws. A rock that big was an easy target. A bottle was better. He had brought one with him, and he set it up behind the erratic, on a waist-high rock. He walked back to a point where the bottle was hidden by the erratic. Using flat rocks he sent spinners out in a trajectory that brought them curving in from the side, so that it was possible to hit the concealed target. This was very important for the rock fights that he occasionally got involved in; usually he was outnumbered, and to hold his own he relied on his curves and his accuracy in general, and on a large number of ammunition caches hidden here and there. In one area crowded with boulders and crevasses he could sometimes create the impression of two throwers.

Absorbed in the exercise of bringing curves around the right side of the boulder – the hard side for him – he relaxed his vigilance, and when he heard a shout he jumped around to look. A rock whizzed by his left ear.

He dropped to the ice and crawled behind a boulder. Ambushed! He ran back into his knot of boulders and dashed a layer of snow away from one of his big caches, then with hands and pockets full looked carefully over a knobby chunk of cement, in the direction the stone had come from.

No movement. He recalled the stone whizzing by, the brief sight of it and the *zip* it made in passing. That had been close! If that had hit him! He shivered to think of it, it made his stomach shrink.

A bit of almost frozen rain pattered down. Not a shadow anywhere. On overcast days like this one it seemed things were lit from below, by the white bulk of the glacier. Like plastic over a weak neon light. Brittle huge blob of plastic, shifting and groaning and once in a while cracking like a gunshot, or grumbling like distant thunder. Alive. And Alex was its ally, its representative among men. He shifted from rock to rock, saw movement and froze. Two boys in green down jackets, laughing as they ran off the ice and over the lateral moraine, into what was left of Watertown. Just a potshot, then. Alex cursed them, relaxed.

He went back to throwing at the hidden bottle. Occasionally he recalled the stone flying by his head, and threw a little harder. Elegant curves of flight as the flat rocks bit the air and cut down and in. Finally one rock spun out into space and turned down sharply. Perfect slider. Its disappearance behind the erratic was followed by a tinkling crash. 'Yeah!' Alex exclaimed, and ran to look. Icy glass on glassy ice.

Then, as he was leaving the glacier, boys jumped over the moraine shouting 'Canadian!' and 'There he is!' and 'Get him!' This was more a chase than a serious ambush, but there were a lot of them and after emptying hands and pockets Alex was off running. He flew over the crunchy irregular surface, splashing meltwater, jumping narrow crevasses and surface rills. Then a wide crevasse blocked his way, and to start his jump he leaped onto a big flat rock; the rock gave under his foot and lurched down the ice into the crevasse.

Alex turned in and fell, bringing shoe-tips, knees, elbows and hands onto the rough surface. This arrested his fall, though it hurt. The crevasse was just under his feet. He scrambled up, ran panting along the crevasse until it narrowed, leaped over it. Then up the moraine and down into the narrow abandoned streets of west Allston.

Striding home, still breathing hard, he looked at his hands and saw that the last two fingernails on his right hand had been ripped away from the flesh; both were still there, but blood seeped from under them. He hissed and sucked on them, which hurt. The blood tasted like blood.

If he had fallen into the crevasse, following the loose rock down ... if that stone had hit him in the face ... he could feel his heart, thumping against his sternum. Alive.

Turning onto Chester Street he saw the man in the black coat, leaning against the florid maple across the street from their building. Watching them still! Though the man didn't appear to notice Alex, he did heft a bag and start walking in the other direction. Quickly Alex picked a rock out of the gutter and threw

313

it at the man as hard as he could, spraying drops of blood onto the sidewalk. The rock flew over the man's head like a bullet, just missing him. The man ducked and scurried around the corner onto Comm Ave.

Father was upset about something. 'They did the same thing to Gary and Michael and Kathryn, and their classes are even smaller than mine! I don't know what they're going to do. I don't know what *we're* going to do.'

'We might be able to attract larger classes next semester,' Mom said. She was upset too. Alex stood in the hall, slowly hanging up his jacket.

'But what about now? And what about later?' Father's voice was strained, almost cracking.

'We're making enough for now, that's the important thing. As for later – well, at least we know now rather than five years down the road.'

Father was silent at the implications of this. 'First Vancouver, then Toronto, now here – '

'Don't worry about all of it at once, Charles.'

'How can I help it!' Father strode into his study and closed the door, not noticing Alex around the corner. Alex sucked his fingers. Stella poked her head cautiously out of his bedroom.

'Hi Stell-bell,' he said quietly. From the living room came the plastic clatter of Mom's typing. He walked down the long hallway, past the silent study to the living room. She was hitting the keys hard, staring at the screen, mouth tight.

'What happened?' Alex said.

She looked up. 'Hi, Alex. Well – your father got bad news from the university.'

'Did he not get tenure again?'

'No, no, it's not a question of that.'

'But now he doesn't even have the chance?'

She glanced at him sharply, then back at the screen, where her work was blinking. 'I suppose that's right. The department has shifted all the new faculty over to extension, so they're hired by the semester, and paid by the class. It means you need a lot of students . . .'

314

'Will we move again?'

'I don't know,' she said curtly, exasperated with him for bringing it up. She punched the command key. 'But we'll really have to save money, now. Everything you make at the market is important.'

Alex nodded. He didn't mention the little man in the black coat, feeling obscurely afraid. Mentioning the man would somehow make him significant – Mom and Father would get angry, or frightened – something like that. By not telling them he could protect them from it, handle it on his own, so they could concentrate on other problems. Besides the two matters couldn't be connected, could they? Being watched; losing jobs. Perhaps they could. In which case there was nothing his parents could do about it anyway. Better to save them that anger, that fear.

He would make sure his throws hit the man next time.

Storms rolled in and the red and yellow leaves were ripped off the trees. Alex kicked through piles of them stacked on the sidewalks. He never saw the little man. He put up flyers for his father, who became even more distracted and remote. He brought home vegetables from work, tucked under his down jacket, and Mom cooked them without asking if he had bought them. She did the wash in the kitchen sink and dried it on lines in the back space between buildings, standing knee deep in leaves and weeds. Sometimes it took three days for clothes to dry back there; often they froze on the line.

While hanging clothes or taking them down she would let Stella join her. The cat regarded each shifting leaf with dire suspicion, then after a few exploratory leaps and bats would do battle with all of them, rolling about in a frenzy.

One time Mom was carrying a basket of dry laundry up the pantry stairs when a stray dog rounded the corner and made a dash for Stella, who was still outside. Mom ran back down shouting, and the dog fled; but Stella had disappeared. Mom called Alex down from his studies in a distraught voice, and they searched the back of the building and all the adjacent backyards for nearly an hour, but the cat was nowhere to be found. Mom was really upset. It was only after they had quit and returned upstairs that they heard her, miaowing far above them. She had climbed the big oak tree. 'Oh, *smart*, Stella,' Mom cried, a wild note in her voice. They called her name out the kitchen window, and the desperate miaows redoubled.

Up on the roof they could just see her, perched high in the almost bare branches of the big tree. 'I'll get her,' Alex said. 'Cats can't climb down.' He started climbing. It was difficult: the branches were close-knit, and they swayed in the wind. And as he got closer the cat climbed higher. 'No, Stella, don't do that! Come here!' Stella stared at him, clamped to her branch of the moment, cross-eyed with fear. Below them Mom said over and over, 'Stella, it's okay – it's okay, Stella.' Stella didn't believe her.

Finally Alex reached her, near the tree's top. Now here was a problem: he needed his hands to climb down, but it seemed likely he would also need them to hold the terrified cat. 'Come here, Stella.' He put a hand on her flank; she flinched. Her side pulsed with her rapid breathing. She hissed faintly. He had to maneuver up a step, onto a very questionable branch; his face was inches from her. She stared at him without a trace of recognition. He pried her off her branch, lifted her. If she cared to claw him now she could really tear him up. Instead she clung to his shoulder and chest, all her claws dug through his clothes, quivering under his left arm and hand.

Laboriously he descended, using only the one hand. Stella began miaowing fiercely, and struggling a bit. Finally he met Mom, who had climbed the tree quite a ways. Stella was getting more upset. 'Hand her to me.' Alex detached her from his chest paw by paw, balanced, held the cat down with both hands. Again it was a tricky moment; if Stella went beserk they would all be in trouble. But she fell onto Mom's chest and collapsed, a catatonic ball of fur.

Back in the apartment she dashed for her blanket under the table. Mom enticed her out with food, but she was very jumpy and she wouldn't allow Alex anywhere near her; she ran away if he even entered the room. 'Back to square one, I see,' Mom commented.

'It's not fair! I'm the one that saved her!'

'She'll get over it!' Mom laughed, clearly relieved. 'Maybe it'll take some time, but she will. Ha! This is clear proof that cats are smart enough to be crazy. Irrational, neurotic – just like a person.' They laughed, and Stella glared at them balefully. 'Yes you are, aren't you! You'll come around again.'

Often when Alex got home in the early evenings his father was striding back and forth in the kitchen talking loudly, angrily, fearfully, while Mom tried to reassure him. 'They're doing the same thing to us that they did to Rick Stone! But why!' When Alex closed the front door the conversation would stop. Once when he walked tentatively down the quiet hallway to the kitchen he found them standing there, arms around each other, Father's head in Mom's short hair.

Father raised his head, disengaged, went to his study. On his way he said, 'Alex, I need your help.'

'Sure.'

Alex stood in the study and watched without understanding as his father took books from his shelves and put them in the big laundry bag. He threw the first few in like dirty clothes, then sighed and thumped in the rest in a businesslike fashion, not looking at them.

'There's a used book store in Cambridge, on Mass Ave. Antonio's.'

'Sure, I know the one.' They had been there together a few times.

'I want you to take these over there and sell them to Tony for me,' Father said, looking at the empty shelves. 'Will you do that for me?'

'Sure.' Alex picked up the bag, shocked that it had come to this. Father's books! He couldn't meet his father's eye. 'I'll do that right now,' he said uncertainly, and hefted the bag over one shoulder. In the hallway Mom approached and put a hand on his shoulder – her silent thanks – then went into the study.

Alex hiked east toward the university, crossed the Charles River on the great iron bridge. The wind howled in the superstructure. On the Cambridge side, after showing his pass, he put the heavy bag on the ground and inspected its contents. Ever since the infamous incident of the spilled hot chocolate, Father's books had been off-limits to him; now a good twenty of them were there in the bag to be touched, opened, riffled through. Many in this bunch were in foreign languages, especially Greek and Russian, with their alien alphabets. Could people really read such marks? Well, Father did. It must be possible.

When he had inspected all the books he chose two in English – *The Odyssey* and *The Colossus of Maroussi* – and put those in his down jacket pockets. He could take them to the glacier and read them, then sell them later to Antonio's – perhaps in the next bag of books. There were many more bagfuls in Father's study.

A little snow stuck to the glacier now, filling the pocks and making bright patches on the north side of every boulder, every serac. Some of the narrower crevasses were filled with it – bright white lines on the jumbled gray. When the whole surface was white the crevasses would be invisible, and the glacier too dangerous to walk on. Now the only danger was leaving obvious footprints for trackers. Walking up the rubble lines would solve that. These lines of rubble fascinated Alex. It looked just as if bulldozers had clanked up here and shoved the majority of the stones and junk into straight lines down the big central tongue of the glacier. But in fact they were natural features. Father had attempted to explain on one of the walks they had taken up here. 'The ice is moving, and it moves faster in the middle than on the outer edges, just like a stream. So rocks on the surface tend to slide over time, down into lines in the middle.'

'Why are there two lines, then?'

Father shrugged, looking into the blue-green depths of a crevasse. 'We really shouldn't be up here, you know that?'

Now Alex stopped to inspect a tire caught in the rubble line. Truck tire, tread worn right to the steel belting. It would burn, but with too much smoke. There were several interesting objects in this neat row of rock and sand: plastic jugs, a doll, a lampbase, a telephone.

His shelter was undisturbed. He pulled the two books from

his pockets and set them on the bench, propping them with rock bookends.

He circled the boulder, had a look around. The sky today was a low smooth pearl gray sheet, ruffled by a set of delicate waves pasted to it. The indirect light brought out all the colors: the pink of the remarkable snow algae, the blue of the seracs, the various shades of rock, the occasional bright spot of junk, the many white patches of snow. A million dots of color under the pewter sheet of cloud.

Three creaks, a crack, a long shuddering rumble. Sleepy, muscular, the great beast had moved. Alex walked across its back to his bench, sat. On the far lateral moraine some gravel slid down. Puffs of brown dust in the air.

He read his books. *The Odyssey* was strange but interesting. Father had told him some of the story before. *The Colossus of Maroussi* was long-winded but funny – it reminded Alex of his uncle, who could turn the smallest incident into an hour's comic monologue. What he could have made of Stella's flight up the tree! Alex laughed to think of it. But his uncle was in jail.

He sat on his bench and read, stopped occasionally to look around. When the hand holding the book got cold, he changed hands and put the cold one in a pocket of his down jacket. When both hands were blue he hid the books in rocks under his bench and went home.

There were more bags of books to be sold at Antonio's and other shops in Cambridge. Each time Alex rotated out a few that looked interesting, and replaced them with the ones on the glacier. He daydreamed of saving all the books and earning the money some other way – then presenting his father with the lost library, at some future undefined but appropriate moment.

Eventually Stella forgave him for rescuing her. She came to enjoy chasing a piece of yarn up and down their long narrow hallway, skidding around the corner by the study. It reminded them of a game they had played with Pongo, who would chase anything, and they laughed at her, especially when she jerked to a halt and licked her fur fastidiously, as if she had never been carousing. 'You can't fool us, Stell! We *remember*!'

Mom sold most of her music collection, except for her favorites. Once Alex went out to the glacier with the *Concerto de Aranjuez* coursing through him – Mom had had it on in the apartment while she worked. He hummed the big theme of the second movement as he crunched over the ice: clearly it was the theme of the glacier, the glacier's song. How had a blind composer managed to capture the windy sweep of it, the spaciousness? Perhaps such things could be heard as well as seen. The wind said it, whistling over the ice. It was a terrifically dark day, windy, snowing in gusts. He could walk right up the middle of the great tongue, between the rubble lines; no one else would be up there today. Da-da-da ... da da da da da da, da-da-da ... Hands in pockets, chin on chest, he trudged into the wind humming, feeling like the whole world was right there around him. It was too cold to stay in his shelter for more than a minute.

Father went off on trips, exploring possibilities. One morning Alex woke to the sound of *The Pirates of Penzance*. This was one of their favorites, Mom played it all the time while working and on Saturday mornings, so that they knew all the lyrics by heart and often sang along. Alex especially loved the Pirate King, and could mimic all his intonations.

He dressed and walked down to the kitchen. Mom stood by the stove with her back to him, singing along. It was a sunny morning and their big kitchen windows faced east; the light poured in on the sink and the dishes and the white stove and the linoleum and the plants in the window and Stella, sitting contentedly on the window still listening.

His mom was tall and broad-shouldered. Every year she cut her hair shorter; now it was just a cap of tight brown curls, with a somewhat longer patch down the nape of her neck. That would go soon, Alex thought, and then her hair would be as short as it could be. She was lost in the song, one slim hand on the white stove top, looking out the window. She had a low, rich, thrilling voice, like a real singer's only prettier. She was singing along with the song that Mabel sings after she finds out that Frederick won't be able to leave the pirates until 1940.

320

When it was over Alex entered the kitchen, went to the pantry. 'That's a short one,' he said.

'Yes, they had to make it short,' Mom said. 'There's nothing funny about that one.'

One night while father was gone on one of his trips, Mom had to go over to Ilene and Ira and Gary's apartment: Gary had been arrested, and Ilene and Ira needed help. Alex and Stella were left alone.

Stella wandered the silent apartment miaowing. 'I *know*, Stella,' Alex said in exasperation. 'They're *gone*. They'll be back tomorrow.' The cat paid no attention to him.

He went into Father's study. Tonight he'd be able to read something in relative warmth. It would only be necessary to be *very careful*.

The bookshelves were empty. Alex stood before them, mouth open. He had no idea they had sold that many of them. There were a couple left on Father's desk, but he didn't want to move them. They appeared to be dictionaries anyway. 'It's all Greek to me.'

He went back to the living room and got out the yarn bag, tried to interest Stella in a game. She wouldn't play. She wouldn't sit on his lap. She wouldn't stop miaowing. 'Stella, shut up!' She scampered away and kept crying. Vexed, he got out the jar of catnip and spread some on the linoleum in the kitchen. Stella came running to sniff at it, then roll in it. Afterwards she played with the yarn wildly, until it caught around her tail and she froze, staring at him in a drugged paranoia. Then she dashed to her refuge and refused to come out. Finally Alex put on *The Pirates of Penzance* and listened to it for a while. After that he was sleepy.

They got a good lawyer for Gary, Mom said. Everyone was hopeful. Then a couple of weeks later Father got a new job; he called them from work to tell them about it.

'Where is it?' Alex asked Mom when she was off the phone.

'In Kansas.'

'So we will be moving.'

'Yes,' Mom said. 'Another move.'

'Will there be glaciers there too?'

'I think so. In the hills. Not as big as ours here, maybe. But there are glaciers everywhere.'

He walked onto the ice one last time. There was a thin crust of snow on the tops of everything. A fantastically jumbled field of snow. It was a clear day, the sky a very pale blue, the white expanse of the glacier painfully bright. A few cirrus clouds made sickles high in the west. The snow was melting a bit and there were water droplets all over, with little sparks of colored light in each drip. The sounds of water melting were everywhere, drips, gurgles, splashes. The intensity of light was stunning, like a blow to the brain, right through the eyes. It pulsed.

The crevasse in front of his shelter had widened, and the boards of his bench had fallen. The wall of ice turning around the boulder was splintered, and shards of bright ice lay over the planks.

The glacier was moving. The glacier was alive. No heated dam would stop it. He felt its presence, huge and supple under him, seeping into him like the cold through his wet shoes, filling him up. He blinked, nearly blinded by the light breaking everywhere on it, a surgical glare that made every snow-capped rock stand out like the color red on a slide transparency. The white light. In the distance the ice cracked hollowly, moving somewhere. Everything moved: the ice, the wind, the clouds, the sun, the planet. All of it rolling around.

As they packed up their possessions Alex could hear them in the next room. 'We can't,' Father said. 'You know we can't. They won't let us.'

When they were done the apartment looked odd. Bare walls, bare wood floors. It looked smaller. Alex walked the length of it: his parents' room overlooking Chester Street; his room, his father's study; the living room; the kitchen with its fine morning light. The pantry. Stella wandered the place miaowing. Her blanket was still in its corner, but without the table it looked

322

moth-eaten, fur-coated, ineffectual. Alex picked her up and went through the pantry, up the back stairs to the roof.

Snow had drifted into the corners. Alex walked in circles, looking at the city. Stella sat on her paws by the stairwell shed, watching him, her fur ruffled by the wind.

Around the shed snow had melted, then froze again. Little puddles of ice ran in flat curves across the pebbled tar paper. Alex crouched to inspect them, tapping one speculatively with a fingernail. He stood up and looked west, but buildings and bare treetops obscured the view.

Stella fought to stay out of the box, and once in it she cried miserably.

Father was already in Kansas, starting the new job. Alex and Mom and Stella had been staying in the living room of Michael Wu's place while Mom finished her work; now she was done, it was moving day, they were off to the train. But first they had to take Stella to the Talbots'.

Alex carried the box and followed Mom as they walked across the Commons and down Comm Ave. He could feel the cat shifting over her blanket, scrabbling at the cardboard against his chest. Mom walked fast, a bit ahead of him. At Kenmore they turned south.

When they got to the Talbots', Mom took the box. She looked at him. 'Why don't you stay down here,' she said.

'Okay.'

She rang the bell and went in with the buzzer, holding the box under one arm.

Alex sat on the steps of the walk-up. There were little ones in the corner: flat fingers of ice, spilling away from the cracks.

Mom came out the door. Her face was pale, she was biting her lip. They took off walking at a fast pace. Suddenly Mom said, 'Oh, Alex, she was *so scared*,' and sat down on another stoop and put her head on her knees.

Alex sat beside her, his shoulders touching hers. Don't say anything, don't put arm around shoulders or anything. He had learned this from Father. Just sit there, be there. Alex sat there like the glacier, shifting a little. Alive. The white light.

Down and Out in the Year 2000

After a while she stood. 'Let's go,' she said.

They walked up Comm Ave toward the train station. 'She'll be all right with the Talbots,' Alex said. 'She already likes Jay.'

'I know,' Mom sniffed, tossed her head in the wind. 'She's getting to be a pretty adaptable cat.' They walked on in silence. She put an arm over his shoulders. 'I wonder how Pongo is doing.' She took a deep breath. Overhead clouds tumbled like chunks of broken ice.

Before I Wake

In his dream Abernathy stood on a steep rock ridge. A talus slope dropped from the ridge to a glacial basin containing a small lake. The lake was cobalt in the middle, aquamarine around the edges. Here and there in the rock expanse patches of meadow grass gleamed, like the lawns of marmot estates. There were no trees. The cold air felt thin in his throat. He could see ranges many miles away, and though everything was perfectly still there was also an immense sweep in things, as if a gust of wind had caught the very fabric of being.

'Wake up, damn you,' a voice said. He was shoved in the back, and he tumbled down the rockfall, starting a small avalanche.

Now he stood in a large white room. Glass boxes of various sizes were stacked everywhere, four and five to a pile, and in every box was a sleeping animal: monkey, rat, dog, cat, pig, dolphin, turtle. 'No,' he said, backing up. 'Please, no.'

A bearded man entered the room. 'Come on, wake up,' he said brusquely. 'Time to get back to it, Fred. Our only hope is to work as hard as we can. You have to resist when you start slipping away!' He seized Abernathy by the arms and sat him down on a box of squirrels. 'Now listen!' he cried. 'We're asleep! We're dreaming!'

'Thank God,' Abernathy said.

'Not so fast! We're awake as well.'

'I don't believe you.'

'Yes you do! Here, look at this.' He took a large roll of graph paper and slapped Abernathy in the chest with it, then unrolled it over the floor. It was covered with black squiggles.

'It looks like a musical score,' Abernathy said absently.

The bearded man shouted. 'Yes! Yes! This is the score for the

327

symphony our brains play every day! Very apt! Now here's the old score, see the violins yammering away for sixteen hours? That's what used to be ours, Fred; that was consciousness.' He yanked hard on his beard with both hands, looking anguished. 'Then there was a sudden drop to the basses, bowing and bowing and bowing, like there. Blessed sleep. And during the night we heard from the mid-range instruments, horn and oboe and viola, spinning over the ground bass with their little improvisations, which got longer and longer until one filled the hour before the violins started blasting again, yes, Fred, it's perfectly apt!'

'Thank you,' Abernathy said. 'But you don't have to yell. I'm right here.'

'Then *wake up*,' the man said in a furious low voice. 'You can't, can you! Playing the new song like all the rest of us. Look at it there – eighty percent REM sleep, mixed indiscriminately with consciousness and deep sleep, turning us all into dream-walkers, into waking nightmares.'

In the depths of his beard, Abernathy saw, all the man's teeth were incisors. Abernathy edged toward the door, then broke for it and ran. The man leaped forward and tackled him, and they tumbled to the floor.

Abernathy woke up.

'Ah ha,' the man said. It was Winston, administrator of the lab. 'So now you believe me,' he said sourly, rubbing an elbow. 'I suppose we should write that down on the walls. How to wake up from the midst of dream. If we all start slipping away like you, we won't even remember what life used to be. It'll all be over then.'

'Where are we?' Abernathy asked.

'In the lab,' Winston replied, voice filled with heavy patience. 'We live here now, remember, Fred? Remember?'

Abernathy looked around. The lab was large and well-lit. Graph paper recording EEGs was scattered over the floor. Black countertops protruded from the walls, which were cluttered with machinery. In one corner were two rats in a cage.

Abernathy shook his head violently. It was all coming back. He was awake now, but the dream had been true. He groaned, walked to the room's little window, saw the smoke rising from the city below. 'Where's Jill?'

Winston shrugged. They hurried through a door at the end of the lab, into a small room containing cots and blankets. No one there.

'She's probably gone back to the house again,' Abernathy said.

Winston hissed with irritation and worry. 'I'll check the grounds,' he said. 'You'd better go to the house. Be careful!'

Fred was already out the door.

In many places the streets were almost blocked by smashed cars, but little had changed since Abernathy's last venture home, and he made good time. The suburbs were choking in haze that smelled like incinerator smoke. A gas station attendant holding a pump handle stared in astonishment as he drove by, then waved. Abernathy didn't wave back. On one of these expeditions he had seen a knifing, and now he didn't like to look.

He stopped the car at the curb before his house. The remains of his house. It was charred almost to the ground. The blackened chimney was all that stood over chest high.

He got out of his old Cortina and slowly crossed the lawn, which was marked by black footprints. In the distance a dog barked insistently.

Jill stood in the kitchen, humming to herself and moving black things from here to there. She looked up as Abernathy stopped in the side yard before her. Her eyes twitched from side to side. 'You're home,' she said cheerily. 'How was your day?'

'Jill, let's go out to dinner,' Abernathy said.

'But I'm already cooking!'

'I can see that.' He stepped over what had been the kitchen wall and took her arm. 'Don't worry about that. Let's go anyway.'

'My my,' Jill said, brushing his face with a sooty hand. 'Aren't you romantic this evening.'

He stretched his lips wide. 'You bet. Come on.' He pulled her carefully out of the house and across the yard, and helped her into the Cortina. 'Such chivalry,' she remarked, eyes darting about in tandem.

Abernathy got in and started the engine. 'But Fred,' his wife said, 'what about Jeff and Fran?'

Abernathy looked out his window. 'They've got a babysitter,' he finally said.

Jill frowned, nodded, sat back in her seat. Her broad face was smudged. 'Ah,' she said, 'I do so like to dine out.'

'Yes,' Abernathy said, and yawned. He felt drowsy. 'Oh no,' he said. 'No!' He bit his lip, pinched the back of the hand on the wheel. Yawned again. 'No!' he cried. Jill jerked against her door in surprise. He swerved to avoid hitting an Oriental woman sitting in the middle of the road. 'I must get to the lab,' he shouted. He pulled down the Cortina's sun visor, took one of the pens from his coat pocket and awkwardly scrawled *To The Lab* on it. Jill was staring at him. 'It wasn't my fault,' she whispered.

He drove them onto the freeway. All thirty lanes were clear, and he put his foot down on the accelerator. 'To the lab,' he sang, 'to the lab, to the lab.' A flying police vehicle landed on the highway ahead of them, folded its wings and sped off. Abernathy tried to follow it, but the freeway turned and narrowed, they were back on street level. He shouted with frustration, bit the flesh at the base of his thumb. Jill leaned back against her door, crying. Her eyes looked like small beings, a team trying to jerk its way free. 'I couldn't help it,' she said. 'He loved me, you know. And I loved him.'

Abernathy drove on. Some streets were burning. He wanted to go west, needed to go west. The car was behaving oddly. They were on a tree-lined avenue, out where there were few houses. A giant Boeing 747 lay across the road, its wings slewed forward. A high tunnel had been cut through it so traffic could pass. A cop with whistle and white gloves waved them through.

On the dashboard an emergency light blinked *To The Lab*. Abernathy sobbed convulsively. 'I don't know how!'

Jill, his sister, sat up straight. 'Turn left,' she said quietly. Abernathy threw the directional switch and their car re-routed itself onto the track that veered left. They came to other splits in the track, and each time Jill told him which way to go. The rear view mirror bloomed with smoke.

330

* * *

Then he woke up. Winston was swabbing his arm with a wad of cotton, wiping off a droplet of blood.

'Amphetamines and pain,' Winston whispered.

They were in the lab. About a dozen lab techs, post docs, and grad students were in there at their countertops, working with great speed.

'How's Jill?' Abernathy said.

'Fine, fine. She's sleeping right now. Listen, Fred, I've found a way to keep us awake for longer periods of time. Amphetamines and pain. Regular injections of benzedrine, plus a sharp burst of pain every hour or so, administered in whatever way you find most convenient. Metabolism stays too high for the mind to slip into the dreamwalking. I tried it and stayed fully awake and alert for six hours. Now we're all using the method.'

Abernathy watched his lab techs dash about. 'I can tell.' He could feel his heart's rapid emphatic thumping.

'Well, let's get to it,' Winston said intently. 'Let's make use of this time.'

Abernathy stood. Winston called a little meeting. Feeling the gazes fixed on him, Abernathy collected his thoughts. 'The mind is an electro-chemical action. Since we're all suffering the effects of this, it seems to me we can ignore the chemical and concentrate on the electrical. If the ambient fields have changed ... anyone know how many gauss the magnetic field is now? Or what the cosmic ray count is?'

They stared at him.

'We can tune into the space station's monitors,' he said. 'And do the rest here.'

So he worked, and they worked with him. Every hour a grinning Winston came around with hypodermics in hand, singing 'Speed, speed, spee-ud!' He convinced Abernathy to let droplets of hydrochloric acid fall on the inside of his forearm.

It kept Abernathy awake better than it did the others. For a whole day, then two, he worked without pause, eating crackers and drinking water as he worked, giving himself the injections when Winston wasn't there.

After the first few hours his assistants began slipping back into

331

dream-walking, despite the injections and acid splashings. Assignments he gave were never completed, or botched. One of his techs presented him with a successful experiment: the two rats, grafted together at the leg. Vainly Abernathy tried to pummel the man back to wakefulness.

In the end he did all the work himself. It took days. As his techs collapsed or wandered off he shifted from counter to counter, squinting sand-filled eyes to read oscilloscope and computer screen. He had never felt so exhausted in his life. It was like taking tests in a subject he didn't understand, in which he was severely retarded.

Still he kept working. The EEGs showed oscillation between wakefulness and REM sleep, in a pattern he had never seen. And there were correlations between the EEGs and fluctuations in the magnetic field. Some of the men's flickering eyes were open, and they sat on the floor talking to each other or to him, but they appeared too exhausted to move. Once he had to calm Winston, who was on the floor weeping and saying 'We'll never stop dreaming, Fred, we'll never stop.' Abernathy gave him an injection, but it didn't have any effect.

He kept working. He sat at a crowded table at his high school reunion, and found he could work anyway. He gave himself an injection whenever he remembered. He felt very, very tired.

Eventually he felt he understood as much as he was going to. Everyone else was lying in the cot room with Jill, or were slumped on the floors. Eyes and eyelids were twitching.

'The earth, the sun, the solar system – we all move through space filled with dust and gas and fields of force. Now there's much more than there used to be. The read-outs from the space station show that, show signs of a strong electro-magnetic field we've apparently moved into. Perhaps it's the shockwave of a supernova, something nearby that we're just seeing now. Anyone looked up into the sky lately? Anyway. Something. And this field has thrown the electrical patterns of our brains into something like what we called the REM state. Our brains rebel and struggle towards consciousness as much as they can, but this field forces them back. So we oscillate.' He laughed weakly, and crawled up onto one of the countertops to get some sleep.

* * *

He woke and brushed the dust off his lab coat, which had served him as a blanket. The dirt road he had been sleeping on was empty. He walked. It was cloudy, and nearly dark.

He passed a small group of shacks, built in a tropical style with open walls and palm thatch roofs. They were empty.

Then he was at the sea's edge. Before him extended a low promontory, composed of thousands of wooden chairs, all crushed and piled together. Out near the tide line there was a human figure, seated in a big chair that still had seat and back and one arm.

Abernathy stepped out carefully, onto slats and lathed cylinders of wood, from a chair arm to the plywood bottom of a chair seat. Around him the gray ocean was strangely calm; glassy swells rose and fell over the slick wood at waterline without a sound. Insubstantial clouds of fog, the lowest parts of a solid cloud cover, floated slowly onshore. The air was salty and wet. Abernathy shivered, stepped down to the next fragment of weathered grey wood.

The seated man turned to look at him. It was Winston. 'Fred,' he called, loud in the silence of the dawn. Abernathy picked up a chair back, placed it carefully, sat.

'How are you?' Winston said.

Abernathy nodded. 'Okay.' Down close to the water he could hear the small slaps and suckings of the sea's rise and fall. The swells looked a bit larger, and he could see the thin smoky mist rising from them as they approached the shore.

'Winston,' he croaked, and cleared his throat. 'What's happened?'

'We're dreaming.'

'But what does that mean?'

Winston laughed wildly. 'Emergent stage one sleep, transitional sleep, rapid sleep, rhombencephalic sleep, pontine sleep, activated sleep, paradoxical sleep.' He grinned ironically. 'No one knows what it is.'

'But all those studies.'

'Yes, all those studies. And how I used to believe in them, how I used to work for them, all those sorry guesses ranging from the ridiculous to the absurd, we dream to organize experience into memory, to stimulate the senses in the dark, to peer into the future, to give our depth perception exercise for God's sake! I mean we don't know, do we Fred. We don't know what dreaming is, we don't know what sleep is, you only have to think about it a bit to realize we didn't know what consciousness itself was, what it meant to be awake. Did we ever really know? We lived, we slept, we dreamed, and all three equal mysteries. Now that we're doing all three at once, is the mystery any deeper?'

Abernathy picked at the grain in the wood of a chair leg. 'A lot of the time I feel normal,' he said. 'It's just that strange things keep happening.'

'Your EEGs display an unusual pattern,' Winston said, mimicking a scientific tone. 'More alpha and beta waves than the rest of us. As if you're struggling harder to wake up.'

'Yes. That's what it feels like.'

They sat in silence for a time, watching swells lap at the wet chairs. The tide was falling. Offshore, near the limit of visibility, Abernathy saw a large cabin cruiser drifting in the current.

'So tell me what you've found,' Winston said.

Abernathy described the data transmitted from the space station, then his own experiments.

Winston nodded. 'So we're stuck here for good.'

'Unless we pass through this field. Or – I've gotten an idea for a device you could wear around your head, that might restore the old field.'

'A solution seen in a dream?'

'Yes.'

Winston laughed. 'How I used to believe in all our rationality, Fred. Dreams as some sort of electro-chemical manifestation of the nervous system, random activity, how reasonable it all sounded! Give the depth perception exercise! God, how small-minded it all was. Why shouldn't we have believed that dreams were great travels, to the future, to other universes, to a world more real than our own! They felt that way sometimes, in that last second before waking, as if we lived in a world so charged with meaning that it might burst with it ... And now here we

334

are. We're here, Fred, this is the moment and our only moment, no matter how we name it. *We're here.* From idea to symbol, perhaps. People will adapt. That's one of our talents.'

'I don't like it,' Abernathy said. 'I never liked my dreams.'

Winston merely laughed at him. 'They say consciousness itself was a leap like this one, people were ambling around like dogs and then one day, maybe because the earth moved through the shockwave of some distant explosion, sure, one day one of them straightened up and looked around surprised, and said "*I am.*"

'That would be a surprise,' Abernathy said.

'And this time everyone woke up one morning still dreaming, and looked around and said "*WHAT AM I?*" ' Winston laughed. 'Yes, we're stuck here. But I can adapt.' He pointed. 'Look, that boat out there is sinking.'

They watched several people aboard the craft struggle to get a rubber raft over the side. After many dunkings they got it in the water and everyone inside it. Then they rowed away, offshore into the mist.

'I'm afraid,' Abernathy said.

Then he woke up. He was back in the lab. It was in worse shape than ever. A couple of countertops had been swept clean to make room for chessboards, and several techs were playing blind-folded, arguing over which board was which.

He went to Winston's offices to get more benzedrine. There was no more. He grabbed one of his post-docs and said 'How long have I been asleep?' The man's eyes twitched, and he sang his reply: 'Sixteen men on a dead man's chest, yo ho ho and a bottle of rum.' Abernathy went to the cot room. Jill was there, naked except for light blue underwear, smoking a cigarette. One of the grad students was brushing her nipples with a feather. 'Oh hi, Fred,' she said, looking him straight in the eye. 'Where have you been?'

'Talking to Winston,' he said with difficulty. 'Have you seen him?'

'Yes! I don't know when, though . . .'

He started to work alone again. No one wanted to help. He

335

cleared a small room off the main lab, and dragged in the equipment he needed. He locked three large boxes of crackers in a cabinet, and tried to lock himself in his room whenever he felt drowsy. Once he spent six weeks in China, then he woke up. Sometimes he woke out in his old Cortina, hugging the steering wheel like his only friend. All his friends were lost. Each time he went back and started working again. He could stay awake for hours at a time. He got lots done. The magnets were working well, he was getting the fields he wanted. The device for placing the field around the head – an odd-looking wire helmet – was practicable.

He was tired. It hurt to blink. Every time he felt drowsy he applied more acid to his arm. It was covered with burns, but none of them hurt very much anymore. When he woke he felt as if he hadn't slept for days. Twice his grad students helped out, and he was grateful for that. Winston came by occasionally, but only laughed at him. He was too tired, everything he did was clumsy. He got on the lab phone once and tried to call his parents; all the lines were busy. The radio was filled with static, except for a station that played nothing but episodes of *The Lone Ranger*. He went back to work. He ate crackers and worked. He worked and worked.

Late one afternoon he went out onto the lab's cafeteria terrace to take a break. The sun was low, and a chill breeze blew. He could see the air, filled with amber light, and he breathed it in violently. Below him the city smoked, and the wind blew, and he knew that he was alive, that he was aware he was alive, and that something important was pushing into things, suffusing every particle ...

Jill walked onto the terrace, still wearing nothing but the blue underwear. She stepped on the balls of her feet, smiled oddly. Abernathy could see goose-pimples sweep across her skin like cat's paws over water, and the power of her presence – distant, female, mysterious – filled him with fear.

They stood several feet apart and looked down at the city, where their house had been. The area was burning.

Jill gestured at it. 'It's too bad we only had the courage to live our lives fully in dreams.'

336

'I thought we were doing okay,' Abernathy said. 'I thought we engaged it the best we could, every waking moment.'

She stared at him, again with the knowing smile. 'You did think that, didn't you.'

'Yes,' he said fiercely, 'I did. I did.'

He went inside to work it off.

Then he woke up. He was in the mountains, in the high cirque again. He was higher now and could see two more lakes, tiny granite pools, above the cobalt-and-aquamarine one. He was climbing shattered granite, getting near the pass. There was lichen on the rocks. The wind dried the sweat on his face, cooled him. It was quiet and still, so still, so quiet . . .

'Wake up!'

It was Winston. Abernathy was in his little room (high ranges in the distance, the dusty green of forests below), wedged in a corner. He got up, went to the crackers cabinet, pumped himself full of the benzedrine he had found in some syringes on the floor. (Snow and lichen.)

He went into the main lab and broke the fire alarm. That got everyone's attention. It took him a couple of minutes to stop the alarm. When he did his ears were ringing.

'The device is ready to try,' he said to the group. There were about twenty of them. Some were as neat as if they were off to church, others were tattered and dirty. Jill stood to one side.

Winston crashed to the front of the group. 'What's ready?' he shouted.

'The device to stop us dreaming,' Abernathy said weakly. 'It's ready to try.'

Winston said slowly, 'Well, let's try it then, okay, Fred?'

Abernathy carried helmets and equipment out of his room and into the lab. He arranged the transmitters and powered the magnets and the field generators. When it was all ready he stood up and wiped his brow.

'Is this it?' Winston asked. Abernathy nodded. Winston picked up one of the wire helmets.

'Well I don't like it!' he said, and struck the helmet against the wall.

Abernathy's mouth dropped open. One of the techs gave a shove to his electro-magnets, and in a sudden fury Abernathy picked up a bat of wood and hit the man. Some of his assistants leaped to his aid, the rest pressed in and pulled at his equipment, tearing it down. A tremendous fight erupted. Abernathy swung his slab of wood with abandon, feeling great satisfaction each time it struck. There was blood in the air. His machines were being destroyed. Jill picked up one of the helmets and threw it at him, screaming, '*It's your fault, it's your fault!*' He knocked down a man near his magnets and had swung the wood back to kill him when suddenly he saw a bright glint in Winston's hand; it was a surgical knife. With a swing like a sidearm pitcher's Winston slammed the knife into Abernathy's diaphragm, burying it. Abernathy staggered back, tried to draw in a breath and found that he could, he was all right, he hadn't been stabbed. He turned and ran.

He ran onto the terrace, closely pursued by Winston and Jill and the others, who tripped and fell even as he did. The patio was much higher than it used to be, far above the city, which burned and smoked. There was a long wide stairway descending into the heart of the city. Abernathy could hear screams, it was night and windy, he couldn't see any stars, he was at the edge of the terrace, he turned and the group was right behind him, faces twisted with fury, 'No!' he cried, and then they rushed him, and he swung the wood slab and swung it and swung it, and turned to run down the stairs and then without knowing how he had done it he tripped and fell head over heels down the rocky staircase, falling falling falling.

Then he woke up. He was falling.

Zürich

When we were getting ready to leave Zürich I decided to try to leave our apartment as clean as it had been when we moved into it two years before. An employee of the Federal Institute of Technology, owners of the building, would be coming by to inspect the place, and these inspections were legendary among the foreign residents living in the building: they were *tough*. I wanted to be the first *Ausländer* to make an impression on the inspector.

Certainly this wasn't going to be easy; the apartment's walls were white, the tables were white, the bookcases and wardrobes and bedtables and dressers and bedframes were white. In short practically every surface in the place was white, except for the floors, which were a fine blond hardwood. But I was getting good at cleaning the apartment, and having lived in Switzerland for two years, I had a general idea what to expect from the inspection. I knew the standard that would be applied. My soul rose to the challenge, and defiantly I swore that I was going to leave the place *immaculate*.

Soon I realized how difficult this was going to be. Every scuff from a muddy shoe, every drip of coffee, every sweaty palm, every exhalation of breath had left its mark. Lisa and I had lived here in our marvelous domestic chaos, and the damage proved it. We had put up pictures and there were holes in the walls. We had never dusted under the beds. The previous tenant had gotten away with things, having moved out in a hurry. It was going to be difficult.

Immediately it was obvious to me that the oven was going to be the crux of the problem. You see, once we went over to some American friends to have a home-like barbecue, the grill out on the balcony up on the fifth floor in the town of Dübendorf, looking out at all the other apartment blocks, the fine smell of barbecued chicken and hamburger spiraling out in the humid summer sky, when there was the howl of siren below, and a whole fleet of fire engines docked and scores of firemen leaped out – all to combat our barbecue. One of the neighbors had called the police to report a fire on our balcony. We explained to the firemen and they nodded, staring coldly at the clouds of thick smoke filling the sky, and suddenly it seemed to us all that a barbecue was a very messy thing indeed.

So I never bought a grill for the balcony of our apartment. Instead I broiled our teriyaki shish-ka-bob in the oven, and it tasted all right. We use a fine teriyaki sauce, my mother got the recipe out of a magazine years ago; but it calls for brown sugar, and this was the source of the problem. When heated, the liquefied brown sugar caramelizes, as Lisa and her chemist colleagues are wont to say; and so on every interior surface of the oven there were little brown dots that refused to come off. They laughed at Easy Off, they laughed at Johnson and Johnson's Force. I began to understand that caramelization is a process somewhat like ceramic bonding. I needed a laser, and only had steel wool. So I began to rub.

It was a race between the flesh of my fingertips and the brown ceramic dots; which would the steel wool remove first? Flesh, of course; but it grows back, while the dots didn't. Only the miracle of regeneration allowed me to win this titanic battle. Over the course of the next two days (and imagine spending fifteen hours staring into a two-foot cube!) I muscled off every single dot, hour by hour becoming more and more enraged at the stubbornness of my foe.

Eventually the victory was mine; the oven was clean, a sparkling box of gray-black metal. It would pass the inspection. I stalked through the apartment in an ecstasy of rage, promising similar treatment for every other surface in the place.

I attacked the rest of the kitchen. Food had suffused into every nook and cranny, it was true; but none of it had caramelized. Stains disappeared with a single wipe. I was Mr Clean, my soul was pure and my hands all-powerful. I put Beethoven on the stereo, those parts of his work that represent the mad blind energy of the universe: the *Grosse Fugue*, the second movement of the Ninth, the finale of the Seventh, and of the *Hammerklavier*. I was another manifestation of this mad blind energy, cleaning in a dance, propelled also by the complex and frenetic music of Charlie Parker, of Yes, *Salt Peanuts* and *Perpetual Change*. And soon enough the kitchen gleamed like a factory display model. It would pass the inspection.

The other rooms offered feeble resistance. Dust, what was it to be now? 'I am the mad blind energy of the universe, I vacuum under the beds!' Cleaning lint from the vacuum I sliced the very tip of my right forefinger off, and for a while it was hard not to get blood on the walls. But that was the most resistance these room could offer. Soon they shone with a burnished glow.

Now, inspired, I decided to get *really* thorough. It was time for details. I had been going to leave the floors alone, as they appeared clean enough to pass; but now with everything else so clean I noticed that there were little dark marks around the doorways, little dips in the grain of the wood where dirt had managed to insinuate itself. I bought some wood polish and went to work on the floors, and when I was done it was like walking on ice.

I dusted off the tops of the bookcases, up near the ceiling. I put spackle in the nail holes in the walls. When I was done the walls were all smooth, but it seemed to me that I could see a little discoloration where the spackle had gone. A few moments' pacing and inspiration struck: I got some typewriter white-out from our boxes, and used it as touch-up paint. It really worked well. Nicks in doorways, a place where the wall was scraped by a chair back; typewriter white-out, perfect.

In the evenings during this week of cleaning frenzy, I sat with friends, drinking and feeling my hands throb. One night I overheard by chance an Israeli friend tell a story about a Swiss friend of hers who had unscrewed the frames on her double-hung windows, to clean the inside surfaces. I shot up in my chair, mouth hanging open; I had noticed dust on the inner sides of our double-paned windows that very afternoon, and figured it was something I wouldn't be able to do anything about. It never would have occurred to me to unscrew the frames! But the Swiss know about these things. The next day I got out a screwdriver, and unscrewed and polished until my wrists were like cooked spaghetti. And the windows sparkled from all four surfaces. They would pass the inspection.

On the morning of Inspection Day I walked through the big rooms of the apartment, with their tan leather chairs and couches, and the white walls and bookshelves, and the sun streamed in and I stood there transfixed as if in the dream of a cognac advertisement, in air like mineral water.

Glancing at the long mirror in the foyer something caught my eye; I frowned; I walked up to it, feeling uneasy as I often do around mirrors, and looked at it closely. Sure enough, some dust. I had forgotten to clean the mirror. As I went to work on it I marveled: you can see the difference between a dusty mirror and a clean one, even when – staring at the paper towel in my hand – there is only enough dust to make a thin short line, like a faint pencil mark. So little dust, distributed over such a large surface – and yet we still can see it. The eye is that powerful. If we can see that, I thought, why not ourselves? Why not everything?

So I strode around the cognac advertisement in a state of rapture; until I remembered the sheets, down in the washing machine. All would have been well, if not for the sheets. All through the week I had been washing those sheets, downstairs in the basement. Red plastic laundry basket filled with linen: we had seven bottom sheets, seven pillow cases, seven big duvet cases. The duvets were fine, as white as cotton. But the bottom sheets, the pillow cases ... Well. They were yellowed. Stained. Alarming evidence of our bodies, our physical existence: oils, fluids, miniscule scraps of us rubbed into the cloth like butter, ineradicably.

Certainly, I thought, the Swiss must have methods for dealing with evidence as serious as this. So I had gone out and bought bleaches. Recalling the bleach ads from back home, I trustfully assumed that the stained linen would emerge from one trip through the wash gleaming like lightning. But it wasn't so. Wash after wash did nothing to change their color. I went out and bought a different kind of bleach, then another. Two powders, one liquid. I upped the doses on each of them. Nothing worked.

And now it was the morning of Inspection Day, and I had recalled the sheets in the basement, and my rapture was shattered. I hurried downstairs, walked down the long concrete underground hallway to the laundry room. I saw that the building would stand for a thousand years. It would resist ten megatons. The washing machine was trilingual and as big as a truck. I brought it online, gave it its pre-run check-off for the final attempt, set my array of bleaches on top of the machine. It was the fourteenth time I had run things through this week, and I had the procedure streamlined; but this time I stopped to think. I looked at the three different kinds of bleach on top of the dryer, and I had an idea. I took the largest cap and turned it open end up, then poured in liquid bleach until the cup was half-full. Then I poured in some of both of the powders.

Synergy, right? Singing a little tune in praise of the mysterious force of synergy, I took the pencil from the sign-in book and stirred the mix in the cap vigorously. It began to bubble a little, then to foam.

Only at that point did I remember my wife, the chemist, yelling at me for mixing two cleansers together in an attempt to get a bathtub clean. 'If you had mixed ammonia and Ajax it would have made chloramine gas and killed you!' she had said. '*Never* mix stuff like that together!'

I left the cap of bleaches on the dryer and ran out of the room. From the concrete hall I stared back in, sniffing carefully. Glancing down I noticed the pencil, still clenched in my hand; and the bottom half of it, the part that had stirred the bleaches, was as white as a stick of chalk. 'Ho!' I exclaimed, and retreated farther up the hall. Synergy can be a powerful thing.

After some thought, and a closer inspection of the pencil, which now had a pure white eraser, I returned to the washroom. The air seemed okay. I was committed at this point, I had to meet the Swiss challenge. So I tipped the capful of bleaches carefully into the plastic opening on top of the washer, and I stuffed our yellowy bottom sheets and pillow cases inside, and I closed up the washer and punched the buttons for the hottest

water available, ninety degrees centigrade. Walking back upstairs I noticed that the very tip of my left forefinger had a white
patch on it. Back in the apartment I found it wouldn't wash off.
'Bleached my flesh!' I exclaimed. 'That stuff is finally working
the way it's supposed to.'

An hour later I returned to the washroom apprehensively,
hoping that the sheets had not been eaten to shreds or the like.
On the contrary; when I opened the washer door there was a
glare as if several camera flashes had gone off right in my face,
just like in the ads; and there were the sheets, as white as new
snow.

I hooted for glee, and stuffed them in the dryer. And by the
time the inspector rang the bell below, they were dried and
ironed and folded and neatly stacked in the linen drawers of the
bedroom wardrobe, looking like great hunks of Ivory soap.

I hummed cheerfully as I let the inspector in. He was a young
man, perhaps younger than myself. His English was excellent.
He was apologetic, defensive; it was a boring task for both of us,
he said, but necessary. No problem, I replied, and showed him
around the place. He nodded, frowning slightly, 'I must count
the various items in the kitchen,' he said, brandishing an
inventory.

That took a long time. When he was done he shook his head
disapprovingly. 'There are four glasses missing, and one spoon,
and the top off the tea kettle.'

'That's right,' I said happily. 'We broke the glasses and lost
the spoon, and I think we broke the tea kettle, though I can't
remember.' These things didn't matter, they didn't have to do
with the essential challenge, which concerned not number but
order; not quantity, but quality; not inventory, but cleanliness.

And the inspector understood this too; after listening to my
admission, he shook his head seriously and said, 'Fine, fine;
however, what about *this*?' And with a satisfied look he reached
up into the back of the top shelf of the broom closet, and held
out before me a short stack of grimy kitchen towels.

In that moment I understood that the Inspector wanted
dirtiness, in the same way that a policeman wants crime; it's the
only thing that can make the job interesting. I stared at the

346

kitchen towels, which I had completely forgotten. 'What about them?' I said. 'We never used those, I forgot they were up there.' I shrugged. 'The previous tenant must have done that to them.'

He stared at me disbelievingly. 'How did you dry your dishes?'

'We stand them in the drainer and let them dry on their own.'

He shook his head, not believing that anyone would rely on such a method. I recalled the Swiss friend of ours who dried her bathtub with a towel after showering. I shrugged stubbornly; the Inspector shook his head stubbornly. He turned to look in the broom closet again, to see if there were any other forgotten treasures. Without forethought I quickly reached behind him and touched the stained kitchen towels with my bleached forefinger.

They turned white.

When the young inspector was done searching the broom closet, I said casually, 'But they're not that bad, are they?' He looked at the kitchen towels and his eyebrows shot up. He regarded me suspiciously; I just shrugged innocently, and left the kitchen. 'Are you about done?' I asked. 'I have to go downtown.'

He prepared to leave. 'We will have to see about the missing glasses,' he said, voice heavy with dissatisfaction.

'And the spoon,' I said. 'And the tea kettle top.'

He left.

I danced through the sparkling air of the empty apartment. My work was done, I had passed the inspection, my soul was pure, I was in a state of grace. Weak sunlight lanced between low clouds, and out on the balcony the air was frigid. I put on my down jacket to go into the city center, to see my Zürich one last time.

Down the old overgrown steps and through the wintry garden of the ETH, past the big building housing the Chinese graduate students. Down the steep walkway to Voltastrasse, past the Japanese fire maple and the interior design store. I touched one red rose and was not particularly surprised to see it turn white. My whole fingertip looked like paraffin now.

Down at the Voltastrasse tram shop, in the wind. Across the street the haunted house stood, a pinkish wreck with big cracks in its walls; Lisa and I had always marveled at it, there was nothing even remotely as derelict as it anywhere in Zürich. It

was an anomaly, an exile like we were, and we loved it. 'I'll
never touch you,' I said to it.

A Number Six tram hummed down the hill from Kirche
Fluntern and squealed to a halt before me. You have to touch
a button to get the doors to open, so I did so and the whole tram
car turned white. Usually they are blue, but there are a few trams
painted different colors to advertise the city museums, and there
are some painted white to advertise the Oriental museum in
Reitberg, so I assumed that this car would now be taken for one
of those; and I climbed aboard.

We slid off down the hill toward Platte, ETH and Central. I
sat in the back of the tram and watched the Swiss in front of me,
getting on and off. Many of them were old. None of them ever
sat in seats beside each other until all the seats had been filled
by single parties. If single seats were vacated at a stop, people
sitting next to strangers in double seats would get up and move
to the single seat. No one talked, though they did look at each
other a little. Mostly they looked out the windows. The windows
were clean. These trams on the number six line had been built
in 1952, but they were still in factory perfect condition; they had
passed the inspection.

Looking down, I suddenly noticed that each pair of shoes on
the tram was flawless. Then I noticed that each head of hair was
perfectly coiffed. Even the two punks on the tram had their hair
perfectly done, in their own style. Shoes and hair, I thought,
these will reveal the wealth of a nation. These extremes reveal
the soul.

At the ETH stop a Latin American man got on the tram. He
was dressed in a colorful serape, and thin black cotton pants,
and he looked miserably cold. He was carrying an odd thing that
looked like a bow; it was painted crudely, in many colors, and
there was a small painted gourd attached to it, where you would
hold the bow if it were meant to shoot arrows. The man had
long lanky black hair that fell loosely over his shoulders and
down the back of the serape, and his face was big and broad-
cheeked; he looked like a *mestizo*, or perhaps a purebred Indian
from Bolivia or Peru or Ecuador. There were quite a few of them
living in Zürich. Lisa and I often saw groups of them on

Bahnhofstrasse, playing music for change. Pan pipes, guitars, drums, gourds filled with beans: street music performed right through the winter, with the players and audience alike shivering in the snowy air.

When the tram started to move again, this Latino walked to the front of the car and turned around to face us all. He said something loudly in Spanish, and then began to play the bow and gourd instrument, plucking it rapidly. Moving one thumb up and down the metal bowstring changed the pitch of the sound, which reverberated in the gourd, making a kind of loud twang. The resulting sound was awful: loud, unmelodic, impossible to ignore.

The Swiss stared resentfully at this intrusion. This was not done; I had never seen it before, and neither had the others aboard, it was clear. And the sound of the primitive instrument was so insistent, so weird. The disapproval in the car was as palpable as the sound, the two vibrations battling each other in tense air.

The tram stopped at Haldenegg, and several people got off, more than would usually; clearly some were just escaping the musician, and would get on the next tram to come along. Newcomers, unpleasantly surprised, stared at the man as he twanged away. The tram doors closed and we moved off again, down the hill to Central. The captive audience stared at the musician, as belligerent as cows eyeing a passing car.

Then he broke into song. It was one of those Bolivian or Peruvian hill ballads, a sad tale dramatically told, and the man sang it over the twanging of his absurd instrument in a hoarse wild voice, expressing all the anguish of the exile, lost in a cold land. What a voice the man had! Suddenly the ridiculous twanging made sense, it all fell together, this voice in a foreign language cut through all the barriers and spoke to us, to each and every person on the tram. That kind of singing is impossible to ignore or deny – we knew exactly what he was feeling, and so for that moment we were a little community. And all without understanding a word. What power the voice has to express what really matters! People shifted in their seats, they sat up, they watched the singer intently, they smiled. When he walked up and down the tram, holding out a black felt hat, they dug deep into their pockets and purses and dropped change in, smiling at him and saying things in Swiss German, or even in High German so he might perhaps understand. When the doors hissed open at Central, they were surprised; no one aboard had noticed our arrival.

The Swiss! I had to laugh. So closed in, so generous ...

Then as each person touched the white parts of my white tram, they went white themselves. Chairback or railing or overhead support, it didn't matter; they touched the tram and left it as white as porcelain figures of themselves. And no one at Central paid any attention.

As we left the tram together, I touched the musician on the shoulder, in a sort of greeting, or an experiment. He only looked at me, eyes black as obsidian; and it seemed to me that the vivid colored thread sewn riotously in his serape actually grew more brilliant, more intensely colorful: little rainbow crosshatchings, scarlet and saffron and green and violet and pink and sky blue, glowing in crude brown woolen cloth. Without a glance back, the musician walked off into the Niederdorf, Zürich's medieval town.

I crossed the bridge looking down at the white swans in the gray Limmat, feeling the wind rush through me, buoyant with the memory of his music and my apartment's purity. I walked down Bahnhofstrasse seeing it all again, seeing it fully for the first time in a long while and the last time in who knew how long, perhaps forever, and my heart filled and I said, 'Ah handsome Züri my town, my town, I too am one of your exile sons,' and I caressed the granite blocks of the stolid elegant buildings and they turned white as wedding cakes under my hand, with a keening sound like violins played backward. When would I ever see it again like this, with its low pearl gray sky rushing overhead in the cold wind, with the Alps at the end of the Zürichsee standing up like cardboard cut-out mountains, steeper than mountains could ever be? I touched the tram tracks and they turned to white gold, in a wide street of glazed sugar. And I walked down this white street looking in the sparkling window displays of the rich merchants, the jewelry and clothing

350

and watches all perfect and gleaming, and, as I traced my fingers over the window glass, as white as white opals.

In among the narrow alleyways of the medieval town I wandered, touching every massive building until it seemed I walked in a silent world of milk and baking soda, saying good-bye with every touch. To consciously be doing something you loved, for the last time! Past St Peter's church which was already alabaster before I touched it, past Fraumünster and across the river to Grossmünster with its painfully spare interior, like a tall empty warehouse made entirely of white marble ... Then back across the river again, on a paper bridge. And looking down the gray Limmat I saw that much of Zürich had turned white, bleached by my touch.

I came to the lakefront at Burkliplatz, touched the steps and suddenly the fine little park and the boat docks gleamed like soap carvings. The beautiful statue of Ganymede and the eagle looked like they had been molded out of white ceramic, and in Ganymede's outstretched arms it seemed to me a whole world was being embraced, a rushing world of gray sky and gray water where everything passed by so fast that you never got the chance to hold it, to touch it, to make it yours. Can't we keep anything? These years of our life, we were happy, we were here, and now it was all white and clean and still, turning to marble under the touch of my hand. So that in the pure rapture of final things I walked down the white concrete ramp to the lapping lake water and crouched down and touched it; and before me I saw the whole lake go still and turn white, as if it were an immense tub of white chocolate; and in the distance the magnificent Alps were white; and overhead the rushing clouds pulsed white and glowed like spun glass. I turned around the saw that the city's transformation was complete: it was a still and silent Zürich of snow and white marble, white chocolate, white ceramic milk, salt, cream.

But from a distant street I could still hear that twanging.